The Magic Horseman

by Freida Kilmari

Cover: Angela Fristoe at Covered Creatively
Proofreading: Square Peg Editing

Content Guidance

Violence

This books contains scenes of graphic violence, including death scenes, and deals with this both emotionally and physically.

Profanity

This book contains excess profanity from all characters.

Sexual Situations

This book contains explicit sex, including MM, FF, MF, MMFFM, and MMF scenarios. Kink List: bondage, choking, DP, mild s/D, and vampirism.

Dark Themes

This book has a graphic depiction of grief. This book deals with gender identity issues, war, loss, and death.

Chapter One

Emergency Message:
Dhaka, New York City, Delhi, Shang Hai, and Cairo at
War

None of us move. Silence. Not just from us, but from the explosion's aftermath and the armies beyond. It's as though the world has come to a screeching halt and we're caught in its puppet strings, unable to move. To do anything.

I . . .

But . . .

"Nine," Dea whispers.

I still can't move. I want to go to him. To the Angel of Death crying at my feet.

But it seems Connie and Arrie are having the same problem because they're frozen behind me. Statues barely breathing. Barely moving.

Just when I thought I would be stuck in this frozen moment forever, Arrie moves and places a hand on my shoulder. "We can't stay here." He crouches to Dea and steals a shocked breath at his tear-soaked face. "Sorry, dude."

Dea stands, wipes his face despite the tears that continue to fall, and clenches a fist. "I know."

"But . . ." Connie behind me sobs, then growls. "I'm gonna kill him."

"No," I say, barely a whisper.

But they hear me because their heads all snap to mine at the same time.

"Hon, he needs to die."

My brother's face swims across my mind, flashing that sly grin, speaking those false words of comfort, and anger courses through me. White hot anger. "I'll be the one to kill him."

"It doesn't have to be you." She finally moves her feet in my direction and wraps an arm around my waist. "Any of us can do it for you."

Dea's still staring at the space where Nine was, where he faded, so I twine my fingers through his and squeeze. "Dea," I whisper, "we need to secure the city."

But he doesn't say anything. He just keeps staring into nothing. Into the space that used to hold our everything.

Arrie runs out of the alley and comes back five minutes later, dragging a Vampire I've not seen before. "Report."

The Vampire looks at us with a frown and then announces, "We secured the city. Then, when Aki, the Fae Queen, and Prince Phillipe teleported in, all hell broke loose. But they left the moment Aki burned the scroll."

"They left?" Arrie asks, frustration ebbing at his features. His fists clench, his knuckles white from strain, and I get the feeling he's holding it all back for us. "So the city is still secured?"

"Yes," the Vampire says. "We can move into the defensive strategy if you're ready?"

Arrie nods. "Oversee the defense of the city."

The Vampire nods and speeds away to carry out his orders.

Arrie looks at Dea not responding, at me, then at Connie, and sighs as a lone tear escapes his left eye. "Connie, take Dea home." He turns to Dea and places a hand on his shoulder. "Dude, if you can, please assist the healers and doctors stationed at the hospital. Many are wounded."

Dea nods in slow motion and then turns to Connie and grabs her hand.

Connie takes out two crystals and smashes them at their feet, holding my gaze the entire time. Anger. That's what flows through her bright green eyes. And I know exactly what she's trying to tell me: don't check out. We need you.

I know.

But I'm not sure I know how to deal with the swirling emotions inside of me. Fear. Guilt. Anger. Frustration. Rage. Grief. Overwhelming dark sadness. And it's all fighting for attention, each one wanting me to break down, lash out, crumple to the floor, launch headfirst into the next fight.

"Hey . . ." Arrie grabs me by the arms and yanks me into him. "Shh . . ."

And there, in the safety of the most confusing man I've ever met, guilt and grief take over as tears spill in rivers while sobs hack at me.

But it's the droplets falling onto my shoulders that have me snapping my head up to look at the man holding me. Streams of tears trace his angles and pour off his jaw. I can tell he's struggling to focus, struggling to stay afloat.

But we have to.

We can grieve later.

Right now, we have to make sure all the Vampire cities are safe.

"Arrie"—I reach up to stroke the tears off his face—"we need to go. This isn't the only city."

He shakes his head, clearing his focus, and stares those ice-blue eyes into mine. "Okay. Let's go." He grips my hand and grabs teleporting crystals from his pocket.

We visit each city together, ordering the start of the defensive strategy now that each city is safe, and we eventually land in Dhaka, where Lucien meets us immediately.

"The city is secure, the dead are being transported to their families, and we have already sent the wounded back to *Sheruta*. I've set up a perimeter and coordinated with local councils and law enforcement to keep your strategy in place,

Arrie. And . . ." He looks at our blank expressions and grim faces and shivers. "What's wrong?" He turns to face me and frowns. "Magic?"

The words leave my lips in a desert emptiness, void of emotion and expression. The only way I know how to shove them off my tongue. "Nine's dead."

Lucien staggers back and catches himself on the nearby lamppost. "But . . . I thought . . . How?"

Arrie waves the question away. "It doesn't matter. He's gone." He steels a business-like expression and clenches his hand laced within mine. "Continue with the plan here. If you need one of us, you know where to find us."

Lucien looks at us with pity. "Go home. We can handle things from here."

We turn to teleport away, and just as we're about to vanish, Lucien looks at me with sad eyes. "I'm so sorry little Horseman."

I snap my eyes away from his just as we land in the house's garden, the weight of home wrapping around me like a blanket. But I can't fall down yet. "I'm going to help Dea at the hospital."

"Okay." But he doesn't let go of my hand. "I need to help co-ordinate what we do from here." He looks at me with this pained expression, like letting go of me is the same as removing the ground from under him.

And I just don't know what to do with that look. With the reverence in his eyes. "You need to find Connie. She can help with co-ordination efforts."

He nods then shakes his head. "How are your energy levels? Need any blood?"

I almost laugh. Because of course his focus is on making sure we're all fed. "I had plenty of enemy blood. It didn't really do much, but I'll be okay for a bit."

"I'll come to the hospital with you then. Maybe Connie's there."

She's probably not, but I think Arrie just doesn't want to leave my side. Who knows what's going through his head. I barely know what's going through it on a normal day. Much less after . . .

This.

CHAPTER TWO

VAMPIRE CITIES ATTACKED: WHY? 'READ ALL ABOUT IT'

The hospital is a small building; we built a special attachment unit for especially for this battle. Well, we politely asked the *Sherutan* residents for help. They were all happy to do their part—especially those who weren't fighting.

Its sprawling mass of buildings, wings, various levels, and wards could confuse the best cartographer, however, and we quickly find ourselves lost.

"Do you think he didn't make it? That he's at home?" My eyes find Arrie's in a frown.

"I don't know." His hand squeezes mine for what feels like the thousandth time as we walk down a series of corridors.

We started in the emergency department, thinking he would be there, and then wandered various wards, trying not to think about how Nine won't be here. Recovering.

Because he's already dead.

In the distance, my hearing picks up on a soothing voice with a lilt that always reminds me of home. "You will start feeling better soon."

"Dea!"

"Where?"

"This way." I drag him down a series of corridors, probably confusing the hell out of him, until we reach the Fae ward. "There you are."

Dea spins to face me and lifts the side of his lips. "Hi." He turns back to the room of Fae stretched out on various beds. "If you need anything, I will be onsite for the next few hours. But with your magical healing abilities and mine, you should recover before then."

The Fae smile at him and then continue nattering amongst themselves.

I grab Dea's hand while Arrie places a comforting hand on his shoulder. "Anything I can do to help?" My fangs descend, reminding him that my blood can heal at a miraculous rate.

"You will be most helpful in the emergency department, Angel."

He's on autopilot.

Just going through the motions expected of him.

"Okay. Then let's go." Arrie drags us both in that direction. "Err . . ." Then looks around confused, clearly lost.

Dea sighs. "It is this way." He guides us left, and we soon find ourselves in a busy ward with hundreds of different species, all moaning and groaning in pain, some at death's door, others not even conscious. "I did the best I can. But my healing abilities take time to work."

"How many patients?"

A nearby nurse answers me in his rush to see to all the patients. "2,167 total, ma'am. Sir." He rushes to apologize, but I wave him off. He doesn't have the time.

"That's a lot of wounded," Arrie grumbles.

"Yes, it is," Dea agrees. Exhaustion lining his eyes.

"You tended to all of them?" Surprise laces my voice. He nods. "Go lie down." Since it wasn't a suggestion, I shove him in the exit's direction, toward home. "I'll handle this."

Dea turns to leave, but Arrie says, "If you see Con, send her my way."

Dea nods and leaves—at a regular pace. Rather than his usual fazing.

A series of scary beeps echoes from my left as nurses shout orders and a doctor rushes over, shouting more orders. "He's going into cardiac arrest."

I yank a dagger out of my thigh holster and slice a two-inch cut into my palm, letting the blood flow. There's water in blood, right? Giving it a shot, I use my water Witch magic to stream some of my blood to the patient, whose mouth is covered by an oxygen mask. A nurse removes it, and I give two drops to the dying Fae and wait.

"His vitals are stabilizing."

Alright.

I wander my way into the center of the ward and cut my palm again, sending various streams of blood along all the beds, dropping small amounts into patients' mouths to speed up their healing.

It's not until I'm halfway through the emergency department that I start to get dizzy, a little light-headed, and a headache forms. "Shit."

"Here." Arrie shoves his wrist into my face.

And I bite down.

All the nurses and doctors are frozen in shock, some removing masks and others opening unconscious patients' mouths.

As I get to the last patient, I remove Arrie's wrist from my mouth and pull my blood back into my body.

"Wow," a blonde-haired nurse from beside me exclaims. "That was brilliant."

Light-headed, I smile. "Thank you."

But my body is fading, bright silver circles spotting my vision, and before I can find somewhere private, I pass out into powerful arms.

Chapter Three

Pixies Spotted on Camera Fighting Alongside Horsemen

A flurry of activity bursts through my sleep-addled brain, coming in short bursts.

"Right, but we can't do that to the cities. They're some of the largest cities in the world, and not just for us Vamps." Lucien's voice. "They need to stay open."

"Then," a familiar grumbling from beneath me says, "we'll have to use resources to keep those defenses in place."

Connie chimes in next. "But we still need to take back New Orleans. We can't be stretched this thin."

"Whaa . . . ?" My eyes open to a familiar scene. A meeting. "What's going on?"

"Finally awake, little Horseman?"

"After saving over two thousand troops, yeah."

Lucien winces then smiles. "Heard about that. Not so little anymore, huh?"

"Ah," I wince, "my head feels like an army of horses have run it over with a thousand Arries on their backs."

"Here." Connie reaches over from my left with a tissue, then points to her mouth.

Oh. I wipe away the blood and let go of Dea's wrist, who sits to my right, his angel wings sitting behind us. Expression blank.

The Vampire king and Prince Lucien sit on the couch opposite, along with the Shifter and Witch representatives. But instead of a meeting room at the embassy, we're all sat in one of our lounges. For some reason.

"We were just discussing how to upkeep the defense of the five cities, hon."

"Ah, I see." Well, I'm gonna need a minute. Maybe five. "I'll be back momentarily." I jump to my feet and leave, clicking the door shut behind me.

Fuck.

Nine's dead.

I Vampire speed to the garden, where rain descends on *Sheruta* for the first time in a few weeks. Fitting. But no amount of rain washes away the pain lancing through me, filling my every pore and any available space.

Black wings wrap around me in the rain as hot breaths trail down my neck. "Angel . . ." Voice strained, his arms wrap around my waist as hot tears collide with chilly rain on my shoulder. "I . . . I'm so sorry."

"No. I . . . I don't—"

"I know." He sighs into me. "I know."

"But we need to take back New Orleans. Somehow. How are we supposed to do that without him?"

"I am more worried about how I am supposed to breathe without him," he whispers.

Oh, Dea.

I turn in his arms to face him, slamming my lips to his, hoping to provide a little comfort. Even if it won't take the pain away.

"Angel," he mumbles between gasps. "I do not know what to do now."

"Me either."

But I know what we have to do. And that'll have to do for now. "C'mon, we should head back inside. I just needed a moment. Nine won't be the only loved one to die if we don't continue with the plan."

I guide us back inside, air dry us off, and drag us back to the lounge, where everyone awaits us. "Right, someone tell me the problem."

Korby smiles at me before saying, "Well, we'll use up eighty-five percent of our combined resources if we keep defending the cities this heavily. But we need to take back New Orleans."

"Korby!" I didn't notice her earlier. "You're okay." I rush to her side and grab her in a giant bear hug. "I was so worried." For just a moment, my smile is genuine.

"Yes," Lucien says, "well, I had to rescue her from a small army of Fae she couldn't handle by herself."

"Oh, bite me." She shoves a middle finger in Lucien's direction, then frowns when she looks at me again. "I'm so sorry."

The smile vanishes at those words. "Me too."

"We all are," Alpha Cal says. "If there's anything we can do." The offer seems genuine, but none of us know what to say. What to ask for.

My boyfriend is dead. What could they possibly do?

I clear my throat, pulling myself out of my thoughts. "For now, focus on holding the cities and recovering. Once all of your soldiers have recovered, we'll reconvene."

Arrie looks up from the floor. "I will consider the resource problem and come up with an appropriate strategy, then set the date for New Orleans."

Everyone gets up to leave, but Korby stays behind. "If you need a break from training, I understand. But I'm staying here in *Sheruta* indefinitely, so I'm available whenever you're ready." She shrugs. "Or just for coffee."

"Thank you." I need to wind down. I feel like I'm holding myself together with the thinnest of threads, and any minute now it'll shatter, emotions gushing like a river.

But it doesn't snap. And maybe that's the problem with grief. It feels like you're one step away from falling into your own grave, but instead, you're always holding on. Grasping for life out of some instinct to survive you didn't know you had. Forever doomed to walk on the edge.

Once everyone's left, we all collapse into a pile on the couch and breathe in silence. Dea wraps his wings around us all, Arrie holds my hand in a death-like grip, and Connie rests her leg atop my lap, where I'm stroking warm hands up and down them.

"What now?" Connie asks, an empty curiosity in her voice.

Dea stays silent, and I don't have an answer, but Arrie shrugs. "I have no idea."

CHAPTER FOUR

WERE THE SUPERNATURAL COUNCIL IN LEAGUE WITH THE FAE QUEEN?

Wake up, eat breakfast, go for a walk, do some yoga, read, go to bed. Wake up, eat breakfast, go for a walk, do some yoga, read, go to bed. Wake up, eat breakfast, go for a walk, do some yoga, read, got to bed.

Like an empty shell, I walk around my life hollow, still waiting for that last thread to snap and for the tears to come, the screaming agony you see on the movie screen. But it's like I've forgotten how to breathe, only living because there isn't anything else to do.

I see the way Connie and Arrie look at me, waiting for the tears, for the moment when they can help, do something, mix my grief with theirs. Like the entire house is holding its breath, waiting for an emotional nuclear explosion.

We've been sleeping separately, all going about our days individually; though, I've noticed Arrie is always close. Somewhere nearby, ready to help. He's being . . . supportive, and I don't know what to think about that. I guess friends are supportive in times of grief. But he's grieving too. And I'm worried he's suppressing it to help the rest of us.

He loves by caring for others, but sometimes he needs to be cared for too.

With that thought in mind, I wander from my favorite couch in my library to the one around the corner that Arrie's curled up on. He's resting his head on the arm, a pillow wedged underneath, and his eyes are slipping shut as a blanket rests over his torso.

He's exhausted.

He's been cooking, caring for, and providing emotional support to the entire team without a second thought. As though that's where his instincts lie.

I don't care how much of an asshole he's been or what secret he's hiding or why he won't be with me; at the moment, all I care about is finding a slice of peace for us all to lie in. Arrie included.

There's no space on the couch, so I sit on the floor in front of him and open my book back up.

Eventually, after a few pages, he lays an arm over my shoulder, his hand dangling by my book. "Killer . . ." he mumbles in his sleep. "I miss you."

My breath hitches.

Looking over at the nearest clock, I realize it's four am and I should probably try to shut my brain off and get some sleep. The bedroom's not far, so I get up to leave.

But Arrie grabs the hem of my tee and frowns. "Where you going?" Sleep murmurs his voice.

"To bed. It's very late."

"Oh." He lets go of my tee with a sad smile. "Okay."

I sigh. "You can come with me, if you like?"

He looks up at me, his ice-blue eyes melting my purple ones into a puddle of goo. A furrow in his brow. "I . . ."

"We're friends, right?"

He nods.

"Then come sleep next to me so I get hugged by a bear while I attempt to sleep peacefully."

He nods, a smile creeping across his face. The first I've seen in weeks. And ever so slightly my heart warms, its frozen form thawing for just a moment.

The duvet wraps around us as Arrie grabs my waist and wraps me in the squishiest of hugs. "Go to sleep, Killer." Then he places a gentle kiss to the back of my head and nods back off.

He . . . kissed me.

But . . .

Why?

I ponder that question as sleep takes me, and I don't wake up once, I don't have a single nightmare, and for the first time since I slayed an army, sleep takes me in its arms and rocks me to peace.

The soft aroma of mangoes washes over me in the morning, and I peel my eyes open to find Connie wrapped in my arms in front of me, her eyes fixed on the ceiling—or a memory that lies within, perhaps—as a few tears slip from her eyes.

I lean forward and kiss them away as more fall.

Arrie groans awake behind me and leans over. "Mornin'."

Connie sniffs but smiles—or tries to. "Morning." She turns to lie on her side, facing me, and grips my lips with hers, pulling me into her, breathing me in.

Usually, she'd be making some kind of advance or sexy remark by now, but I don't think that's her purpose today. I think she just needs me.

Arrie turns to leave, but I grab his hand and pull away from Connie. "Stay. Please?"

He looks at me, pain in his eyes, but nods.

So we stay in my bed, all cuddling under the duvet. There are some tears, some sobs, some smiles, and even a couple of light jokes. But the important thing is we're together.

"How's Dea doing?" Connie asks me, hope and concern drifting across her green eyes.

"I have no idea." I look up at the ceiling. "He won't let me into his room."

"Me either," she says.

"I've been leaving plates of food outside his room, but he

hasn't touched them." Arrie strokes circles across my tummy while Connie lies in the crook of my neck. "He needs to be with us." He looks down at me. "At least with you. He shouldn't go so long without touching his mate."

"His Angel is probably needing you, hon."

"You think I should barge in there anyway, privacy be damned?" But isn't that a little . . . invasive?

My fingers worry themselves stupid, until Connie grabs them and wraps hers through mine. "Yeah, I do. Who the hell has privacy in a mating bond anyway?"

I chuckle. But she's right. Dea's always nosing his way into my emotional business for the better. Maybe it's time I do the same. "Okay, okay. I'll go see him."

"I'll bring you both breakfast," Arrie says.

"I'll come check on you both in a bit. I'm gonna take a walk."

I sit up and hug her, hoping to remind her that she's loved. But maybe actions aren't enough right now. "I love you."

She raises my chin with a finger so that our eyes meet. "I love you too. Never forget it. I'm just a little . . ."

"Empty?" I suggest.

She nods.

Arrie looks at us both and smiles. "Grief's empty, like a vase waiting for its flowers. It comes and goes in waves, never really disappearing but sometimes giving you breathing room."

I turn to face him. "But it doesn't mean you can't love. It's possible to be grieving and in love."

He frowns, as though he's never thought of it like that before, then gets up and heads out, probably to make breakfast.

"Go on," Connie says. "Go be with your Angel."

Chapter Five

Prince Phillipe Joins Fae Queen in Magical War

The black door in the corner with the giant hinges and the splintered wood stands as a gate in front of me. Locked.

"Dea, please let me in."

Silence.

"Dea, we need to let each other in. We can't just shut everyone out when we're hurting. You taught me that. You're my mate, and I need you, and I know that you need me too."

C'mon, come on, come on . . .

I don't know what else to say.

I'm not good with words like he is. I don't know what to say to make the pain go away, or if the words for that remedy even exist. And I want to respect his privacy, but sometimes people shut you out and you need to be a little forceful to get them to let you back in. Especially after trauma. And especially when you're angel mated to them and need regular touch.

"Dea, please. I—"

The door unlocks on silent hinges.

And I step through.

The room is pitch black, shadows in every inch of space, and the only light shines from two galaxy pinnacles huddled on the floor in the corner.

"Dea?" I close the door and kneel next to him, a hand gently raised and placed on his shoulder. "I . . . I'm here."

His body looks melted, like an ice cube that's met its temperature match, leaking the last of its endless water onto the floor. His eyes meet mine, and for the first time, I want to look away. I don't want to drown in their sadness. Because the only thing staring at me right now is a man on the brink of breaking in two with no way of stopping himself from falling over the edge.

Tears prick the edges of my vision. I don't have the right words, nor do I know what to do, but I lie next to him and yank Dea's head to my shoulder.

I don't think I can make this okay.

Because I'm just as broken, and I don't even know how to put back the pieces of myself—or even know who that is enough to grab a diagram. But I'm gonna try anyway, because he needs me. Because he's a part of my everything. And I can't lose another piece of my world.

Dea's fingers claw into my back as sobs wrack his chest

and tears fall down my shoulder in waterfalls, gushing pain onto bare skin. "I . . . cannot . . . breathe."

"I know." My arms wrap his body in a tight hug, grabbing on with everything I have. "I know."

I can't even imagine how much pain must be wrecking him right now; they were lovers for hundreds of years. You don't just get over that. Whenever Dea entered a room, Nine would light up, like Dea was the switch to his happy. They connected in a way that I can only dream of understanding. Let alone achieving.

My feet stand of their own accord, and I grab Dea's hands in mine as our eyes connect. "Let's lie down."

With tears streaming down his face, a crease in his brow, and lips that won't stop trembling, he nods and allows me to pull him to his feet.

I guide him to the bed and sigh. The last time I was in his bed was between them both. Nine's absence cuts like a knife. Before settling us into bed, I strip the sheet and duvet cover and ask the house for something else. Anything else. Then I remake the bed and settle us under the black cotton sheets.

Dea sighs into my neck as he nuzzles close. "Nine hated cotton. It is why my sheets are always silk. He liked how they felt against his bare skin."

So many tiny details I didn't bother to learn and will never get to.

"I wanted to marry him." More tears slide down my cheeks. "Marry you all. Somehow. Someday." But that dream is fading, drifting into the impossible. It was always all or nothing with them, but I was naïve. There's still something in the nothingness, and right now, that something is the man listening to my pain while not knowing what to do with his own.

"I should have . . . married him centuries ago." More sobs escape his lips as the words fade into the empty air. "Should have said so many more words. Done more . . ."

I wrap my arms and legs around his torso and drag his head to my shoulder. "I know. He loved your words."

Connie and Arrie are outside the door, waiting. Listening. And when I concentrate, I can hear Connie's small hiccups and sobs and Arrie's hand brushing over her back.

"Arrie and Connie are outside. Want them to come in?"

Dea shrugs, words no longer able to escape past the tears. "You can come in."

Arrie pushes the door open with a look of trepidation on his face. I don't think I've ever seen him scared before, but clearly the idea of Dea's pain terrifies him. Connie's tucked under his arm, shuddering. But when she meets my gaze and looks at Dea, she runs over to the bed and jumps under the sheet on Dea's other side, her arms wrapping tight around his torso.

Arrie climbs into the other side, settling behind me. I can sense his hesitation, but he eventually settles an arm around my waist and tucks his head into my neck. I don't draw attention to the pool of tears slowly forming on my neck, nor do I move an inch while his chest contracts into silent sobs.

I have no idea what happens next—what we are without Famine in our relationship—but I know one thing for certain: we will deal with this together.

Dea's bed the next morning is a pile of limbs, tears, and sadness—a puddle of grieving people. Arrie is missing. I wonder where he went? I miss the warmth of his arms wrapped around my waist, even the slide of his tears on my shoulders was a comfort, knowing that we finally share something, even if it's pain.

Connie snores gently on Dea's other side, her arm still wrapped around his waist, her face scrunched up. I hope she's not having another nightmare—they've been getting more frequent of late.

"Arrie is going to get breakfast," Dea says, his voice raspy, as though all the tears have dried his throat. Though after a few days of crying, I guess it would. "He said he would bring it back to bed."

"Okay." I don't know what else to say. The dreaded silence of grief suffocates me, as though the world stopped turning the moment Nine died and we all stopped breathing. "Dea . . ."

"It is okay," he whispers. "You do not have to fill the silence; I think it is just going to have to hurt for a while."

Just as I open my mouth to respond, Arrie walks through the door, two trays in hand, the frilly apron he always uses tied around his waist. His usual grump of a smile plastered on his face. Pretty sure the man doesn't have a smile. "Breakfast."

Connie whines under her breath, a little whimper I would label cute if I didn't know she could spear me with an arrow from three hundred meters away. "Is it morning already?"

I rest my hand on hers on top of Dea's stomach, a grounding touch in the floating silence. "Afraid so. But Arrie brought breakfast."

"Hmmm?" She sniffs the air and smiles a beautiful smile I haven't seen since we laughed for the first time yesterday. It's weird what you notice, what you miss—the small things, the odd bits and pieces you never took notice of before. A smile is beautiful.

Arrie rests the two trays at the bottom of the bed and climbs back in beside me, scooting under the duvet. "It's not much, but it's . . . something."

I rest my spare hand on his knee and offer a weak smile, little more than a tremble, really. "It's perfect."

Connie brings the trays forward, digging in, but no one speaks. No one really knows what to say. Dea doesn't touch the food, he just looks at it with a sneering disdain written on his face, as though he completely forgot food was a concept and that its very existence insults him in some way.

"I wonder when Lo will be back?" He's been gone a while, and I'm not sure when he was due back, or if he'll return at all, but I miss my little library dragon. I miss my friend.

I miss my boyfriend.

Tears slide down my face, not entirely unexpected, but

it's not as though I can stop them from falling. Cascading like small waterfalls. Like a flashing red light signaling where my thoughts have traveled.

Everyone looks to me, worry etched across their eyes with matching sad smiles. I think it's supposed to be sympathy. Pity. But I'm not sure.

Arrie's heavy, gentle hand rests on my shoulder as he whispers, "I'm right here."

My eyes meet his icy blue ones, and I don't know what to say. He's never been here before. Never gone out of his way to provide comfort or love or support. Why now?

The confusion is clearly written across my face, because his eyes dart away and return to the breakfast tray on our laps. After swallowing a mouthful of berries, he asks, "What now?"

Connie shrugs and whispers, "I don't know." She takes in a big breath, as though deciding finally that this is the moment she can speak something that's been on her mind for a while. "We need to tell the public."

I don't know what to say to that. She was somehow thinking of her job, thinking of all the little things that need to be done, like public announcements. I'm not sure I even have the energy to string a mental sentence together, much less focus on my job, which is probably a bad sign for the world, considering, you know, my job is to save it.

Connie jumps from bed, anxious energy running through her, and yawns. "I think . . . I think I need a distraction. Something to focus on. To give my attention to. To take my mind off . . ." She trails off, vocally gesturing to the painful elephant in the room that sits on top of our vocal chords, squashing us into silence.

No one seems able to say his name, his death, or anything remotely similar, as though just the very thought is a curse.

Is this when people are allowed to break down? I usually break down over the smallest of things, but right now I just feel numb.

Dea slides the tray down the bed and crawls back up to rest his head on the pillow and bury his face in the duvet. I don't think he's ready to face a world without Famine yet.

What is it people do now? Move on? Focus on something else? Drown in grief? I'm not sure which option I wish to land on yet.

"Anyone want to help run errands?" Connie rubs her hands together expectantly, her eyes begging mine, begging any of us to join her. "Please?" The hair stopping at the middle of her back, currently sticking out in all kinds of angles, reminds me just how much she's been through recently. How much she has been through in such a short space of time.

"Sure."

Dea whines gently beneath me, an almost silent breath I'm sure the others probably heard. I wash my hand beneath the duvet and rest it on his back, rubbing gentle circles, soothing his rugged breaths.

I don't know what to do. They both need me, but I can't be in two places at once, and Connie's right, she needs to expel her energy.

"I'll stay with him," Arrie suggests, his voice barely a whisper.

I look to him, surprised. And then a gentle smile washes over me. A genuine smile. One of relief and gratitude, and maybe, just maybe, my relationship with Arrie is on the mend.

Chapter Six

The outside world is spinning on. I don't know what I expected, but a part of me wanted to see cities burning, people screaming, and my friends struggling—the world mirroring my mind. But, of course, it doesn't.

Connie doesn't let go of my hand as we walk to the embassy in companionable silence, each of us squeezing in thirty-second intervals. Reassurance. A team. That's what we are today.

"So," I start, breaking the silence, "we have an agenda today?"

Connie shrugs. "Nothing specific. We just need to check in with everyone, make sure the cleanup's gone to plan, that the wounded are doing okay, and nothing's gone to shit in the meantime."

"And I can ask about Lo."

Connie smiles sadly. "He's a dragon. He might have just taken off, hon."

I nod, the realization that I don't know Lo that well and he has no reason to return hitting me like a fresh wave of grief. "I know." My voice is quiet, barely a whisper. "But I just . . . want to know."

She squeezes my hand.

See, reassurance.

Teamwork.

And we have friends we need to check in with, like Prince Lucien, Korby, the Vampire king, my Fae trainer, and everyone else I've met on this journey. I want to make sure they're still doing okay.

We reach the embassy with somber expressions, our hands still grasping each other's, and walk to the offices upstairs, where we see Red.

Who looks at us with surprise. "Oh, umm . . . Hi." She smiles weakly as us. "I didn't know you'd be here so . . . soon."

So soon after Nine's death.

Because we should still be in mourning.

When I say nothing, Connie chimes in. "We're just wanting to make sure everything's okay. And we want a final report."

She nods, a business-like demeanor returning. "Right.

We're collaborating on that report, hence why I'm here." She gestures to herself and the building. "And as for the Witches, we're doing okay. Minimal losses overall." Her gaze meets mine. "Which we have you to thank for. You kept our losses low, and for that I'm grateful." She bows her head low—respect.

I bow in return. "No need to thank me. I was just doing my job."

She looks at me with a small smile. "But your powers are something else, girl. Err . . . boy. I mean—"

I hold up a hand, stopping her ramble. "It's okay. Genuinely. But I prefer ve/they."

"Noted." She spins on her feet. "I'll take you to the Shifters and Vampires for a better update."

Red walks us into a large meeting room upstairs, but rather than step through into board meetings and paperwork, we step into chaos.

Voices hurl themselves across the room, a lion is growling in the corner, and five Vampires have their fangs out, including the king.

But despite all that, I smile, because on the table is a small Lo chasing a familiar rabbit. Korby.

"Lo!" Surprise and joy enter my voice, and I feel floaty for a minute, like the sun. "You're okay."

He leaves his rabbit conquest behind him as he flies over and lands in my hand. "Of course. I am a dragon."

Well, he's not wrong. "Yeah, but I worry anyway."

He smiles through sharp little teeth. "I am sorry. I should have checked in sooner, but when Lucien told me what happened, I thought it best to give you all privacy."

I poke a finger at his nose. "Well, next time interrupt my depression to let me know you're still breathing, please."

He lifts a wing and does his best salute. "Yes, Magic."

A panther in the corner shifts back into a man I recognize and immediately Vampire speed to. "Nigel!" I feel so guilty that I haven't really thought about anyone else over the last few days. Shit. I'm terrible goddaughter. "You're okay."

He wraps tight arms around me and squeezes, then breathes me in. "I'm here, kid. Right here." He takes a step back and gestures to the room. "Keeping your friends from murdering each other."

I chuckle, then look around the room. Frowning. "What the hell is going on?"

No one speaks, no one even breathes, but Connie smiles at me from the doorway with a thumb's up.

The lion in the corner shifts, and Alpha Cal looks at me with a scowl on his face. "We're trying to decide how best to split resources."

Seriously, it's been a few days, and they can't make a single decision on their own? Fuck my life.

"Well," I start, "what are the top priorities?"

"My Shifters are spread too thin. If the Fae attack, we can't protect our own."

Prince Lucien speaks up, frustration ebbing his tone.

"We're sneaking blood supplies into New Orleans as best we can and keeping the defense system in place for the main Vampire cities."

Red, who's standing next to Connie, smirks at the room and meets my eyes. "We're monitoring the Fae, but there aren't enough Witches to go around."

I breathe. Deeply. And then breathe again. "Bring all our wounded from every city here. Fill up the hospital and bring all the medics, too. That'll free up some of the defenses and reduce pressure on the soldiers."

Prince Lucien smiles while Alpha Cal bows his head.

"That is a good plan, Magic," Rufus says. "But where do they go then?"

I rub a stressed hand through my pink hair. "Back to their respective homes. If they want to keep fighting with us, they can. But no one has to." But they're right. We are spread too thin. We simply don't have enough numbers to go around. But what if it isn't about numbers? "We're not using our soldiers most effectively," I mumble.

"What do you mean?" Alpha Cal asks.

"I mean, we've split everything up by species, but just like the battles, we're best when we utilize all our skills. Mix everyone up. Vampires would be great alongside Witches to monitor the Fae. They have better vision and senses, are quieter than mice when they want to be, and have night vision. Take some fairies with you if they don't mind. Vary up the species defending the cities, and then thin the numbers so we can also protect the Shifter strongholds. Biggest Shifter groupings take priority, Alpha." I turn to Connie. "In the meantime, we need to prepare to take back New Orleans."

She looks at me shocked. "Magic . . ." She sounds uncertain.

"I know." I take a deep breath, trying to remain calm. "I'm not ready either, but the world can't wait just because ours has stopped spinning." My voice lowers into a whisper. "Besides, Nine would hate that people are suffering because of him."

Everyone in the room falls silent—no one even breathes—and everyone bows their heads, avoiding looking at either of us. No one knows what to do.

I turn to the room with a brave face. "I know that it's difficult, and we've all lost people, but we can't take too long to recover. While we get stronger, so does the enemy. We can be ready to go in a few days if we use teleporting crystals."

"Are you sure?" Alpha Cal asks us. "We need you at your strongest for this." He turns to face Connie. "They need you."

I know that. I do.

But how I am supposed to retake an entire city guarded by the Fae army and the Supernatural Council without Famine?

Chapter Seven

The Horsemen: What Do They Want?

"I need you," I whisper to the night sky, wishing he were here. He'd know what to do. "I don't know what to do now. Well, I guess I do know what to do, but I don't . . . I can't . . ." I sigh. "I just don't know."

"Spiraling out loud, Killer?"

"It's the only way he can hear me." I look to Arrie's ice-blue eyes that pierce the night and a tear slips free. "I could really use his advice right now."

He sits next to me and gazes up at the stars too. "I think he'd tell you to just be yourself. Trust your own judgement. Fate gave you to us for a reason." He moves my chin to face him and spears me with an expression I don't know how to interpret. "You are our greatest gift."

"Our?" It slipped free before I could stop it. Shit. "Sorry, forget I asked."

He stays silent, not answering. Thank the goddess.

But he lies beside me, staring into the night sky, his familiar, comforting presence flitting around me like a blanket on a cold winter's day. "I miss him."

I barely hear it, the confession slipping from his lips. But when I do, it burns hotter than fire, searing me with its flames.

"I wish I could just . . . forget," he whispers. "I wish I was never chosen."

I shoot up and curl my legs underneath me. "Don't say that. If you weren't chosen, I'd be left with some talkative shitty little twink of a Horseman of War. I already have two of those." I hitch a breath. "One. I have one of those." Tears fall from my eyes before I can stop them, slipping into needing comfort rather than giving comfort. "Everyone . . . needs me, and . . . I'm just . . . crying."

Arrie's arms wrap around me, his head resting atop mine. Our white hair mixing underneath the moonlight. "You don't need to be happy to comfort someone. Your tears are comforting too."

When I'm dry crying, no tears left, Arrie pulls me away from him and smirks. "Want to be the first to have a go on my Christmas present?"

I nod. Words not forming.

He pulls me to my feet and guides me to the back of the garden, where I asked the house for a racetrack and a new fancy car just a week ago.

We get in, strap ourselves with the seat belts (I don't have time to regrow limbs right now), and Arrie shoots us across asphalt.

"You know," he says, "I've never gotten such a splendid gift." His face shifts, sourness forming on his lips. "Not for a long time, anyway."

That's more than he usually says. So maybe he's getting closer to that something I can feel between us on the horizon. Maybe he's ready? No, I won't push him. I don't want to go backward.

"Magic?" He briefly meets my questioning gaze. "Do you think maybe I can start sleeping in your bed again?" He takes a deep breath. "It feels more lonely without Nine around."

I smile, something washing through me. Something that feels a little like love. "Always." I put a hand on his knee. "You never have to ask."

"If you need me to leave for any intimacy with Con and Dea, you can just say, and I'll—"

"We'll be fine, Arrie. We are not lacking for room options."

He laughs, and it vibrates through me like nothing I've ever felt before. It swirls around me and ignites everything inside me, pushing out the bad feelings, the grief, the guilt, and the anger. And for a moment in time, I'm so happy, I feel like I'm soaring through the skies.

"Besides, we're not exactly in the right headspace for sex

right now."

Arrie frowns. "Sex can be a good healer. Besides, you have needs they should think about." He grins, a sly look crossing his lips. "We do not want to go down that road again."

Something tells me he'd do it on purpose and watch me suffer just to be the one I tear apart in a frenzy.

He swerves us around a corner with a sharp twist of the steering wheel, and I squeal, thrill soaring through me. "Ahh, Arrie!" My fist tightens on the passenger side door's handle.

"I'm just using the gift you gave me."

The smirk in his voice forces a smile to my lips.

"Besides, you'll live."

Assuming no one steals my seal and destroys it, sure. Ever since Nine, I feel more vulnerable, less immortal. Any of my team could be next, any of them could leave me, and I wouldn't be able to stop it.

The car slows to a halt, and Arrie rests a hand on my knee, a shadow of him touching me. He looks at me and brushes the tear out of my eye.

"What if the rest of you die, too? What if you all leave me?"

Arrie stops breathing and looks at me, a stolen breath held between us. "I'm never going to leave you, Magic." His giant hand cups my cheek as his fingers slide through my hair. "I'll fight beside you forever." He bows his head and screws his eyes tight shut without taking another breath, and before I know it, he's leaning in, eyes wide open and staring at my lips like they're the last ones on Earth he'll ever get to kiss. To feel against his skin.

He lights me up like electricity, an alive pulse racing through my veins that I'm too slow to do anything but feel. I'm at this man's mercy, too weak to do anything but experience him. I should push him away, have a conversation, maybe ask if this is what he really wants, but I don't. Can't. His lips are too glued to my soul.

His other hand slides up my thigh and grips my waist, then yanks me toward him. I straddle him in the driver's seat, his hardened arousal grinding into mine, all while not breaking contact, not taking a breath.

But when his hands run over my chest and starts to fiddle with my shirt buttons, I grab them. "Arrie . . ." I take a deep breath. "We're moving a little fast."

"Oh, right." A small groan slips from his tight lips as he grabs my hip and burns me with a fiery stare. "I've missed you."

I feather my lips across his, reminding him I'm always his. That I'm waiting for him. "I miss you too."

He presses his forehead to mine and breathes heavy. "Thank you."

"For what?"

"Going slow. Stopping me. Being patient. Forgiving me and—"

I shove a hand over his lips and smirk. "If you think you're off the hook that easily, then maybe you don't know me as well as you think you do." His eyes widen with worry. "If you want my forgiveness, then you'll have to earn it." I release my hand. "But I'm not going to punish you by being angry and avoiding you and treating you like shit. What you did hurt, even knowing there's a reason and things I don't know, but I love you too much to sit here and keep breaking you."

Chapter Eight

EMERGENCY REPORT: HORSEMAN OF FAMINE DEAD

By the time we get to bed, Dea is already asleep, so we join him. Connie's doing her own thing, but I'm worried. She only sleeps every few days, which means she's alone for most of the nights. Alone in her grief.

"Maybe I should stay up with her," I whisper to Arrie, trying not to wake Dea. "She's gonna be alone."

Arrie rests a heavy hand on my chest. "Shh, Killer. Con will be fine. Just get some sleep."

"But she needs me too."

Dea rolls over and rests his head on my shoulder. "You cannot fix all of our pain. We are capable adults."

It's the first real sentence he's spoken since we got back home, and it's to give me wise old sage advice. I roll my eyes.

Of fucking course it is.

The door opens slowly, silently, and Connie walks in with a small smile on her face. "I'm flattered. You're all talking about me." She crawls up the bed and sits in my lap. "Look at me." She meets my eyes. "I've been sleeping for less than these guys for a *very* long time, babe. I'm used to having my alone time." She leans in and swipes her lips briefly over mine—a quick burst of affection with all the power of a longer kiss. "Now, get some sleep."

I yawn but drag her down into bed with me, enjoying her warmth, her lying on top of me, a solid weight while I drift off.

"You know," Arrie grumbles, "if Nine were here, he'd be suggesting some kind of orgy."

"If Nine were here," Connie responds, "we'd already be having an orgy."

We all chuckle, but Dea slips back inside himself and buries his face in my neck.

I kiss his hair and whisper, "Do you want me to switch to my female form, so our angels can touch?"

Dea whines a little, clearly unsure, but eventually nods. "But it is not because I want you only as a female. I love both forms, and—"

"Shhhh," I whisper into his hair. "I know." I switch forms, and Connie squeals as I lose a few inches and move about on the bed some, but she holds steadfast nonetheless. "Besides, I have more holes for orgies this way."

44

Everyone chuckles, even Dea.

"Arrie?" I ask the dark room.

"Hmmm?"

"Can I tell them about earlier?"

"Tell us what?" Connie asks the room, suddenly alert. "You have to tell me now. Girl code."

Arrie nods against my shoulder, but his hand tightens into a fist against my leg.

"I don't have to, you know. When I ask a question, it's me giving you a genuine option."

"Oh," he says. "Well, okay then."

"Sooooo, that's a yes, then? Or a no?"

Connie groans from on top of me. "Listening to you two trying to have a conversation is painful."

Arrie punches Connie in the arm, who punches right back.

"Yes, you may tell them."

Dea is silent, but he's awake; I can feel his breathing. Connie, on the other hand, is leaning on her elbows, which are placed beside my shoulders, while she stares at me with child-like glee.

"Arrie kissed me tonight."

Connie's jaw drops, and Dea raises his head. Interest piqued. "Really?" he asks.

"Uh-huh." I nod, a smile forming on my lips. "We didn't chat about it or anything, but—"

"Magic reminded me to go slow."

"Wow, big guy"—Connie pats him on the head—"well done. Didn't know you had restraint in you."

He growls at her, and the deep vibration of his voice shoots right through me. My insides squeeze, and I do my best to not squirm, but apparently Connie notices anyway, since she just laughs at me."

"Well, well, well . . ." She looks at me, devilishly beautiful, and smirks. "I learn new things about you every day."

"Shut up." It comes out more as a mumble, and the guys look bewildered, but we both just giggle. They're used to us by now. Taking a deep breath, I force the words out of my mouth. "I'm scared."

"About what?" Arrie asks.

"Life without him." I sigh. "Sex without him. Thinking without him in my mind. It's so empty, it echoes. Like my thoughts are just shouting back at me." I look at everyone, a somber expression thrown across their features again. "Sorry, I turned everything sad again."

"It's okay, babe." Connie strokes my cheek with a soft thumb. "We're all allowed to just randomly be sad."

Arrie and Dea snuggle in on either shoulder, Connie curls up between my legs, and we all fall asleep together. Well, all minus one.

Chapter Nine

PRINCE LUCIEN SPOTTED GOING TO *SHERUTA* THROUGH PORTAL

Connie, Arrie, and I sit at the embassy the next day, discussing specifics over strategy, how to retake New Orleans with the least number of casualties possible, and how to mingle our forces for maximum efficiency.

Arrie paces the room, his vision that shining, zoned-out look he gets when he's using his battle strategy mode. "Move half the fairies from New York unit four to Delhi unit eighty-seven. Schedule half the Vampire troops from all cities to support the Shifter cities, then move thirty-eight percent of the Shifter troops to the Vampire cities, remove Lo from active defense, and reinforce Cairo with the eighteen Witches from Dhaka."

Connie and I aren't much use right now. Arrie's in the

limelight. And what a hot limelight it is. My jeans are getting a little strained over here. So I shift to my female form.

"Hot, isn't it?" Connie whispers into my ear.

Vampire eyes shoot our way, but I ignore them.

"Yup."

"Gonna tap that later?" she whispers back.

"Nope."

She frowns, huffs down a whine, and goes back to paying attention.

Dea's at home, still in bed. And I don't know what to do. He needs time. And in any other circumstance, I'd let him wallow for years until he's ready to poke his head back above water. But we need him in this war. There's no way we can do this with just the three of us. But I don't want to be the reason he's pushed before he's ready. I don't want to watch him snap.

"Stop spiraling," Connie whispers.

Arrie stops talking and looks my way, a question in his gaze. "You okay?"

I nod, but I don't smile.

The real answer is I'm not sure what okay feels like anymore. But that doesn't matter. I have to be there for Dea. For Connie, who was struggling before. And for Arrie, who needs me to remain by his side while he figures himself out.

I can't fall apart right now.

I look around, my gaze falling on the ambassadors in turn and then on the empty Witch seat. Blood boils in my veins.

I'm gonna kill him.

And I'm gonna enjoy it.

A few screams pierce my zoned-out hearing, and I look around. Shit. The couple of chairs around me are on fire. Shit, fuck, shit.

Water, Magic. Water.

Before I can generate a stream, one of the Witches, Nana, I think, puts them out with a scowl. "Watch your emotions next time."

I frown at her.

Then I frown at the empty chair again and point. "Someone fill that seat."

"We're working on that," Red says with a gentle look. She's a fire Witch. She gets it.

"Sorry everyone."

Everyone grabs new chairs, and the meeting rekindles with little fuss. Other than Lucien laughing at everyone's horror. But we all ignore his crazy.

By the time we're done, we have a plan. All that's left is a date. And for that, we're gonna need a little reconnaissance.

"Who's up for some spying on the SC?" I ask everyone while we're sat drinking cocktails in the sun, the balcony doors open. "I promise fun times ahead."

Everyone chuckles.

Red sticks her arm up. "You know I'm game."

Lucien shakes his head, a smile of affection on his face aimed toward Red. "I'll go with you."

My eyebrows reach the ceiling.

"What?" He shrugs. "Always up for spying on my big brother."

Something tells me that's not the reason he's going.

"Can I go with?" Nigel asks, having joined the drinks after our meeting was over. "I'm a bit bored doing not much right now."

"I thought Rufus was keeping you busy?" After he officially quit his job with the Supernatural Council, Rufus made him part of his right-hand team here on *Sheruta*. A way to look connected with Earth, I think.

Nigel shrugs. "It's just a little . . . stuffy."

Lucien grabs Nigel's hand and shakes it. "Happy to have you on board, Nige."

Nige? Since when is the little prince friends with all my people?

Connie's quiet next to me, her silence having fallen the moment the meeting was over. I wonder how she's really doing? Between Bandio Bontanos, our new relationship, and Nine, she's probably been through more than the rest of us recently. I hope she's doing okay. Well, as okay as she can.

I squeeze her hand and nestle hers in my palm.

She looks to me with a sad smile. And I know that look. That's the look she has when she's remembering Nine.

"Okay," I start, "we're gonna head home. Red, please lead the team. Be safe. Don't take stupid risks. We'll check in later." I help Connie out of her seat, and Arrie and I lead us back up the winding path to home.

This is the first day we've left Dea alone, and I won't lie, I'm scared what I'll find when we get back home. "I'm worried about Dea," I mumble.

"Me too." Arrie grabs my other hand. "This reminds me of what it was like when Haji died, but worse because there are more memories with Nine."

"And we're all sad too," Connie says, "so we can't . . . be as supportive."

I look to Arrie, then to Connie, and think of Dea . . . I need to help them through this. I need to be there for them. I can't let them fall.

"Well, at least we're one step closer to freeing New Orleans." Arrie speeds up, clearly wanting to get home. "It's awful reading all the news stories about how much those Vamps are suffering."

"The sooner we can free that city, the closer we are to dealing with this mess."

I snort. "Sorry, but we're a long way off peace. The SC need to be retired, the Fae need to adhere to the law or face consequences, the humans need to either get on board or shut up whining, and the Witches need to come out of the closet." I take a deep breath. "Anyone know how I'm supposed to fix any of that?"

Arrie looks at me with certified confidence. "You'll figure it out, Magic."

Connie tightens her grip on my hand. "You always do."

"Yeah, but I usually break something first."

Chapter Ten

VAMPIRE KING SPOTTED VISITING WOUNDED AT NEW YORK CITY GENERAL HOSPITAL

Once we reach home, we're greeted with a whirlwind of magical pressure, and I drop Arrie's and Connie's hands and race to Dea's room at top Vampire speed.

I can hear Connie and Arrie following, equally worried.

"Dea?" I half yell through the popping feeling in my ears. "Dea!" The door to his room is half blown off its hinges and papers, potion bottles, and pillows fly around the room in a whirlwind of madness. And at the center of it all is a black ball of feathers huddled on the floor. Screaming. "Dea!"

I race to the center, dodging a pillow and smashing two glass bottles to the ground. The moment my hand finds its way beneath his wings he's using to protect himself and my skin makes contact, I breathe a sigh of relief.

And everything freezes.

There're pillows in the air, along with sheets of paper, books, and anything else previously stacked neatly in the room.

"Dea . . ." I yank on his arm and get him to a sitting position, wipe the tears from his face, and shove my arms around him. "I'm sorry. I won't leave again."

His usually golden skin burns red as painful magic pulses out of him. "No . . ." he groans. "Please, make it stop."

Arrie and Connie rush to my side, and Arrie growls. "Dea, stop being so stupid. Go and help whoever needs helping."

Connie's hand flattens on his shoulder. "The more you fight it, the more it'll hurt. Go."

And that's when I realize what's happening. Dea's being called to a lost soul. To help guide them to the otherworld gates. The gate Nine's currently waiting behind.

With a soft voice, and being as gentle as I can, I whisper, "This is your job. Without you, they'll be lost. They deserve happiness in death, Dea. We all do."

"No, I . . ." His skin glows red hot again. "Argh!" He grips his hair hard, yanking at it. "I do not want to carry another crying soul to their afterlife. To watch their loved ones cry and be the reason they are being left behind!"

Arrie grumbles something and then translates. "This is a really shitty time for a soul to get stuck."

It mustn't happen very often because I've not seen this

before.

"Please, Dea. Go." I grab his hand and rub soothing circles on its palm. "I'll be right here for you when you get back, with tea, blankets, movies, books, and as many blowjobs as you like."

Arrie chuckles. "Hear that, dude? Unlimited access to Killer's mouth? Who'd turn that down?"

I look to him and blush. Then I return my attention to Dea. "In either form."

He snaps his attention to me and then looks sheepishly to the ground. "You do not have to do that just for me."

I lift his chin up. "Trust me, I'll be getting some too."

His lips tilt up ever so slightly, and a small breathy laugh escapes. "Tempting the Angel of Death with blowjobs and tea?" He sighs, clearly not wanting to go still. "Fine. Deal."

Everything in the room crashes down, and the moment he closes his eyes, he pops out of existence.

"Wait, what?"

Arrie laughs at me while Connie helps me to my feet. "Yeah, it usually teleports him to Earth, and then he can fly to the person at the speed of light like a homing pigeon."

"But faster." Connie gestures to the mess. "I think we should clean this up for him."

"I'll get started on some food." Arrie wraps a quick arm around my shoulders and squeezes, then he rushes off to make something no doubt delicious.

Connie and I are left to clean up Dea's room. We could

call one of the maids, but we're funny about them being in our spaces. We still clean our own rooms. The maids just collect the washing.

Connie looks around the space and sighs. "He doesn't really like his job." She asks the house for trash bags and starts collecting things that flew out of the waste bin and picking up the broken glass.

"Why?" I grab the books and start re-shelving them. "I mean, he didn't kill them."

She runs a hand through her hair, and I once again feel guilty when it ends at her waist rather than her ass. "It's not that he feels guilty; he doesn't enjoy watching their loved ones crying and screaming or the emptiness of the soul. He says they're as blank as paper when passing."

I shudder. "Does that mean Nine's blank? Empty?"

Connie looks at me with a grimace. "That's probably why he doesn't want to go. He won't see him. He doesn't actually go through the gates—just guides them to the door and opens it."

"But just knowing that Nine's beyond them . . ." Alone. Without any of us. Blank and empty. While the world needs him. While we need him. While I need him.

Tears creep down my face as I shelve the last book.

"Sorry," she whispers as she wraps her arms around my chest.

My shoulders shake, and for a moment it feels as though my knees might not keep holding me up. "It's okay. I asked."

I take a deep breath and turn in her arms. "You were just answering my questions." My lips meet hers, our gentle tears mixing between our teeth and lips. "I always want you to be honest with me."

She nods. Understanding. "Let's keep going. It'll be nice for this room to be clean for him. You know how he gets about his clean space."

I chuckle and wipe the tears away. "Yeah. He's a bit of neat freak."

"A bit?"

We both laugh as we do our best to return the room to its usual impossibly clean standards. We do okay, I think. But I'm sure Dea will move things around and readjust when he returns.

"Come on"—she grabs my hand—"let's go for a walk." She guides us outside into the bright and sunny weather of *Sheruta* and toward the rainbow forest, where I used to spend my mornings trying to punch Arrie in the face. Good times. "I'm sorry for being so checked out over the past few days."

She avoids my eyes, even when I try to meet them, so I squeeze her hand. "Stop apologizing for having emotions. You needed space and love, like being left to your walks and work but being consistently reminded that I'm here."

Her eyebrows raise. "Got me all figured out, huh?"

"Maybe a little of you." We pass the clearing I used to do hand-to-hand combat training in. "It's my job to understand you. To help you."

56

"Don't push yourself too hard, hon. You need space too."

But they need me. Changing the subject, I whisper, "I hope Dea's okay." He seems so broken, so unrelentingly upset. And I don't know how to fix it. Or make it even the slightest bit better, and I'm worried that there isn't a way to do that. "It's like I've lost them both."

I can hear the loud swallow of Connie's throat and feel the squeezing of my hand. She opens her mouth, then closes it again, then opens it, then closes it. Seems she doesn't know what to say either.

"It's okay," I reassure, "I don't need comforting words."

We walk all the way through the forest, enjoying the light filtering through rainbow-colored leaves pattering onto the floor in small bursts. We tiptoe past the unicorn herd toward the northern edge, and I stop to observe them. But they're as calm and placating as usual—all grace and no anger. As though they were plucked from a dandelion's heart and placed into the body of a silver cloud on a cloudless day.

I wish I were as peaceful.

There's this simmering rage deep inside me. One I can't seem to let go of. And just when I think I've gotten a handle on understanding it, of reining it in, it explodes into a million shards of glass. Like the fiery chair incident. And when I nearly choked Felicity to death.

Connie leads me up a familiar hill, past familiar rabbit holes, and we sit underneath a familiar *Shinto*. "It's peaceful up here."

"Yeah, I know. We can see everything: the forest, the town, the house, the fairy gardens." I take a deep, earth-scented breath and let it calm my soul. "It always reminds me that I'm home."

Connie rests her head on my lap and reaches up to twizzle the white strands of my hair through her fingers. "You're more comfortable with your male form now." It isn't a question.

"Yeah. Dea helped. But I also don't really want to grieve with Vampire emotions. Not if I have a choice to avoid it."

"Makes sense." Her palm lies flat against my cheek as she strokes my eyelid and smiles at me. "I know it hurts, and it'll continue hurting forever, but I'm so proud of how you've handled this." She leans up and places a gentle kiss as soft as rose petals against my lips. "The rest of us are falling apart, and while you're struggling, you're holding up for us." She whispers her lips against mine. "Thank you."

I smile against her, a sad smile I'm not sure could really signal happiness. "I'll always be here for you." I guide a gentle hand down her front, along the outline of her breasts, and then inch my fingers along her the edges of her tank.

She arches into my touch, a breath racing out of her mouth. Her hands reach out and grace their silken skin down my cheeks and round my neck, where she grips hard. Then pulls my face to hers. "Kiss me." Her voice needy, her eyes hazy.

I slide my tongue past her lips, caressing her mouth with

a growing need, while my fingers play with the edges of her top and shorts, teasing.

Her hips arch into me, seeking, needing. "Magic . . ." she moans into my mouth.

"Hmm?" I say between kisses. I slide my mouth down her neck as my fingers slip up her top, her skin like silk, caressing every inch of my hand like rivers of scorching sand.

"Fuck me." She opens her eyes and pierces those earthy greens at me. "Please." Her mouth tipped open, her eyes begging, and her pink lips wet from my mouth, I lay her on the grass and straddle her waist.

"Anything in particular you'd like?" I whisper into her ear, my hands finding their way to her breasts once again and skimming beneath her bra.

"You." Her hands grip the sides of my head and yank me to her lips. "Inside . . . me," she gasps between breaths.

"I've been waiting for you to ask."

I've been purposefully gentle with all the team these last few days, not trying to pressure them or push them before they're ready, but now Connie lies before me, her tank top above her bra, her breathy moans caressing the air, and her legs parting beneath me. I sit between them and expose one nipple to the warm air.

Her chest arches toward me as a small whine slips from her mouth, so I take the nipple into my mouth and slide my tongue in soft circles while my hand exposes her other nipple for me to play with.

I want this to be perfect for her.

So I use my knees to widen her legs, to spread them in front of me, as I grind my rapidly hardening dick into her clit and hear her moan my name on the wind.

"Magic . . . please."

No way am I giving in that easily.

I seal my lips around her nipple and suck, continuing to use my tongue. My fingers on the other nipple pinch tighter, pulling slightly.

"Ahh, yes."

Her back arches off the ground as far as it can go as her legs wrap around my waist and pull me harder against her, increasing the friction.

The stiff material of my jeans feels more like a steal trap at this point, caging me in and squeezing the prisoner. But I continue on, not wanting to give Connie want she wants just yet. Wanting to relish every moan and sigh, capture them like falling stars.

I let go of her nipple with a pop, remove her tank top the rest of the way off, alongside her bra, then trail my lips south. Kissing every inch of skin along the way, paying attention to her pristine glow, to the way her hips slide beneath my hands, to the top hem of her shorts and how much I want them out of the fucking way. So I undo the button and gently wiggle them down her hips and throw them off.

Lying beneath me is a beautiful as sin woman in nothing but a pair of green lace panties, with golden blond hair trailing across lush green grass, looking at me as though I'm the most beautiful person she's ever seen. As though she's never looked in the mirror.

"You're beautiful," I whisper. I part her legs wide, placing a foot either side of my hips, and lick around the lace of her panties. Tickling, teasing.

My hands travel back to her breasts, rolling her nipples between my fingers in the same way Dea does to me. My dick aches to be free, to be slipping inside this woman, making her moan my name without a care for who hears us.

Connie squirms beneath me, trying to get my lips closer to her. "More," she demands.

And I oblige, sucking her clit through the material and tasting her. "So good." I lick my lips and swallow the taste, savoring the feel of her in my mouth.

Her fingers wrap around the edges of her panties, and yanks she them down her thighs, shoving my mouth away for a moment. Green eyes flash deviously at me, and a wicked grin to match.

She knows exactly what she's doing.

We pull her panties off the rest of the way and throw them to the floor, then I'm right back between her legs, eager for more. As my tongue darts out and wanders upward, past her opening and through her lips, to find its way to her clit.

"Shit," she curses and shoves her hips into my face. "Yes, please, more."

I've never been this turned on, this needy, this insistent

about where I want my cock to be, but it's going into this woman soon, or I'm going to burst.

But first, I lick, suck, and nibble, enjoying the thrashing, moaning, and cursing slipping from Connie's lips as she loses control. Loses the battle of seduction.

My fingers find their way up her thigh, slipping through leaked wetness and gliding into her warmth, stretching her walls. And fuck, if I didn't want it to be me in there, her walls clenching my dick instead of my fingers. A groan slips from my lips as I suck a little harder and curve my fingers, looking for that perfect spot.

When I find it, she thrusts into my hand, chasing the rising tide.

"Don't stop."

"Don't plan to," I growl. My tongue and fingers work in tandem to keep her moans rising higher, her hips thrusting faster, and I follow her cues and speed.

Her hands grip my hair, keeping my face buried in her, riding her hips against my mouth like I'm her personal sex toy. "Yes, yes! Fuck, yes." Her walls spasm and clench hard around my fingers, but I don't stop moving them. And I don't let her clit go, continuing to suck.

Her legs tighten as her thighs clench and she shoves her hips into my mouth harder, faster. Riding the high as she moans.

As the orgasm subsides, her moans get slower, breathier, and her legs unclench as she gently pulls my head away and up toward her face. She smiles at me. "That was fantastic. I'm kind of jealous you made me come so hard your first time."

"Well, it is easier when you also own a vagina."

"True." Her lips slant against mine as our foreheads touch and our tongues dance in tandem to a relaxed, needy rhythm. She pulls away and smirks. "Now fuck me."

Jumping to my feet, I yank my jeans and underwear off.

"The t-shirt too," she commands. "I wanna feel those abs against me."

I shove it off and then bow. "As my lady commands."

We both giggle, the light shining in her eyes and bouncing off of me in a way that relieves the ache of grief and sadness.

Connie rises to her knees and crawls toward me, her mouth parting, her tongue licking those plump pink lips. And I know what she's going to do before she does it. Her lips kiss the head of my cock, licking the pre-cum and swallowing.

My eyes follow her bobbing throat as my balls tighten and my hand grips her lovely blonde hair, encouraging her to swallow me further. "More."

Her green eyes meet mine in a devious glare, and I watch as her lips descend, swallowing inch after inch, until my cock is touching the back of her throat and she's taking a deep breath in through her nose and swallowing.

"Damn." Her throat encloses around my dick, a tight channel constricting, wet, and then she starts to hum. "Shit." My hips buck, pulling out and then back in.

But she just continues to kneel, swallowing with each

thrust. And I realize that she's had a lot of practise with this and used to fuck Arrie, and I can't imagine him holding back. She can take my weak-as-shit male form pounding her throat.

So I grip her hair tighter and keep her head in place, then pull most of the way out before diving back in. Pleasure rolls through me in waves, each tight, warm swallow filling me up and making me clench.

My thighs tremble.

And I thrust harder, faster, chasing the feeling that's rising on the horizon, biting at the heels of my sanity. Causing my knees to buckle and my breath to run in ragged gasps. "Connie . . . I'm gonna—"

She yanks my dick out of her mouth and jumps to her feet. "Not yet."

A low whine escapes my throat, my hips still wanting to buck. "Connie . . ."

"You want me?" she asks. I nod. "Then come get me." She takes a step back, her brows raised in defiance, and smiles. "Fuck me like you own me."

I grab her arm in a bruising grip and yank her back to me, her skin against mine, the air wrapping around us, the sun beating down on our backs. "Then c'mere."

She kisses me hard, her tongue plunging into my mouth and taking control, but I fight back, kiss harder, and shove her to the grass. The hiss that escapes her lips when I suck at her nipples in turn tells me just how oversensitive they are from earlier, but I don't care.

Her legs wrap around my waist and pull me in, lining my dick up against her dripping entrance, and I slam home.

We both moan, mine being muffled by the neck I'm nuzzling into, but hers echoing around us, her head flying back onto the grass.

"Yes, right there." Her thighs clench around me and encourage me to move.

So without breaking contact from her clit, I slide out and back in, relishing in the warmth now surrounding me.

The world seems to break away for a while as my focus pins itself to her, to our bodies connecting, to the pleasure rolling through me. To the moans she's screaming into my ear.

"Shit, you feel so good."

She tightens around me with a wicked smile.

And I moan. "So tight."

I rock my hips, trying to get that perfect angle for her and continue grinding, and I'm rewarded by a gasp and a shout.

"Magic!"

Her walls tighten slightly as her moans get louder, and I know she's close.

But I'm right behind. So close. I thrust into her harder, balls slapping against her ass, my dick slamming against the back of her.

"Fuck," she groans into my ear, "I'm gonna come again."

"Yes, come for me."

She spasms, tightens, clenches my dick like it's a lifeline as her hips grind against mine.

But it's her screams that send me over the edge, thrown like a cannonball, moaning louder than intended, as I pin her arms above her head and use her. Fill her up. And make her mine.

Just as she requested.

Chapter Eleven

Arrie's laying the table when we walk in, hand-in-hand, red-faced, fully clothed, and he smiles when he sees us. A knowing smile.

Yeah, he probably heard us, but whatever. I don't care. That was some of the best sex I've ever had. And I didn't once worry about having a penis or being in my male form. I just enjoyed it.

I'll call that a brilliant win.

"Had a good time?"

Arrie lays the plates and some of the serving dishes out on the giant dining room table, but instead of the usual five, there's four. And suddenly, all the wind under my sail is gone.

Deflated.

"Yeah," Connie says gently, "it was fun being railed by Magic's dick."

Oh my goddess, Connie. I just look at her, surprise in my eyes, hoping to convey that.

"What? It's not like ve doesn't have a dick."

Arrie coughs and focuses his look. "She's right. It's fine. Totally normal. Not even worth a conversation."

"Really?"

"Really." He smiles at me, but there's something there, lurking underneath, something he's not sharing.

I can tell.

"If you say so." I grab his arm as he goes to pick up a giant plate of crispy tacos. "Are you okay?"

He chuckles. "Yes."

I look at him dubiously, a question in my brows.

He sighs and runs a hand through his hair. The feeling is there, on the tip of his tongue, but he usually shrugs or swallows it and just says nothing.

"You can tell me, big guy." I rub his shoulder. "It's important to communicate, remember?"

"I'm just a little . . . jealous." He looks away as he says it and picks up the taco plate to place it on the table.

"Oh." Jealous? So he wants me? Well, of course he wants you, Magic. He kissed you with those 'come fuck me' lips in the car just the other night. "Sorry, I didn't mean to make you feel left out, I just—"

"It's okay." He looks at me with a smile. "Seriously."

If he says it's okay, then I'm going to choose to believe him. Because I think I'm beginning to understand that communication is always honest with this man, hence why he chooses to say nothing a lot.

Connie and I help him lay the table, and just when I'm about to ask where Dea is and wonder if he's okay, he pops into the kitchen on an exasperated breath.

"Dea!" I run to him and wrap my arms around his neck. Then shift into my female form and let him breathe me in at the crook of my neck, like he usually does. Besides, I like his Angel form touching me like this. "I love you."

A couple of silent tears slide down my shoulder, but he looks at me with a peaceful kind of sadness on his face and wipes them away. "I love you too, Angel." He lifts my knuckles to his lips and drops a light kiss. "Always."

"Good. Now come eat." Connie points to his share with a demand in her voice that brokers no argument.

He switches out of his Angel form and sits on his chair and stares at Nine's with a heart-breaking look of disappointment on his face, but I grab his hand and rub circles over his thumb, trying to distract him.

He needs to eat.

"I made tacos," Arrie says, clearly trying to help. "You like tacos."

Dea snaps his gaze to Arrie's with a small smile. "I do like tacos." And he grabs a tortilla, some meat, some salsa, and a couple of sides, and I breathe easy as my Angel of Death eats for the first time in days.

In a vague, bland voice, Dea whispers, "The soul was a woman in her twenties—Fae—who refused to leave Earth because the queen demanded she always stay by her side."

Connie looks like she's trying not to vomit, and Arrie looks pissed. I don't know what I am, though.

Connie explains, "The Fae Queen can order her people around, a little like how Nine's magic worked, but I've never seen it transcend death before."

"Me either." Dea shrugs. "Probably just a one off."

I file that potential problem away for later, maybe a question for my Fae trainer, and dig into the tacos. Arrie's tacos. Hehe, Arrie's tacos. Can tacos be butt cheeks or just frontal flaps?

Goddess, I'm tired.

Connie coughs after finishing her first taco and announces, "We are waiting on Red, Lucien, and Nigel to get back from scouting, which we think should take a few days, and when they do, we'll set the date for taking back New Orleans."

Dea looks at her. "So soon?"

She shrinks, following both Arrie and I shrinking, and looks at him with pity in her eyes. "I know, but they're suffering. They can't wait for us to get our shit together."

Dea nods, understanding, but clearly not wanting to follow through with that plan, anyway.

I grab his hand again, reassuring him everything's going

to be okay. "If you like, you can stay here."

Arrie nods. "I can probably create a strategy without you, dude. If you're really not up for it."

Dea looks to me, to Arrie, and then to Connie, and then slumps in his chair. "I do not know." A worried hand rakes through his uncombed hair.

"Dea?" My hands shake slightly under the table. He looks at me. "Have you considered maybe seeing a grief counselor?"

His shock registers, then a small amount of anger, until eventually he looks at me and smiles a genuine smile. "If you think that is for the best, then I will give it a try."

"I think we'd all benefit from counseling, to be honest, but you're not coping. The Dea I know would never let other people suffer just because life's gotten a bit hard."

"A bit hard?"

Yeah, even I heard that one. For fuck's sake.

"He is dead, Magic. And he is not ever going to be undead. He's not coming back." He gets up and storms off, probably back to his room, the echo of his sliding chair the only thing I can still hear.

"Shit." Could I have said that better? Should I have not said it at all? What about different words?

"Shhh." Connie's hands are on my shoulder. "He's just upset because he knows you're right."

"And he hates that he's let himself fall so hard." Arrie gets up and sits next to me, in Nine's empty chair, and rests a hand on either knee. "That you're doing so much better than him, despite you being the emotional one."

"That's just because I don't feel anything."

Arrie and Connie both look at me with worried expressions.

"I feel numb. I cry sometimes, in bursts of sadness, and I have small moments with all of you, but overall, I feel nothing." I take a deep breath. "It's like I'm waiting for the tidal wave to hit."

"Oh, hon, I'm so sorry." She looks at me with guilt, nibbling on her bottom lip. "I just assumed you were holding up okay." She swears under her breath. "I'm so used to Nine telling me how everyone's doing when things get like this. I'm shit at doing it myself."

Arrie's low laughter filters through the air like a small rumble. "Sorry, it's just we're so shit at this without him."

Connie and I laugh too, and soon we're laughing and crying and falling apart and flying all at once. A cocktail mix of emotions we don't know how to navigate.

"Yeah, we are." I wipe my eyes and get up, stubborn pride soaring through me. "Now, if you'll excuse me, I've got an Angel of Death boyfriend I need to apologize to."

"Want us to join you?" Arrie asks. "Or do you want to be alone?"

"Errm . . ." I fidget my hands. "Can you both come with me?" I feel stronger as a unit.

Chapter Twelve

That familiar black door with the old hinges—the ones we asked the house to fix for us after Dea's outburst—stands I front of me. In front of us. But this time, it stands open, like he expected us to follow. Or he's hoping for us to follow.

"Dea?" I enter the room, never really sure what I'll find these days, but I'm pleasantly surprised to find Dea rearranging things. Putting them back where they actually belong. I look to the bookshelf. "I see you didn't like the order I had going on?"

He looks at me with a small smile. "Sorry, Angel, no." He drops the duster he'd just picked up to start cleaning with and circles me with those strong arms. "Angel, I am so sorry for yelling."

Connie and Arrie stand near, both not looking too sure where they should be standing or sitting or looking. But Dea invites them into the hug, and soon I'm surrounded by all three of them. Their strength, their unity, their family. And something about it finally breaks me.

"I hate this!" My fists ball at my sides. "I don't have the energy to help any of you. But I need to because you need me." Heaving breaths wrack my body as the tears fall in sobbing waves. "Dea needs my Angel form to feel grounded, especially right now, and Connie needs me to be strong and keep touching her and flirting with her and being there for her, and Arrie is requiring so much patience that I just don't have right now. And I don't know what to do." All of their arms stay around me, strong and unyielding. "I just want Nine back. He'd know what to do."

My knees can't keep me up anymore, and I fall, my body finally cracking. But Arrie catches me. He wraps his arms around me and holds me tight as he carries me to the bed we've all been sharing, laying us down on the cotton sheets.

"I'm so sorry, Killer." His gruff voice is soothing, like a deep earthly rumble that grounds me to the present.

"We've been expecting too much of you." Connie lies on top of me, her weight a comforting presence on the anxiety boiling beneath my surface. "You have as much grief as we do."

I shake my head. "That's ridiculous. You knew him for

two thousand years. I only had a few months." My hands grip the sheets. "Of course your grief hurts more."

Dea lies on my other side, his wings having come out, so he lays one over us all. "Grief does not work that way. It is not measured in years known or love felt. Just because we had him longer does not entitle us to more tears; you have every right to be grief stricken."

"But . . . but . . . ." I swipe the tears away frustrated by them. "For fuck's sake, I thought I'd outgrown this emotional nonsense." I've been doing so well.

Connie giggles at me and places a hand on my cheek. "You'll never outgrow your emotions. They're made to be felt."

"And just because you feel them harder than most," Dea adds, "does not make you any less of an adult."

"You're allowed to fall apart, cry, and have breakdowns, Killer. We might be immortal, but we're only human."

I look to Arrie, unsure of how to reply. "So you're sounding like Dea now? Giving advice?"

He shrugs. "Maybe."

"Then you can lead the team," Dea adds, "since Magic and I seem to be incapable right now."

"Ve's doing a great job," Arrie argues. "We're just waiting on some intelligence and then we can plan the New Orleans take over."

Dea looks to the ceiling as he lies flat on his back. "I'll join you."

"Are you sure?" Connie asks, curling up between my legs. "You don't have to. Neither of you do. Arrie and I can do it alone."

Dea and I look to each other, then laugh.

"What?" she asks, genuine surprise lacing her words.

I grab her face between my hands and smile. "As much as I love you, I am not leaving New Orleans to the pair of you. The city won't even be standing by the time you're done."

"Pfft."

Arrie shrugs. "Could use some reconstruction."

"Not on our dime," Connie says. "With Nine . . . gone, our finances aren't refilling like they used to."

"Oh yeah." That was all Nine, too. "He did so much for us."

"Too much," Dea says.

"We don't have to change, though." I take a deep breath. "Sometimes having three partners is hard work, but I wouldn't change it for the world. I want you all to continue leaning on me."

"I don't want to be an inconvenience," Connie admits. "I know how much Dea needs you right now. I can take a step back, if you think that's—"

"No." I don't elaborate.

"Ooookay, I guess that's that."

Arrie stays silent, not offering anything, but I know that's because he isn't ready. And I will never push him.

Dea nuzzles into my neck. "I am going to rely on you all,

rather than just you, Angel."

"That's acceptable." I chuckle to myself at a funny thought. "Do you think Nine's looking down on us somewhere and thinking finally, they have some communication without me."

Dea chuckles, and Connie and Arrie follow suit, and soon we're all laughing.

I know, it's weird for four grieving people to laugh, but the truth is that your other emotions don't switch off just because grief is taking the steering wheel. And that's okay. Laughter is meant to be heard in times of hardship. Otherwise, how are you supposed to come through the other side?

Chapter Thirteen

Are the Horsemen Trying to Rule the World?

Today, I asked Connie if she could contact Korby and my Fae trainer, so I could do something instead of moping around. And with some luck, they both arrive first thing in the morning.

"Magic!" Korby throws her arms around me, my pink hair swaying with the weight. "It's so good to see you."

My Fae trainer smiles gently at me, but when I catch her doing so, she frowns and looks away.

"It's good to see you too, Mrs. No Name."

Korby raises her eyebrows. "Huh?"

"Oh, she won't tell me her name." I shrug. "Says it's unnecessary."

Korby also shrugs, but then she runs into the kitchen and

puts her hand on the side and closes her eyes. In a few seconds, a steaming cup of Starbucks coffee enters her hand. "Ohmygod, ohmygod, it's true! Wow. The house is magical."

A familiar almighty thump echoes across the ground from outside, followed by a rush of tornado-level wind.

"Lo." I run out to great him. "Lo!"

He snorts, that gruffly thing he does when he laughs. "Hello, Magic."

Korby and my Fae trainer stand behind me, and I get the feeling something's happening.

"What's going on?"

"We have agreed," Lo says, "to train you together."

"All three of you?"

"Yup." Korby laces her arm through mine and drags us closer to Lo. "See, you need to start using your abilities together, rather than separately. So we brought as many people as we could to help."

Lo lowers his head. "Nigel is going to help you gain strength in your shift when he returns."

"Anyone available to help me with unlocking my earth powers?" I've managed to gather air, water, and fire, but no such luck with earth. It would seem it's as stubborn as a mountain.

"I can help with that," the earth Coven Witch says from behind us.

I turn around to face the older woman and her walking stick. "Hello." I bow low, respecting my Witch elder.

She waves a hand through the air, disregarding it. "No need for principle. We're here to help." She sits on a nearby tree stump near a fairy den and smiles. "But that was a long walk up that hill."

"In that case," Korby says, "go grab your staff."

I Vampire race to my room and grab the charm bracelet its sleeping form takes and then race back outside. I'm back before of them have taken a breath.

"Damn you're fast," my Fae trainer says.

"Have you not seen Magic's female form abilities before?"

She shrugs. "Sometimes. But never their Vampire stuff."

Korby looks to me in question.

"I've just never had a need for it during our sessions before. I've used some Witch magic though."

"C'mon." Korby drags me into a nearby empty space between a few fairy dens and the rainbow forest. "Let's begin."

Korby drills me for nearly an hour on all the various forms, footwork, and positions we've practised in both forms, and by the time we're done, my male form is panting and sweating in the morning sun.

"You can work harder than that," my Fae trainer says. "Put the same amount of discipline into this that you do my puzzles."

"Or engaging with your partners," Lo says.

I blush, but everyone chuckles, even Mrs. No Name.

"Wanna try this while flying?" Korby asks.

"What? How?"

Lo lowers his wing, and Korby climbs on. "C'mon," she says, "I wanna ride a dragon!"

Giving her this moment, I fly into the air and meet her bo staff's tip in the air as Lo gently rides through the clouds. I have to focus on keeping my balance in the air, directing myself, and dodging Korby's attacks. And that doesn't even consider going on the offensive.

Lo dives lightly, and Korby loses her footing, slipping near the wing. But just as I reach out with my air magic to save her, she finds her footing once more and is back to attacking me from the wing.

"Come on, Magic! You can do better than that!" The wind nearly steals her words from me at this altitude, but I rush the air toward me so I can hear her.

"Fuck off! This is hard work." Seriously, I'm doing a lot right now. Back off.

"We can go back to the ground if it's too hard." A hand on her hip and smirk across her lips, she knows what she's doing. Baiting me.

"Nope. Not gonna happen."

I fly over her, trying to attack from the higher ground, but she slides down Lo's wing and reaches up, spinning her staff and knocking mine out of my grip.

I race to catch it before it reaches the ground and then attack again, but this time from Lo's tail, trying to use the wind to my advantage. It flies me forward in a wind tunnel as I move the air into a tornado and spin my staff in a move that's designed to confuse Korby.

It works, because Korby takes a step back and looks at me with a moment of panic.

When my wind tunnel hits her, I grab her by the arm and lift her off of Lo as the dragon gets caught by the blast and it sent soaring through the air. Now Korby is dangling by the arm a hundred feet off the ground. Squirming in my grip.

"Don't make me drop you, Korby. Stop wiggling!" I lift her into my arms, where she feels safer, and fly us gently to the ground.

Korby's feet and hands reach the ground at the same time as she kisses the earth. "I'll never leave you again, I swear." She turns to face me with an angry scowl on her face. "What the hell were you thinking?"

"That I wanted to win?"

A smirk crosses her lips. "That was awesome! Terrifying but awesome."

My Fae trainer walks up to us and smiles. "You could just drop people from high in the air."

"Wouldn't work on everyone." I shrug. "Vampires won't die, flying Shifters can fly, air Witches can fly, and who knows what spells Fae can use to arrest their fall."

She weighs up my argument. "Fair points." She sits on the ground and starts weaving a spell around her, encircling herself in runes. "Your task today is to try to reach me."

I change forms and sit crossed legged outside her circle of complicated looking runes. "Okay."

"You can use any skills available to you. Your only clue is that I have used runes and only a single ingredient to create this defensive spell."

Only a single ingredient and runes? That isn't enough, surely? But analyzing her rune circle tells me one thing: this was designed to specifically keep me out.

Bullshit. That's what this is.

She sits inside, eyes closed, meditating or some shit. The perfect Fae. Little Mrs. No Name. I swear, when I find out who she is . . . I'm gonna kill her.

I get to work decoding the runes, finding out what they all do and how they all link together. What their purpose is. But there are a dozen runes here, and they're all complicated. I've never even seen some of them. But I don't have to have seen them before to figure out how they work.

Three of them contain the structure—a sphere—and ensuring it goes all the way around her and that no one can get in or out who isn't her. One of them is barring my DNA specifically from getting in (male and female). There are two runes linking the structural runes and one binding ingredient that's kind of holding them together, since there are so many. The other six are supporting runes, providing a metal-like resistance to the barrier, making it fireproof, waterproof, and earthquake-proof, amongst other things.

"I don't know how to dismantle this." If I know what the ingredient is, I can start to figure out how to deconstruct the entire thing, and it'll fall apart; which is one of the weaknesses of binding ingredients used in defensive spells. They rely on the attacker not knowing or understanding Fae spells. Which will work great against a different species, but not so much against your own.

"Think, Magic. The answer is sitting right in front of you."

"Huh?"

Okay, okay. Let's start over.

We have the structural runes, which I could attach the binding runes to and then it would change shape or start to deconstruct, but there's no real way to know how or in what way, so it feels like a dangerous thing to do. We have one rune that is barring me from getting in as a male or female, so shifting won't help.

Wait a minute.

Yes, shifting will help.

I shift into a falcon and fly through the barrier with ease, then shift back into a man. "Your spell doesn't keep my animal forms out, because my DNA changes when I shift, even if you take into account both my human forms."

She opens her eyes. "That did not take you as long as usual. It seems you are learning Fae logic." She dismantles the spell and everyone claps. "You cannot be contained by a regular barrier spell, since you can shift into any animal form at will and there's no Fae alive who can incorporate every animal's DNA into a barrier."

"Assuming I haven't drained my Fae energy, of course."

84

She looks at me confused for a moment.

"I struggle to shift and move and even really breathe when my energy is drained. The magical energy I experience in each form affects my form in total, not just my specific species. So a lack of blood in my female form affects my Witch magic, too."

"I see. So there's a limitation there, then." She mumbles something more to herself as she turns away and sits back where she was earlier.

"Earth magic?" I spin to face the resident Witch.

"Maybe after lunch?" Korby asks.

Lo hums his agreement.

"Okay, so lunch and then earth magic?"

The earth Witch smiles and nods. "At your own pace, Magic. It has been a trying time."

Indeed it has.

Chapter Fourteen

"Nothing—and I mean nothing—is better than ramen after a workout."

"You are absolutely right." I slurp my ramen soup at the bottom of the bowl, curtesy of Arrie, and lean back. Full. But still tired.

"How're you doin', hon?" Connie walks into the kitchen, her hair tied into two buns on top of her head and wearing nothing but a skimpy bikini.

"Err . . . fine," I drool. "Good, I mean, I'm doing great."

"Cute, huh?" She twirls. "Picked it up this morning on a shopping trip. Sounds stupid, but shopping makes me happy. And it felt good to have a slice of normal."

I hug her and give her a long kiss, trailing a hand I hope no one can see along her ass. "It's never stupid to do things that make you happy." I kiss her forehead and wink. "Besides, I like it."

"Of course you do, it's your favorite color."

The black material grazes along my hip as she walks out of the kitchen and goes to sunbathe—probably by the pool.

"You two are cozy," Korby taunts.

"Yeah, we are."

"How's the rest of your harem doing?" she asks, eating a second bowl of ramen.

"Arrie's okay, doing as best he can, and Dea is . . . struggling. But he's better than last week."

Korby puts her bowl down and smiles. "You included Arrie that time."

Huh? "Oh, yeah. Guess I did."

She waggles her eyebrows and laughs. "C'mon, dish the dirt."

I rejoin her at the table, finding the sight of an excited earth Witch and a bored Fae trainer hilarious. "He kissed me the other night. But we're taking things slow. There's something there still. Something . . . blocking him, I think."

"He's a man, child. He'll figure it out. You just have to give their brains a little longer to work." She smiles at me and grabs my hand. "Now, are we ready to try unlocking that earth magic?"

I sigh because no, I'm never ready to try unlocking a

Witch magic. They're a pain in the ass. Every. Single. Time. But I smile gratefully and whisper, "Yes." As she guides me outside, I ask, "Where would you like to work?"

"Anywhere will do. It's all earth."

Right. Earth is like air—always around me. It's versatile like air, too. Unlike fire and water, which I can only summon through concentration because I have to create it most of the time.

There's a part of me that's excited to connect to the earth and learn its magic. Even as a mortal, I was fascinated by earth Witches. They're a life of the very fundamentals of Witch magic and what makes up their being. Lucky. I was stuck with death magic I somehow knew how to control; but that control is lost now. And relying on Aki's teachings seems a little foolish, even for me.

We sit on the ground, and she grabs my hands with a stern look. "You are a Witch, so you should be able to feel the magic all around you, the earth beneath your feet giving you stability."

I've always been quite attuned to the earth, finding peace within it whenever possible. I hope this is easier than the others.

"I associate earth with peace of mind, but then I used that for water, so maybe that's not quite right." I search myself, letting the feeling of my surroundings fill me up. "It's like this presence in my soul, making my chest expand and my brain relax. But I don't know what that feeling is."

"Love," my Fae trainer intervenes.

"Love?"

"That's an interesting association," she says, her hands on the ground beside me. "But I can see how the earth could mean love to someone who has been in search of it their whole life."

"Even as a child, I'd prefer to be outside when seeking happiness or peace, near hilltops and rivers and mountains. Maybe that love has always been there, even before I was immortal. Is that possible?"

"I do not know, child. You Horsemen have your own magic that you guard closely."

With good reason. I broke that closeness and look what happened? Nine died.

"Now is not the time for pity parties!" Her scowl scolds hot, and I flinch. "Now is the time for focus."

Right. Focus.

In this form, I can hear everything: the trees swaying, the bugs titter-tattering, Connie sunbathing, Arrie doing his weird yoga dance routine in the forest's clearing, the fairies in their nests . . . It's all so beautiful. Like a whole world I'm connected to and can tune in to at will. "So why can't I just move a rock or rumble the ground?"

"Because you're trying too hard," she says. "Let it become you, not you become it."

Let it become me? What does that even mean?

I try to relax, set the will to sink into the ground aside, and just exist, waiting, hoping beyond hope, but nothing clicks into place. Nothing moves. I'm still just me.

No extra powers.

Yet.

We keep trying for the rest of the afternoon, breaking it up with some bo practise and more Fae magic puzzles, Lo occasionally dropping in to cause mischief. But by the time the sun drops beyond the horizon, I've still not unlocked any kind of earth powers. But I have had a good day, perhaps the first full good day since Nine's passing.

Everyone says goodbye, and I find my way up to Dea's bedroom, expecting to find him in bed, but he's at his desk, furiously writing with a pencil that's barely long enough to call a pencil.

"Hello Angel," he whispers while he continues to work. "Come in."

"I can leave you be if you're busy."

He lifts his head and smiles at me. "It is okay. I was just working on an old project to pass the time, maybe distract myself a little."

"That's a good plan. Did it work?"

He shrugs. "It gave me some energy, but no, Nine is always on my mind."

I sit on his lap and let him play with my hair, slide his arms up my sides, entwine his fingers with mine, and just exist with me. "Do you want to watch a movie? Maybe have something to eat? Or do something else?"

"A movie sounds wonderful."

"Connie!" I listen out for her response, honing my ears in.

"Yeah?" She sounds out of breath.

Wonder what she's doing? "Movie night?"

"Always. I'll grab Arrie."

Chapter Fifteen

What Next? The World Waits with Bated Breath

The next morning is a whirlwind of noise: Arrie makes us breakfast in bed with a complimentary glass of forest-tasting blood, Dea immediately works on his project, diving in headfirst, and Connie goes for a run. So I'm left alone with Arrie in Dea's bed while Dea sits at his desk, not really paying attention to the real world.

"Anything you wanted to do today?" I ask Arrie.

He looks sheepishly to the ground and runs a nervous hand through his hair. "Well, I was wondering if you'd like to go on a date with me?" His voice is barely a mumble, but it's there. "I know we're all a little emotionally frazzled, and I don't mean to rush you, but I'd like to start making things up to you. Apologize properly."

Dea stops what he's doing and turns to face us—more specifically, Arrie. A thunder rumbling across his face. "What are your intentions?"

Arrie looks at him in surprise, a wordless, open-mouthed shock dropping his jaw. "I . . . Well, err . . ." There's that nervous and frustrated hand traveling through his hair again. I can see the anger rising, his cheeks flushing, his fist curling.

But I grab it and thread my fingers through his.

"Because you cannot lead ve on again. If you go on a date, it has to be serious. It has to be because you want it to lead somewhere."

"I know that!" he snaps. "I'm not a fucking idiot, Dea."

The growl that escapes his lips has my thighs clenching and my mouth dropping open. "But it'll be slow." I grab Arrie's hand. "As slow as you need. Even if that means just dating for the next thirty years."

I'm done pushing this man. It needs to be his choice. I want to be his choice.

Arrie nods, a grateful blush creeping across his face. "I don't think I can go thirty years without touching you, Killer." He leans over me and pushes me back into the mattress. "So I'm gonna have to get my shit together." And he kisses me. But this isn't gentle or teasing, like Connie. This is demanding. A white-hot forge of pleasure crashing into my mouth, forcing my tongue to dance with the devil and never let go.

But when he does let go, I'm breathless, and I have to stop myself from rocking my hips into his. Because if we go down that road, we won't come back from its burning sands, and we'll never reach a good emotional place.

For once, I'm going to do this the emotionally healthy way. I'm going to date, kiss him at the front door, talk about our interests, go for long walks, and build something with this man who has very much stolen my heart.

"I would love to go on a date with you."

"Meet me at the front door at three pm. Wear warm clothes."

I nod, not really sure what to say, as he leaves the room.

I turn over and bury my head in a pillow, letting loose a squeal of excitement. Arrie is taking me on a date. A date!

I don't think I'm even mad at him anymore. I try to be, but he's really putting in some effort, apologizing, and trying to treat me better. But if he thinks for a second he's going to get away with not telling me what his deal is, he's got another thing coming.

"Excited, Angel?" The bed dips as Dea sits next to me.

I nod, my head still buried in the pillow and my legs fighting the urge to kick around.

He chuckles in my ear. "Good. You're allowed some good memories and happiness."

I lift my head and ask, "Even if Nine isn't here? Even if I'm supposed to be mourning him?"

"Even then. You can be happy and sad, just like you can be anxious and happy, at the same time? Remember that." He lies on his back and wraps me up in his arms. "And remember this." He slams his lips against mine, pushing me back into the bed, as his form changes and his wings burst over the sides.

My legs instinctively wrap around his hips, and I grind against him, need coursing through me. "Mine," I whisper as I nip at his lips and suck at his neck.

"Yours." Dea looks at me with all the reverence in the world, as though I'm the sun in his universe. "We don't have to have sex if you would rather wait?"

This team has unleashed something inside of me, and I'm no longer seeing the benefit of waiting to be okay. "So long as you're ready, I'm ready." I reach into his bedside drawer and pull out the birth control potions I know he keeps there—just in case. I down one and then return to his attention. "Sorry, I've not been taking them recently." I just forgot in all the emotional hysteria.

"Arrie told me you had fun with Connie the other day?" He traces light fingers along my collarbones and the edges of my bra. "Want to tell me about that?"

"We were just taking a romantic stroll through the garden, and we sat at the *Shinto* and things got a little out of hand. In my defense, though, she practically begged me to fuck her."

"Connie begged, huh?" He grips the lace of the bra with his teeth and tugs, revealing my nipples. "That is not like her."

"I know." I groan as he takes one into his mouth and teases and sucks. "She's usually so teasing and more of a leading lady, but she begged, so I licked her pussy, then she sucked my dick . . . And fuck, she sucked it all the way down her throat. She has some talent, that lady."

Dea's fingers delve between my thighs and stroke up my entrance, then back down, and back up, but never entering. "Tell me more."

"I was just about to come, but she pulled away and asked me to fuck her, so I pinned her legs to the garden floor and fucked her as hard as she'd let me."

Dea groans, a golden brightness in his eyes. "I want to see you fucking her one day."

"Really?"

"Really." He punctuates that with a sharp press of his fingers into me. "But right now, you are mine." His fingers delve in and out of me, caressing my insides with accurate strokes of silken goodness. "Say it."

My eyes shoot open and meet his golden galaxy ones. "I'm yours." He adds another finger, stretching me further, shooting pleasure through my entire body. "In whatever form you'd prefer."

His fingers stop, and he looks at me. Like, he really looks at me, and my breath catches in my throat and my body lights on fire, and I can't move. "I want you in whatever form you feel like being in today." But there's something in his eyes as he says it—something that sets me aflame.

I know what he wants. And now, when my whole world is falling apart and I'm treading the pieces trying to move forward, I just might be ready to give it to him.

I gently pull Dea's fingers out of me and then concentrate on my form, shifting it so that I'm lying on Dea's bed fully clothed in the last clothes I wore in this form, staring at him, silently begging him to fuck me.

His hand rests on the button to my jeans, a question in his gaze. "Are you sure?"

The vulnerability in his gaze gives me pause. "Dea?"

He looks up, meeting my sure expression.

"I wouldn't have offered if I wasn't sure." I slip my eyes to those lips, to the piercings on either side, and add, "But I like it when you order me to do something. It takes the indecisiveness out of the equation."

A wicked grin spreads across his face, and he snaps his hands onto my wrists quicker than lightning. "In that case, stay still for me, Angel." He pins my hands above my head and leans over me, his black hair dancing along the sides of my face. "Just let me know if you want me to stop."

I nod, words not wording, and spread my legs, letting him settle between them.

The smile fades from his lips and is replaced by something far more exciting—desire. It radiates off him like a flood I can taste in the back of my mouth, lingering even after I swallow every drop.

He rips his belt from his skinny jeans and wraps it around my joined wrists, then one of the bedposts, laying me out diagonally across the bed. "Now, be a good little angel and lie there quietly." Dea stands up and leans one hand on the canopy frame, staring at me. His eyes lick me up and down as he bites the corner of his lip, playing with the piercing there. "You look delicious."

But instead of doing something, he just stands there, looking beautiful, staring at me like I'm his next meal. But he doesn't do anything.

Just when I think he might stare at me all morning, he moves to grasp the bottom of his t-shirt and pulls it over his head. Revealing the delicious body beneath. Now it's my turn to stare—and maybe I try twisting on my bonds a bit. (Don't judge me, he's gorgeous.)

A small laugh escapes his lips, and I just know he's loving my struggles. I want to touch him. And the cocky bastard knows it. I want to run my hands over the lean muscles leading down beyond his jeans. To unbuckle the clasp and . . .

"Dea . . . I wanna—"

"I know. But you cannot right now," he says with a gleeful smile.

My cock is straining against my jeans, begging me to touch it, to give it some kind of attention. Begging anyone to. But I can't move my hands when they're tied up like this.

Dea slides his hands to his jean buttons and undoes all three at a time, one at a time, piece by piece, and I hate it. Love it. Can't stand it but don't want to look away. He bores holes into my eye sockets while sliding his jeans off his legs and tossing them aside.

"You okay there?" he asks as his fingers slide along the

98

edges of his underwear.

I shake my head, no. I'm not okay. I need him to touch me.

"Whatever is the matter?"

I tug at my restraints again. "Touch me."

"Hmmm, maybe." His hand slips inside his underwear and grasps his dick. A groan escapes his lips as he leans on the canopy again, his naked body stretched out before me.

My mouth opens of its own accord, wanting nothing more than to swallow those moans. And maybe the cause of them.

As if reading my mind, Dea shucks off his underwear and straddles my waist. "Suck it." He presents his cock like a leaking gift on a silver platter.

And like the good little angel I am, I open my mouth with a moan and nod.

"Good Angel." He slides up closer to my head and rests the tip on my lips. "Now relax that tight little throat of yours." As I open my mouth wider, he slips the silky softness in, and we both groan at the same time. "Fuck, yes."

I raise my hips up, trying my best to find friction despite the clenching tightness of denim caging me in, and I meet Dea's hand.

"I've got you, do not worry." He massages my dick through my jeans.

And I'm so relieved, I forget that I'm supposed to be focusing on swallowing. On somehow taking this guy's dick all the way down without suffocating. But fuck, his hand feels so good.

Pleasure rolls through me, and I forget all about the cock in my mouth as I moan unashamedly.

"Take a deep breath."

I inhale.

Dea pushes further in, enough to tickle my gag reflex, and shit, I don't think I can do this. I'm gonna look like an idiot.

"Swallow."

My throat goes to constrict, spasm, and—

Dea grips my dick. Hard. Hard enough to hurt. Too hard. "Swallow."

Going against my throat's need to spasm, I swallow.

Dea pushes in further, and before I know it, he's pushing at the back of my throat and ordering me to swallow again.

I follow his orders, and Dea shoves his cock down my throat.

"Good, Angel. You're doing so well." His voice purrs. "Just lie there and keep taking my cock." He pulls out slightly, so that his dick is only just past the back of my throat, and then slides it back down.

The groan that escapes his mouth sets my body on fire. His head falls back as his hand grabs my hair in a punishing grip. "Yes, just like that." His hand tightens on my dick, and I moan. "God, yes."

My dick is leaking and my underwear is soaking, and I just want him to strip me naked and fuck me already.

But Dea just picks up the pace and fucks my face hard

into the mattress. "Fuck, Angel . . . You are so tight." The pace is brutal, slamming down the back of my throat, but I stay relaxed, watching his face scrunch and his fists grip my hands tighter. But then his gaze meets mine, and he stops and pulls out. Gently. "You did so well." His hand caresses my cheek. "So well."

His hand roams down my t-shirt and buries itself underneath, where he travels across my smooth skin, setting tiny sparks alight every inch of the way. "Now, come here." He unzips my jeans and cups my balls around my underwear. "Let's get all this clothing off of you."

"Yes, please." I'm still breathless, but I manage to eek the words out in a small, breathless puff.

He slowly inches off my jeans, then my underwear, and stares in disbelief at my dick. As though he didn't fully believe it was really there before. "You're so big."

Oh. "I . . . err . . ." Is thank you the right phrase here? "Thanks?"

Dea chuckles. "It is definitely a compliment." He looks at me again and licks his lips. "Nine would have loved being fucked by you."

"Really?" Tears sting my eyes.

Dea looks at me and wipes the wetness away. "Oh yes. Remind me to tell you of the time I once fucked him with my dick and a dildo at the same time."

My eyes widen. "You can do that?"

Dea laughs. A full-on belly rumble that has my mouth

smiling and my eyes watering again. "With enough prep and lube, yes." My dick twitches at the thought, and it does not go amiss by Dea, who smiles at me with raised eyebrows. "One day." Soft fingers trail across my jaw and trace my small smile.

His hand wraps around my cock with wonder, and he traces a thumb over the sticky head, making me buck and gasp. "One day, I'll persuade Arrie to fuck you in the ass at the same time as me. Really stretch you open."

My dick leaks more pre-cum at the thought, but my mind has a hard time imagining that. "Sounds like a lot of pain."

Dea rests his lips against mine and breathes, "I'll always make you feel good, Angel." His face lifts away with a golden glint in his eyes. "I'll only hurt you if you ask for it."

With a wink, he layers kisses across my jaw, nips at my neck, and licks lines of pleasure across my chest. Every touch is like lava in my veins, setting my body on fire and dousing my brain in fog.

I can't think.

I can't do anything but feel.

And fuck if this isn't the most relaxed I've been in days.

Dea takes a nipple into his mouth while his hand slowly jacks me up and down. His tongue flicks and circles as his hand twists and squeezes, and a series of long, unintelligible moans escape my lips while passionate fire torments me.

I edge closer, my body ready to explode, but I don't want to come like this. I want this gorgeous man to fuck me. And I want to watch as he comes undone while buried inside me. I want to feel what Nine felt every time he was with our Angel of Death.

"Dea . . ."

"Yes, Angel. Come for me."

"No, wait. I want it to be . . . you." Dea's hand stops moving, and despite it being what I want, the lack of movement and friction makes me frown and groan. "I want you to fuck me like you did Nine."

Chapter Sixteen

Everything Sucks: 'A World at War' Peace Study

He looks at me with a curious and hurt expression, and shit, maybe that was insensitive.

"I'm sorry, I didn't mean to take away the privacy or important memory. I just wanted to know how he felt. I want it to be you, Dea. It was always meant to be you."

"It is okay." He takes a deep breath and looks at me. "I am not offended. It is just . . . hard." He grazes a soft finger down my cheek and smiles. "But I want to share him with you. You had so little time together. And it is unfair."

I wiggle my hips and grind my dick against his, letting our soft, velvety skin slide against each other.

And he groans, surprised. "I am definitely fucking that pretty ass of yours today."

My whole body clenches—in excitement, in fear, in anticipation—and I exhale a breathy sigh. "Yes, please."

A deep, throaty chuckle escapes Dea's mouth, and it vibrates through me. Everything in me aches. All I want is for this man to fuck me into oblivion and make me forget and remember.

"Now," he rumbles, his voice edging back into familiar, commanding territory, "spread your legs." He folds my knees up and then parts them, spreading me out before him.

Not only are my balls and dick right in front of him, but my ass is prime time right now, and I won't lie, it feels a little exposing. Cool air rushes along my hole, and my dick twitches in need.

Dea lowers his head to my groin and then travels lower, lower, until he's past my dick and licking stripes up my balls. "Just relax, Angel." His hands grip my thighs like vices and pin them apart, forcing them to give him more room. "I have got you."

He can have me for the rest of time if this is what follows.

He sucks a testicle into his mouth and hums, sending pleasure vibrating through my balls and straight up my cock like lightning. And I can't stop leaking, it seems, because it's starting to trail down my stomach in a small stream Dea runs a finger through.

He does the same thing with the other testicle, and I'm in heaven, moaning, writhing, tugging on my restraints with complete abandon, all traces of embarrassment and rational thought having flown out the window.

"Dea, oh my goddess." There's a growly edge to my voice as I say his name. "Don't stop."

Dea's mouth widens as he sucks both balls in at once, and my whole body tightens with need thrumming through me in waves that douse the edges of my sanity.

I can't think.

I can only feel what this man is doing to me.

But Dea stops, and I groan, until his hands release my thighs and gently spread my cheeks and his tongue is traveling another path. A very different, very new path.

Unexpected nerves shoot through me.

But Dea continues, licking up toward my exposed hole and flicking a quick circle.

"Mmm, yeah."

"You taste divine," he groans. His tongue laps at my hole, eager and hungry.

And the sparks that shoot are new, bright and golden, like fireworks, and I plant my feet firmly on the bedsheets, refusing to move them. Because I might just combust if he stops what he's doing.

His hands slide under my ass and yank me closer to him, so his nose is pressed against my ass crack and his tongue is piercing my hole.

And oh my goddess, the stretch is sooooo good. "Fuck."

Dea shoves his tongue deeper, as deep as it'll go, and I let out a tiny scream of pain and pleasure mixed—an echo of what's the come.

My hands grip my restraints, my toes curls around the messed-up sheets, and my eyes screw shut as the pleasure rockets up, builds, and needs somewhere to go. Anywhere.

Fuck, I wanna jack myself. I need to . . .

Dea wraps a hand around my dick, swirls his thumbs over the wet head and spreads it around, then jacks me in harsh thrusts. His tongue still buried inside my ass, licking every part of me I never thought I'd be comfortable enough to share.

"Mmmm . . . yes yes yes."

I can feel my balls start to tighten as my hips rock, seeking more friction, more speed. More something.

But Dea pulls his hand and tongue away.

"No, wait—"

"Shhhh, Angel." He places two fingers over my lips. "I will get you there. I promise."

"Please," I whine, looking straight into those golden eyes that are burning brighter than I've ever seen them.

Dea looks at me like I'm his next meal, his careful composure slipping like a landslide. He reaches over my head to the nightstand, where he pulls a bottle of lube I've not seen before. This one's blue, rather than the usual red.

My confused expression has him smiling as he explains, "Anal sex is best with gel-based lubricant." He holds up the bottle. "This is the same one I used that night with me and Nine."

That night flashes through my mind, Dea in my ass, Nine

in front, and both hammering away at me like a personal sex toy. A whiny groan slips my lips.

"Yeah, I liked it too." Dea lathers two fingers in lube before returning to my spread legs. "I loved the sounds you made then, and how tightly you gripped me." He strokes a finger around the edge of my hole, and it quivers in response. "And I love how responsive you are."

A single finger pushes in, and it feels like he's stretching me beyond measure. There's no way he is going to fit. But we've done this before, and I trust him to do it again.

"Relax, Angel. Just bear down, it'll make it easier." I follow his instructions as he takes my dick in his other hand, no doubt distracting me. "Just think about how good it will feel to have my dick buried in your ass."

The image those words conjure up brings more pre-cum to the surface, spilling over. Dea leans down to lick it off, and I buck into his mouth.

He adds a second finger, slowly delving deeper, until he's gently lapping them in and out, fingering my ass. His grip on my dick tightens, and I rock my hips to the rhythm he's set, fucking myself on his fingers and into his fist.

"That's it, Angel. Such a good little boy."

His words take me aback. That's the second time he's said that, and I hum in response. Maybe I do like that?

"You are doing so well." He adds a third finger, then a fourth, and soon I'm throwing myself onto his hand, desperate for more. But he pulls his hands away and breathes a kiss across my starved lips.

I lean into him, but he's gone before I can get anything more.

He reaches for the lube again and spreads it over himself, and I watch as his hand rises and falls up his cock, twists and squeezes in the way he likes. His head falls back and his legs spread slightly. "Going to fuck you so good," he groans.

"Mmmm, yes," I whine, pulling against my restraints because it's mine. His cock is mine and I want it now. "Gimme."

Dea looks at me and smirks, that cocky grin telling me he knows exactly what he's doing. "You want it?"

I nod, words escaping me.

He grabs my thighs and pushes them to my chest, then lines his dick up and slowly pushes through my ring.

Blinding pleasure shoots through me, along with a slice of burning pain, but I bear down, and he pushes farther in.

"Fuck," he swears, "you are so tight."

"So good," I pant. "More."

He groans as slides the rest of his dick into me, his balls lying flat against my cheeks. His golden eyes meet mine in a wicked glare. "Hold on."

I grab the leather of my restraints, and he holds my thighs to my chest as I take a breath and steel myself.

The thrusts are harsh, punishing, like Dea can't bear to be soft and gentle right now. And as his hair flies around his face, his grip tightens on my thighs, and moans spill from his lips, he looks like a wild man, some wild thing whose humanity has long since left him.

He pushes my thighs against me tighter, causing my hips to shift higher off the bed, and something in me lights up like a Christmas tree. "Shit, yes." I throw my head back as a series of long, unintelligible words string my lips on a moan. "Don't stop."

His thrusts harden, becoming harsher by the second, until the only sounds in the room are skin slapping against skin and our combined moans as his balls slap my ass and my hole quivers in pleasure against his slick cock. Lips slam against mine as he breathes into me. "Never going to . . . stop."

"Ohh, mmmm, yes." My dick twitches uncontrollably between us as a stream of cum leaks and my balls tighten. "Oh goddess! Yes! Gonna . . . !" My orgasm hits me like a freight train as my hips rock into his dick and my hole squeezes tight. Ropes and ropes of cum shoot across my chest.

"Oh fuck." Dea watches my face with rapture. "So fucking tight." His hips lose rhythm as a frenzy overtakes him, and he's slamming into me hard enough to have me gripping my restraints to hold on. "So close." Golden light shatters the dark room as he opens his eyes to meet mine. He holds that gaze as he shoots his orgasm into me and keeps on pumping, riding out his orgasm.

He eventually slows, and he slumps on top of me, spent.

"That was . . . amazing," I say on a breath.

"Yes. Yes, it was."

Chapter Seventeen

The Horsemen Polycule: Exposing the Scandalous Romance

"Soooo," Connie says, her usual give-me-all-the-details voice coming in strong, "things with you and Arrie are going somewhere?" She holds up another outfit choice from the pile I had the house summon.

But I shake my head, no. Too pink. "Yeah, I think." I take a deep breath and rummage through the pile to find those cute jeans I had in my hands earlier. "I'm thinking of maybe bringing it up with him tonight. You know, just to make sure we're both on the same page. But I don't wanna scare him off or anything." I scratch my head, confused about the jeans and Arrie. "He's a bit skittish."

Her laugh bounces off my ears, and I look up to see her

golden smile beaming my way. Her hair is in two long plaits today, tapered at her waist with two green bows that match the green of her eyes. And damn if her boobs don't look perfect in that tank top.

She laughs again. "My eyes are up here, babe." She points to her face, and I blush. "And you got enough sex from Dea earlier."

"Only in my male form," I whine. "My vagina is lacking said attention."

She snorts and then laughs, and I follow. But she looks at me with serious eyes. "Tell me everything."

What is with these people and making me recount my sex life? "Well, I was in my other form, but we talked about it, and I decided I wanted to finally take the plunge, so we had sex in my male form instead."

"And?"

"And . . . it was great."

"That's all the detail I get? Who topped who? Did he go all controlling on your ass?" She waggles her eyebrows. "Pun intended."

I laugh but sigh. I swear, these Horsemen. "Yes, he went all controlling on my ass. He also taught me to deep throat. It was great." I return my attention to the giant pile of clothes on the bed. "Now, I really really need something I can wear that'll be sexy but good for cold weather. How cold are we talking? Is he taking me to Scotland, Canada, Russia, or The Artic? Why is he never specific!"

"Because I did not want to give away the surprise, Killer." Arrie's standing in the doorway, leaning against the frame, looking phenomenal in a pair of low-rise jeans and nothing else.

"Oh, I didn't see you there." I cringe. "Sorry."

He moves to stand beside me, placing an arm around my shoulders, and glances at the pile. "What is it with you four and clothes?" He steals a breath. "Three, I guess."

The room falls silent. Just like it always does whenever one of us brings Nine up in conversation or forgets that we're now only Four Horsemen, not five.

It's the kind of silence that cuts like a knife through your sanity, where you wonder if you'll ever feel normal again and what normal even is now that a part of your foundation has come crumbling down.

I'm allowed to be sad and happy.

I'm allowed to be sad and happy.

I'm allowed to be sad and happy.

My eyes squeezing shut, I repeat Dea's advice in my head over and over again, my fists clenched and my body shaking.

"Heeey, shhh . . ." Connie rubs soothing hands over my shoulders while a firm, steady presence stands at my back, heavy hands silently on my waist. Grounding me. "It's gonna be okay," she whispers in my ear, like a gentle lapping of the ocean against my shore.

I need to . . . be there for them. Not crumble into the wind. I need to . . .

"Whoa, Killer." Arrie grumbles something under his breath. "Calm down."

Suddenly their comforting touches are gone and Connie is standing a few feet away nursing her hand. Arrie is behind me, but only by a couple of steps.

"You're flaming," he explains.

I look down at myself and see the flames licking my skin, and then I notice the heat, the slight sting, and I yelp. "Shit." I hiss, then work on calming myself, and empty the equivalent of a river over my head. When I'm left shivering, hands trying their best to warm me up, I curse. "Fuck's sake. Now I'm cold."

Arrie wraps strong arms around my shivering frame and lifts me into his arms, then throws a scowl Connie's way, and she's off, running into my bathroom. The sound of water pattering the tiles hits my eardrums.

"She's turned the shower on for you," Arrie whispers, his voice deep and rumbly and sending shivers rumbling through me. "You'll warm up in there. And you won't get a cold."

"But won't we b-b-be late?"

He laughs. "There's no timescale for our date. We'll be fine."

"Okay." I look up at him and smile—well, I try to. "Think you can pick out an outfit for me and then ask the house for something for my male form too?"

He frowns. "You want me to pick out clothes for you?"

"If it's not a problem. I'm not used to cold weather."

"I'll try." Arrie deposits me in the bathroom.

Where Connie helps my shivering hands disrobe and shoves me into the warm spray before leaving to help Arrie. The water warms my skin first, prickling along my edges, until the heat seeps deeper, warming my insides. And by the time I've shaved, washed my hair and body, and dried—twice—I step out of the bathroom to find Arrie holding up three pairs of boots with a frown.

"Need some help there, big guy?" I twizzle the towel around my long pink hair with a smile.

"I think I have a good outfit picked out . . ."

He sounds unsure, and goddess, if his frown and concentration isn't the cutest thing. "I'm sure I'll love whatever you've chosen." After all, I don't need to look perfect for this man. I can just exist.

"Well, I left the male one on the chair over there." He pointed to the chair next to the fireplace. "And I'm still finalizing the female one."

I walk up to the male one and smile. It's a lot of layers, a windbreaker, with a good hat and gloves. "Seriously, I have no idea in what order to wear all of this." I chuckle. "Your dates need to come with instructions."

Arrie looks at me with concern and frustration in his face.

"It's not a criticism. It's just a joke."

His face fades into a smile.

I switch into my male form. "But seriously, you'll need to tell me how to put all of this on."

"Oh. Right." He walks up to me and points out the first layer. "The layers better help keep the heat in, so start with underwear and thermals." Then he layers me up piece by piece until I'm standing in my bedroom looking like a human penguin. "Perfect."

"I feel like a marshmallow."

His laugh echoes across the room and licks candy up my insides. "Now, let's get you dressed into your female clothes. I had to ask Connie about the best bra options. I do not know how breasts work."

N'awww . . . Aaaaaaand now I'm melting like a marshmallow. "That's okay. I'm sure you figured it out."

Again, we start with underwear and thermals, and then shove a few layers on, including hat and gloves and a windbreaker.

"Remind me again where the hell we're going?"

Arrie looks at me with a smirk. "Nope."

I grumble, a groan slipping through. "Teleporting crystals, though, right?" Please, don't make me have to deal with portals. They're much, much worse.

"Of course." He grabs two from his pocket. "Ready?"

I grab hold of his arm with my gloved hands and nod. "Ready."

And soon we're swirling into the aether and I'm doing my best to not puke. But before I know it, we're landing on a snow-covered plain that's covered in white for as far as the eye can see. And my eyes can see pretty damn far.

116

"Wow." I step away from him and look around, startled. "Is this somewhere in the arctic circle?"

"Iceland." Arrie's own layers stare at me when I turn around. "It's my homeland." He wraps his arms around my waist and leans down to place a gentle kiss to my head. "I thought I would share my favorite places with you. That's what you do on a date, right? You share yourself with some-one you want to connect with?"

"That's . . . right."

This is it. This is him opening up.

This is Arrie meeting me halfway.

Chapter Eighteen

Horsemen Absent in Recent Days: Are They Admitting
Defeat or Nursing their Bruised Ego?

The aurora borealis glimmers above us, and I'm mesmerized by its beauty, and for a second I forget the other beauty standing right next to me. "It's like a night rainbow sliding across a net of fireflies."

Arrie hums. "I've always loved how your mind works."

I turn to face him, his eyes lit in a midnight rainbow.

"I was always jealous that Nine got an instant all-access pass." He grits his teeth and steels his breath. "He always knew what you were thinking."

"Trust me, he often hated it."

Arrie raises a brow at me.

"He never said anything, but sometimes dealing with my

inner turmoil hurt him. He often took walks or focused on something else to take a break. I was always feeling guilty."

Arrie rests his arms on my shoulder as we both stare up at the glowing night sky. "He loved you."

Loved. Past tense.

"And I love him."

Does he still love me in the afterlife? Does it still count if I'm alive and he's not? Can I still say he loves me? Or will it always be loved from here on out?

I guess I'll never know the answers to those questions.

"What are you thinking?"

He . . . wants to know what I'm thinking? "I was wondering if he still loves me in the afterlife."

Arrie stops breathing for a moment, then blows out a harsh breath. "Yeah, probably." A tear drops onto my hood. "He has to."

I spin in his arms and look up into his face. But the hurt I see on his face slashes me in two, cuts me into pieces and burns them at the stake. "This is about more than Nine, isn't it?"

He closes his eyes and nods. "I promise to try to open up. It's just . . . hard."

I nod, understanding. Well, I guess not. Not really. But I can see he's struggling. "What part is hard to you?"

He flinches, and the by the curling of his fist, I can tell I've offended him.

"Wait, sorry. That came out wrong. I didn't mean it spitefully. I was being genuine. What part are you struggling with? Is it trusting me? Thinking about the pain?"

Through clenched teeth, he whispers, "Getting the words out."

What has this man been through that even getting the words out hurts?

My hand reaches out to his cheek and lands there, like coming home. "I'm not going anywhere. My love isn't fragile."

The smile that cuts through the pain lights up brighter than the sky, and my knees go weak. But he keeps me on my feet. As always. "Then we best get going. We've got a trek to the hotel."

A trek? In this weather. Fuck that.

Air whips around us, settles into the familiar pattern it's used to when flying myself and Arrie, and we lift into the air.

"How about a lift?"

"I was hoping you'd say that." He points in the right direction, and I do the heavy lifting.

So we fly and cover the few miles in a few minutes, whereas it would have taken a good hour or so on foot. Thank fuck for magic. We fly past fjords, distant mountains, and I take us up high enough we can see the aurora more clearly.

"It's beautiful here."

I land us firmly on the ground at the front doors, where Arrie walks in, clearly comfortable, and smiles at the man at the check-in desk.

"Arrie, my man." He walks toward us with a smile and one-arm hugs Arrie. "How're you doin'?"

"Good." He shrugs, clearly blowing off the question. "Is our room ready?"

"It is. This way." He guides us to the elevators, where we rise on the middle floor and are guided to the room at the end of the corridor. "Here you are." He hands him the keychip and walks away. "Enjoy your night."

"Thanks." Arrie unlocks the door and strides in. "This is one of the safe houses I manage."

"But it's a hotel?"

"Sure. But it caters to specific clientele that pass my checks. Besides, this way, we can ask for room service if we're struggling."

That does make sense. And it runs itself, basically. So Arrie has very little management to actually do. Clever War.

"I'm impressed." Taking a gander around the room, it's all dark wood and faux fur throws, with a balcony against the wall full of windows on the far side. "Really impressed."

The bed, however, stands four poster in front of a wall with a mosaic of wooden carvings. An art style I recognize.

"You made this?"

"How can you tell?" His hand cups the back of his neck, a flushed embarrassment flooding his face. "It could have been anyone."

"No one carves like you." I throw my bag on the bed and sit on the edge, taking it all in. "It's so . . . warm." A little like home but not.

"Thank you."

Neither of us know what to say next. Or do. Because we're both looking at each other, then glancing around the room again, hoping we'll catch onto something we missed before.

"I have not . . . done this before."

"A date?"

He nods. "I'm not sure what to do now." He shrugs. "I have plans for us tomorrow, though."

"Okay. So how about we order some room service and watch a movie? That way, you don't have to struggle to hold a conversation if you don't want to." I look sheepishly to the ground.

He stands in front of me and redirects my gaze back to his with a single strong finger. "I like you. And I love listening to you talk. I even enjoy conversation with you. But . . . I dunno"—his shoulders bunch as he struggles to get the words out—"I've always enjoyed conversation-less socializing more."

"I know. And I'm okay with that. I like your silence. You don't have to force a conversation with me. I want you to just be yourself." I stand and place my hands on his chest. "And I want to learn who that is."

Something on his face shifts—he goes from uncertain to confident in half a second—and suddenly his face is above mine, leaning in, pressing me back onto the mattress. And when his lips meet mine, a pressure explodes in my chest.

Rips me apart from the inside. And brings his weight crashing down upon me as we splay across the bed.

His hands shove my shoulders into the mattress with a huff as his thighs trap my legs together beneath him. His tongue plunges into my mouth like he can't breathe me in fast enough, can't get enough of me.

And I squirm beneath him, trying to move, to grab him or move against him or something. Anything.

But he pins my shoulders harder, his grip like iron, as he pulls away. His eyes are lust-shot, and a small whine slips from his silence as he stares at my lips with longing. "Fuck." He looks like he's going to tear in two. But eventually, with a groan of frustration, he pushes off of me and storms into the bathroom, slamming the door shut behind him.

A small laugh escapes me, understanding his mood for the first time. He's horny, but he's trying to go slow. Emotions first, sex later. Clearly, something he sucks at.

And I'm going to make it as hard as possible.

Time for your punishment, Arrie.

Luckily, Connie was in charge of packing my bag.

I pull out the pajamas and don them, making sure to forget the bra. Oops. So when Arrie comes out of the no-doubt cold shower, he notices me lying on the bed in a tank and shorts, nipples pebbling through the thin material, he wipes a frustrated hand down his face.

"Really?" He stands there, not daring to move.

"What?" I gesture to myself. "This is what Connie packed

for me."

He mumbles something in Norse with clenched fists and storms over to me, crouching on the bed. "You really have it in for me, don't you?"

"What? You mean it's cruel to lead someone on while watching them suffer? Oh no." My hand covers my mouth in a mock gasp. "I wonder how that feels."

An actual, real life growl rumbles from deep in his chest. (I shit you not.)

And it does nothing but make me smile. "I'm sure you can keep it in your pants till morning."

He mumbles something else in a strange language—not Norse, English, or Japanese—and lies on the bed in a huff. Sulking.

"N'awww . . . You'll be alright. Promise." I place a small kiss to his cheek and switch on the plasmascreen. "What you wanna watch?"

Chapter Nineteen

Despite Arrie's sulking, we snuggle and watch some dorky romance I'm sure he hates, but he sits through and even laughs from time to time. And then we spend the night cuddling. (I swear, it was just cuddling.) And every time his arm shifted or his body moved, I was reminded of the fact that this was the first time we'd shared a bed alone.

Alone and, in Arrie's case, needy.

But today, apparently, he has a plan.

And I'd be lying if I said I didn't want to know what that plan is.

After I'm dressed in more layers and warmer than a dragon's ass, we exit the hotel and head to a place we can hire snowmobiles. Yes. An actual snowmobile. That I get to drive!

Yay.

"Ready?" Arrie asks, sat on a larger snowmobile next to me.

"Never been more ready for anything in my life."

He chuckles before shutting his visor and starting the engine and setting off.

And I follow.

Don't worry, I had a demonstration on how these things work. I'll be fine. And besides, the chance of me actually dying from a snowmobile crash? Slim to none. I'll be fine.

Arrie leads us across sheets of snow, up and down various hills, through a couple of copses of trees, and down into a valley where, at the very bottom, a group of ruins lays. He stops and hops off, then gestures for me to do the same. "You okay?"

"Uh-huh." I pull my helmet off and yank my hood up. "Just catching my breath. That was awesome."

"Maybe one day I'll take you rock climbing." He wraps an arm around my shoulder. "With our strength, we can probably scale Everest."

He's right, we probably could. "That would be great."

"I'll add it to the list."

I look around, trying to decipher why we're here. It's nothing but ruins and snow all around. "Arrie, where are we?"

He wanders over to a ragged stone jutting out of the ground. "This was my home."

His home? But . . . Oh, his home when he was mortal. This was where his wife and children played. Where they all slept. Where he watched them from a distance as they grew old and died while he remained the same.

"Houses were nothing more than wooden huts with fancy features back then. But it was home. For a while."

"What did the village look like?"

Arrie guides me to the edge. "This was the entrance. It used to be an archway." We walk through and along what I assume was once a path. "This was the main path, and we used to have merchants here. They'd have their wares outside their houses." We take a left. "The chief used to live up there. That's what the large circle of ruins is. I married his daughter."

"Of course you did." I sigh. I have to live up to the daughter of a Viking chief? Seriously?

"Well, she was very beautiful. And strong." He gazes into the distance, and for a minute, I lose him to memories. And I have a feeling those memories haven't diminished over time like most people's. "And behind us was just more houses, a few open houses for things like drinking and socializing."

He walks me through the rest of the village, reminiscing about where things were, what life was like, and how they celebrated, commiserated, married, and died.

"She was twelve when we married. I was fifteen."

"What?" I squeak. That's insane.

"Marriages were arranged back then from a young age,

since there was no guarantee we'd live very long."

"Guess they didn't account for immortality, ey?" I meant it as a joke, but I don't think it landed like one. "I'm sorry, I didn't mean too—"

"It's okay."

But it kinda isn't, is it? Whatever this place is to him, whatever is haunting him from his past, it's wrapped up here. And it's clawing at him, holding him back. Holding us back. But I can't just wave my magic wand and wish it all away this time. All I can do is be here and hold his hand.

My fingers entwine with his in a tight grip. "Thank you for sharing."

"Maybe next time, you can take me somewhere important to you?"

Somewhere important to me? "I'm not sure I have anywhere that's important to me other than *Sheruta* and home." I shrug.

"Nothing at all from your mortal past?" He's standing right next to me, holding a conversation, but he's not really here. The words are empty—just something comforting to fill the space with. "There must be something."

"Arrie, all that stuff . . . My mortal life . . . It's not me anymore. It's like looking back on a whole different person. Yes, it happened, and I lost people, and I still have memories, but they're just that now. Memories. My life here as a Horseman is the only life I value." Actually, one person does spring to mind. "Well, I guess except Nigel."

"Hmm." I'm not even sure what that sound means, but by the look on his face, it seems to be a disagreement. "I'm not sure I can ever be like that."

"The past is a part of us, but it shouldn't be a part of our present. If it was meant to be here with us, it still would be."

He looks at me with these searing eyes, anger and fear and tears all intermingling into a maelstrom of emotion you'd miss if you weren't looking hard enough. But I do. And I don't miss. And it breaks a part of me I didn't know was beating.

"You really think that?"

My voice goes quiet and my body shudders. "I have to." Otherwise, I'm still just a killer.

He nods, understanding where I'm coming from. "It's different."

"How?" My hand rests on his shoulder as my other's thumb circles his hand I'm still holding. "What can't you let go?"

"Nothing," he mumbles.

"C'mon, that's not true, and we both—"

"All of it!" He throws his arms around us with an angry scowl. "Everything!" His breaths harshen as his fists clench, and I practically see the rage boiling beneath. "I should have been here, Magic! Here. With my tribe. My wife. My children. They were my whole world!" A heavy breath rushes out of him as he falls to the floor. "But I wasn't. So when invaders from the south ransacked the village, I couldn't do anything. I was one of the most powerful beings alive, and I couldn't even save my own family.

"Dea always said that it would get easier over time. That the pain would diminish—maybe not entirely, but enough to live with. But it's been over two thousand years, and it still feels like that first day I found them here, bodies mangled, raped, and beaten."

He stands and looks at me, fresh anger slicing my way, and whispers, "And every time I kiss you, every time I even look at you inappropriately, all I can feel is her. Her judgement, her hurt that I'm kissing someone else, her jealousy." He laughs harshly, like he hates me, but I just stand there. Silently. "She would have hated you."

I want to say something. But what? What do you say to someone in so much pain?

For a moment, I swear I can hear Nine's voice in my head. Telling me, *You tell him you love him.* But it's not Nine, because if it were, there'd have been an obviously tagged onto the end. Maybe even an eye roll.

"Probably, I am stealing her man." I look at him with vengeance in my eyes and a snarl on my lips. I grab his hands and shove his fingers through mine, forcing us together. "Look, I'm not going to patronize you by pretending to understand, but I'm not going anywhere. There's no fight to be had here. You already have me. You just need to embrace me."

"She loved these." He picks some purple flowers that are growing out of a crag between two rocks. "They're Artic Thyme flowers. Violet purple . . . Just like your eyes." He sighs. "I don't know what to do."

A frustrated hand runs through his hair, but I catch it and raise it to my lips. "Nothing." I shrug. "You don't have to do anything. You think I'm going to be annoyed that you aren't over your ex-wife? Arrie, it's okay that you've been in love before. And it's okay if that love was an epic for the ages. It's okay that you're broken and hurting. All you need to do is love me."

"You make it sound so easy."

"Because it is."

"But I . . . still love her."

I laugh, because this is actually a little funny if you think about it. "I'm literally fucking your ex casual hookup while telling her I love her every day. Do you really think I'm going to be jealous of a woman who's not with us anymore?"

"But I'm broken. I can't offer you what the rest of the team can. I can't be your one and only. There'll always be someone else who means just as much to me. Another woman."

"I. Don't. Care." I don't know how to get this across any clearer. "I just want the chance to love you." To hear him say it back. Just once.

"And if I'm thinking of her when I'm kissing you?" He steps closer, his fist clenched. "When I'm inside you? What then?"

"Then walk me through the memory so I can help you remember." His hands grab my hood and yank it down, and then all of a sudden, his face is blocking the sun and his lips are cutting off my air supply and everything in me is singing as my hands grasp at the back of his windbreaker, trying to hold on. Trying not to get swept up in the waves of his emotion. With slashes of tongue and the sting of tears, he kisses me with everything in him. Laying it all out for me. And there's no way I'm letting go.

Call me a glutton for punishment, but I will happily continue being on the other end of this man's mood swings for the rest of time.

"Arrie," I gasp between breaths. "I'm sorry I made it so hard for you. That I didn't just ask sooner."

A raw, deep laugh interrupts the moment. "Sorry? You have nothing to be sorry for. I knew I was hurting you, and I just kept doing it. I should have stopped. Or at least just talked to you. But I'm shit at all that."

"You seem to be doing great today."

He pulls back and returns my hood up to my ears. "I am . . . trying for you."

And goddess dammit, if that doesn't turn my insides to mush and makes me want to kiss him again. "I know, but I didn't help. I just kept reacting instead of thinking."

"You were going through a hard time."

"Well, now we all are, so I can't just keep reacting anymore. I need to be more responsible than that."

His knuckles graze my cheek. "You don't need to do that for us. I love that you just react in whatever way you need to. It's beautiful."

132

"But I just cry all the time and get annoyed and frustrated with myself."

His head tips back and laughs. "Yeah, you do. It's great." He links his arm through mine with a smile, and together, we head back to our snowmobiles and leave about a million tons lighter than when we arrived. "Let's go."

About an hour later, we enter a town not far from the hotel, where Arrie takes me on a tour through the shopping district, past frozen ponds, and then treats me to the best lunch I've ever had. At one of his restaurants, of course.

We're sitting at the front at a small table next to the window, where I'm a little fixated on the beauty on the other side.

He's been quiet since we arrived at lunch, but it's a peaceful kind of quiet. Not the inner-turmoil he's trying to hide, kind. After the last bite of his toasted steak sandwich, he wipes his mouth with a cloth napkin and smiles at me. "I'm thinking of opening a bakery."

I blink in surprise. "A bakery?" I lick my lips. "You mean, I could have access to your brownies on tap?"

"I'll bake you a batch every morning, if you like?"

"Shut up and marry me now."

We both laugh, disturbing the couple behind us. Oops. (Not sorry.)

"But seriously, what kind of bakery? Got a theme yet?"

He shrugs. "Kinda. I'm thinking of opening a Vampire bakery. Mixing blood with baked goods so you can eat without feeling yuck."

He's designing a line of cakes and snacks for me? Awwww . . . That's so sweet.

"You look like you're going to melt all over my restaurant's floor."

Wiping the small tear from my eye, I take a deep breath. "I just might." Seriously, no one does big gestures like this man. The books—all of which had non-cisgendered characters—the Christmas present, the date, the conversations he's struggled through, and now this.

He really does care, doesn't he?

He was holding back because he wasn't ready to move on. And seeing him now, everything makes sense. He wants me, but he's been pushing me away because it hurts to feel like he's betraying her. But in doing so, he's hurt me.

The memory of his words, his insults, his leading me on and then shoving me away . . . It still stings. But he's trying. And right now, that's enough for me.

"Magic?" Arrie grabs my hand. "You okay? We can leave if you want to go home?"

I shake my head. "No, no. Sorry. I was just thinking about . . . us." Looking back to where we were a few months ago, I'm actually proud.

"The verdict?" He looks at me with tense anticipation.

But he doesn't need to.

I lean over and place a kiss to his cheek. "I'm proud of us."

"Me too." He leans forward and whispers in my ear, "Want to be my official taster?"

"Fuck yes." I lean back and look at him. "And Arrie? If you ever get frustrated and angry and you don't know what to do, just come find me and tap my shoulder."

He raises his eyebrows.

"I can handle you."

"You think so, hmm?"

I look him up and down. "Definitely."

Chapter Twenty

New Orleans Locked Down: The Insiders' Stories

We spent the rest of daylight hours in the hotel, cuddling, kissing, and watching terrible daytime TV. But when night fell, I raced onto the balcony in nothing but my shorts and strappy pajama top to see the aurora light up the sky.

But fuck, it's cold out here.

I light a fire in my hands and let it warm me up.

"Come here." Arrie wraps his arms around me from behind and rubs hands along my upper arms. "You're freezing for a Vampire."

"Still a Witch."

The lights shine above us, illuminating the world in a gentle, distant rainbow, and I'm floored. Again. Like it's thrumming through me and I'm coming alive.

"I should have taken you here sooner. Sorry."

"I'm here now. And we can always come back."

"I'll take you anywhere you want to go."

I turn in his arms. "Road trip? You know, the old-fashioned ones, by car."

He looks surprised for a moment and then softens his lips into a gentle smile before slanting them against my forehead. "That sounds beautiful."

"Really?"

"All your ideas are beautiful."

I hold a finger to his lips. "Not all of them. I shouldn't have faked our attack on the Vampires, and I shouldn't have just let you walk away." I look at those ice-blue eyes and fall more in love by the second. "Next time, I'll just pin you down and tie you up until you tell me what your deal is."

Arrie spins us around and slams me into the wall. "If anyone's going to be tied up, it'll be you." His hips pin mine in place as his hands travel up my waist and around my curves and land on my shoulders. "Trust me, I'm not the type to bottom."

Yeah, I kinda guessed that. "Guess you'll just have to be a little more flexible. Remember, I'm just as strong as you."

"The fuck you are," he growls. He yanks me up and into his arms before pinning back against the wall and holding up my ass with a single hand.

Our lips connect, messy, teeth clashing, groans echoing off the stone, and when his hand travels under my tank top, I arch into his touch.

A voice barges into the moment that I recognize. "Arrie? Magic?" Connie runs into the room and onto the balcony in a huff. "Sorry, but you need to come home." She takes one look at our embrace and waggles her eyebrows at me. "Dea this morning wasn't enough for you, huh?"

"That was in my other form," I explain as Arrie lets me down with a grumble. I gesture to my boobs and vagina and shrug. "This me is still horny."

Connie and Arrie both chuckle as I rush to get dressed and grab our crystals to take us home.

"I swear," I mumble, "this emergency best be important."

As we teleport into my bedroom, Dea shoots off my bed and looks at us with this serious expression I've come to fear. "The SC are going to bomb New Orleans."

"Wh-what?" I stumble, but Arrie catches me by the shoulder. "But why? How?"

"We do not know either of those things." Dea stands in front of me and places a reassuring hand on the other shoulder. "But Lucien and Red overheard the plans when they snuck into a meeting they absolutely should not have snuck into."

Connie's leaning against my doorframe, smirking at me and Arrie. "So we need to free New Orleans before that happens."

"Do we have a date?" Arrie asks, his no-nonsense tone back in full force.

"Three days." Dea's grim expression tells me we're not prepared for anything in three days.

But we don't have a choice. "Then we'll have to move our plan into action and free New Orleans in two days." I glance at Connie and smile. "But we'll need to stop the bomb, too."

"Otherwise they'll just bomb the city when it's free."

Realization dawns. "That's why they shut down the city." Everyone's eyebrows raise in question. "To limit the number of Vampire casualties. If any of the rogue Vampires got caught in the blast, the Fae Queen would lose her alliance."

"So she infiltrated the SC, probably with Aki's help, in order to have access to their forces." I sigh, guilt welling. "They're just as much a victim in this as we are."

"If only we could expose the bad eggs in the Supernatural Council . . ." Connie imagines, a slight wistfulness to her voice. "Then we could get rid of them and start fresh."

Arrie holds up his hand, stopping her thoughts. "One problem at a time. For now, we need to help New Orleans and give the Vampire king his kingdom back."

An hour later, we're sitting around a table with the entire embassy, delivering the bad news. Everyone looks a little broken. But Lucien looks like he's going to yank his brother's brains out with a hook and eat them for breakfast.

"I'm gonna kill him," he growls. His knuckles glow white with clenched rage as his fangs descend (again) and his eyes radiate blood red violence. "They're our people! How could he be so evil?"

No one knows what to say, not even Dea.

"For now," I attempt, "we need to focus on evacuating the city. Just in case we fail." Everyone nods their agreement. "Which means we either need to infiltrate the city or take it back." I look to Arrie working in the corner, papers spread out before him, a frustrated hand working through his hair.

He doesn't look happy.

And that doesn't fill me with confidence.

"How we doing, big guy?"

Arrie looks over to me with a weak smile. "Not great. There's simply not enough of us while we're protecting the cities, even with a more even spread of power amongst our forces."

Connie turns to look at him. "So we do it covertly. We find an in and an out, and we evacuate the city quietly."

Dea sighs. "We have no way to know how many are stuck. We do not know if we will have enough time. It could be a few hundred or a few thousand."

Felicity chimes in with some helpful information. "Well, we had ninety-six thousand Vampire residents in New Orleans. Of them, only twenty-three thousand are accounted for outside of the Rogue Faction, which have thirty-one thousand Vampires. Which leaves forty-three thousand Vampires unaccounted for."

Arrie sighs. "That's too many to evacuate quietly. We'll never do it in two days."

"And," I chime in, "that doesn't account for the Witches, humans, and Shifters left behind."

Lucien slams his hands on the table. "Then we have to take back our city!"

I turn to Arrie. "We need to make it work. Somehow." I get up and sit beside him, running a hand down his stressed back. "Where are the problems?"

"There are too many entry points. We can't cover them all." He points to various points on the map. "There are two roads coming in north, water on the west and east sides, the rest of the urban area going south and southwest, and the bayou southeast. That's too much ground to cover. And we only have so many Witches and *Sherutan* Fae to cover the water, even with your help." He grips the map with frustration. "And water isn't your strongest element."

A shadow looms over the paper pile, and I look up to meet Lucien's stern eyes. "We don't need perfect, War. Just find us a solution that will result in as few casualties as possible."

We both look at him with a grimace.

"The best result I can find wipes a third of our army."

The room falls silent.

"That's twenty thousand people," Connie argues. "That's . . ."

"Yeah," Arrie agrees.

"But if we do nothing," Lucien argues, "then we lose over forty thousand people."

His math is right. Sucky, but right.

No one ever said this war would be easy.

I stand up, fists curled at my sides. "Arrie, tell everyone the plan."

Connie gasps. "But—"

"This is our job, Connie." I gesture to everyone in the room. "This is why we exist. This is why our armies exist. They're willing to sacrifice their lives for the greater good, but the innocent Vampires stuck in New Orleans didn't sign up for that. We have to get them out."

Dea clears his throat. "While you are all doing that, I will stop the bomb."

My eyes widen. "No. Not alone."

He rests a hand on my shoulder. "I am the best chance we have. I can find out where the bomb will be coming from, stay invisible, then stop it." He looks to Arrie in question.

And damn him, he just nods, agreeing with him. "You're our best chance, dude."

"Then it looks like we're going to war. Again." Rufus, the ever-knowing, ever-pissing-me-off Shifter, huffs. "Will *Sheruta* always have to help Earth's wars?"

I sigh, because I don't have the time for this. Or the patience. "Feel free to leave, Rufus. This is a voluntary position." I swing my arm toward the door and raise my eyebrows.

He remains seated, arms crossed, a huffy look on his face.

That's what I thought.

"What about Aki?" Connie asks, shooting me an apologetic look. "What's his goal?"

142

"Us." I look to the table. "I'm so sorry. He's moving all the pieces to start a war to lure us out so he can get to us." And to stop any of us from dying, I'm going to put as much protection on our seals as possible. No one is dying on me again. "I'm sorry you're all at war because of me."

"Don't give yourself all the credit, Magic," Red says. "Aki's just poking at already created holes."

"If it's anyone's fault, hon, it's ours." Connie looks to me with a soft, guilty expression. "We should have stepped in way earlier than we did. We should have been here for all species, including humans, from the get go."

"If anyone spots Aki in the battle at New Orleans, come find me." I look everyone in the eyes. "It's important you do not engage him." He wields death magic stronger than me, but I can at least defend myself. They can't. "He's more powerful than you know."

And I just happen to have given him more power for a Christmas present. What was I thinking? Now he knows all my spells and charms.

Connie gets to her feet and looks at everyone. "Get your armies ready. We move out tomorrow." She turns to Arrie. "We need that plan as soon as you're ready. Mobilize everyone the moment you can."

"Is there a spare office I can use?" Arrie asks Lucien.

Lucien nods and helps him carry all the paperwork out. Both men silent. I get the feeling Lucien's silence will break soon, and it'll break like a tidal wave I'll contain somehow.

Chapter Twenty-One

While everyone else is either preparing, helping Arrie or the embassy, or having some quiet time with family, I'm staring at the vault in my library. Inside are four seals—War, Death, Conquest, and Magic—that I've triple-checked are there and real, but I'm still trying to puzzle out a way of protecting them.

So I called for help.

I'm nervous to let anyone else know about the seals, but I need to make sure none of us die this time. If nothing else, so I can sleep soundly at night.

A knock on my study door has me sweating. Nervous doesn't begin to cover it. I shift into my female form and

Vampire speed myself to the door, where I open it with a small smile.

"Come in."

My green-skinned Fae trainer looks at me, then at the library, then back at me. "Well, what in the world do you need me for? There's got to be more magic knowledge in this library than the rest of the world combined."

Despite the terror looming on the horizon, I laugh. "I know, but I don't have the time to study up. It's quicker with a teacher."

"I guess." She sighs. "What did you bring me here for?"

"Umm . . . Yeah, about that. I need your help, but it's a secret, and I can't tell you too much about it."

Her eyebrows raise. "I can't help if I don't know what I'm dealing with."

Fair. Annoying, but fair.

"I need a protection spell or some kind of Fae trickery to hide something from any prying eyes."

"Well, that shouldn't be too hard." She picks up a book on a shelf and huffs in amusement. "Do you know how much a copy of this is worth?"

I shrug. "Not really."

Lo flies toward us, his tiny dragon form carrying a stack of books on its back. My little dragon librarian. "Oh, hello." He puts the pile of books back where they belong and then turns to face me. "You did not tell me we were having visitors."

"Sorry, Lo." I cringe. "I just need her help with something important."

"Anything I can help with?" he asks.

"Nah, probably not. We won't be long." I guide us both back toward the vault deep in the library and gesture at its metal door. "I need to protect this and what's inside."

"I can build a protection spell for the room, but I can't do anything for what lies inside without knowing what it is." She shrugs. "Your choice."

"You don't understand how important this is. The last time I showed someone what's inside, Nine died."

"So what lies beyond this door is the key to your immortality?"

I nod, not daring to speak.

"You probably shouldn't have told me, but it's okay. I'll keep your secret." She grabs a chair from the corner and drags it to in front of the door. "I'll do my best to seal the door and lay some booby traps."

"Thank you." I place my hand on the door, and with a silent wave of stale air, it opens. "If you don't mind, I'm going to stay."

She nods, then gets straight to work, examining the material, the placement of everything, and getting a good feel for the space. Then she proceeds to spend all day layering various runes, ingredients, and words together, on top of each other, winding through each other. And by the time she's done, I'm exhausted just looking at her.

146

"I don't know anything in the world more protected." She steps back and takes a last look at her handiwork. "If anyone even touches it that isn't specifically you, you'll know."

"How does that work? Is it linked to my DNA or something else?"

"It's linked to your magical essence. Not just your death magic, not just your DNA, but everything that makes your magical signature yours." She looks me dead in the eyes and smiles. "No one can copy it, not even your evil twin."

I snort-laugh at the moniker. Evil twin. I guess he kinda is, isn't he?

"In fact, even your harem can't get in. You'll be notified the moment they try. Though I can add their signatures if they want me too."

"I'll ask them." I guess it'll probably be best. It's their immortality too. "Thank you."

She looks at me with pride in her eyes and a gratefulness I'm not used to coming from her. "Despite the fact I usually hate people, I've come to rather enjoy your company, Magic. Maybe some day, I'll let you know my name."

"That would be lovely."

"But I'm more than exhausted, so I'm going home to bed. Tomorrow's the big day, after all."

I walk her to the door in surprise. "You're fighting with us?"

Her hand lies on my shoulder. "Always."

A rustle and a creak of the floorboards behind me causes

me to spin on the spot. Dea sits on a chair in the dark corner by my closet. "What was that about?"

"You okay?" I thumb point toward the door. "She was just working on a protection spell for the seal vault and laying some booby traps. No one can get in now, not even you lot. But she can add you to the spell, if you'd like." I huff out a sigh. "I watched her the whole time, assessing her work and making sure she didn't steal a seal."

Dea chuckles. "It's okay, Angel. I trust you."

"Well, I trusted Aki last time, and look how that turned out."

Dea wraps his arms around me and breathes me in. "It's okay. That wasn't your fault. None of us knew. Not even Nine."

He's finding it easier and easier to say his name, as though the pain is becoming more bearable. And I'm happy, but I'm also kind of sad. Nine's meant to be mourned forever. He's not someone who is ever meant to be gotten over.

"Soooo," he says, mystery and wistfulness edging his voice, "how did your date with Arrie go?"

I give him a questioning look.

"What? Curious boyfriends want to know."

I lie on the bed and breathe heavily, relaxing into my own bedsheets. "It went well. He took me to the village he lived in when he was mortal. He shared the story with me and told me why he's been struggling. He feels guilty. Like he's cheating on his dead wife." A small tear leaks down my cheek. "But

I don't really think I got through to him. I just think he's tired of not letting himself love me."

"Maybe desperate want is something he needs to break through that barrier." Dea lies beside me and snuggles into my shoulder. "Maybe he just needs you."

"Uh." Tears flood my face. "This is . . . so much harder without Nine." I relied on him to nudge me in the right direction, like my sexy fairy godfather who also happened to enjoy making his family happy. "He . . ."

"Shh, Angel." He scoops me up and scoots us up to the top of the bed, where he sits me between his legs and lets me cry into his chest. "I know. It hurts. And you have been so focused on helping me through, helping Arrie through his problems, holding Connie's hands, fighting this war, you have not had time to grieve." Magic surrounds us for a second, and then black wings emerge beneath us and the chest I'm spilling tears onto glows gold. "But you can lean on us, too."

"But . . . I . . . don't want you to . . . break." Sobs interrupt each word, making my voice come out in hoarse breaths and hiccups.

His hands run under my t-shirt and sizzle across my bare skin, where our connection shoots up me like fireworks, and everything is cooler, softer, less intense. "I will not abandon you, Magic." His finger lifts my chin so our gazes meet. "I will not check out on you, no matter how bad things get or how broken I am. You are mine to protect."

Lo flies out of the library and lands on my shoulder,

curling up and scorching small flames out of his nostrils as he breathes. Which is his way of saying I love you, I think. "Emotional control is not a strength. It's a weakness. It is a human way of saying 'I am not allowed to exist in this time and space, so I will tamper it down'. Showing emotion, acting, processing it, and then moving on is strength."

And I know that. But I cry so much. I'm sure everyone's annoyed with me, thinking I'm pathetic or maybe crazy. I do jump from crying to screaming to boiling in rage in the space of a single morning.

What would Nine say?

He'd probably spout some nerdy wisdom about how emotions work, and then Dea would chime in with some pearly words that would make me reconsider my entire emotional reasoning.

Yeah, that sounds about right.

Connie and Arrie wind up on the other side of the bed after coming home from their tasks for the day, and they both add to the cuddle pile, Arrie being the one on my right while Connie lays between my legs, like usual.

"Sooo . . ." Connie says the moment I stop crying, "what were you and Arrie getting up to when I interrupted?"

Lo snorts. "Uck. I'm gone." He returns to the library, probably to sort through more books and continue cataloging them. "Bye."

"What was that, Angel?"

"Hmm?" I look up to Dea, whose eyes are a sparkling

night sky full of mischief and wonder.

"What were you two getting up to?"

"Leave ve be, dude," Arrie gruffs. "They don't have to announce every part of their sex life."

"Trust me, big guy"—I pat his leg— "Dea will not stop asking until I tell him. He's possessive like that."

Arrie just huffs, but the small smile tugging at the corners of his lips warms me. It's like he's back. The man that used to flirt with me, the one who pinned me to the rock that day we were rescuing Connie and kissed the ever-loving-fuck out of me. He's mine. Or, at least, he's going to be.

I proceed to tell both Connie and Dea every detail of our date, from the aurora to the hotel to the food to the trip to the village—which Arrie remains silent on, but he agrees to let me tell them everything he said—and when I'm finally done, a smile lights up my face. And I'm happy.

A part of me is still missing, and I'm not sure I'll ever recover from that, but I can be happy and lost at the same time. After all, I have three very good reasons to be happy right here.

Chapter Twenty-Two

Black gates surround me, as tall as the sky and as full of magic as I've ever felt. But it's strange magic. It's suffocating my senses, like a pressure forcing me to the spot that I can't shake off.

It's stealing my air, and I can't breathe.

Shit, why can't I breathe?

Panic grips me, but I take an imaginary breath, stabilizing myself, and try to think straight.

Where am I?

These gates look somewhat familiar, like I've seen them before. Maybe in a drawing. That's it! I've seen these in Dea's drawings in one of the textbooks in my library. These are the Black Gates to the Otherworld. Where Dea brings lost souls to help them cross over.

This is where Nine is.

But why am I here?

Magical pressure constricts like a snake, winding around me, and I still can't breathe. But the magic is . . . Fae. I think. It feels like something I know. Something I've felt before.

I wake up with a gasp, clawing at air as my lungs splutter, and all three of them surround me, touching me, calming me; and Arrie, ever the pragmatist, asks the house for a glass of water and a brownie.

The terror chases me, even as my eyes open and the nightmare subsides. Everything's so hazy.

"You alright?" Connie asks, sitting in front of me.

Dea rubs soothing circles on my bare back. "Would you like to talk about it?"

I shake my head. Words not wording. Thoughts not thinking. I'm just frazzled.

"How about some morning yoga?" Arrie asks, proving yet again that he has been paying attention.

But I shake my head again. Instead, I get up, throw on a nightgown, and head to my library. There's something I need to know.

Lo would be flying in the morning sun by now, so I'm alone for the moment.

Perfect.

I shift into my female form and sprint around the library, heading to the section I need. Fae magic. I only have a couple of hours until I'm needed in New Orleans, so I have to be quick.

My eyes scan title after title, my Vampire speed helping, until I eventually land on the right volume. I was flicking through its contents page a few weeks ago, and right under section three lies THE AFTERLIFE'S BLACK GATE. I flick to the right page and scan the introductory paragraph, deciding this is what I'm looking for.

WHEN HEADING TO THE WORLD BEYOND THIS ONE, YOU'LL BE GREETED BY THE BLACK GATE—A PIECE OF FAE MAGIC FOLDED OVER A THOUSAND TIMES THAT WILL ONLY OPEN FOR THOSE WITHOUT A BODY—AND YOU WILL PASS THROUGH. DEATH SPOKE WORDS OF PEACE WHEN ASKED HOW SOULS COPE. THAT IT IS A NATURAL PROCESS WE INNATELY KNOW HOW TO DO.

Fae magic? The gate to the Otherworld is made of Fae magic? And what does this term mean here . . . folded? How can a spell be folded?

"Angel?" Dea fazes to my side, and I close the book in haste, placing it back on the shelf. "Are you okay?"

I shake the thoughts from my mind. "I'm fine. Sorry for scaring you."

Arrie and Connie walk from around the corner, frowns on their faces, arms crossed over their chests.

"I just wanted to look something up."

"And what would that be?" Dea asks, stern contemplation lacing his words. He saw the book. "What would Fae magic have to do with your bad dream?"

I look into those galaxy eyes and shudder. I can't tell him.

Not yet. If I get his hopes up and it doesn't work, it'll crush him all over again. Besides, I have to deal with New Orleans first. "I need you to trust me." I look to Connie and Arrie. "All of you. It'll be best if I don't mention it until after we free New Orleans. We need our minds clear, and I need more time to research. Please. I just need time to process before sharing."

Connie nods, followed by Dea, but Arrie looks at me with a frown. He doesn't like this. Which makes sense. I hated it when he did it to me, too. But I watch his frown melt off his face and be replaced by a look of trust, his eyes meeting mine.

"Fine," he grumbles.

"We don't have time for this," Connie complains in a huff. "C'mon, I'm not going to war on an empty stomach." She marches toward the kitchen, dragging the rest of us with her. "But don't worry, Arrie. We'll just ask the house for food."

"I can cook."

"You are such a perfectionist," she whines, "it'll take way too long."

He huffs and throws himself into his usual chair in front of me. Dea on the left head, Connie on the right head, and an empty seat next to me where Nine used to sit. None of us have the heart to get rid of it.

The sheer number of slices of toast I eat should be illegal, but hey, I have two mouths to feed. I am, officially, eating for two. I chuckle to myself, and the team all look at me like I'm crazy, but I don't care. For the first time in days, I have hope. And that's enough for now.

"So," I turn to Arrie and ask, "what's the battle plan?"

"We're going to have to divide and conquer again, but across the same city, so we can swap and change as needed." He looks at Nine's empty seat. "We'll have to use a magicom system to communicate."

We all follow his sad gaze and realize at the same time that it's because Nine can't relay messages anymore. Because he's not here.

"Magic, you're taking the water fleet and protecting the east along with strong water Fae and Witches. I'm taking the northside with the two main roads while Connie will be taking the city to the west." He sighs, struggling with something. "We'll have to leave the southside to Lucien and the Demons. It's their territory anyway."

That does not fill me with confidence. No one but Lucien has heard from the Demons since the last battle, but he assures me he's been in contact. And I'll just have to trust him, I guess.

But I get why Arrie is worried: we're leaving an entire area of defense up to someone else. But I don't think Lucien will let anything happen to his city or his people.

I get up from the table and dust the toast crumbs off my hands. "Okay. Let's do this."

We all head to the armory to grab weapons and gear, setting ourselves up, and I shove the stuff on that I wore back in Dhaka. It's been mended. So it should hold up okay. And then we meet in the back garden by the firepit.

I'm the last one there, of course, because I had to change twice. But once I'm there, we teleport to the rendezvous point just outside the city, where the heads of our army await.

Lucien is the first one to notice us, followed by Red, then the Vampire king himself. Who I'm surprised to see.

"Your Majesty, you shouldn't be here." Shock laces my tone. "It's dangerous." And he's old, though I don't say that out loud.

"I appreciate your concern, Magic, but I am neither too royal nor too *old* to defend my city and my people." He gives me a pointed look, telling me he knows exactly what went through my mind. "These are my people. I want to help defend them."

Lucien chuckles at my shock. "Clearly, you've never seen Father in action. He's not Vampire king for nothing." His gaze bores into me, a look I know well. Lucien will protect his father. Regardless of the outcome of the battle.

Red looks at me with a serious expression. "All armies are in place and awaiting our orders."

The rest of the leaders teleport to their designated places in the battle plan while I look at Dea, Connie, and Arrie with no small level of trepidation. "I . . ."

"Shhh." Dea rests a hand on my face. "We are going to be fine."

Connie nods and wraps her arms around me, then dances her tongue with mine. "Don't get injured. I have celebratory plans for us." She winks at me and then teleports away, far too happy to be about to go to war.

Arrie lays a comforting, heavy hand on my shoulder. "You still need to plan our second date, Killer. Don't hold out on me."

"Don't do anything stupid," I try to tell him. "I need all of you alive."

He teleports away with a nod I don't quite believe, and then I'm left facing Dea, who has yet to leave my side.

"I will be back as soon as I can, Angel." He nuzzles my neck as he shifts, his Angel form exploding into the midday sun. "I promise, I will not get hurt and leave you behind."

"And I'll be here when you get back. Waiting."

I wasn't nervous before, but the butterfly storm has started churning in my gut, ready to burst forth from my mouth in a torrent of acid.

What if he dies too?

Shut up, Magic. He'll be fine.

Besides, we have a plan. Well, the start of one.

As he vanishes into thin air, I'm left alone staring up at the sun and taking a deep breath. "I can do this." The crystal smashes at my feet, and suddenly I'm spinning toward the ocean, falling fast.

I catch myself in the air and fly to the few ships floating in the water blockading the valley.

The first person I notice is my Fae trainer, who meets me right away. "We're ready whenever you are."

I nod, my head dizzy and my body shaky. "We'll wait here

for now."

"Magic, can you hear me?" Arrie asks over the comm in my ear.

"Loud and clear, Arrie. How about you, Connie?"

"Coming in strong."

"Good luck." I take a deep breath and turn to my army. "It's gonna suck today. We're outnumbered and have a next-to-impossible task ahead of us. But water is the strongest element, and there's no option of breaking. No choice to lose. Everyone in that city is counting on us."

"Stand by for countdown," Arrie says.

"Formations!"

"Five, four, three, two, one. Go!"

"Charge!" I carry my voice on the air so it reaches the other six boats.

We all manipulate the water to carry our boats toward the port as quickly as possible. Everyone is holding on, trying not to fall into the water, staying brave and strong despite being terrified. And when the port comes into view, I step forward and raise all the boats, lifting the water into a tidal wave, and crash us onto the dock.

Water spills everywhere, crashing through buildings, hurtling down streets, but I set us down gently.

It wasn't enough to hurt any Vampires, but I'm hoping it'll get rid of a wave of Fae in one fell swoop.

One can hope.

We jump off the boats and charge the streets, disarming

and knocking every guard unconscious that we see, clearing this entry point. But it's a few miles long, and we eventually have to spread out.

"Magic, don't hold back!" my Fae trainer yells as we head south with a small army of Witches and Fae behind us. "Now isn't the time for nice."

Not sure I know how to be nice to these assholes anymore.

There's a fence surrounding the city, and I pull it down as we go, yanking it to the floor at multiple points to gain us entry and everyone trapped inside an exit.

A small contingency of Fae and Vampires charge us, but my Fae trainer intercepts, hurtling them off their feet before they get within ten meters. Then she quickly draws a few rune circles on the ground in magical energy and rumbles the earth beneath us.

I use one of the spells on my staff and keep the enemies down while barging the nearest building with a ball of energy, sending it collapsing around us, crushing the enemy but dodging where we stand.

"Let's go." I run forward, waving everyone to follow me. "We have to reach Lucien before we can stop."

Easy for me to say, I'm a Vampire, but these Witches and Fae have human-like stamina. They can't run for miles without needing a breather. And eventually, we have to stop to let everyone catch their breaths.

"Magic, you should . . . go on," my trainer says. "We shouldn't hold you back."

I shake my head. "If Arrie thought that was the best strat-egy, then he would have suggested it. We stick to the plan."

She nods, understanding. Agreeing. Or, if neither of those, she's at least following orders. I don't really care which right now.

"We need to keep going."

The Witches condense water from the air for everyone, providing small balls for everyone to drink.

"Remind me to get one of you to teach me that trick."

"Still a Horseman in training?" one of them teases.

I rush air at her hair, sending it flying in all directions. Ev-eryone laughs. "Seriously, I'm hundreds of years away from being anywhere close to the others."

"Pfft," a guy with pink hair says. "They're light-years from you."

Everyone nods, but I just stand there mentally aghast. They really think that? Not the time, Magic. Not the time.

"C'mon." I wave us farther south, following the fence. "We need to clear the perimeter. Then the real fight begins."

We jog as fast as we all can as a group, tearing down the fence and freeing the city. Physically speaking. We still have to remove the army from inside and get everyone to safety.

Eventually, my Vampire hearing picks up on a group of voices in front of us I recognize. Shouting. And sounds of a fight fluster through the air.

"They need help!"

We all run faster, but I get there first, throwing daggers at two Vampires ganging up on Lucien.

He looks our way with surprise and a fanged, red-eyed smile. "Good to see you, Magic." He pats my shoulder with a genuine display of affection. "Thank you."

The Witches and Fae take care of the other six enemies while I help the king to his feet. A little dirty, but none worse for wear. "You doing okay, Your Majesty?"

His red eyes greet me, and the amount of power leaking from this one man scares me to a standstill for a moment—alongside everyone else in my group. "Never been better."

The salacious glee dripping from those words reminds me that despite his diplomacy, he's a Vampire. A pissed off, tired, hungry Vampire.

Lucien barks at two of his men. "Head west to meet the two teams. Make sure they've succeeded and join their ranks."

Everyone is heading anti-clockwise, sending two Vampires to the next team. So while we wait for two Vampires to head our way, we refuel.

The king looks at his son with pride and surprise. I think he'll make an excellent king someday, but I don't say that out loud. It might be my plan, but I'll need to do some buttering up first. Something tells me he won't take up the mantle easily.

One of the blood vials from Arrie graces my lips with a delicious lavender scent trailing down my throat. Fuck, I didn't think I'd get anything from anyone but Arrie. He's a little possessive about feeding me, which I now realize is because he's jealous. Not just intentionally being a dick. But blood from any of them is phenomenal.

I wonder what Connie tastes like?

I shake that thought from my head, because there's no use fixating on something I'm never going to chase.

Lucien taps his datachip and smiles. "Thirty seconds till we storm the city."

This next part of the plan is gonna get messy. We need to take out the army and any opponents by any means necessary. As quickly as possible.

Tapping my comms, I ask, "How's everyone doing?"

"Clear and waiting," Connie says, a smirk to her voice.

"Getting . . ." A huff sounds through the earpiece. "There."

Connie chimes in, "Thirty seconds, Arrie."

"Fuck off, Con."

Their banter makes me chuckle, and when the king looks at me questioningly, I wave his concern away. "Arrie's still fighting."

Lucien laughs. "Really?"

I shrug. "Connie and I are waiting for him."

"Okay," Arrie says, "we're good on the north side."

I nod to Lucien. "Count us down, Prince."

He descends from fifteen, and when he reaches one, we sprint into the city, staying as a unit for the moment.

Vampires run around the outside of our group, defending our position, scouting ahead, while Witches, Fae, Demons, and some pixies stay in the center, throwing magic shields and spells around, protecting our position.

But after a mile or so with no encounters, we come to a standstill.

"Hey, Connie? Have you encountered anyone yet?"

"Nope."

Arrie hmmms. "Where is everyone?"

"I'll check it out." I turn to face my group. "Stay here. Lucien's in charge. I'm going to fly around and see what's going on."

Everyone nods, understanding, and Lucien looks a little surprised by his assignment, but he straightens and nods nonetheless.

I lift myself into the air and fly ahead, beneath the clouds so I can see everything, but nothing greets my eyes. Even when zoomed in. The city is totally empty.

"Guys," I say over comm, "there's nothing here. The city's empty."

"No," Arrie says, "there must be at least the trapped residents somewhere, even if they evacuated their people out."

I fly back to Lucien and turn to the king. "Is there any kind of underground tunnel system in New Orleans? Somewhere you could trap thousands of Vampires if needed?"

He thinks for a moment, then turns to Lucien. "The drainage system."

"With water in?" I ask.

He nods.

"Perfect." A smile grows across my face. "Take me to the

nearest entrance."

Lucien stops his father when he takes a step, and he instead orders a random Vampire to run with me the few miles to a small maintenance door with a no entry sign.

I thank him, and he runs back.

My hand meets metal when I touch the handle, but a shot of energy zaps me like lightning. "Shit." I yank my hand back and switch forms. My hand hovers over the door, analyzing the spell, and I smile. "I know this spell." It's a defense spell aimed at keeping people out unless they have their DNA stored. It's similar to how my trainer's village barrier works, but with a fancy electrocution rune built in. And the great thing about this is that I know exactly how to get through it.

I add my magical DNA signature to the storage rune, and boom, I'm opening the door and jogging down the stairs beyond.

It's dank. It's dirty. And it's small.

And I hate it.

But it's all I've got right now. If the Vampires aren't here, then I don't know what to do.

After a few twists and turns, walking over piles of what I hope are snapping twigs, I gag at the stench now built up. Water trickles ahead of me, and I know I'm close. When a small opening with a metal grate greets me, I smile. Water.

I dip my hand in without thinking—well, trying not to think about it—and send my energy through the stream, taking note of anything and anyone the water touches.

C'mon, c'mon, c'mon . . .

"There!" Hundreds of people at what I think is the center of the city spreading out. No, thousands. "They're all here."

Well, at least we don't have to round them up.

"I've found them," I say over comms.

"Well done," Arrie praises, and I preen. "Where?"

I cringe. "In the underground sewage system spreading throughout the city. But there's a spell on the doors. I don't know how to get the Vampires out." I couldn't just add thousands of DNA signatures to the spell—that would take days. We don't have days. "I don't know what to do."

"Gosh, Magic," Connie says sarcastically, "if only there was an expert in Fae spells on your team."

Right! "Oh yeah, of course. Right. I'll be back. Hang tight."

I switch back to my female form and sprint back to Lucien and the team. "Found them."

The king's face lights up.

"Only, there's a problem." I turn to my Fae trainer. "There's a spell on the sewage maintenance doors, similar to the one on your village, but it zaps you every time you touch it."

She cringes, fear creeping across her face. "I . . ." She turns to the Vampires looking at her with such hope in their eyes and steals herself. "I'll take a look."

I fly us both there this time, trying to save time.

"Magic," she warns, "I'm not sure I can do this."

I look to her, utterly bewildered that she'd lose hope so quickly. "We can do this."

"No, you don't understand. I designed that spell so that you can't really break it. You can get a few people through it, but to break it, you'd need a team of Fae and several weeks of time to unweave everything."

"Oh." I place us on the floor in front of the door as my smile drops. "I see." I face her, resolve firming my feet to the ground. "Can we at least take a look?"

She rests a hand on my shoulder and looks at me with a worried expression, as though she's already made up her mind, but smiles anyway. "Maybe it's something different."

We both touch the spell over the door, weaving our hands through its intricacies, both of us looking worried, until she pulls her hand back and hangs her head.

"I really . . . I really am sorry." She lifts her head, a sad, lost expression in her features. "I designed that spell for the queen. I . . . It's all my fault."

"No, it's not." My hands rest on her shoulders. "It's hers. You are not responsible for the hatred of others."

There must be another way to get them out. Something that doesn't involve breaking the spell.

Think, Magic. Think.

"Argh!" My hands clench at my sides. "If only I could teleport them." I fiddle with the charm bracelet at my wrist that's hiding my staff and smile. "Maybe I can?"

She looks at me in surprise. "What do you mean?"

I snap my staff into existence. "Nine programmed these charms with all kinds of spells, but he left this one blank." I point to the purple crystal sitting in the cradle. "Told me to use it for whatever would be most useful to me."

"And you want to turn it into a teleporting crystal?" She looks the staff up and down, studying it. "I don't know. Maybe with some time and study, but on the fly . . ."

"Yeah, you'll be surprised the amount of shit I get done under pressure." Like creating a teleporting crystal that doesn't have to break and can transport anyone within its rune circle radius. I press the button on my comms. "Arrie, how much time do we have?"

"I'd say around four hours. Why?"

"Sweep the city clear, then get everyone together near me."

"Hear that, Connie?" I ask.

"Loud and clear."

I smile at my trainer, a wicked gleam of studious excitement. "What? We're gonna need some guinea pigs."

Chapter Twenty-Three

An hour later, after every team sweeping the entire city clear, we're gathered in the center, the army spread out around us in a protective circle.

"Sooo," Connie squeals, "what's the plan?"

I haven't seen her this excited in forever.

"Well, I can't break the spell on the door." I look to the floor, embarrassment flooding through me. "It'll take me years to get that good at Fae magic, and we don't have the time."

Lucien looks at me with worry, but the king smiles, asking, "But you have another plan, yes?"

"Of course." A deep breath. "I'm going to teleport them all out."

"At once?" Connie asks, looking impressed. "You can do that?"

I shrug. "No idea." I meet her gaze, then the king's, and exhale. "But I'm going to find out." I snap my staff into existence. "Nine built this for me with my powers in mind. This top crystal"—I point to the amethyst in the cradle—"can be whatever I want it to be. So I'm going to make it into a teleporting crystal I can reuse."

My Fae trainer beams at me. "If we make it produce an area radius, we can transport as many people as we can fit into the circle." She worries her bottom lip between nervous teeth. "With enough power."

"Let us worry about that." Arrie places a firm hand on her shoulder. "What do you need from us?"

"Time. And guinea pigs."

Arrie turns to the leaders of each group and yells, "Form a perimeter around the city. No one gets in or out without confirmation from me directly. Understood?"

Everyone nods an affirmative, and my knees go weak as a spark of something else shoots through my body. Damn, he's hot barking orders.

"Uh-huh," Connie agrees when she sees my flushed cheeks. "I know." She wraps an arm around me before giving me a quick kiss and setting off with her soldiers.

"Arrie?" Meeting his gaze, I lean into his embrace. "Can you contact Dea and see how he's doing? I'm worried."

A sympathetic grimace flashes across his otherwise stoic

170

face, and he nods.

One by one, everyone leaves, and I'm left alone with the smartest Fae I know to figure out how to transport forty-three thousand people in as few trips as possible out of the city.

"So," she starts, "what first?"

"We need to figure out how to make a teleporting crystal that's activated without needing to be smashed on the ground. Once we've done that, we can figure out how to transport more than one person per crystal. Ask me again after that."

Her green skin glows under the warm sun, but her smile is anything but beautiful; it's cunning, like she's ready to flay the magical rules into pieces and refuse them to her will.

Between us, we can do this.

We have to.

Hunkering down on a nearby bench, I hand over my staff and allow her to analyze it. She whistles. "This is some magic." She looks to me with raised eyebrows. "Famine was amazing."

"Yeah," I sigh, "he was."

This would be the perfect time to ask her questions about the Black Gate. But I don't have time for that. It'll have to wait. C'mon, Magic, you can't be that selfish. The job has to come first.

"This is just an empty Witch's charm made from a powerful stone that looks like amethyst but isn't. It's boosting the magic somehow."

"Right," I say. "And here you can feel the threads tying

it together." I grab a regular teleporting crystal out of my pocket and hand it over. "Smashing the crystal on the ground serves a purpose: it links the spell to the current location. But it doesn't have those linking tendrils because it's just a regular crystal."

"Maybe we can use them to spread outward to seal the location, kind of like a tracking spell."

I run my hand over the stone and grab onto the tendrils tight, then coax them outward, seeing what they do. But after a few seconds, they return to the stone and leak black ooze throughout the gem.

"It's relaying the information," she confirms. "Good. Now we just need to make it select location information only." She plays around with some runes, mutters a few spells, and eventually, something I've never heard of sticks. She hands the staff back. "There."

"You're making this look easy."

She shrugs. "It is so far." In answer to my incredulous face, she says, "When you've studied Fae magic as long as I have, you pick up a few things. You're still a baby."

"Well, this baby Fae needs more training." I analyze the staff, working my magical energy over her spellwork, wondering how it works. But I don't have forever, so I only get the basic gist. "Now, how to transport as many people around me as possible." I tie three runes together, then build two more on top of that, linking them with a basic linking spell and sitting them on top of the gem.

"Here." She rummages around in her cloak pocket and produces some glowing moss in a vial. "This will help."

I take it from her and hold it up to the light. "What is it?"

"Pretorium."

"It's kinda pretty."

She laughs, her voice a little strange with the unusual sound. "It's extremely rare, because it possesses the properties needed to magnify any spell tenfold, so it was farmed to basic nonexistence a long time ago."

"And you just happen to have some hidden in your cloak?"

She shrugs. "Never know when you might need a magical bomb. I keep a little of this and that on my person."

Of course she does.

"If you place this onto the rune circle you just made, it'll magnify it around you, allowing it to trap anyone in its circle."

"How big can it go? How many people can it catch?"

"No idea. Never put it with a signature circle before."

"Won't it use it up every spell?" That would be a nuisance. Especially if it's as rare as she says it is.

"Yeah, but I hear Witches have a natural way with earth and imbuing it into charms. Maybe there's a way to imbue the crystal itself with the pretorium, and then you can just link any spell you like to it."

"I . . ." She's just given a Horseman a magical power expander. "What were you thinking giving this to me?"

"You're a good egg, Magic. You're going to change the world. I can feel it. And I want to be one of the people in your team that made it happen." She punches me in the shoulder. "But don't waste that." She points to the vial. "It's all I have, and I can't get more for you right now."

"Right. Don't spill the glowing gogo juice. Got it."

I lift the crystal out of its cradle carefully and place some of the moss in the center, then the crystal on top of that. Now all I have to do is get the rune circle to draw power from the pretorium.

Once we're sat there staring at what we think is a teleporting crystal strong enough to transport an army anywhere in the world—Earth and *Sheruta*—I don't know what to say. It felt kinda . . . easy. But I don't want to say that out loud lest I jinx us. I guess without her it wouldn't have been easy, would it?

"Test it out?" She looks at me questioningly.

"Right."

I stand to my feet, prepared to teleport myself, but she stops me. "You should teleport me first. Just in case."

"Can't do that. It'll take me with it because I'll be at the center of the spell circle."

"Huh." She blinks at me, astonished. "Should have thought of that."

"It's okay. You just fried your brain trying to play 'guess that spellwork' with the Horseman of Magic. You're allowed to have senior moments."

I duck just in time to miss the punch she tries to land on me. Then I shift into my female form, ready to activate the charm and send power through it. Probably won't take much for just two people, but it'll be a good beta test.

"Ready?"

She nods.

And then we're glowing bright purple and hurtling through the aether. But it's taking too long. We're not even seeing any signs of the destination yet.

"Magic?!" she screams, pain lancing her voice.

I try to turn in the aether, and eventually manage it with a bit of air magic. A gasp slips through my lips.

She's slowly tearing into pieces in the aether, her form disassembling.

"Shit."

What's going wrong?

Why isn't it just teleporting one signature from one location to another.

"Reassemble the rune circle you made!"

I grab the gem with one hand and filter through the matrix of the rune circle with the other, checking everything. But everything's here. I double, triple check. Nothing's missing.

"You forgot the stability rune!" she screams into my ear.

I count the five runes and internally scream at myself for being so damn stupid. I quickly whip up a stability rune and attach it to the circle, then breathe more magic into the gem and fuel the alternation to the spell.

"There."

We hurtle toward the kitchen at home at record speed, but neither of us land on our feet. In a heap on the kitchen floor, my Fae trainer looks at me with a face like thunder. "That hurt!" She huffs and takes a deep breath. "You can't make mistakes like. We're not all immortal like you."

"I know, I . . . I'm sorry." I avoid her gaze, scared of the disappointment I'll see if I raise my head. "I was so focused on getting it right, I didn't even think about keeping it all together."

She sighs a long, deep breath and grabs my hand. "I'm not dead, don't worry." She helps me to my feet. "And now we know it works. Let's get back."

Chapter Twenty-Four

New Blood Pill Could Put End to Feeding Dens

The journey back goes off without a hitch, and we're suddenly back in the center of New Orleans with a tested plan.

"Arrie?"

"Yeah?" he rumbles in my ear.

"Any problems?"

"A few on Connie's end, but she's got it covered. I couldn't get through to Dea. I'm sorry."

My breath hitches. "Okay. Let's focus on the here for now." I take a deep breath and refocus. "Ask the king if he still wants us to teleport them all to the next city."

A few seconds later, Arrie reaffirms the plan.

I look to the Fae beside me and nod. "It's time."

We race to the nearest sewer entrance and steel ourselves.

This is it. I'm saving a city.

The sewer is just as disgusting this time around as it was the first, and I have to hold my breath to wade through the water, trying my best to ignore what's floating around down here.

"This is the most disgusting thing I've ever done."

"Yep. Me too."

We eventually find our way to the edge of the group just as a fight breaks out.

"Well," I hear one of them say, "we have to do something!"

"Please," I try to shout, "I'm here to help."

Everyone turns to us with fear and surprise, but some with outright hostility, and I suddenly realize that there's a lot of nonsense circling about me right now, and it won't be an easy feat getting everyone on board.

"I can teleport everyone to safety."

"You're that new Horseman, right?"

"Why would you help us?"

I steel a breath and swallow my frustration. "Because it's my job."

"Ugh." My Fae trainer shoves past me and looks everyone in the eye. "Look, there's a bomb coming to wipe New Orleans off the map. Yes, we have someone trying to stop it, but in case they can't, we need to get you all out of here. Now. I know you cannot trust Magic, but you need to try, because without them, you're going to die."

I need to remember to ask her to write any future speeches. Straight to the point, not messing around, and everyone just magically listens.

"A bomb?"

Worried shouts echo down the chambers, where hundreds more Vampires are trapped.

"Please, let me help you."

They all stay silent as they begrudgingly nod their assent.

"Now, is everyone here, even the non-Vampires?"

Lu pushes through. "Magic? Is that you?" It's the human from before. "Are you really here?" Tears in her eyes and a wobbling lip, she falls toward me. "You came!"

"I promised I would. I'm sorry it took so long."

A few others come forward, thanking me, when I notice a familiar face from when Aki and I were last here. "You're the charm Witch, right?"

"Yeah, yeah I am. Got caught up in this mess again, as usual."

I grimace. "Yeah, sorry. But I'm here to get you all out."

"Then what are we waiting for, an invitation?"

"Well, I was trying to get everyone's consent, but it's—"

"Consent? Magic, we're trapped in the sewers with a bomb on the way. Quit being ridiculous and just teleport us already. They'll thank you later."

"Err, right." I shift forms and grip my staff tighter. "I need to be in the center as much as possible, so could you lead the way?"

He grabs my arm and drags me through the throngs of dirty people, desperate faces lit up in glimmers of hope, and goddess only knows what in the disgusting sewer water. "I don't know where the exact center is, but the crowds of people are thickest here."

"Okay, that'll do." I look to the surrounding Vampires and hope to the goddess that I don't disassemble them on the way. "I need everyone to pack themselves in as tightly as possible."

People shuffle to me, squashing me from all sides as a panicked kind of hope washes through the crowd. Questions of "what's going on?" and "are we really getting out of here?" fill my ears, but I ignore them. I need to concentrate.

I slam my staff on the ground and send my Fae magic into the crystal, encouraging those tendrils attached to the rare stone to seek out our location. "C'mon, c'mon." Then I shoot as much magic as possible into the staff and watch every rune on the side light up as the crystal spins in its cradle, the moss glows brighter, and the rune circle I created echoes around us in a large enough radius that we'll be taking hundreds at once.

And then we're gone, shooting through the aether. I try to remain concentrated on Baton Rouge. But fuck, it's hard directing more people than I can see, and my mind wants to wander and think about other things, but it can't. I can't. Right now, we need to help these Vampires. I can think about my own issues later.

I gather myself, take a mental breath, and concentrate on

our goal location. I've been to Baton Rouge before, so it's not too hard, and before I know it, a vast green space opens up in front of me.

Yes!

We hurtle toward it, and the aether spits us out with more force than usual—I need to look into that—but we're safe. Hundreds of Vampires are safe.

Vampire officials come out of the nearest office building to meet us, and volunteers from all species start handing out blankets, water, synthetic blood tablets, and anything else they think will be useful.

They're in safe hands here.

I teleport myself back to the sewer, and do the same thing again forty-three times, each time dumping them onto the green that's managed to clear somewhat each time I come back. And when I teleport myself back for the final time, I land in my Fae trainer's arms in complete exhaustion.

"I can't believe you did that. So reckless." She half carries me out of the sewer system. "You shouldn't use all your magic like that."

"There's a leyline beneath us. Just need to . . . recharge."

"Magic, Connie, we have a problem," Arrie says in my ear. "The bomb is hurtling toward us."

I look up and see a giant magical ball of green light heading our way, still a few miles out. "Everyone's been evacuated."

"Okay, then send your armies home," Arrie commands

everyone. Every soldier has a teleporting crystal, so I assume they use those. "Then meet in the center square."

I shift forms, so I have slightly more energy, and manage to drag us to the meeting point, where Connie, Arrie, Red, Lucien, and the king await us.

"What took you so long, little Horseman?"

I scowl at him. "I have just teleported thousands of Vampires in a mere forty-three trips, so if you could hold your judgement, little prince, that would be fantastic."

The surprise on everyone's faces hurts just a little.

"What? You didn't think we could do it? I'm hurt."

Connie wraps an arm around my shoulders, and I slump into her. "Always knew you had it in you, hon."

"Now," Arrie says, breaking the moment, "what to do about that bomb."

"It looks like Fae magic," my trainer says. "Powerful Fae magic."

Arrie looks to me with a grimace, then an idea lights up his eyes. "You share an energy source, yes?"

"Huh?"

He sighs. "Your forms share a single energy source? Didn't Nine say something like that a while ago?"

"Kinda. I'm tired and exhausted in this form too, but not as much."

"So if you fuel up, you can fly up there and help Dea?"

I look to the sky, to the glowing green ball, and watch Dea fly around it, trying to do something. But he's failing, because it's mere minutes from hitting us.

"I can try."

Arrie holds out his wrist expectantly, and without missing a beat, I sink my fangs in and drink my fill, letting the energy gained soothe me and the pleasure flood through me. Though I'm careful to let neither show in public.

Once finished, I shift forms and take a look. "I'm tired, and I don't have a lot of magic left, but I can certainly take a look and disable a few spells."

"It might not be that simple, Magic," my Fae trainer says. "Would you like me to come with you?"

"No. You should all leave." I look to the king. "Especially you, Your Majesty."

He goes to argue, but Lucien grabs two crystals and smiles at me. "Save our city, Magic."

"I'll do my best." I turn to my trainer and place a hand on her shoulder. "Get to Baton Rouge and see if you can help there. That way, you're within calling distance if I need any help."

She nods, then teleports herself away.

I'm just about to tell Connie and Arrie to leave when they look at me with raised eyebrows. Immortal, Magic. We're all immortal.

"Be careful," Connie says, worry trying her lip.

Arrie doesn't say anything; he just looks at me, and I know. I know he's worried. And he's feeling more than he knows how to communicate.

Without another word, and while trying not to cry (and failing, but shh, let's not spill those beans), I fly up, soaring myself faster than I'd previously managed. "Dea!"

Dea looks up and meets my gaze with relief. "Magic." He collapses into my arms and hugs me. "I have no idea what to do." He gestures to the bomb soaring next to us. "I was not expecting . . . this."

"Yeah, us either. But I'm here to help." I shift forms, and Dea catches me.

"I have got you, Angel." His voice caresses my ear and rushes straight to places that shouldn't be so thrilled I'm in my boyfriend's arms while next to a magical bomb. "Whatever you need, just tell me."

I analyze the bomb and exhale in frustration. There's so much here that I don't recognize, but I have to do something. Okay, Magic, start with the bits you do know.

There are plenty of explosion spells, of course, but there's also something that looks like a homing device, some kind of DNA recognition, and plenty of ingredients swimming around in various crystals and potions that I've never seen before.

I don't have the knowhow to break this.

There must be something else I can do.

I turn in Dea's arms and bite his neck, taking him by surprise. He falters, and we swoop low in the air for a minute before his wings catch us as he moans.

"Magic . . ."

Once done, I look up at him and smile. "Sorry. Just fueling up." I could really use Connie's blood too, but I'll just have to make do. I shift forms and untangle myself from Dea's grip. "I'm gonna smash it to pieces."

Dea's eye widen. "Magic, I am not sure that—"

I place a single finger over his lips. "I have neither the time nor the knowledge to do anything else. So this will have to do." I shrug. "I'm immortal. We'll be fine."

"There is no one left down there, I assume?" I nod my agreement. "We could just . . . let it go."

"This is their home. Their royal home. I can't let that happen. I promised Lucien I'd do everything I could."

He mumbles something that sounds like "that damn Vampire", but I can't be sure. He's gotten good at mumbling things beneath the volume my Vampire hearing can detect. The controlling asshole.

"Then I will get the others up here to help. We have a greater chance of pulling this off together." He flies to the ground at top speed and returns with both Connie and Arrie in his arms.

"Here." I create boards of air for them both, like the one I made for Connie that time at the Fae palace. "Use these."

Connie hops on like a surfer and quickly finds her balance, whereas Arrie takes a few seconds longer, his bulky weight making it harder.

"Are we really doing this?" she shouts.

"Yup."

Dea scowls at me, then sighs. "It appears so, yes."

Arrie laughs, like full-on belly laughs with shaking shoulders and a wicked grin. "Then let's go!" He draws his battle-axes and roars.

Connie grabs her short sword, Dea draws his daggers, and I call up two great fireballs and increase their density.

We're getting closer to the city, we're running out of time, and the pressure of the situation is crippling, but I can't crumble now.

Right now, I need to help save New Orleans.

"Now!"

All of us rush the bomb, throwing daggers, fireballs, strength, and swords at it, doing anything we can think of to break it apart to cause some damage. But nothing works.

Shit.

Calling up my Vampire strength, I charge through the air, faster than a bullet, and rush the structure. Crash. The impact dents the outer case, and it slows.

"I did something!"

Arrie gets ready next, and his eyes meet mine. He nods.

I rush the air around him and send him hurtling into the bomb. His battle-axes crack the dents, splitting the weird metal in half.

Connie and Dea are holding back, giving us space.

When we finally break the metal casing off, we get our first good look at the inside. It's made of some kind of light or white fire.

Maybe I could soak it dry?

Kill the fiery substance?

Let's try.

I turn toward the ocean to the east and drag a decent-sized ball of water, then throw it at the bomb.

Clouds of steam sizzle as the speed falters more.

"Do that again!" Arrie shouts.

"Yep." I'm sweating, panting, and unable to keep myself balanced in the air, but I take a deep breath and call water from the ocean in waves. Wave after wave, enough to drain the coast dry. "Hold on!"

Everyone moves out of the way, Dea dragging them both at maximum flight speed away from me.

I circle the water around me into a tornado and point the apex directly at the bomb.

It crashes around me, sizzling and sparking, angry and white. Hot fumes steam. Angry burning sounds spurt. But eventually, when I'm nearly out of water, the bomb is drowned and hurtling to the ground.

I catch it a few meters before it hits the ground—just in case. And I send all of the leftover water, including the now-flooded areas of New Orleans, back to the ocean.

"I hope that didn't affect the wildlife or the sea level too much." Oops. Didn't think of that.

Tiredness overwhelms me instantly, as though all the energy I had is slipping away with the adrenaline.

I'm looking up at the clouds. Why is the sky falling?

Chapter Twenty-Five

Emergency Announcement: Bomb Headed for New Orleans Stopped by Horseman of Magic

"You think they'll be alright?" Connie asks.

An unfamiliar voice answers. "Yes. Magic will recover with time. They used all their magical energy. It would kill a mortal."

"Well, then we're lucky Killer here is immortal." Arrie laughs under his breath.

And I release a long exhale as my eyes begin to open. "Did we win?" I croak, my voice hoarse from disuse.

Arrie chuckles under his breath, a huff of a laugh filtering through the fog in my brain like a beacon. Clearing the muggy thoughts. "Yes, we won. New Orleans is safe."

"Safer than safe," Connie says. "Dea is helping oversee

the rerunning of the city. The Vampires have their home city back. Congrats."

My eyes peel open and see Arrie run a stressed hand through his hair. "Yeah," his gruff voice meets my ears. "Dea got a little possessive and wouldn't let the doctor near you, so I had to send him back. Sorry." His eyes flash an apology, a look I'm not used to seeing on his gorgeous angles and ice-blue eyes.

"Oh." I could just imagine Dea doing that in his Angel form. All black wings and gold body protecting me from literally zero threats. The idiot. "Is he okay, d'you think?"

The doctor leaves just as Connie sits beside me and runs soothing hands down my bare neck and chest. "I think he's doing the best he can."

Arrie lies on my other side and runs a hand over my bare leg. "He'll be alright with you by his side."

"You think so?" I ask, eyeing him up. "You don't think he's just slowly dying alone in a corner of his mind?"

"Is that how he feels to you?" Connie asks. "As his mate."

I shrug. "I don't know. I think he can feel me a lot better than I can feel him. But yeah, it kind of feels like he's pushed everything into some dark corner of his mind and is just running on every emotion, ignoring his needs." A shiver runs through me. "I'm scared for him."

"Me too, hon." Connie lies down and snuggles into my side.

"What if . . . I could bring him back." The words tumble

out of my mouth before I can catch them, and it's too late to shove them back in. They're out there.

"What?" Connie asks.

"What if I could bring Nine back?" I look to her, searching her eyes with mine, looking for an answer somewhere in those green depths. "What if I could fix everything?"

"No." Arrie doesn't offer up any more words or actions, just a tight squeeze of my thigh with his monster-sized hand.

"Why not?"

"Too many unknowns, hon. You'd be risking everything—and not just for us, but for the world, too. For a future you don't know you can achieve."

"But I could bring him back. I could . . . I could . . ."

"Shhh," Connie whispers. "Get some rest. We can talk about it later."

"Can you send Dea up when he gets back?"

They look at me like I've grown a second head. "Just to cuddle." Goddess. I wasn't going to give him false hope. I'm not the evil twin.

"Of course."

I drift off to sleep as they leave, and at some point during my nap, Dea snuggles into bed with me, one of his wings laying on top the duvet like a second blanket. "Shh, I am here, Angel."

My nose snuggles into his neck and inhales the smoky lavender scent I always associate with calm and tranquility.

"Did everything go okay?"

"Uh-huh." His head is rested on top of mine. "The king is back in his palace, Lucien is overseeing everything else, and I've made sure we have some of our forces protecting the city."

"We can't protect the cities forever."

"No, we cannot."

"So what now?"

His hands run over my bare skin, his touch sending a million little zings pinging across my body, as he whispers, "I do not know."

But I do.

I know.

Now, I want to get my boyfriend back.

Chapter Twenty-Six

New Orleans Evacuated: Read All About It

It takes a couple of days to get my strength back, but once I do, I'm in my library researching the Black Gate and everything I can find on the Otherworld.

Lo helps, finally happy to be the one helping me for a change. "Are you sure this is what you want to do, Magic? It seems dangerous, even for an immortal . . . What's that word you taught me? Badass?"

I giggle, a little slip in my focus, before I return my attention to the task at hand. "Yes, I'm sure."

"Okay, then."

Lo now knows more about this library than I do, having had more time to explore. He's like my personal little librarian. Though, I guess he's only little because he's choosing to be—and because I threatened to drown him if he tried barging through these shelves in his regular size.

The book in front of me is a journal entry from Dea dated a thousand years ago. THERE IS NEVER A TIME WHEN HELPING A SOUL CROSS TO THE OTHER SIDE IS SOMETHING I WILL NOT WANT TO DO. IT IS MY GREATEST PLEASURE AND YET MY GREATEST BURDEN. BUT I MUST ADMIT TO BEING POORLY PREPARED AT TIMES TO HANDLE THE IMMENSE EMOTIONAL BURDEN OF BEING AROUND A PERSON'S DEATH SCENE. FOR THAT IS WHERE I AM CALLED. NOTHING HURTS MORE THAN WATCHING A MOTHER SCREAM FOR THEIR CHILD OR WATCHING A LOVER CRUMPLE UNDER THE WEIGHT OF IMPENDING LONELINESS, BUT BEARING WITNESS IS WITHIN MY DUTY.

Oh, Dea. It must be so hard for him to simply do his job. He really was handed the worst ability, wasn't he? Thank goddess Nine didn't need help passing. I think that would have killed him. It certainly would have killed me.

The book from earlier is spread out in front of me, and I've been trying to decipher what it means all damn morning but failing.

"What the hell is a folded spell?"

Ding, dong.

Someone's at the library door.

(Yes, I installed a doorbell.)

"I'll get it," Lo says, flying that way.

A few minutes later, Mrs. No Name Fae Trainer walks through the stacks toward me with a small, rare smile on her face.

"Anything I can help with?"

She opens her mouth, looks at the books I'm reading, and then closes her mouth, the smile falling from her face. "Or maybe there's something I can help you with?" She sits in the seat across from me. "Magic . . ." Her eyes meet mine, her warm green skin glowing in the daylight filtering through from outside. "The Black Gate? I know the legends. They're famous among my people. But if you're looking them up for the reason I think you are, then stop."

"So is it true? Did the Fae really create the gate to the Otherworld?"

She sighs. "No one knows. It happened before our history records began. But maybe." She drags one of the books and a translational bookscreen toward her and begins looking through the text with me.

"Hey," I ask, seeing it mentioned again, "what's a folded spell?"

"It's a type of concealment. You can fold parts of your spell away so other Fae can't read them. But it's a difficult technique few can master." Her head never rises from the pages, her eyes flicking back and forth over the lines of text.

"Hmmm . . ." I flick another page. "Can you do it?"

She looks to me with curiosity in her eyes. "Yes. And yes to your next question, too. I can teach you." She gestures for me to hand over the book I'm reading, and once she's flicked through the text herself, her head falls into her hands with a sigh. "Folded spellwork." Her head raises from her hands with slow movements. "Magic, I care about you. I didn't think I would, but you've become my friend. So I mean this with love: I'm not teaching you folded spellwork if the outcome is you risking your life to bring your dead boyfriend back."

"What?" a quiet, familiar voice echoes from behind me.

Fuck.

"You can bring him back?" Dea asks, still not stepping out from the bookcase I didn't even know he was hiding behind. "Really?"

"I . . ." I look to my trainer and scowl. "I don't know."

"But you think you can?" He steps out from his hiding place and walks toward me. "You think you can bring Nine back?"

"Dea . . . I . . ."

"Stop coddling me!" He flinches at his own raised voice. "Sorry, sorry." His hands run soothing lines down my arms in apologies not voiced. "Sorry. I just . . ."

"I didn't want to tell you because I don't know." I gesture to the books. "This is so complicated. And I don't even know how much of it is true or just fabricated legend." My eyes drift from his to the floor. "I didn't want to get your hopes up."

"But I want to help."

"If it doesn't work, it'll be like losing him all over again."

My Fae trainer interrupts, coughing. "Even if you do drag his soul out of the Otherworld, what then?"

"I honestly have no idea," I admit. "But something about

that just feels right." Just like it did in my dream. "Arrie and Connie don't agree. They said it's too dangerous."

"They would," Dea gruffs. His hand strokes my cheek. "They just do not want to lose you after losing him. They are still hurting, like we are."

"But that doesn't mean it's not the right choice."

"Risking your life," my Fae trainer says, "for something you have no idea how to accomplish is never the right choice."

I turn to her. "Why do you think I'm here with a thousand books, trying my best to gather as much data about the Otherworld as possible?" Inhale. Exhale. "Just because I sometimes act like one does not mean I'm a child."

Her hands raise in surrender. "I never said you were."

"No, but everyone looooves treating me like one." My hands clench at my sides. "And it drives me fucking batty."

Dea snickers.

I spin, throwing an accusatory stare his way. "What is so funny?"

"Batty. You could turn into a bat if you really wanted."

For goddess' sake.

But the laughter spilling from his lips is like a dam breaking, and he can't stop, and then I can't help but join in. And even though we shouldn't be laughing, should be continuing this serious conversation, I shift into a bat and make everyone laugh, even stubborn old greenie over there.

I shift back to human and say, "Okay, okay."

They both slowly stop laughing, wiping tears from their

eyes.

"So, I'm going to try. Whether everyone agrees or not. I couldn't live with myself knowing that I might have succeeded but was too scared to try." I turn to face Dea. "But you have to know that it might not work. In fact, it probably won't. We have to be prepared to fail."

He cups my jaw. "We are losing nothing if you fail. I will go with you and ensure you return safely." He turns to look her in the eyes and smile. "Does that satisfy you?"

She nods, clearly still unhappy.

"Good," I say, "then let's get to work."

Chapter Twenty-Seven

Horsemen Refusing Comment About New Orleans

All three of us spend hours pouring over textbooks, and I get the basic rundown on how folded spells work. Though I'm unsure I can actually create one. But it doesn't matter. I just need to know how to undo one or edit one or fiddle with it so I can remove a soul from inside to outside the door.

If I can manage that, then I can bring Nine home.

But what I do when I drag his soul back down to Earth is another question I don't have the answer to.

Will the teleporting crystal even work on a soul without a body? Can I even get him back to *Sheruta*?

What about Connie and Arrie? Will they hate me for doing exactly what they didn't want me to do?

This is insane.

Completely and utterly insane.

My craziest plan yet.

"Hey, Angel. Stop spiraling." Dea's gentle head rests atop mine. "We will be fine. We can do this."

"It's just . . . I have so many unanswered questions. Questions I'll never be able to answer. There are parts of this plan we'll have to make up as we go along."

"Uh-huh." He nods. "That is about the gist of it with you."

A scowl rips across my face.

"It really is," my Fae trainer says. "Your powers are basically limitless. I don't think you were created to be like the other Horsemen."

"In what way?" I ask, confused. I'm a part of the team. Just like the others.

"The others have specific powers designed to help specific problems. But yours are infinite. You can combine all types of magic to solve all kinds of problems. You've basically put them out of a job." She gestures to Dea. "The world doesn't need them anymore. It needs you."

"See, even grumpy agrees." Dea wraps his arms around my waist. "Look, even if we do not manage to bring him back, we tried. We owe him at least that much."

"Then you can be the one to tell Arrie."

Dea chuckles. "Yeah, he will not be happy." His fingers lace mine as he sighs a deep breath. "But we will tackle it together."

Another few hours, and we're all exhausted. So we head down for dinner, where Arrie and Connie are spreading out a lush evening spread of tacos and cheesecake. But it's Arrie's tacos and cheesecake, so it's elite. Not that tacos on their own (without the Arrie-level awesomeness) aren't great.

"I'm going to head back home for a few days. I need to rest." Her green skin does look duller than usual, and her bloodshot eyes echo how I feel.

"Are you sure?" Connie asks. "You're more than welcome to stay."

Lo flies into the kitchen. "Is that tacos I smell?" He settles into a spot on the table Arrie set for him.

"I'm sure. I'm exhausted." She says goodbye to everyone and leaves out the backdoor, heading home.

"So," Connie turns to me and asks, "what have you been doing all day cooped up in your study?"

I look to Dea and wince. "How about we eat first and then chat about that?" Because I'd like to get through dinner without Arrie throwing a fit.

"Because that's not ominous." Connie wraps an arm around my shoulder and places me in my seat. Next to Nine's seat. His empty seat. "Whatever it is, I'm sure it'll be fine."

Uh-huh. Absolutely. Fucking perfect.

The usual silence pervades dinner, the emptiness sitting next to me an all-consuming presence none of us can ignore.

"I found an interesting book today," Lo says, breaking the silence. "It was talking about how powerful Witch magic is when used together, combining their powers. Is that true?"

Dea looks to Lo and smiles. "Witches have a strong sense of community. They build entire homes out of mountains and caves and streams while weaving their magic together."

"Maybe we could ask for the local Witches help to create something more beautiful and permanent for the pixies in the northern forest?" Lo suggests. "They're just camping out there for now, waiting for someone to tell them to leave or to need to move."

"Oh, I should have checked in on everyone by now." Fuck. I've been so busy focusing on my team and New Orleans I forgot about everyone. "The Demons too. Glowy. Everyone. I'll check in on them all tomorrow."

"We can all go, if you like?" Connie suggests. "Though, I do have a few things at the embassy to take care of first."

Dea looks at me. "I'll continue with the research." Then he looks back to his plate and avoids the growing elephant in the room.

Arrie shrugs. "I can come along, if you'd like some company?"

"I don't mind."

"Okay." Connie slams her knife and fork down. "Out with it." At my eyebrow raise, she explains, "Whatever is ruining this dinner, whatever has you so worried and quiet, spill it."

I look to Dea, and together, we take a deep breath. "We're going to the Otherworld and bringing Nine back."

Everyone falls silent, no one even taking another bite—it's

like I've stopped time.

"Okay." Connie takes a deep breath. "We should talk about this."

"It's not up for debate." Her eyes flinch, hurt, and I immediately regret my choice of words. "I'm sorry. I'm sorry that this means risking my life and that you're worried and that we don't agree. But I'd do the same for any of you. I have to at least try. Even if I fail, I owe him that much."

Connie clearly struggles, tears brimming her eyes, but she chokes it back. "I hate this." A shuddering breath exhales out of her, like defeat. "Like I have to choose between wanting you to be safe and saving him." She smashes her hand on the table, frustration rubbing tiredness into her beautiful eyes.

"I don't want you to go." Arrie looks me dead in the eyes as he says it, fists clenched. "If it means losing you, I don't want to save him."

Dea snaps, his wings popping into existence. "What do you mean you do not want to save him? Arrie! How fucking could you?"

"What do you want me to say, man? That I understand? That it hurts but I am okay sending my partner to their death? He's gone! But Magic is right here." He points at me, as if proving his point.

"He has been with us for two thousand years!"

"You think I don't know that?" His voice is quiet, deadly, on edge. As though he's going to explode at any moment. "I want him back too. But not at Magic's expense."

"It's not your choice," I tell him, because it isn't. "The only reason I'm talking it through with everyone is because last time I didn't, you all yelled at me."

"And brought back a murderous evil twin," Connie ever-so-unhelpfully points out.

Dea exhales. "I get it. You are scared. But Nine is scared too. Scared we might not come for him. Scared that we will give up and abandon him." Tears sting his eyes. "I need to go and get him, and I cannot do that without Magic."

But Arrie, ever the pissed-off Horseman of War, storms off, not wanting to listen to another word.

Chapter Twenty-Eight

Sheruta: What Is It and Can I Visit?

Knocking on that door is like standing on the edge of a cliff—unsure if I'm going to fall off or step back. But today is all about flying, and I can't do that if I don't leap first.

Knock, knock, knock.

"Arrie?" No answer. "Can I come in?"

The door swings open, and a tower of muscle stands between me and the other side.

"Are you just going to stand there, or are you going to let your partner into your bedroom so we can talk like grownups?"

Frustration slashes across his face like an unmovable iceberg. Frozen. But he steps aside and gestures a wide arm for me to enter. With a sigh. But I'll take it.

Baby steps, people. Baby steps.

Arrie thumps the door closed behind us and stands with his arms folded across his chest and that same frustrated scowl frozen on his face. He opens his mouth, then closes it. Opens, then closes.

He doesn't know what to say.

Okay, then I'll start.

"I'm sorry." Genuinely. "I'm so sorry I'm doing something I know will hurt you, and I'm sorry that there's nothing you can say or do that'll change my mind."

His eyes meet mine with an upheaval of emotion, like he can't quiet decide how he feels. Or maybe he feels more than one thing. (Seems unlikely.) Fists clenched, eyes screwed shut, he focuses on breathing. In, out. In, out.

But nothing he does makes his fingers uncurl or his eyes reopen, and I realize that maybe his anger is something he can't just breathe away. Maybe he needs some way to release it.

So I grab his curled fist and lift it to my mouth, biting down. Forest-scented blood trickles down my tongue in waves as a loud thump meets my ears, and I open my eyes to see Arrie's splayed hand on the wall and his eyes fixated on me with enraged fury and heat and lust.

And finally, when I'm nearly done, he uses purposefully gentle fingers to tuck a loose strand of hair behind my ear.

I unlatch my mouth from his skin and stare at him with a bloody smile. "Alright. Gimme your best shot, old man." I widen my stance, bring my fists to my center, and focus my weight onto the balls of my feet. "You wanna let out that energy, I'm all ready to go."

"Magic . . . I'm not going to—"

"I'm going to the Otherworld with Dea, regardless of how you feel, to save Nine. With or without your blessing," I remind him.

That stubborn face flits to one of rage and frustration in an instant, and his splayed hand forms a fist once again—one that comes swinging my way.

I meet it with crossed arms, but the force sends me skidding backward a few feet.

Ragged breaths meet my ears.

"That all you got?" He doesn't move, doesn't speak. Frozen. "Don't pretend like you haven't wanted to punch me in the face since the moment I got here."

Quick as lightning, his hand grips my throat and squeezes, cutting off my oxygen supply. "You're just going to leave us? To leave me? For Nine? For someone who's already dead that you have no idea if you can bring back!" His voice edges louder the more he speaks. "Why is he more important than us?"

He's not. I would do the same for any of them. But I can't say that because he's lifting me off the ground by my throat—thank goddess I don't need to breathe—and my dangling feet squirm.

I kick outward, landing a foot to his steel abs.

But he doesn't move.

Of course he doesn't.

So I flail and kick upward, landing a blow to his chin that knocks his head back and loosens his grip enough for me to unwind his fingers and fall to the floor.

His eyes snap back to mine, furious. "Since when did Nine become top in the relationship."

"He isn't. Wasn't." I take a breath and back up. "Isn't."

"Then why risk us losing you for him?"

I don't say anything. Because there's nothing I can say to that. I'll risk it all because I love him, just like I love all the rest of them. Just like they love me.

So even if the world burns, I'll make the choice to risk it all.

"Why?" He throws a fist my way, but I block. Then another that I dodge. "Why can't you just be happy with the three of us? Or at least try." Tears brim his eyes. "Are we not good enough for you?"

That question catches me off guard, and he swings his grip to my shirt, which he catches and uses to yank me toward him. He snarls in my face, a growl escaping that vibrates through me.

I wrap my legs around his torso and squeeze.

But he unravels them and throws me across the room.

I fly through the air, too fast and too sudden for me to think about catching myself, and I land in the wall next to the door. Half in, half out. "Owww . . ."

Arrie charges at me, a seven-foot tower of ice-cold fury,

and I brace for impact. But he stops in front of me and grabs my legs, ripping them open. He pins my knees to the wall, resting his hands underneath, holding me in place.

Oh, fuck.

His icy blue eyes meet mine, and I swear they're a shade darker, more teal ocean than ice cold. But the look he gives me is half feral anger and half uncontrolled lust, and a full-body shiver racks me head to toe.

"Why?" he asks.

Again, I don't answer.

I don't know how.

A growl rips from his teeth, vibrating through his lips. And before I can protest or try to get out of his grip, he buries his head up my skirt and grabs my panties between his teeth.

The sound of ripping fabric and snarling fills the air as my breath hitches and my brain freezes. This is not where I thought this would go. But it doesn't matter, because without preamble or foreplay, he's spearing me with his tongue, parting my lips with practised skill.

A small sound of protest escapes before Arrie curls his tongue and flicks the tip across all the good nerves. And that protest turns into a moan as I curl my fingers into fists at the wall, trying to hold on to something—anything. But I'm suspended against a wall with nothing but his palms flat behind my knees keeping me up.

"Arrie . . ."

"Shut up," he growls. His tongue pulls out and slashes

upward, lashing at my clit in harsh strokes that are too much too quick.

I try to wiggle free, to move away, but I can't. He's got me pinned.

His wicked gaze flies up to me, and the salacious smile that meets my eyes makes me tense and my body quiver. "Sit there and fucking take it."

Nothing prepares me for the way he dives back up the fabric of my skirt and wraps his lips around my clit and sucks, his tongue circling and my moans and growls vibrating.

Oversensitive sharpness soon turns to waves of molten pleasure as my back arches. "Arrie . . ." His name leaves my lips on a sigh as I push myself into his mouth further.

He grips my thighs and pushes them higher, splitting me open further.

As he sucks harder, soaring my body higher, my legs growing shakier by the minute, my fingers thread through his hair. "Arrie, harder."

The rugged groan that escapes his lips sends a thrill through me like nothing else, and he moves his hands to my ass for a minute while he undoes his jeans. Lips never leaving my pussy.

His tongue circles faster as I clench around nothing. Emptiness filling me.

"Arrie, fuck me." I squirm, trying to move to his rhythm, but it's hopeless pinned to the wall like this. "Please fuck me."

He rips his mouth from me and meets my eyes again.

"No." And then he returns to licking my slit, spearing his tongue into me like it's the last thing he'll ever get to do.

I'm dripping down his chin, but he doesn't care.

He just continues to stab his tongue in and out of me, and when he curls the tip, sparks shoot through me.

"Fffuck," I stutter, my body tensing as my legs shake. "Oh goddess."

He pulls out and licks a stripe up, swirling his tongue around my clit, making me cry out. He finds his way under my hood and stays there, forcing pleasure through me in tidal waves.

My legs try to tighten, yanking against his arms, but he keeps me firmly pressed into the wall.

His lips suck as his tongue flicks, and it's all I can do to hold on as my pleasure crests and I'm thrashing in his arms as the dickhead fucking laughs at me.

"Arrie!"

He lashes his tongue harder, sucking tighter, and I'm gone. Flying off the handle as uncontrolled screams leave my throat. He holds me through, slowing his mouth down as the wave ebbs, prolonging the orgasm as long as possible.

But when I'm done, he looks up at me, his chin coated in my cum and his smile gone, he asks, "Why?"

"Because I love him just as much as I love you. And if it were me up there, and there was a way you might save me, you'd give everything you had to at least try."

Arrie looks at me like he finally sees me, as though something has clicked into place that wasn't there before. And he lets go of my knees and helps me to my feet, steadying my wobbly legs. "You good?" I meet his gaze with a heated, lazy one of my own, and he laughs. "Yeah, I guess you are."

I grab his hand and yank it to my face, where I rest my head and keep his gaze locked in mine. "Arrie?"

"Yeah?"

"Fuck me before I go."

His eyes widen, and it's clear he gets my meaning. If I don't come back and something goes horribly wrong, I want to have good memories, and I want to revel in them forever.

He brushes a palm across my cheek and whispers, "I'll do more than that. I'll make love to you."

CHAPTER TWENTY-NINE

NEW ORLEANS FOOTAGE: VAMPIRE KING AMONG SOLDIERS

Arrie turns me around, and we pass through the Zen garden that is his main bedroom—past the trees, the ponds, the koi fish, and across the wooden bridge—to the bed by the window wall.

"I can close the blinds," Arrie offers.

It's still light out, and while I don't relish the idea of any of the housekeepers seeing me dick deep, the way the sunlight dapples across the gardens and the atmosphere it creates brings me more peace than I knew a bedroom could.

"I'm good, unless you'd prefer to."

He shrugs. "I don't care about things like that." He sits on the edge of the bed and gestures me to follow, then places me on my feet between his open knees. "I'm okay to do this in whatever form you'd prefer."

He'd be okay with that? Really?

"I want you to be comfortable, Killer." He looks up at me, his eyes shining with something more than lust. "Always."

"Except when you're pissing me off. Then you want me angry."

He looks sheepishly to the floor, embarrassment flushing his features. "I like it when you're passionate. It lights you up."

My fingers angle his chin back up to re-catch his eyes, and I'm floored by the emotion I see in them. He looks almost tearful.

"I do not want you to go, but I am willing to respect the reason behind your decision to leave." His fingers thread through mine in a tight grip. "It is not about me."

I place one knee beside him on the bed, then straddle him with the other. "You don't have to be good at sharing." A harsh puff of air escapes me. "Maybe I kinda like it when you're possessive." Something in me likes how close we are, how many words are pouring out of his mouth to meet mine. "Passionate," I correct.

"Yeah?" His strong grip wraps around both my wrists. And he flips me onto my back on the bed, then drags me up toward the headboard, where he deposits me in a heap with a smirk I'm beginning to become addicted to. "Still think you want me in your harem?"

My knees fall to the mattress either side of me, an open invitation. "It wasn't complete without you."

He shucks his jeans all the way off, leaving him in just his underwear standing at the foot of the bed. Staring at me like I'm his next meal. "I like that skirt."

It's a plaid black and white one I paired with a black bralette and knee-highs—a look I know Connie likes. Pretty sure Dea would prefer I walk around the house naked. But it's good to know Arrie likes me in a skirt. Maybe I'll have to wear them more often.

He crawls up the bed and strokes a hand up my leg, dipping underneath the skirt. "Easy access."

A laugh escapes me. "Of course that's what you like about it."

"Maybe one day I'll show you why." The mischievous look in his eyes promises dirty secrets in public places, and goddess am I here for it. "But right now, I want that top off." His jaw snaps shut, his teeth clenching. "Now."

I rush to obey, thrill shooting through me.

It's not the first time he's seen me naked, but it's the first time he's been allowed to adore me in such a state. And while I'm unclipping my bralette at the back, slipping it off slowly, teasingly, he roves his eyes over my breasts. Landing on the hard points of my nipples he worked up earlier.

His underwear grows tighter the more he looks at me, and the outline of his erection has my mouth watering. He follows my gaze and huffs a laugh. "Later. Right now, I want to bury myself in you."

"Leave the skirt on?"

214

He nods, words lost on him. But he crawls overtop of me, his fists landing either side of my face as that hard bulge I was staring at moments ago nuzzles between my legs.

A small gasp, and he's swallowing my sounds like a dying man breathing his last breath, dancing our tongues together, our teeth clashing, my lips numb and plump.

My hands roam down chiseled pecs, abs made of steel, and settle on hips I drive toward me like I'm high on this man. "Take your underwear off."

Instead of listening to me (because goddess forbid he does that), he grinds his hard cock into me, lighting me up and rewarding himself with a moan. He swivels his hips, not stopping, and drops his head to my nipple. And that talented tongue from earlier reminds me just how much practise he has pressing all the right buttons.

"Arrie," I gasp, out of breath and clenching the sheets beneath us. "Arrie, yes. More."

A growl leaves his lips and rumbles across my skin. "I love how you sound." He bites my nipples between gentle teeth just harsh enough to hurt. And my hiss turns into a moan when the pain turns into pleasure. "And it's finally for me. I've been listening to you moan for them for far too long."

"You've been listening, huh?"

"All the goddamn time." Another bite, then a swirl of his tongue as his hips continue to grind against me. "Like a fuck-ing pervert with my dick in hand." He grabs my hands and shoves them into the mattress. "You're infuriating."

All he had to do was be nice to me. Wow. Imagine that. A guy cock-blocking himself.

He lets one of my hands go and pinches the other nipple, setting fire to my body in the best way.

"Ffffuck . . ."

He groans as he grinds faster, picking up the pace with his tongue and fingers. "Yeah, I love the way you sound."

"Then get in me and make me scream already." My voice half sobs, half begs.

And by the way he chuckles around my nipple and pins me to the bed with his hips, he loves it. Which is good news for me, because I'm one of those pathetic people who naturally beg, it would seem. (Don't roll your eyes at me.)

But so far, I've had zero complaints from my lovers.

Eventually, Arrie lifts himself off of me and shucks his underwear off, releasing the hard dick that's been grinding into me for the last fifteen minutes.

Everything in me wants me to wrap my lips around the head and see how long it would take for him to explode down my throat. Or to squeeze around it while he pounds into me.

"Would you like to use a condom?"

"Oh, err . . . If you'd prefer to? I haven't been using them so far." I look away, suddenly unsure of myself. "I'm on birth control and only sleeping with the team, who have only been sleeping with me, so . . ."

"Right. No, that's okay." He shrugs. "I don't mind."

He leans back over me, carrying his weight on his knees

and wrists, then nudges my opening with his dick, grazing it up my entrance like a damn tease.

Instead of begging this time, though, I reach down and grab it, squeeze hard, and watch his eyes roll into the back of his head. Then I line myself up and roll my hips up into him, sinking in a few inches.

Both of us moan, his louder and gruffer than mine. He leans down, resting on top of me, and buries his face in my neck as he slowly enters me further, inch by glorious inch. The stretch burns me alive, flexing my muscles further than before, and soon he's nudging the back of me, a gentle caress that promises more.

"You good?" I ask, after he lies there for a solid few seconds, breathing hard. "Because I really want you to use that strength on me."

His laughter reaches my ears, and I melt in his arms. He places his wrist to my mouth and sighs in relief when I grip it hard. "Best fuel up then."

And I do. I take what I need from him in slow pulls, relishing in the sounds leaving his mouth, the small, slow thrusts he's making inside me. My lips latch on, and I suck harder, leaving us both high.

"God, that's . . . Fuck, don't stop."

So I don't. I keep pulling harsh, long pulls of his blood, leaving plenty of room between each so he won't pass out. "Fuck me."

He nods, then drags his hips all the way back, before

slamming them into me, forcing the bed to close the small gap between it and the window wall. Again and again he slams into me, hitting that delicious spot at the back of me that sings with every point of contact.

But I have to stop drinking from him or he'll lose too much blood, so I lower his wrist and grab his chin in firm fingers and swivel his gaze to mine. "Don't hold back."

He shakes his head. "Never planned to." A growl rips from his lips as he clamps harsh fingers around my hips and lifts them off the bed.

I throw my hips onto him, sinking him into me. His hard dick throbbing against my walls. His uneven breaths mixing with mine.

Skin slaps against skin, fingers grip into hips and sheets, and moans echo throughout the room—and if the others didn't know what we were doing in here before, they definitely do now.

With every thrust of his hips, he grinds against my clit, soaring me to new heights, and when he takes my nipple into his mouth once again, I convulse around him.

"Argh . . . Do that again."

I clench around him, tightening myself.

"Oh, oh god." He yanks me off him and flips me around so I'm on all fours. Then he grabs my hip with one hand and wraps my hair around the other, holding me in place while he fucks me ragged.

My back arches, his cock hitting just the right spot, and I

release my hands from where they were clenched in the sheets and let him hold me up. Use me. Take his fill of me.

"Let me choke you."

I do my best to nod, but I can't—he's yanking my head back too hard. "Yeess," I hiss. "Please."

He yanks on my hair so my back is to his chest and I'm sat above his lap as he rocks into me.

A thick, callused hand wraps around my throat and squeezes, cutting off my air supply. Then a second hand joins it so he's strangling me.

And I can't breathe.

He picks up the pace, ramming into me hard enough so that I can't move. And my back arches deep, deep enough to hurt a little, but the pain spurs me on.

I try to moan, to scream, to make some kind of noise, but my throat is straining against his grip, and all that comes out is pathetic gurgle.

My head goes heavy, dizziness spinning through me, and my head lolls.

"Yeah, that's it. Right there."

He releases his grip, one hand delving to my clit, which he pinches in hard squeezes. His head lowers to mine, the hand around my throat squeezes again, threatening. "C'mon, Killer. Come for me."

He fucks me faster, harder, the wet sound of our bodies joining and our skin slicking and slapping against one another all I hear as my body shatters.

Arrie's fingers pinch harder, enough to send pain spiraling through me. And his hand chokes me again.

Oh goddess. Oh ffffuck. A torrid scream leaks from my throat—raw and ragged—as I spasm around him.

"Yes, yes, yes." Arrie buries my head into the mattress and grips my hips, pummeling into me fast. "Oh god. Fuck!" he shouts as he comes, filling me.

He flops against me, his hips coming to a stop. "Fuck . . ."

I'm too stunned and exhausted to respond, my breaths coming in ragged heaves as he rolls off of me and tucks me into his arms.

Gentle fingers run along my neck with a wince. "That's gonna leave a bruise. Sorry."

My throat is sore, but I manage to croak, "It'll heal."

Chapter Thirty

Governments Call for End to Smear Campaigns Against Horsemen

I spend the night in Arrie's room, plus the following morning, and he dotes on me like I'm his one true love; he cleans me up, puts some cream on my nipples, gives me a throat sweet and some numbing spray for the pain, and keeps me wrapped in a tight ball of blankets and soothing arms forever.

Well, it feels like forever.

But eventually I do have to get out of bed and back to my office.

As I'm getting dressed, Arrie is quiet. Actually, he's been quiet ever since we finished fucking. "Killer?"

"Hmm?" I turn around as I'm trying to find my bralette. "Yeah?"

"Sex is a good communicator."

I laugh, he laughs, and we both stare at each other with loved-up eyes and wonky smiles. "Yeah, it is. But we should try communicating outside of it, too. Maybe next time we can go for a drive. Just meet me by the track out back."

He nods. "I will try."

I run my hand up his arm and smile. "It's okay. We have all the time in the world to learn communication skills." I thumb gesture to the door. "Gonna come help me so I don't kill myself trying to undo a folded spell keeping the Black Gate shut?"

"It's a Fae spell?"

"Yeah. Kinda came to me in a dream."

"A premonition, maybe?"

"Like, Seer magic?"

"Maybe." He shrugs. "You are supposed to have all the Witch abilities."

I guess. "But it's the first I've had if so." Thinking back to some of my nightmares, the possibility that they might not all be from the past sends shivers up my spine. "I hope."

Arrie throws on a pair of jeans and a t-shirt, then joins me as I'm leaving the room. "Let's get you saving your other boyfriend." He still looks hurt, still looks like letting me leave is the last thing he wants to do, but he's encouraging me, anyway.

Because he . . . loves me?

He didn't say it back.

But he might not be ready yet. And that's okay. At his own pace is the pace I want to be at.

We walk into my study early afternoon to find Dea and Connie already pouring themselves over books and printed web pages, not even noticing us enter.

When we sit down to join them, Connie snaps her head up with a smirk. She waggles her eyebrows.

"Yes, Connie." I sigh. "Just . . . yes."

"Eeeeek!" She launches herself at me with arms wrapping around my neck. "Yay!" Her lips meet mine in a slanted kiss that tastes of cherries and coconut (her favorite smoothie). Her tongue tangles with mine in a mess of teasing heat and tingles. She pulls away, breathless, and whispers, "I need you next." She turns around to the guys and shouts. "Bagsy Magic tonight."

"I am not some car you can call shotgun over." I harrumph but smile at her. She's so adorable. "I am a grown-ass person."

"Fine." She looks at me with a serious expression upon her face. "Can we go on a date tonight?"

"Y-Yeah. Sure."

She rolls her eyes. "There. Same thing achieved." She shrugs and moves back to her seat.

Dea looks at Arrie still holding my hand with a small smile on his face before burying his nose back into his book. "Good morning."

"No Fae trainer today?" I ask Connie.

"No. She messaged to say she'll be here tomorrow if we need her. But she needs a rest."

Oops. I may have been overusing her. "Yeah, that's cool. She can take as long as she wants. She's not an employee." I feel guilty. She didn't really have time to rest after the shit in New Orleans. "Maybe I should send a fruit basket or something."

"A fruit basket?" Arrie asks, confused. He slumps into a chair and analyzes the white board of key notes we started to take yesterday but they've added to this morning. "What is a fruit basket?"

"A basket of fruit?" Was that not obvious?

"And what does the fruit basket do?"

Err . . . "It makes her feel appreciated and not taken for granted?"

"You do not sound sure, Killer." He lifts the nearest book into his hand and delves into reading.

I . . . What?

Three hours later, I'm starving and no closer to working out how to get my ass through the gate. "I still think Dea could just drag any of us through."

Dea's fingers massage his temples. Frustrated. "I. Do. Not. Know. If that. Will. Work." He lifts his gaze to mine. "I have never taken anyone but dead mortals through the Otherworld Gate."

I shrug. "Guess I'll be the guinea pig."

Arrie growls from beside me. "Just because you fucked me into submission does not mean I am going to let you go off with half a plan and a pile of pointless hope." He points the papers in his hand. "We'll figure this out before you leave, not as you go."

"Wow." I breathe in amazement. "That's like the longest paragraph I've ever heard from you."

He squeezes my wrists together in a nod to the position he had me in against the wall, and I flush.

Connie laughs to herself. "Might as well have added a "Yes, Daddy" for good measure."

I wrinkle my nose. "I'm not *that* submissive." I look to Dea. "Am I?"

He wraps an arm around my shoulder and places a soft kiss to my forehead. "There is nothing wrong with being naturally submissive." He gestures go himself and Arrie. "Especially with us as boyfriends."

Arrie's hand lands heavy on my thigh.

I look to Connie, who's looking at the three of us with some kind of look I can't interpret. "Ready to go on our date?"

She looks at me with wide eyes and a giant smile. "Yes, yes, yes!" Then jumps to her feet. "What do you want to do tonight?"

"Did you have anything in mind?" She usually does, and I'm happy to go along with the plan.

"Ohhh, the tickets!" She runs out of the library and

comes back a couple of minutes later with the concert tickets I got her for Christmas waving in the air. "They're for tonight. I totally forgot."

"Then what are we waiting for?"

She looks at what we're both wearing and scowls. "Better clothes for a start."

I sigh, then giggle. "I'm going to get to see you naked before we leave, aren't I?"

She slaps me on the butt as she grabs my hand and yanks me along behind her. "Babe, you're gonna get a round two before we leave."

Arrie and Dea snicker as we leave, promising to keep up the research while we're gone. And I give a silent look to Arrie, telling him to keep an eye on Dea. He's doing better than before, but grief is fickle—it rises and falls as often as the sun.

"So," Connie starts, "what you thinking?" She rifles through my wardrobe and drawers until she's gotten a few options for me to try out. "Something more shorts and knee-highs or something more dress and tights."

"As long as there's a choker, I'm down." My words flash Arrie's hands gripping my neck across my mind, and I absently rub the bruise that's basically faded.

"Is that . . .?" My flush meets her gaze, and she squeals. "Tell me everything!" She chucks the tights she had in her hands onto the bed and drags me to the chairs in the corner. "Now."

"Well, I went up to talk about things, to at least try some

226

communication. But he was too angry, and he was struggling to feel anything else. So I drank his blood and punched him in the face."

Connie's eyes go wide as she gasps. "You . . . punched him in the face?"

"I tried to. He blocked. But we fought for a little bit, letting some of his anger out, but then he changed the game and . . . threw me into a wall, pinned me there, and went down on me."

"That does not explain the bruise on your neck, hon."

"It didn't really end there."

Her hands ball into excited fists that she calms down with a few breaths, her braids bouncing everywhere. "There's more. There's more. Okay, okay. There's more."

I giggle, because she's being ridiculous, but I carry on with the story, anyway. "When we were done, and he finally understood why I'm leaving to get Nine back, I asked him to fuck me." I'm just leave out the part where he said he'd make love to me and then utterly destroyed my vagina. "So he did."

"How? In what way?"

"You are very into my sex life."

Her hands throw themselves into the air in exasperation. "I am your sex life."

True.

"Well, first we were just having sex normally, with him on top, but then he flipped me over onto all fours and . . ."

"Oh my god, he pulled you to him by the throat, didn't

he?”

I just nod, embarrassment flooding me, my eyes wanting to look anywhere but at Connie. Which is stupid. She's seen me in all kinds of positions.

She squeals again. “Does that mean he'll be with us sometimes when we're all together together?”

I shrug. “I dunno. We haven't talked about it. But assuming he wants to, yeah.”

Connie's eye light up like Christmas Day morning, but she looks over to the clock on the wall and to the clothes on the bed, then sighs. “We need to get a move on.”

So I try on a few outfits in both forms, test them out, and settle on a pair of shorts with a long skirt flowing down the back of them that I've wanted an excuse to wear for weeks. Paired with a black tee, a harness, a choker (obviously), and my hair wavy down my back.

“Maybe I should change my hair color soon?” I suggest as we head to Connie's room to pick out something for her.

“Ohh, what you thinking?”

“Maybe something like the midnight sky or galaxy kind of colors?”

Her room looms ahead, and when we enter, Connie darts straight for her wardrobe and pulls out a short dress on a hanger. “I've had it picked out for weeks.”

It's strappy, short enough I'm sure I'll see plenty of ass tonight, and a kind of burgundy color I wouldn't pick out for someone else. But on Connie, it'll look amazing.

She's amazing.

When she's pulling the tight dress down her body—one I can't stop staring at (and maybe there's a little drool, but shh)—she asks, "When you getting your hair done? Can I come with? Ohh, maybe I should change my hair color too?"

"What kind of color?"

"I don't know. I've never dyed it before."

Now it's my turn to choke in surprise. "Really? Like, never? Not in two thousand years?"

She shrugs. "I really like my hair. It's beautiful. But maybe changing it up might be fun. Besides, it'll just grow back out."

"There are color removing spells nowadays, anyway. If you hate it, I can just make one and change it back."

"Sold!" She laces up her boots and finishes her lipstick, then turns around to me. "Okay, I'm ready."

My charm bracelet snaps into my staff as I wrap an arm around her waist and teleport us to Madison Square Garden. Thankfully, I've been here before. Otherwise we would have had to fly here from somewhere and ruin our hair.

The normally blue lights up the side of the building flash different colors—pink, blue, green, orange, then red—in sequence as the queues move slowly in through the doors.

The queue takes ages to get through, but eventually we're buying drinks from the bar and fighting our way through to the front of the crowd, where we cradle our two beers each like they're our lifeline. But one look at Connie downing one of hers, and I guess I have to get rid of one.

Oh well, bottom's up.

Beer is gross by the way—0/10 don't recommend—but it does the job. And by the time the warmup acts are done and I've found a new all-girl rock group to listen to in the future, the main act lights up the stage, and I get to watch as Connie loses her shit.

She sings along, dances as best she can in the space, and screams and shouts at all the right moments—or whenever she damn pleases, it would seem. She wraps her arms around me from behind, pushing me into the railing, and shouts into my ear, "This is the best Christmas present ever! I'll say thank you when we get home! Or sooner if you're lucky."

I only just caught that last bit, but the words lick flames up my neck and melt me into a pile of goo. Public sex? Hell yes.

I think.

Maybe.

Oh, what the hell. Connie'll persuade me and I'll love every second of it. That seems to be how this goes with the team. And I'm happy to just be along for the ride.

The two Fae members of the band fly through the air while singing all the high notes, the skirts flowing in the wind. The rune circle on the floor lights up, changing the color of all their outfits simultaneously, and the crows roar.

But as the song continues and the chorus repeats for the second time, Connie slips a hand up my skirt and layers kisses down my neck.

Wait, here?

Like, right here, right now?

But before I can overthink things, her fingers are sliding past the edges of my thong and delving low, cupping, and sliding into me with a gasp. She latches her lips onto my neck, clearly trying to match Arrie's bruise that's since faded, and sucks and nips and licks as her fingers curl and the palm of her hand grinds.

I look up onto the stage and find none of the women are looking our way anyway—and around us are only other adults. So I stop worrying and rock my hips into her hand, chasing the feeling now pumping through my body in time to the music.

She tries to whisper something in my ear, but I can't catch it, as the music changes and they play another of their songs I've heard Connie listening to.

Music pounds through me as notes hit my ears and Connie's fingers play me like an expert, her fingers pressing firmer and her hand grinding faster. My gasps get lost in a sea of voices.

Connie pulls my head back to meet hers, and her gaze catches me on fire as her lips suck mine in a frenzied passion I have no struggles meeting.

Oh, shit.

My body drowns as my head falls back onto her shoulder, the guitar solo ripping through the air, rendering my screams unheard. Pointless. But Connie laps them up, and when I've stopping convulsing around her, she grabs both sides of my panties and tears them in half, removing them from my body and tucking them into her pocket with a wink.

She then leans into my ear and shout-whispers, "Don't worry, I'm not done yet."

Chapter Thirty-One

Horsemen of Conquest and Magic Seen at Concert

Crowds of people disperse as the concert ends, and while we take ages to exit the arena, we hold hands and chat all things music.

"Soooo . . ." Connie squeals. "Who are we seeing next time?"

I laugh, because only Connie would ask that. "Well, we could see that Fae band you like?" Their show is supposed to be full of magic as well as music. "That sounds like fun."

"Ohmygod, yes. Seeing 'In Flight' live would be a dream!" Her giddiness is infectious. She looks to me and asks, "Remind me why we're not just teleporting ourselves outside?"

"Because I'd drag everyone within the spell circle's radius with us." I gesture to the crowds of people around us. "And I don't wanna scare them."

She chuckles to herself, probably finding the idea of teleporting a bunch of random strangers without telling them hilarious. I am not such a demon. Well, I might do that to Arrie—but he's an asshole, so that doesn't count.

"What are you chuckling at?" She nudges my shoulder.

"Just thinking about teleporting Arrie to Alaska without telling him."

"Have you been before?"

I shake my head. "Be worth the trip, though."

"Even better if you make sure he's not got any teleporting crystals on him. He'd have to fly back to the main portal."

"Oooh, you're evil." I lean in and kiss her forehead. "I love it."

I picked the hotel this time, and knowing Connie, I went extravagant. Exclusive. If I were with Arrie, I might have picked somewhere we could camp, but I'm not. Connie likes finer things, so I'm going to provide the finest.

We weave out of crowds and find ourselves in a street with a large enough space that I can teleport us to the hotel doors, then I collapse my staff back into a charm bracelet and wrap my arm through hers.

"Well, that's easier."

"Yup." I gesture to the grand revolving door of the Highlight Hotel. "Your chamber awaits, my lady." I gesture her in as she giggles.

The bellhop notices us straight away and guides us to reception, where we're given a room key and a smile; we don't even have to provide our names.

"Seems you're well known now," Connie suggests. "Well, I guess after our interviews and all the video footage, people just know us." She looks to the floor, her eyes floating with something definitely not positive while her smile vanishes for a second. "We'll never get back to being anonymous, will we?"

We both enter the elevator, guided by our silent bellhop.

"I don't think we should be, but if we stay out of the way for a few hundred years, we'll just be a piece of history." I wrap an arm around her shoulders and guide her eyes to mine. "If that's what we want."

I'd do anything for the team. For my family.

The bellhop clears his throat as the elevator dings. "Follow me, please." He guides us to a room at the end of a winding hallway, the doors to which are double, made of aged wood, and have an endless plating of gold swirling all around them. "Your rooms, Magic." He nods to me, then to Connie. "Conquest." And turns away on his heels.

Unlocking the door with the fancy keychip covered in artwork made of vines, we step inside.

There are vines in the ceiling, weaving through the beams like they were carved from a tree, and the vines drape in some places, with the occasional piece hanging all the way to the floor.

"Ohhh, now that's a nice bed," Connie says as she jumps on the four-poster opposite the window. She spreads her arms wide but doesn't manage to touch the edges. The brown and gold bedsheets beneath her crumple as she rolls to standing and rejoins me. "You okay?"

"I don't think I'll ever get used to staying in places this amazing. It feels like I have a rich sugar daddy."

"Or four." Connie exhales slowly. "Three."

Both of our eyes crumple as they close, inhaling our breaths together. I tangle my fingers with hers.

"C'mon," I say on a sigh. "Let's check out the bathroom." I drag her through the door behind us and breathe another sigh of relief when I see a claw foot tub big enough for the both of us.

As Connie stands in front of the mirror, I run the hot water and put in all the bubbles, salts, and silky goodness I can find in the caddy provided by the hotel. I slowly take off her dress, remove her bra and panties, then grab a makeup wipe out of my purse and wipe her face clean. All the while her mind is somewhere else; Nine, Bandio Bontanas, or somewhere else in her past, I don't know. But I'm going to stay here.

Her eyes refocus on the present, exiting their distant gazing, and she looks down to find me wiping the last of her foundation off. "Sorry."

My hand cups her cheek. "You never have to apologize for existing, Conquest."

"I know. I just feel I ruin our dates sometimes. When I can't pull my thoughts in and I just . . ." Her words trail off, probably unsure how to complete the sentence.

"You could never ruin our dates. I love you even when you're sad." I grab her hand and walk her toward the bathtub that's now full and appropriately bubbly. "Maybe even more so because that's when you need my love the most."

Connie doesn't say anything as I help her step into the tub, and when I follow, I nest her between my legs and let her head fall back onto my chest, her hair spreading out in the bubbles next to us. I wander my hands over her chest, through her hair, across her forehead, and lie with her in the water, relaxing. Allowing the heat to light the chill on fire and set the grief aflame.

"You know, I used to be a badass."

I laugh, because that's ridiculous. "You're still a badass."

"Maybe the badassery is taking a break."

"Breaks are good," I mumble against her forehead before placing gentle kisses there. "They let you know who you are."

"Maybe," she says as she turns around to face me, hovering her naked body inches above mine, her breasts pressed against mine, "I want to be more of a lover than a fighter for a while."

"Yeah?" I push her hair back so I can see her beautiful face better. "And who will I have to compete with for all this loving attention?"

She smiles, and goddess, it lights up the room. "No one. I'm all yours. Always."

"Then let me love you," I whisper across her lips before letting them brush together in a hint of passion. "Let me make you feel like you're on top of the world."

A small laugh escapes her lips on a sigh. "You've been spending too much time around Dea." Her knees kick open my legs as far as they'll go, before she grabs them and throws them over the side of the bath and her hands grope my breasts before mumbling, "Been learning all the good words."

"I'll say whatever it takes to make you smile and get you in my bed, Connie." I sigh as she takes my lips in hers again. "I'll wax poetic or talk dir—"

Her fingers pinch my nipples, then roll them around, and a moan slips free as my hips shift forward, seeking friction.

"That sound is all the motivation I need." One hand slips beneath the water and cups my pussy, a finger resting teasingly on my entrance. "I'll let you love me, but only once I'm done with you."

My head falls back onto the bath's rim, and she sinks a single finger into me, hooking it just right, and slowly rubs circles as she presses her palm into my clit. It's slow—so slow it's barely there—but it's doing things to my head, making it spin with its arms out as music dances in my ears.

She bends her head to my neck and laces kisses up to my ear, shivers traveling down my body. "I want you to eat me after I'm done with you. I want you to bury your tongue in me while you get yourself off. And I want to watch you do it."

She adds a second finger, slowly, and speeds up ever so slightly, almost unnoticeable, but she grinds her palm harder—short, fast circles.

My bent knees start to shake as they clench the sides of the tub, and she grins, delight filling her face.

"That's it, babe." Her forehead rests on mine, her nose toughing my own. "Take it."

My hips grind into her hand, picking up enough speed to slosh some of the water over the sides of the bath. "S-s-shit."

Connie squeezes my nipple before rolling it around between her fingers, then she bends her head over my arched chest and sucks the other into her mouth. Her teeth grazing my nipple slightly.

My hips buck as her fingers move fast, sending lightning through me, and my legs squeeze the sides of the bath. "Connie . . ." I spasm around her fingers, gushing into the water, as my whole body lights on fire. My hips thrash, chasing the orgasm as my screams echo off the tiles.

"Fuck yes," Connie mumbles around my nipple.

I grind and buck and thrust until the sensation subsides and I'm nothing more than a wet, panting mess in a bathtub only half filled with water. No bubbles left.

Chapter Thirty-Two

The Four Horsemen: A History

She carries my dripping body to the bed, where she throws me onto the covers and stands at the end. Lording over me. "I'm not done with you." She crawls between my legs and peppers kisses to my knees, up my thighs, and stops at the junction between them and my throbbing pussy. "You can play with me all you want another day, but tonight, I want you to myself before I have to hand you back to the guys and share."

I can't manage a single coherent word, so I just nod my head and let it fall to the mattress. All I can do is feel the heat of her hands on my thighs and the wet, firm tongue that's licking the outside of me, cleaning me up.

Her tongue dips in, then out, then back in, but not far

enough. Just enough to tease.

"Connie . . ." I groan, hands grabbing her hair and pulling her back to me.

"Such a needy Vampire," she chuckles. And as she says that, my fangs slip free from my control. "I love that you can't control it. That I'm making you wild." Her mouth returns to its mission, teasing my lips, running her tongue up past my slit and to my clit, where she rubs quick, harsh circles that make my eyelids flash silver and my fists clutch the bedsheets.

Too much. Too much, too quickly. I hiss with oversensitivity, but she doesn't care.

She wraps her lips around my clit and sucks, her tongue flicking quick flicks.

My hips come off the bed as I moan, thrusting into her face, and she slips her hands beneath my ass and holds me to her, not allowing me to pull back.

Pulling one hand away, she hooks three fingers inside me and yanks them back out, then shoves them in. Hard. Fast. As though she can tell I want it rougher than the bathroom.

"Ah, goddess. Yes!"

My hips shift in what little room Connie allows them to have, holding me to her as she sucks my clit between her teeth.

The room spins as my eyes clench shut, my fangs and pussy throbbing in tandem. The obscene sounds coming from her working me spur me on, and before I know it, another orgasm crests. "Fuckfuckfuck," I hiss between clenched teeth. My hips buck in her hand as she continues pumping me, riding me through.

As the orgasm subsides, she sets me down on the bed and lays her head on my stomach her hips shifting into a grind on the bed every now and then.

Fuck. No.

I'm never leaving this woman wanting.

She's mine.

I flip her off me and pin her to the bed, our eyes meeting. I'm sure mine are red, and when I realize this, I look away, shutting them.

"No, don't look away."

"Connie, it's okay if you'd prefer—"

"Shh. It's okay. I want you to look at me."

And so I meet her green eyes, her perfect smile, and her flushed cheeks, and I kiss her, tasting myself on her lips as I grind into her.

Her tongue licks up and down my fangs, re-stoking the fire, but I take back control and pin her hips against the bed to match her arms. She can't move. Or escape.

And while I can see a flicker of fear pass her eyes every now and then, the roaring lust I see in them surpasses any concerns I might have.

She bites her lip, and my eyes track the movement. "Just . . . don't bite me."

"I won't." I layer a kiss to her neck, allowing her to writhe beneath me, trying to gain some kind of friction between us, to please herself. But I stay just out of reach.

242

"Magic . . . Babe?"

I lift my head, concern filling me.

She laughs and flips us over so I'm beneath her again. "You really fell for that?"

"That was a dirty trick."

Her legs split mine apart, then her knee presses hard onto me, and I shameless grind, seeking friction. Pleasure. Her.

"Don't worry," she whispers. "I'll get you off again." She straddles me and crawls her way up my body so she's kneeling over my breasts. "But first you're gonna open up."

My mouth slips open, my tongue shamelessly seeking her out, wanting her taste to mark it.

She parts her knees farther open, lowering herself onto my face, and the moment my tongue can reach her, I lick a stripe from top to bottom as she grabs hold of the pole in the center of the bed top. She uses it to rub herself over my mouth, her skin over my fangs, her juices coating my tongue. "Get yourself off," she groans. "Please."

I reach my hand around her, finding myself still dripping, and shove as many fingers as I can inside me, desperate to feel that high.

Connie looks over her shoulder and moans. "Yeah, like that." She grinds against me, using me like a personal sex toy.

But I do my best to keep up, to spear my tongue inside her, to suck on her clitoris like she did mine, to avoid piercing her with my fangs that are running through her folds with every grind of her hips. I seal my lips over her clitoris, not letting go, even as she tries to pull away.

And her moans inch toward screams as my name slips from her lips. "Magic . . ." She slams her hips back down and rides me, grinding against my mouth as I flick my tongue around, inside, and across.

Her sounds shoot through me, making me convulse, as my fingers pierce into me harder, faster. As I remember her mouth on me, my legs wrapped around the side of the bathtub, my dick buried inside her while we laid naked in the gardens.

"Magic, shit, yes," she groans as her moans reach fever pitch and her juices explode into my mouth.

My hand moves faster as she uses me, and my legs shake as I moan, not able to hold it back, which only seems to heighten her orgasm, the vibrations sending her wild as she slams her pussy into my mouth and I suck and lick as hard and fast I can.

"MMMMMagic!"

Her screams send me over the edge, and before I know it, I'm grinding and thrusting onto my hand, my hips bending off the bed. Fuck, fuck, fuck.

Her grinding slows to a halt, and my hand stills as my butt falls back onto the bed.

"Fuck yeah," she says on a sigh as she flops next to me. "We're doing that again."

"Uh-huh," I manage before sleep exhaustion takes me.

Chapter Thirty-Three

Arrie's arms wrap tight around my waist, his nose nestled into my neck. "Don't die, Killer." His heart pounds against my back, rapid, thrusting beats that unsteady me and halt my breath. "Just come back alive."

Connie wraps her arms around the front of me, meeting Arrie's torso at my back, and she breathes me in. "I'm scared. But I know you have to go. I'm just sorry I can't be there with you."

Dea stands next to us, his wings folding around us all, then dropping to the ground. Silent. He doesn't need to say anything.

Connie looks up at me and runs her hand through my

white hair. "Bring him back."

I smile, my tongue stuck in my throat.

"We will." Dea hugs us with his wings and then backs off, dragging me with him. "Come on."

I untangle myself from Connie and Arrie and let Dea drag me out the back door, where I portal us to Earth and reform my staff into its charm bracelet form.

Dea sweeps me onto his feet and wraps a golden arm around my waist for security. "Ready?"

"Ready."

He shoots us into the sky, high enough to be soaring near the clouds, and everything below looks so insignificant, but it's mine to protect. Ours. It's a world that's ours to protect.

But we can't do it without Famine.

"It is going to get hard to breathe."

Right.

I write a rune pattern on my throat, then swallow a bayus leaf, and mutter a small incantation. As I breathe my next breath, an air bubble forms around my head. A pocket of air that recycles my exhales into oxygen for me to inhale.

We spend a good hour flying in what seems like a random direction, but Dea knows where he's going. He has been doing this for two thousand years. I trust him.

Eventually, after boredom passed long ago, a black dot grows in the distance. It looms ever closer. Bigger and bigger. Until I'm breathless from its magnificence and wide-eyed from its beauty.

The spell wraps around its entirety, forming a black shimmer over a pair of gates made from something that looks like plasma, something equally made from the leyline energy.

"Get me closer. I need to touch them."

Dea's breath hitches, fear no doubt coursing through him. But he obeys.

And soon I'm touching the energy that makes up the Black Gates to the Otherworld. Beyond this is the land of the dead. And the severity of what I'm about to do settles on my heart like a lead weight.

A complex, almost unreadable spell graces my fingertips. I could spend years and never finish unraveling it. Multiple generations of Fae created this from a time long before records began—from a time before myth.

I try to file through the basics, see the building blocks, but they're buried beneath tangled webs of interweaving spellwork I can't decipher. "It's really old. I can't really read much of it." I sigh, defeat washing over me. I don't know if I can do this. "Even the runes are foreign."

"Breathe, Angel." He rubs my shoulder and places a gentle kiss to my neck. "I know you can do this."

He's right. I can do this.

I was made for this.

Or remade.

Whatever.

After a few deep breaths, I shove all the tangled network of spells aside to see if there's anything underneath; and there, beneath centuries of spellwork, is a single, seemingly innocent rune.

I graze a single finger of it, and glowing blue lines upon lines shoot out from the gate, scattering in all directions, beyond what the eye can see.

"What are they?" Dea asks.

I spin us around a little, getting a better look, and gasp. "They're the leylines. The Black Gate is powering the leylines."

"But that is . . . impossible."

"Well, they had to come from somewhere."

Dea wraps both arms around me tighter and spins us back to the gate. "I just assumed they were natural, like the Earth."

"Even the Earth was made from something, Dea."

"I guess so."

I shrug. "We just don't think about it because it happened so long ago." Grazing my hand along the rune, I take a deep breath. "Right, Magic. Focus."

The rune seems innocent enough, but upon closer inspection, it seems like it's one rune made of many, as though someone just took various parts of many runes and glued them together to create some kind of rune hybrid. The level of knowledge and skill this one aspect of the spell took is simply insurmountable.

I'll never be this good.

At least not right now.

And that's not me being pessimistic; that's me knowing

my current limits. I can't rewrite this rune or rub it out or replace parts of it. It's simply beyond me. So I'll have to do something else. But I do take a mental picture of what it looks like, because I'm gonna study the shit out of this piece of orgasmic beauty later.

"You okay there, Angel?"

"Huh?" I whip my head around to look at Dea's smiling face. "Oh, yeah. I'm fine. Just concentrating."

"Uh-huh."

Weaving out from that single monster-mash rune are three lines of spells—all different—formed of various smaller runes, some of which I recognize, some of which rings some bells, and some of which I've never seen before. There's also a green glow around them, which I've come to notice is what happens when an incantation is used. Usually I can kinda feel it, like an echo, when I run my hands through it, and when doing it to this one, it's like a loud shout. Like it hasn't been heard in years and it's excited to finally see me.

It vibrates around my hand.

"Hey, little fella. Wanna tell me what your incantation is? You'd be being super helpful."

"What the hell are you doing?" Dea whispers in my ear.

I ignore him. I don't have the brain space right now to explain how this spell feels alive, and how it feels like it's communicating to me. And I don't know how to say that without sounding insane.

Ergo, I'm saying nothing.

The spell vibrates harder, tickling my hand and sending vibrations up to my elbow.

"You like it when I talk to you, huh?"

It vibrates harder, sending further tingles up to my elbow. It tickles, and I want to yank my hand away, but I don't want to offend the spell. Maybe if I can find a way of getting it to answer yes or no, I can narrow down the spell somehow?

"Ready to help?"

The vibration tickles my hand again.

"Okay, vibrate for yes, do nothing for no. Understand?"

More vibrations.

"Alright. I'm trying to find out what you do. How you affect the spells around the three threads. Do you bind them in some way?"

Nothing happens.

"Okay. Do you enhance them?"

Again, nothing.

Maybe . . . "Are you the spell, and the runes are supporting you?"

The vibration starts up, getting faster, and I have to fight the urge to yank my hand away as a giggle escapes my lips.

"Ohh, yay. Okay. Okay." I run my other hand through my white hair and take a deep breath. I file through the three strands, seeing what runes are there, seeing what ones I recognize and what they could possibly mean. "I think this one stabilizes you in some way."

A light vibration tickles my palm.

The other two are trickier to read, focusing on runes that I don't recognize and that look like some kind of older runic language, almost similar to the scribbles I've seen Arrie make from time to time.

"These are like Norse?"

The vibrations start up again.

"But they're not quite the same. They're curvier."

Dea leans in. "But that means they are at least two centuries old, if not older."

"So they predate you?"

"It would seem that way, yes." His wings flap gently, keeping us in the air.

"So the Black Gate existed before you, along with whatever you want to call the land that lies beyond it?"

"Yes." He tightens his grip on my waist. "I simply opened them before. I did not create or destroy them. But they were locked, and no one could figure out how to open them. And there was kind of an army of angels guarding them."

"So you killed the angels and opened the gate, allowing everyone to pass on?"

"Humans were already passing on, but supernaturals were not. So I opened the gate, and then they seemed to be able to open and close at will."

"Can you open it again?"

Dea nods. He flies us up higher, to the center of the gates, and grabs the knocker bigger than his head. "Ready?"

"Ready." I grab his arms tight, my teeth clenched hard,

my knuckles white. "Let's go."

He grabs the knocker and lifts it, then throws it back down. The loud knock that follows shakes the air, sending a gust of wind through us so strong, Dea has to flap to keep us from being blown away. Then he lifts it again. And again.

And the Black Gates, the entrance to the afterlife, opens.

"Remember," he says close to my ear, "you cannot pull a soul back out. And I do not know if I can pull you in."

"I know." I place my hands on the spell the entire time, mapping what changes, looking at the runes that activate and logging what each one does. "But now I have more pieces to this puzzle."

"Huh. That was clever of you."

His praise shoots through me, lighting me up.

And I place my hand again on the three strands shooting out of the monster-mash rune, but something's different. The incantation that seemed alive is now subdued in some way. I look up, winding my way through the tangle of spells that follow those three, and gasp.

Light bulb moment.

It's not subdued, it's spread. The tangled spells are now also green, glowing from the spread of the incantation.

"The knock!" I breathe in, my bubble still keeping me oxygenated. "The knock is the incantation. Because it doesn't have to be words. It can be any sound."

Dea listens silently for a change, taking it all in.

The gates, on the other hand, continue to open as light

spills from beyond. Light that blinds and clarifies simultaneously. Light that, without, would make life feel cold and empty. It's a feeling I've had before, but I can't place. Like a long-lost emotion that reverberates through every life, that one thing that makes us all vibrate with power but no one has ever come up with a word for before.

"What is that feeling?" I mumble.

"It is the feeling of life keeping us alive, the energy that makes our heart beat even when we do not want it to. It is soul-deep love."

"Has anyone else ever felt this besides you?"

"Every soul that passes feels like this and continues to feel like this for all of eternity. It is what we miss out on being immortal."

That's . . . "Is pulling Nine back not selfish, then? If this is how happy he is, how content, then are we doing the right thing?"

Dea chuckles behind me, his chest vibrating against my back. "I am done doing the right thing for the benefit of everyone else. For once, I want to do the selfish thing. Even if that is the wrong thing."

"Okay then, but if I break the world, this is also your fault."

"I am happy to share blame."

"Good."

Dea flies us forward, to the edge of the gate's border, and tries to push us across, but an invisible barrier prevents us.

"*Kutabare*. I can't cross." I run my hands up the spellwork again, seeing if there's some kind of database or barrier spell I recognize. "But I don't know what I'm looking for." I'm hoping to just add myself to whatever spell mojo it has going on, but what prevents living beings from entering a space?

"Maybe it is like an if statement."

"A what?"

"A piece of logic that lets the spell make decisions based on certain information, like your status of being alive or dead."

"Okay, so I'm looking for more of a scanner, then." I run my hands through the threads, and notice a vibration pulling one of the original three. The second one that I couldn't identify earlier. "This one?"

The vibration tickles my hand again.

"Hmm." A concentrating hand strokes through my hair. "Okay." The runes seem to be scanning something, or trying to gather information from an external source. It's like they're pulling our essence inwards, toward themselves, and analyzing it. "So, this is what's scanning us?"

I wish I had a camera or something on me. I'm never gonna remember all this to study later.

But where does it store the information? That's what I need to alter. That's what I need to change.

I trace the information, follow it along the thread, and find it somewhere in the tangle, in a small bundle of knots made of various runes so complicated reading them makes me dizzy.

"Wherever they want to be. This space isn't physical, so it has no space limit."

I look around the empty space, pacing along the stones of the courtyard beneath my feet, and eventually happen upon a fountain; and sat upon that fountain, in a nerd pun t-shirt that reads 'I am Schrodinger's Cat' with clever alive/dead wording underneath, is Nine.

My boyfriend.

He looks up at me, then down at the hand entwined in Dea's, and smiles. *I've been waiting for you.*

Chapter Thirty-Four

"Nine," I whisper. My voice is barely audible, barely edging into existence. But it's there. Meeting his ears.

Dea doesn't move. His hand stays laced with mine, his lips part but no sound comes out, and his body trembles, like an emotional earthquake rumbles through him. "I . . ."

"Oh god," Nine says, standing up, "did you have a massive breakdown?"

Dea lets go of my hand and jumps into Nine's waiting arms. "Nine." His sobs echo around the empty space, joining mine.

Nine looks at me and smiles. *You gonna come here or stand there gawking?*

I didn't think I could do it. I didn't think I could be here.

I know.

I wrap my arms around them both, sandwiching Dea between us, and breathe in the bonfire, lavender, paper smell that is them both together. Both halves of my triad.

"You know," Nine says, "it's been boring as hell waiting for you, bro." He lets Dea hug him for as long as he wants, saying nothing about the snot and tears running down his shoulder or the tighter-than-Earth grip he's squeezing him with. But he looks at me, and those orange-brown eyes bore into mine with the intensity of the sun. "I didn't think I'd get to see you, Sweetie."

"You'd not believe the lock on that gate," I say while wiping my tears away and composing myself. "The spell of the century, that one."

His brows dip in confusion. "Spell?"

"Oh, yeah. The Black Gate is a Fae spell, and it powers the leylines."

His eyes widen, his breath stopping short. "Really?" *That's awesome. You could switch off the leylines and render the Fae powerless.*

Yeeeah, maybe in another hundred years, when I've untangled that spell.

Oh, right.

Are you two done geeking out? Dea asks in our heads, I assume projected by Nine. *Because my eyeliner has never looked this bad.*

I switch forms—

Only, my body doesn't switch.

"Why can't I switch?"

They both turn to me, looking confusing.

"I can't shift back into my female form."

At all?

"Nope." I sigh. "For goddess' sake, I left my handbag with my other form."

Dea raises an eyebrow.

"It had eyeliner in."

Here. Nine grabs the bottom of his shirt and uses it to wipe away the black-stained tears smearing over Dea's cheeks and around his eyes. And when he's done, they just stare at each other.

At the same time, they stretch out their hands to me, and I grab them. They yank me to them.

"It is not complete without you, Angel." Dea looks down at me and smiles in relief, in genuine, heart-throbbing happiness. "It is not a competition."

No, but if it were, I'd win best t-shirt.

Have you seen some of my crop tops? They are works of art!

"This." He points to his t-shirt. "This is something I made up. You can just ask for anything your mind conjures, and it'll pop out at you. Like the house but an upgrade." He gestures to the left (well, I think it's left. Is it left when all around you is white emptiness?), and a house pops up.

A small house with cottage windows and a cute red door, like it popped out of a fairytale book for children and said

260

hello in a cute Disney voice.

Nine, still holding onto our hands, drags us that way with a small smile. "Welcome to my home."

"Home?" Dea asks. "Your home is on Earth, with us."

I run a frustrated hand through my hair. "Yeah, we've come to take you back."

He rushes us to the door and shoves us through, then slams it shut behind us. "I know why you're here." He turns to face us, a solemn expression on his face. "But you can't take me back."

"Well, not yet." I shake my head. "I haven't figured out how to get you past the spell, but with enough time, I can—"

"No, no, no. You don't understand. I can't leave." Nine walks to a small living room and slumps onto the couch. "Angels guard this place. And like the Angels on Earth, they're strong, ruthless, and are numerous enough to form an army."

Dea sits beside Nine and places a hand on his shoulder. "You do not seriously expect us to just turn around and leave, do you?"

I sit on his other side, my hand on his knee. "We came to take you home, and we're not leaving until you do." Nothing will stand in our way. "And we don't have all the time in the world, because we left Earth in the hands of Connie and Arrie."

Nine sighs and lets his head fall into his hands. "They're more likely to kill the entire Fae Court than fix anything. You know that, right?"

Dea smirks at me. "Well, Magic may have mellowed Arrie out a little recently, so maybe not."

"Dea," I groan.

Nine swivels his head my way and smiles. "So you got my message, then?"

Message? Huh? "Oh, when we were at the old village ruins?"

He nods.

"Yeah, I got it."

Figured a little dead boyfriend energy might give you a boost.

"Nine!" Dea slaps his arm. "Do not joke about that."

Too soon, buddy. He turns to me and asks, "Do you have a plan for my body, or are you expecting me to be a ghost in your harem?"

"I am not fucking a ghost for the rest of time, so yes, I have a plan." I try my best to block out the image of me being witchy and hoping for the best, but I don't think I succeed, because he looks at me all stern like.

"That's your plan?"

I shrug. "I'll deal with it later, okay. For now, let's just work on getting you out of here." I look to Dea. "I need you to lead. This is far too precarious to leave up to my stupid brain."

"Agreed." He stands to his feet and starts pacing. "So we need to sneak you out of here, avoid the Angels, and do so without really knowing if we can move you past the barrier?"

"Yup."

That about sums it up, yeah.

"Okay, Magic." He turns to me. "You need to go back to the gate with Nine and see what happens. I will distract the Angels and meet you there."

"That's the best you can come up with?" I ask, incredulous.

"Do I look like Arrie to you?" He crosses his arms over his chest. "He is the one with the fancy battle strategy ability. I am not."

I sigh, running a hand through my hair and along my neck, where it rests as I look up to Nine's living room ceiling. "How many?" I swivel my eyes to Nine.

"Too many to count."

Chapter Thirty-Five

Vampires' World Returns to Normal: A Story of Photographs

"You're the Angel of Death, Dea!" My hands ball into fists, my voice stretches thin. "They should just let you do what you want."

"That is not how it works," he hisses through clenched teeth.

"How do you know that?" I jump to my feet and yell. "How do you know what will happen?"

"I don't!" He faces me as he stops pacing the length of the living room. A stressed hand runs across his neck. "But I am not risking either of your lives trying." His golden eyes pin me to the floor. "I cannot lose you too."

"Err . . . guys?"

"Then don't." I take a deep breath. "Fight to keep us both."

"I do not know how to do that, Angel."

"Guys?"

Dea wraps a wing around me, shooting warmth and comfort through my body. "It is an unknown."

"Everything we do is unknown." My hands firmly on his chest, I push him away an inch. "I never know what I'm doing, everything is on a whim. I just have to trust that Fate knows what it's doing."

Guys! Nine snaps.

"What?" Dea and I yell simultaneously.

Nine just points out the window, which is no longer white nothingness. A white forest with shimmery blue layered over top flicks into existence, trees taller than I can see, with grass and ferns trailing a forest longer than I can possibly imagine.

They're coming.

Dea looks to me, a panicked look on his face, and asks, "What do we do?"

"Soldier up, Horsemen."

Dea grabs one of his daggers out of his belt and throws it to Nine, who catches it with a smirk. He looks at me with a question, but I shake my head.

Instead, I get my hands ready to create some Angel-kicking spells. Not that I know any. But this is a great time to try.

Never know when that might come in handy.

Outside, air circulates in waves of fresh breezes I didn't

know were missing, and the grass beneath my feet wavers as I inhale deeply.

Then, on the edge of the forest's horizon, a line of white soldiers appears, armor the same color as their skin, power the same intensity as Glowy's.

"Dea," I whisper. "Get ready to grab Nine and fly."

He looks to me with panic in his eyes, the golden irises swirling in worry.

"I need you to trust me."

He nods.

"Just try to see if you can pass him through the barrier." I turn to Nine. "Let me know if he can or not."

Nine nods, then offers me his daggers.

I shake my head. "I don't need them. But thanks."

"Remember," Dea warns, "you cannot shift form here. Fae and Shifter abilities only."

"Yup. Well aware of that limitation."

Really?

Yup. But I don't have time to puzzle it out right now. There's kinda an army of Angels heading my way.

"Focus," Dea warns.

One soldier breaks rank and walks forward, heading our way. He storms across the forest floor, his wide strides larger than his body, making his legs look like Blu Tack being stretched. "You cannot leave with the dead, Death." His ethereal voice booms around the space, reminding me that it's actually an empty chasm. "You may only arrive with them."

"He's not supposed to be dead." I step forward, in front of Dea and Nine. "He's a Horseman of the Apocalypse. He was chosen by Fate to help Earth."

"Never the less, he's dead. He is in our charge now." His face is mere inches from mine, the expressionless look turning my stomach and sending goosebumps through my bones. "He no longer belongs to the world of the living."

"He will always belong to the world of the living. He is immortal."

"No one is truly immortal." His hand raises above his head, and the line of Angels draw their swords.

Go. Go now.

The whoosh of Dea's wings crackles through my hair as I smile, a relieved breath releasing from my lungs. I'm positive Dea can just drag a soul out. But if not, I'll do my best to alter the monster spell. Somehow.

The soldier's hand clenches into a fist, and the army charge forward on silent feet, all stretching their legs across the forest floor like creepy weirdos.

The soldier in front of me draws his sword, and I take a step back, conjuring an air spell between my fingers. My staff is in charm bracelet form, but I can grab it if needed. For now, I'd rather use what spells I have available.

I don't want them knowing all my tricks too soon.

His sword swings at me as he takes a step, but just before it meets my head, I breathe into the spell. "*Kūki.*"

A rage of wind slams into the sword and arcs down, swirls

around his body, and picks him up. He flies into the air with a shout. "Put me down, Magic!"

"Gonna let me and my boyfriends go?"

"I cannot."

"Then no. I don't think I will." I get another air spell ready, but this time, I direct it into a tunnel. "*Tatsumaki.*"

I haven't moved from my spot, but soon, the entire army is stuck in a tornado that rips the trees up from their soil-less ground and rages leaves through the air.

Nine's house falls to pieces behind me, the roof flying off and joining the fray.

I wish I could say I feel bad, but I don't.

Nine's home is with us at the house, not here in some cottage all by himself. He waited for us. In a white world with no one else to call a friend—for months—all by himself. He never has to see that house again.

The Angels spinning in a wind vortex are all screaming, struggling to breathe properly, and begging me to let them down. And I will. Eventually. But right now, I need to catch up to Nine and Dea and see how they're doing.

I run in the direction Dea flew, hoping to find the gates. And I keep running. And running. And running. Until I have to stop and catch my breath so hard I hunch over, hands on knees, heaving in gulpfuls of air.

"Shit." Where is the gate?

I look up, breaths still ragged, and see a black dot in the distance. Everything else is white nothingness. So much white,

I can't tell which way is up. But I head toward that dot, keeping my eyes on it, staring it down. I will reach it.

After taking more steps than I care to guess, I reach the looming Black Gates, but Dea and Nine are nowhere to be seen.

Nine?

Can you hear me?

Nothing.

I hope that means they're on the other side and not trapped in some kind of magicless box guarded by more Angels.

Yup. Definitely option number one.

Because I don't know what I'd do if it were option number two.

So I put my hand on the gate and push, and to my surprise, it opens. Just like that.

And just like that, red hair rushes me as wings engulf me.

"You made it," Dea breathes into my ear.

"Yeah, piece of cake."

Nine chuckles. *You got lost?*

Shut up.

They both chuckle as their arms surround me, but Nine's are becoming translucent, his touch fading.

"Nine?" Dea asks, worry etched into his frowning brow. "What's happening?"

I'm returning to soul form.

Dea touches his body, but I can't. Why can't I touch him?

Why can't I just hug my boyfriend? Why is this happening?

"Shhh," Nine comforts. "You knew this would happen."

"We did," Dea confirms. "You said you would know what to do when it does." He stares me down, one eyebrow raised, his lips quirked into an I-told-you-so expression. "Do you?"

"You damn well know I don't!"

I switch forms, enjoying the fact that I now can. I missed the freedom of being myself—someone I've come to realize is persistent, emotional, a little selfish, but full of determination and love.

You finally found yourself, huh?

Maybe I'm still finding myself, but I've certainly found some important pieces.

Dea rests a gentle hand on my cheek, his wings brushing my back. "You will always be finding yourself. Changing. Moving with the times. It is what makes us human." He smiles. "You do not need to continuously look for who you are. All you need to do is live."

Chapter Thirty-Six

No One Has Seen Horsemen in Two Weeks: Why?

For now, we take Nine home. Maybe there's something, or someone, there that can help. He's alive.

He's actually alive.

I watch as Dea and Nine walk side-by-side up the hilly lane that leads to our home, fingers entwined, telepathically conversing the entire time.

They both look back at me expectantly.

And I run to them both, tears finally leaking from my eyes, my own emotion finally coursing through me. "I was so scared . . ."

Dea wraps his arms around my middle, his chest to my back, as Nine looks at me helplessly. His hands ghosting over my skin with frustration.

"I didn't know what to do." Breaths escape my lips in ragged heaves as tears flood my cheeks and drip off my skin. "Everyone needed me to be strong, to lean on. And I didn't know . . . what to do." Exhaustion washes over me, and a half-cry, half-yawn escapes. "I'm so tired."

Nine smiles, a gentle caress of a grin I've missed. *You've done so much for everyone else, all while being too scared to lean on them. You can relax now. I'm home.*

"I am so sorry, Angel." Dea's lips touch my neck and breathe me in. "I was so lost. I knew you needed me, and I was not there."

A warm splash lands on my shoulder, and I laugh. A hearty, belly-deep laugh. "We're such a mess."

"Wanna go add to that mess?" Nine asks, gesturing to the house. "They're waiting."

Connie and Arrie stand at the door, smiles on their faces, Arrie's arm around the back of Connie's shoulders.

"You're back!" she shouts, then runs over. "You brought him back." Her hand covers her trembling mouth, tears escaping her, and she goes to jump at him, but stops. "You're still just a soul?"

For now.

Nine looks at me with all the confidence in the world, but fuck, I really don't know how to give him a solid form.

Arrie stomps over, his usual frown in place of a grin. "So, you're back?"

"As good as new." Nine gestures to himself, his dirty

clothes still worn and ripped from the battle he died in. "Well, soon to be."

"It's good to have you back, dude." Arrie places the hand he wanted to place on Nine on me, steadying my body to the ground. "You done rescuing boyfriends?" He looks down at me, a quiet smirk on his stony face.

"Assuming none of you die again, yes."

Connie laughs. "So do us a favor, and start protecting your lives. I don't wanna be without pussy again."

My cheeks burn bright as I shoot my gaze to the floor.

"Oh, come on," she whines. "You've fucked us all. You can't possibly still be embarrassed by me liking how good you taste."

"Well . . ." Maybe I can? Maybe we're still a few hundred years from me being openly crude with the team.

Don't worry. Fuck us all at the same time, and you'll be well over it.

At the same . . . time?

The dinner table that night consists of the team, Nigel, my Fae trainer, Korby, Prince Lucien, and Red. All wanting to celebrate the return of Nine.

Albeit, they have questions. Lots of questions.

"So, does that mean you can bring anyone back?" Lucien asks.

I shrug. "I have no idea. Probably not." I turn to Dea. "How did you get him through the gates?"

Dea looks at Nine, who looks to me and then everyone

else. "I think it was because I'm a Horseman. I'm not really mortal in the same way you all are."

Is that true?

I don't know. But I don't want them all thinking we can bring whoever we want back.

That would be a dangerous piece of knowledge, indeed.

"How do you intend to give him a body then?" the green Fae asks. "Because he cannot be a ghost for all eternity."

"Well, that is a good question . . ." She stares me down, and I sigh. "I don't know."

Red splutters her drink. "What do you mean you don't know? You did this without knowing?"

"Look," I snap a little too harshly. "I do a lot of things without really knowing how they work. Okay? It's par for the course around here. I was kinda hoping I would just know. But I don't yet." I look at everyone around the table and smile. "But I will try. Even if it takes me a hundred years."

I sincerely hope not. That is a long time to go without sex for.

Oh goddess, how I've missed your mind.

It is a beauty.

You're beautiful alright. Beautiful and smart and funny and you smell amazing.

He looks to the ground, his pasty cheeks slightly reddening. And it's then I remember he doesn't get compliments often, and I enjoy showering him in them.

Nigel raises his glass. "Regardless of the road ahead, here's to Famine. It's really really good to have you back, buddy."

Nine looks to him. "Thanks."

Everyone raises their glasses and cheers.

And we eat a series of amazing small plates served to us with food from one of Arrie's restaurants that we ask the house for—the poor guy needs a break—and everyone agrees it's the most delicious ever.

To Arrie's grumbling dismay.

He likes to be the one to cook the food we gawk at.

And technically this was made by someone else, even if it is his own recipe. And that's not good enough. Apparently.

I rest my hand on his knee on the couch we're snuggling on in the cinema. "It's still your food. But if you really want to impress me, I wouldn't mind brownies for breakfast." I grin up at him, and he cracks a smile.

"Brownies for breakfast it is."

Connie lies between my legs while I rest on Arrie's shoulder. Dea's wings hang behind the couch as Nine lies on him, the only person he can touch right now, and only if Dea's in his Angel form.

But it doesn't matter because we're here. All of us. Home. And for the first time in forever, I breathe an easy breath.

Chapter Thirty-Seven

The Supernatural Council Remains Silent on Issues with Vampires

That night, Connie snuggles into my left, both of us lying on Dea's wing, his other curled around Nine, as Arrie lies behind us all, myself and Dea in his lap. All of us together. And I sleep better than I've slept since before Aki turned into a murdering, raging psychopath and my boyfriend died.

Wow.

It really has been an insane few weeks.

Arrie leaves at the ass-crack of dawn, like usual, and wakes us all up a few hours later with brownies in bed.

"Aww, dude, you didn't have to," Nine jokes.

"Shut up." Arrie chucks a pillow at his head, but it sails right through. "Err . . . sorry."

Nine shrugs but goes silent. "Thanks for the brownies, but I can't eat them yet. I will, however, take a mountain of them the moment I have a corporeal form with which to eat them."

"Ugh." My head hits the pillow as I lie back down, the weight of that task throwing back into bed. "Thanks for the reminder."

"Well, I made the brownies for Magic." He shoves the plate under my nose, and I rise back up.

Risen back from the dead by brownies.

Not a bad way to become a zombie, if you ask me.

God, I've missed your brain, Sweetie.

I grab one off the towering pile and shove it into my mouth with gusto, groaning at the chocolaty goodness now coating my tongue. "Fuck, they're good," I mumble with my mouth full.

Fully refreshed, I hop out of bed, much to the chagrin of the rest of the team, and stand in front of the mirror. What kind of day is it gonna be today?

I grab a dress out of the closet, hold it up in front of me, and frown. Nope. Not a dress day. Maybe shorts and tights? Nope. Not that either. Shoving some sweatpants on, I relax a little but it still doesn't feel right. So I switch forms and get undressed again, then put my male sweatpants on that fit this height. Then look back in the mirror again, the weird uncomfortable feeling in my chest lightening.

"There."

"Is that really how you decide what form to be in for the

day?" Arrie asks, amused.

"Well, sometimes I just know. I wake up knowing how I feel." I shrug, then grab a comb and run it through my hair. "Other times, it's not so clear, so I try a few things on, see how I feel in them, and that usually lets me know where the wheel of gender identity has fallen today."

"Is it always certain?" he asks, sitting on the edge of the bed.

"No. Some days, no matter how hard I try, I can't seem to settle how I feel. Like something is always a little off." I gel my hair into place and then grab some sneakers. "On those days, I just do my best to be as comfortable as possible with looking as close to how I feel as I can."

Dressed, I turn to the team. "I am going for a run. Then I'm doing some yoga, and then I'll get to work on trying to fix my boyfriend." I kiss everyone on the forehead, wave to Nine, trying to not to let the fact that I can't kiss him get to me, and leave.

The mid-morning air is crisp today, a cold wind settling over *Sheruta* for the first time since I've lived here. And the breeze cools my aching lungs when I run harder than my stupid weaker male body allows, squeezing out sharp breaths.

Arrie runs past me, taking the same route, and smiles as he goes. The asshole. Whoever said smiling was the appropriate social interaction while running had obviously never been on a run. Or was a god with already Vampire-like stamina.

I pick myself back up and continue. Just one more lap of

the forest, and then I can start yoga. At least that's on my ass. For the most part.

Just a few more minutes. Nothing too intense.

And when I finally finish, climb the stupid hill, and sit in my *Shinto* shrine, I thank the goddess for the Earth for providing something for me to sit on. Because goddess knows I'm not getting back up for the next century.

Okay. So running isn't fun.

Not even for a Shifter.

But yoga? That's fun.

Big, deep breaths calm my racing heart as I stretch high into the sky and then bend low to the grass, clearing my mind. As I breathe out, a rustle in the nearby trees makes me peek open an eyelid.

"You can come out, Arrie. I know it's you."

He always watches.

But now we're together, he can watch freely and not sneak around like a yoga perv. So he exits the tree he was standing behind, brushing off the foliage from his undershirt and cargo pants, and climbs the hill to sit beside me in silence.

I, on the other hand, continue with my yoga routine, adding in a whole new standing position: the eagle pose.

"I've not seen that one before," Arrie comments.

"It's a garudasana, also known as an eagle pose," I say on a breathy exhale. "I'm getting a little better in my male form," I explain as I move into a warrior pose, "so I thought I'd add some new positions this morning."

"You'll have to teach me one day." His eyes are still closed, hands resting atop crossed knees. "My flexibility isn't great for a warrior."

"Always happy to help make you more flexible," I suggest, sneaking a look at him.

He chuckles, and the deep vibrato of the laugh makes me lose balance in my tree pose and stumble onto my ass, where I land heavy with an oof. "Damn you and your sexy-as-fuck laugh."

I dust myself off and try to recenter, but it's pointless. My mind is drifting too much. Besides, I need to head in and grab an update from Connie. "How long have I been gone?"

Arrie looks up at me, all blue eyes and chiseled chin, and says, "Two weeks."

Connie and I catch up with a working breakfast in my library an hour later, after a shower, a brownie, and a hot make-out session with Mr. Muscular and Charming.

"I've really been gone two weeks?"

She nods, her hand laced in mine.

"It feels like it's been a few hours."

"Well, it was an awful two weeks with just Arrie to keep me company. He was grump as hell without you around."

I flip through a couple of textbooks on magical theory I'd grabbed from the shelves on my way over. "Get up to anything fun while I was gone?" I ask, suggestion lacing my tone. My eyebrows wiggle, and goddess damn it, I'm bad at this.

Sighing at her laughter, I put the book down. "Just tell me the details. I want the juicy details."

She coughs, looking around at anywhere but me, and finally says, "I haven't slept with Arrie since our first date in my bedroom that night."

Wait. "What?" I stumble over her words, tripping up on their meaning. "Why not?"

She shrugs and bites into an apple. Upon swallowing, she wipes her mouth and says, "Just didn't feel right to be using him for dick while dating you for actual feelings. Felt like I should be at least exclusive to emotional connections, even if that was with more members of the team than just you." She shrugs again. "No hate to anyone else, it just didn't feel right for me. So I broke things off with him."

"For me?"

"Hon, I love you. I do. But I wouldn't break things off with another member of the team just for you. At least not without serious pressure from yourself. I love them too. But it's a different kind of love right now. And I think I'm comfortable with that. I broke things off with Arrie for me."

"Soooo . . . group sex is off the table?"

She puts down her apple and looks offended. "Not on your life. I wanna watch you come alive with one of the guys. And besides, group sex is still with you."

"You are a complicated person, Conquest."

"I'm a woman. We're all complicated."

"That you are."

"What you talking about?" Nine asks, floating over the table, a giant grin on his face.

"Whether I'd be up for group sex with everyone."

Nine mimes spluttering a shocked cough, and we all laugh. "Group sex, huh?"

"We've done group stuff before, just not with everyone."

"You're seeing where we all stand with comfortability, aren't you?" He floats into a seat he doesn't quite sit in and places his hands behind his head. "Well, you know I'm game, Sweetie. As long as you and Dea are okay, I'll fuck any of them with you."

"Manwhore," Connie accuses.

"Says the girl who's caused more middle-aged orgies than cupid himself."

"Hey. I was a repressed woman living an immortal life, give me a break."

"And now I'm a ghost."

"Yeah, about that . . ." I look to Nine, apprehension in my eyes, I'm sure. "I have no idea how to give you a physical form."

"I know," he confirms. "But I'll help you try." He looks at the book pages I have open and scratches his chin. "Might need to call for backup, though. I also have no idea what I'm doing."

"In the meantime, I'll update you on where we are with things," Connie says. "The Vampires are returning to New Orleans with help from the embassy, the new artificial blood pill is being distributed for free at the moment while the Vampires get back on their feet." She looks to both of us. "We're footing the cost, but we won't be able to forever. I have offered embassy seats to the pixies and Demons, who graciously accepted, so we're getting those set up."

"What about Glowy?"

"The Angel? I didn't think to since we don't know any other Angels, but I can if you'd like?"

"Just because we don't know any, doesn't mean she doesn't. Besides, there were a couple at the Demon hideout in the bayou."

"Done." She adds it to her list, then places her head in her hands and sighs before announcing, "We have no idea where the Fae Queen and her army are. Nor Aki or the Rogue Vampire Faction. They've vanished."

"Great news," I moan, my face also hitting my hands. "Any chance of scouts finding anything?"

"Already sent out," Connie says, "but so far, no news."

"Great," Nine interrupts, "now we're all caught up, can we please call for magical backup and get me a corporeal form? Not being able to fuck you or eat Arrie's brownies is a damn crime."

Arrie find us just as Nine says that, and he smiles. "Nice to know my brownies are as good as my partner." For just half a second, he stumbles over what to call me, and I can't believe he even put more than a moment of thought into his words.

"That's what I want when I get a body," he says, an idea

coming to him, "brownies, sex, and being bitten." He looks at me, all the confidence in the world on his face. "All three at the same time."

I chuckle, finally feeling a little less embarrassed by conversations of sex with the entire team. "Consider it done." I turn to Connie and smile. "Please make sure everyone is still preparing for whatever is coming next while we think of next steps. I'll consult Arrie and Dea and get back to you. If you could consult the embassy, that would also be of help."

"Consider it done," she says, mimicking me. Just as she gets up and goes to leave, she turns back around. "And I wanna be there to watch Nine's coming home present." Her tongue snakes into my mouth as she fists my hair in her hand and my neck in her other, her heat shooting straight through me. "Don't forget me."

"I could never forget you." Images of me in the bathtub, my legs dangling either side, as she brings me to bliss, sear across my head.

Much to Nine's delight, apparently, as he blows out a breath.

Arrie chuckles in the corner and eyes Nine, who he shares a look with him.

Don't send my sexy to everyone!

Why not? You're fucking us all, anyway.

Well, because . . .

Oh, forget it. Just ask Connie too.

I don't mind, Connie's voice echoes into my head a few moments later. *Not like they haven't seen me naked before.*

Good, Nine says. *Now I can turn everyone on!*

Goddess, I've missed his meddling.

Another hour of pouring through research books, of which Nine can't even touch, and help arrives in the form of Dea, Lucien, Red, Nigel, and my Fae trainer. Between us all, we should be able to at least brainstorm some ideas of where to look next.

"Everyone, grab a seat," I order. "I need your help."

"What with, little Horseman?"

I point to Nine. "He needs a body, and I have no idea what I'm doing." They look at me as though I've just popped my head off my shoulders. "Do I look like the grim reaper's polar twin to you?"

I wonder where the grim reaper came from? Did Dea have a death goth phase?

Phase? Have you seen him?

I look to our boyfriend, whose head of black hair is in a book with a translational bookscreen overtop, and sigh. Yeah, I have.

Uck. You two are disgusting. He looks at me with a smile and clearly holds back his laughter at my face. *Don't worry,* he says with an eye roll, *I find you both lovingly adorable.*

I love you too.

Now, can we please get back to finding you a body?

"Can I reanimate a body and tie his consciousness to it, somehow?" I ask the group.

Again, they look at me with utter astonishment.

"I can't even believe I'm here," Red says. "Seriously, reanimating corpses? What are you, Frankenstein?"

"I am not a monster, thank you," Nine chides as he floats above us. "Does anyone know anything about death magic?"

No one says anything, but Red shifts uncomfortably.

I look to her and ask, "What it is?"

"Well, there's a rumor—more like a legend—in the Witch Coven that earth magic has energy-restoring properties, with legends of famous Witches bringing all manner of things back to life, from plants to whole forests, and sometimes . . . people." She looks at everyone, who is looking at incredulously. "They're just legends. Things we tell children to amaze them before bed."

"But maybe there's something more to them," I suggest, my brain running away from me.

Chapter Thirty-Eight

In a World Dominated by Powerful Supernatural Alliances, Who Can Humans Trust?

Three hours later, after everyone had gone to lunch, the seer and earth Witches of the Coven sit before me in my library, an opposing smile and scowl on each of their faces.

Nine flies over and hovers in front of them.

Each of them scowls, shock and appall plastering their faces in equal measure.

The earth Witch stands up, her cane jamming into the floor. "What have you done?"

The seer joins her, pity and frustration flashing in her eyes. "Magic, this isn't how things are supposed to be."

"Spare me." My eyes roll of their own accord. "I know you aren't going to agree with my decision, but we Horsemen are hardly natural. I did not bring you here to lecture me."

"Then why are we here, child?" the seer asks. "My magic cannot help you here. I cannot foresee the dead."

"Really?" But that dream felt so real, and it was of the realm of the dead. Does that not count? Is it a Horseman thing? "But . . ." I turn to the other Witch in the room, who has so far remained silent. "How true are the legends of your people?"

"I see Red has been speaking of matters she should not. Again." The earth Witch sits back down with a heavy sigh, defeated. "I know not of the past, but I do know that every living being has earth magic running through them. It is the very basis for what we earth Witches use. The energy given off of the leylines that give sustenance to life."

"The leylines power life?"

She rocks her head from side to side. "Not quite. But it flows through life. You Horsemen do not have that thread."

"Makes senses," Nine confirms. "We're basically the walking dead."

"What flows through you five is something else entirely. Something linked to earth magic but not quite. Almost like its polar opposite from the same source." She looks around her in wonder and asks, "Do you have a copy of THE ORIGIN OF WITCH MAGIC?"

I hold up a finger and grab the seeing stone from my desk around the corner, then come back. After a few seconds, I ask it, and the book pops into her lap.

"That is quite handy."

Well, I know what's going on the 'making the world like me again' Christmas list.

She flicks through the book and places it open on a page with a giant diagram on the table. "This"—she points to the large circle in the center of the page—"is the origin of the leyline's power. We know not what it actually is."

The Black Gate.

But I don't think she'll take that very well. So I elect to stay silent.

See, politics.

Improvement!

"And these"—she follows the various lines snaking from the black circle—"are all the various types of magic the leylines produce. Each one is a different type of magic that every Witch can access." She points to each one in turn. "Earth, air, fire, water, charm, and seer."

There are two dotted lines circling the others coming from the very center. "What are those?" Nine asks.

She looks to the seer Witch, who nods. "Those are life and death magic. It's something Angel-descended Witches could do when they used to rule our Coven."

"Angel-descended Witches used to rule? Why?"

"Because they had the power to unite people," the seer Witch explains, "to bring us great power and prestige. Their powers were revered by most of the magical community."

"That was over a thousand years ago, when Angels and

Demons used to rule this Earth," the earth Witch scowls. She points to the dots coming off those lines. "But this is what flows through everyone. Everyone, that is, but you five. And even if you could tap into this power somehow to bring someone's physical form back—which I don't know that you could—that form would be mortal."

Which would put Nine's life at risk in any battle. And I'd have to reform it every time it died.

Not to mention how much trouble Dea would get into having to continuously drag my soul back.

"So, what you're saying is . . . ?"

"You're asking the impossible, dear." The seer Witch stands and places a hand on my shoulder, then looks to Nine. "I'm sorry, but I don't think it can be done."

"You've both given me plenty to think on. If you'd like, I can teleport you both back to wherever you'd like on Earth."

"That would be splendid," she says, a smile on her face. "I'm so sorry we couldn't be of more use."

After sending the seer Witch back to her husbands and the earth Witch back to a mall she was shopping in—which totally explains her bad mood, I'd be angry if I was interrupted while shopping—I settle back into the library with my head resting on a pillow.

It aches.

It really, really aches.

Can Horsemen even get headaches?

Yeah, if we're overstressing. Like now.

"I just don't know what to do. I'm not overworked here. I have two problems, but no solutions to either of them." Unlike before, where I had lots of problems, but not enough time to deal with them all.

"How many people know about your death magic?"

"Aki, you four, Nigel, the Witches might . . . I've lost track." My arm rests over my eyes as my feet kick off their shoes and rest on the couch. "Even if it has to do with my death magic. Nine, I can't use that on you. Even if I wanted to. I know so little about it. Let alone combining it with earth magic—which I still haven't unlocked yet by the way—to create a form for you. And even then, I don't know how to make that form immortal."

Arrie walks up to me and wraps his arms around my middle. "Just kill it."

"What?"

"Kill the mortal form, right?"

I turn in his arms to face him, confused.

"Sometimes you nerds are dumb." He takes a deep breath. "Our mortal forms die before we're made into Horsemen, then Fate takes over. It'll probably just make you immortal again. And if it doesn't, then we know we can drag your soul back and try something else." He shrugs. "No big deal."

"So I just have to make a body. Any body."

"Preferably *my* body, Sweetie," Nine corrects. "I'm rather fond of my dick."

Sighing, I look at him with stern resignation. "Any other

requests to make an already impossible job that much harder?"

"Could you make me taller? Just by a few inches?"

A stressed hand runs down my face just as they come back from lunch, Lucien with his arm wrapped around Red's shoulders, an achieved smirk on his face.

Those two are getting closer and closer every time I see them. I wonder what would happen if a royal Vampire and a Coven Witch got married?

Nigel is laughing with my Fae trainer, who has a brilliant smile plastered across her usually harsh face, and I smile in response. Happy she's settling in, making friends. Maybe she gains something from being part of my training circle after all.

They all gather around, chit-chatting, Red with a brownie in her hand, and Nigel picking up where he left off with the open book on the table.

Red is the one to ask, "What did Aunt Sasha say?" My look of confusion must encourage her to explain, "The earth Witch."

"So your grandma is the fire Witch and your aunt is the earth Witch?" I ask, trying to wrap my head around their family dynamics.

"Yep." She pops the last bit of brownie into her mouth and swallows. "They're twins. My mom is Musa, daughter of the fire Witch."

"Your Coven is complicated."

"We're old." She shrugs, not seeing the big deal.

Getting back to the point, I answer her actual question. "I just sent her and the seer home, actually. They were . . . informative, if not all that helpful."

Nine floats over the table, not even blocking the light. "Actually, they were most helpful. I think the answer might lie in your earth and Angel magic."

My head falls into my hands. "It couldn't rely on a type of magic I have some skill in?"

"Fate's a bitch like that," Arrie mumbles from behind me, settling into a comfy armchair with a . . . Is that the romance book I was reading last week? "She likes to challenge us, to push us past our boundaries and see what happens."

"Well," Nine says, "I'm more of a 'know what's going to happen before you try it' kind of a guy." He sighs, papers flittering over the table. "But I guess I'll have to concede to Magic's usual 'figure it out as you go' method."

"Hey! That's gotten us out of many a bind in the past."

"Like dragging you out of the Otherworld," Arrie remarks.

Finally. A good use for his snark.

Finally using it for you instead of against you. Hey, by the way, you need to show me what happened between you two.

Later.

But just as I say that, images of him fucking me from behind while grabbing my throat flash across my mind in vivid detail.

Fuuuck.

I ignore the annoying voice of my boyfriend in my head and stick my eyes back into the book the Coven Witches had made me grab. Maybe more answers will be given.

Chapter Thirty-Nine

More Attacks on Shifter Communities Bring Doubts as to Horsemen Efficiency in Dealing with Recent Turmoil

A few hours later, and no closer to an answer, Connie and Dea walk in, side-by-side, smiles on their faces.

What have they done?

"We have done it," Dea says. "We have come up with a plan for how to at least weaken Aki and the enemy."

"Really?" Nine asks. "That's what you've been doing all day?"

"Well, as much as I want you to have a body," Connie says. "We need to keep doing our job, too. So we thought we'd help Magic out by solutionizing a different problem." She shoves a giant sheet of A1 paper into my hands with a proud smile on her beautiful face. "Check it out. Meanwhile, we'll check out what you've done and see if we can add to it."

Nine, Arrie, and I pour ourselves over the sheet of paper with Dea's beautiful handwriting on and check their notes. Lucien and Red leaning over our shoulders.

"They want to tackle the SC first?" I ask.

"It makes sense," Arrie adds. "It'll weaken their defenses because they won't have the legal power they once did."

"And most of the SC are being blackmailed or brainwashed, so if we can fix those members, they won't have the majority vote anymore." Nine flies around the table I've laid the piece of paper on, excited. "It's not a bad plan."

Connie calls from a few feet away, "We don't know where Aki is, or what the Fae Queen and the Rogue Vampire Faction have planned, but we do know where the houses and locations of the various council members are."

Dea's got his head in the various notes I made, cross-referencing them with the Fae trainer's, who has found the project as perplexing as everyone else. But we're certain the answer to Nine's corporeal form is by mixing different types of magic.

"This looks promising," Dea says after putting the papers down. "You have clearly used the knowledge at your disposal." He thinks for a minute, then looks at me with a gleam in his golden galaxy eyes. "Have you considered using your death magic to direct the earth magic into a soul and seeing the effect?"

"If we knew more about the effects of that, we would be able to create a better solution," my Fae trainer adds. Agreeing with Dea.

"Wouldn't that be dangerous?" I ask, curious.

Dea shrugs. "To be honest, Angel, I think souls are impervious to most damage. They are not alive. You cannot do much to them." His eyes drift to Nine, who's silently staring at us all, tears in his eyes.

You okay?

I don't want to be the reason you're all in pain. He floats away to somewhere else in the library.

Dea goes to follow, but I grab his hand. "I think he needs some time alone."

Connie hugs me, her arms wrapping around my middle, and Arrie stands beside us, a worried look on his face.

"But what if he wants to go back?" Dea asks.

"He won't," Arrie says, looking confident in his answer.

Lucien, Red, and my Fae trainer all leave, leaving us just with Nigel—who looks sheepishly to the ground. "Listen, Magic . . . I—"

"Don't." I hold up a hand, stopping him. "Don't apologize for something that isn't your fault. He's clearly got issues."

"But—"

"There are no buts." I place both hands on his shoulders and take a deep breath. "You are not to blame for a kid you didn't raise. It was unfair of our parents to place so much on your shoulders."

"If I had taken you both in, maybe he would have turned out better."

"And maybe we wouldn't have turned out at all. Two Angel-descended Witches so close together? It's what killed Mom and Dad." Patting his back, I smile. "You did the best with what you had."

"When this is all over, we should go to Japan and visit them."

"I'd like that."

Nigel hugs me goodbye and leaves, leaving me alone with all four of the team for the first time in forever. And when I turn around and notice them all smiling at me, tears roll down my cheeks.

Dea's shifted into his Angel form so he can hold Nine's hand—who has come back after taking a breather—Arrie leans an elbow on Connie's shoulder, and I just stand there like a lemon leaking juice all over my cheeks with a smile on my face.

"I'm just so happy you're all here." I turn to face Nine, sincerity entering my voice. "I'll find a way. I promise."

He shakes his head with a small smile. "We should prioritize dealing with the SC for now, Sweetie."

Dea looks to him sharply. "But—"

"It's the right move," Nine interrupts. "And you all know it. I can wait."

"But you shouldn't have to," Connie whispers, then grits her teeth. "You've done nothing but serve the people, and we can't even take a couple of weeks to focus on giving you a corporeal form?"

"Afraid not, Con." Nine floats in front of her and raises an open hand. "I'll be here still. Always."

She meets his hand mid-air, not able to actually touch it, and exhales a frustrated breath.

Dea's hand rests on Nine's shoulder and he nuzzles his neck with his nose. "We will fix you."

Nine's hand reaches back and rests on Dea's neck. "I know."

Chapter Forty

Horsemen Embassy and the Supernatural Council:
What's the Difference?

The following day, the embassy meets, including our new additions—our fellow Demon Verity and a pixie named Carter. Since their populations are each solely in one place right now, there's no need for more than one representative. But we can change that over time as needed.

Now our embassy is up to twelve members.

I have a feeling that the more members we have, the more species that are represented, the more difficult our discussions are going to be.

Connie slaps a hand on the table, grabbing everyone's attention, and clears her throat. "We would like to extend an invitation to our resident Angel and chat about adding an

Angel division to the embassy."

"It's getting a little crowded," Rufus mutters.

"The point of the embassy," I clarify, "is to represent every species on the planet. But it'll take time to grow into that. We're lucky we have most of the pillar communities leading the way."

Our single Fae representative from *Sheruta* we've since added to the embassy holds back a lot, I've noticed, and now is no exception. So I make a point to ask him, "How are the Fae doing?"

He clears his throat and looks around the room, everyone's eyes fixed on him. "Well, I think." He looks to the floor, his hands fidgeting in his lap. "They're a little angsty from what their kin are doing on Earth."

Red holds in a laugh and Lucien squeezes her knee.

"They're also nervous how it is going to make them look in the long run. People are becoming afraid and on edge around us Fae, and it's making it hard to feel a part of the community."

Connie and Dea nod (his charm bracelet working wonders). "We understand," Connie says. "Hopefully things won't remain this way. We have every intention of removing the issue."

Everyone snaps their gazes our way.

"And how, Horsemen," Lucien starts, "do you plan on achieving that."

Arrie taps on the wall behind us, and up flashes Connie's

diagram and list. "With this."

On this piece of paper turned plasmascreen wall art is a step-by-step process of how we're going to deal with the SC.

"So we have twelve council members. Of which, the three humans are being compelled, two of the Fae were not aware of the queen's real motives, and all three Vampires are aligned with Prince Phillipe."

"The obvious first start," Dea begins, "is to undo the compelling of the humans."

Nine is float-sitting in the chair with a smile on his face. "I would be happy to offer my assistance. Gotta love wiping away compulsion."

You can do that?

Yup. Centuries of Vampires with compulsion talents equals centuries of practise.

"We will follow this by communicating with the two Fae councilmen and try to reason with them," Dea adds, "which I will be doing myself." He looks to Prince Lucien with a worried look, unsure if this next step will even work. "Then we need to implore the Vampire king to see reason and request a Vampire seat vote. He needs to take a public stance against the SC."

Lucien puts his head into his hands, his long blonde hair falling around himself like a curtain. With a heavy breath, he says, "I will try, but I cannot make any promises."

"Then try hard, Prince," Red says, "because without the Vampire councilmen on our side, what way discussions go with regards to removing support from the Fae Queen's efforts will depend solely on the Shifter councilmen."

The three Shifter ambassadors shake their heads. "We do not like to show open support for any singular movement. We try to remain an open vessel of refuge for all. Defend when necessary, but otherwise remain passive."

"I know," I start, "and I respect your way of life and beliefs, but if it comes down it, people will die if you choose to remain neutral. Your own people are dying, and will continue to do so unless we act."

They do nothing but nod their heads, silently taking on board my words. Hopefully.

Addressing the whole room, I ask for an update on our scouting efforts. "They can't have just vanished! They're an entire fucking army."

Lucien speaks up, reporting on Vampire efforts. "We've scoured the whole of France by this point, offered payment for any information, and nothing."

Dea, hand on chin, at peace with a new puzzle to solve. "All it would take is one charm Witch, and he will have all he needs to create teleporting crystals as often as he likes."

"So they could be anywhere," Red mumbles. "Great."

I flick my gaze to her, asking, "Any charm Witches missing?"

"Not in the Coven, no." She shakes her head. "If there are Witches helping them, then they're from out in the world."

"Have any way of checking on each coven, doing a headcount?"

"Sure. I'll bring it to Coven tonight." She looks to the window, thinking for a minute, then swivels back around. "Should have an answer within a few days, maybe a week."

"So quick?" one of the Shifter ambassadors asks, incredulously.

"There aren't many of us to count."

Nine, we need to find a way to help the Witches after all this is over. See if there's anything they need.

I'll get Connie to write it down.

A few seconds later, she brings out a different notepad and makes a note, then smiles at me, nodding.

"Okay then," I say. "Arrie, go with Nine and keep him safe while he wipes away the compulsion. Take as many teleporting crystals as you need." I look to Dea, then to some of the ambassadors in the room. "I'll need volunteers to go with Dea and I to speak to the Fae. We'll need to go prepared with evidence and a full plan, so only those of you who like the Fae please."

Our *Sheruta* Fae ambassador nods his head "I will join you as a show of Fae strength." A few others join, and soon we have an ambassador envoy ready to go.

"Okay, so Dea, I'll need you here with me working with everyone to create a solid plan. Persuading a Fae is not an easy task." An idea takes root. "Oh, and take Nigel. He might be able to help you."

"Actually," Lucien interrupts, "I need you with me, Magic." He shrugs. "Father likes you. That might help."

"Okay, then Dea, you'll be handling the Fae without me. That okay?"

"I am a Horseman, Angel." He smiles, his dimples melting my insides into goo. Like always. "We will be fine."

"Then, Red and Nana, could you please help the Witches do a headcount?"

Sheruta's Witch ambassador shakes her head. "I've never left *Sheruta*, but I will do a headcount here. You never know."

Chapter Forty-One

It's our first mission since New Orleans, and tensions are running high. The entire embassy is splitting up, dividing ourselves.

"Connie?" I pull her aside once everyone else has left. "I need you to make sure some of our army are here, protecting the embassy. With so many of us gone, we're open to attack. Too open."

"Already on it," she reassures, her hands tapping away at a plasmascreen balanced on her fingertips. "Helpfully, it's kinda hard to get here, even with teleporting crystals."

"Right. You'd need one for every soldier to pull it off. That's unlikely." I breathe a sigh of relief. "Even I'd have a hard time producing that many."

"We could get datachips and reroute it to a private network. It would allow us easy access to the internet on the go, messaging and calling each other as we go, rather than having to schedule it every time, and eventually we could discuss using it as regular citizens."

Dea scowls. "We have always tried not to do that."

"But that was before we were out in the open, public knowledge," Connie adds. "I think I'm with these two on this. Sorry Dea."

Everyone looks to Nine, who shrugs. "I can't get one, anyway."

"You're still a member of the team, ass rat. You still get a vote."

"Then, I guess it's about time we treat ourselves the same as we treat everyone else, and not like we're on some societal pedestal."

Dea sighs, head in hand, looking tired. "I need to go home and change my charm bracelet out before I start planning with everyone else."

"And lunch," I say. "I'm starving."

"I have a new batch of brownies for you to try," Arrie says, a suspicious look in his eyes.

"I'm all up for trying brownies."

"Me too," Connie says.

But Arrie replies, "These are just for Magic. Sorry."

"Oh, I see how it is. Just for the girlfriend brownies?"

Connie jokes.

Arrie laces his fingers through mine, a small but perceivable smile on his usually grumpy face. "Yes."

"You've done it," Connie whispers beside me. "You've melted him."

"Only took a year, too. I was prepared to spend the next century slowly chiseling away at him."

We all leave, taking the walk back to the house for lunch before we have to divide and conquer.

"You know, just once I'd like to have a mission with all five of us."

Dea shakes his head. "No, you do not." He wraps his hand through the one Arrie isn't holding. "If something requires all five of us, the world is either ending or warring so bad that the human population is at risk."

"Dea's right," Nine says. "We should never have a single problem so bad that we need all of us. But problems like this, that are complex, often require us to split up and conquer together."

"There's gonna be a battle, isn't there?" Connie asks hesitantly. "I can feel it."

"Me too," Arrie rumbles. "It's what Aki is waiting for."

"That will need all five of us," Dea adds. His thumb rubs circles over my hand, reassuring me that they'll be here.

"Maybe it's a good thing I'm not corporeal right now." At our confused faces, he explains, "I can use my powers and take zero damage. I'm unbeatable like this."

"I promise I'll fix you." My hands squeeze Arrie's and Dea's. "I promise I won't just leave you like this, unable to touch or feel or interact."

Nine hovers in front of me, floating backward. "I know you will. Sweetie. I believe in you."

"It's just less logical science and more hocus-y pocus."

Once home, Lo flies into the kitchen and lands on my head, smiling, purring away.

"Haven't seen you in a while, Lo. I missed you."

"Mmmmm, been exploring *Sheruta*."

"Everyone want cake and pizza from the pizzeria in town?" Connie asks, the ordering menu on the plasmascreen in her hand.

Everyone agrees, thanking Fate for the opportunity to chill on the couch and not focus on anything.

"Oh," Lo says, interrupting, "I let that Fae lady into the library. The one teaching you spells."

"Oh, she's here?"

"Upstairs. Said she needed your library for some research."

Connie shrugs when I look to her. "Guess I'll go ask if she wants pizza." She walks up the stairs, as exhausted by all the planning, researching and politics as the rest of us.

I carry Lo on my head to the living room, the guys trailing behind me. All of us sit in silence; even Nine floats near the ceiling in complete silence, not mentally chatting to anyone I don't think.

"How long do you think we'll be gone for?" I ask.

"Won't take me long to undo the compulsion. Don't even need to speak to them, just be within eyesight." Nine shrugs, confident his mission will be easy.

"Mine might take a few days," Dea says. "Fae are not known for being easy to reason with. But at least they live within the same part of Paris, so I will not have to do everything twice."

"I don't know how long it'll take me to convince the Vampire king to cast a revote on the Vampire councilmen."

Arrie places a hand on my shoulder. "We will come to you when we're done if you like?"

"Yes, please." Something about going back to New Orleans puts me on edge. Lots has happened to me in that city in the last year; I'll be happy to see the back of it. "I don't really do a lot of missions solo."

Connie comes downstairs, shaking her head. "She's deep in some Fae nonsense up there. I'm just gonna deliver her pizza when it arrives." She crashes into the spare armchair by the window in a huff. "Fuck, I'm exhausted."

"Mmhhmm," I agree. "I need a damn shopping trip."

Dea smiles while Connie grabs the edge of the couch with glee. "Yes. Yup. We're doing that!" She turns to Dea, elated. "Wanna join?"

"Sure."

"It's a date, then." Connie writes something down on an

old-fashioned notepad with a pencil.

Using a little air magic, I blow it over to me and grab it out of the air.

"Hey! No fair . . ."

I flick through the pages and feel my cheeks burn a little hot. She's been keeping note of everything I say I want. In a bullet-point list. Like some kind of ideas book.

Ideas for dates. Gifts. Loving things to say.

"This is why you're so good at gift giving?" I float it back to her with an apology on my face. "You keep track."

Just as she opens her mouth to scold me, the doorbell rings. "Ooh, pizza." She sprints to the door, somehow finding the energy—then again, she's probably not low on physical energy. A pile of pizza boxes towering over her head walk back through the doorway, and everyone laughs.

"How much pizza did you order, Con?" Arrie asks, amazed.

"Enough so that you don't steal any of mine!" she shouts from somewhere behind the boxes.

I help her out with a bit of air magic, spreading them across the floor, looking at all the labels. After a few moments, I find mine—pepperoni with extra chili—and grab it and sit back down.

Connie grabs the two she ordered for the Fae upstairs in my library and delivers them, leaving the guys alone to fight for the rest.

Dea goes to grab the biggest box labeled Meaty Champion, but Arrie growls. Like, legit growls. Like some kind of animal. "Touch it and spend six months growing back your head."

Dea lets it go with a worried glance my way and instead picks up the Hawaiian.

"Ugh," Nine groans. "You seriously need a better palate."

"Considering you are a part of my palette, I would say it is just fine." He shifts into his Angel form and pats his lap. "Come here."

Nine floats down from where he was on the ceiling with a sheepish look on his face, but the moment he settles on Dea's lap, he breathes a sigh of relief. Eyes rolling into the back of his head. Lips parted.

I want to give him that look.

I want to touch my boyfriend.

Connie comes back and settles back onto the armchair with her chosen pizza and cake from the army-sized pile on the floor.

"I . . . I'm so sorry." Tears roll down my cheeks before I can stop them, uncontrollable rivers of grief. The weight of the world pushing them off my chin. "This is all my fault. I trusted Aki. I trusted him. And look what's it done!" Hands shaking, breaths ragged, words spill. "You're floating in Death's lap, deprived of touch, of life. Of pizza! Because I didn't think to be more cautious about who I trust."

None of them move. Connie puts another bite of pizza in her mouth, content to listen and watch until she's needed.

Nine, on the other hand, leaves Dea's lap and settles above me with his legs crossed, inches from my open pizza box. "Now you listen here. And listen good. Because I'm only going to say this once." He waves a hand through my face, and a cold shiver floats slowly through me like a lazy wave. "You are not responsible for the actions of others. Not even if those actions could have been prevented. The responsibility of others falls on them, not you. No matter how much you believe otherwise." He takes a deep breath, despite the fact I'm certain he doesn't need to. "You are simply wrong." Then he smiles and floats back to Dea. *Besides, Dea will just have to get us both off while all tied up.*

Sniffling, trying my best not to look too pathetic, I shove another bite of pizza in my mouth and huff.

Why is he always right?

Chapter Forty-Two

Can the Horsemen Really Neutralize SC and Fae Queen Threat?

Lucien walks into my bedroom the next morning—well, he more swaggers into my bedroom, but still, you get the point—and sits on the couch near the fireplace. "So, persuading my father to take a stand against the SC. A public stand."

"Tall order?" I ask, fluffing my skirt out and removing the last curler from my hair. "Shouldn't he want to support his people?"

"I know you weren't around for when Vampires came out of the closet, little Horseman, but I was. And let me tell you, it was hard. The SC did a lot to smooth things over for us. In fact, the only reason we weren't hunted with pitchforks was because of the years of campaigning the SC did for us."

"So you owe them?"

"Yeah, basically."

Grabbing my charm bracelet and tying it around my wrist, I ask, "Do you believe in holding grudges to a community's detriment, Prince Lucien?"

"No?"

"Good. Then you shouldn't believe in holding an IOU to a community's detriment either. This is silly." Arrie and Nine have already left, and Dea is at the embassy, so I call to my Fae trainer and Lo, "I'm off. Enjoy my library."

"Bye!" I hear them both call, both sounding distracted or otherwise engaged.

I switch my charm bracelet into my staff and bang it on the floor. "Time to go home, Prince Lucien."

Magic swirls around us, the pressure of teleporting overcoming my senses, and I have to hold in the vomit threatening to expel all over Lucien. But once we land, the hedge next to me is not so lucky.

"Magic! That is *my* hedge."

Looking around, I realize I have once again teleported into Lucien's front garden. "Oops. Sorry. Weak stomach."

"You couldn't have teleported us to the Vampire Council building?"

I shrug. "I could have, but it seems rude to just poof into a government building, and I can't be bothered to get arrested again by another pillar community. And I couldn't really remember what the outside looks like, then I panicked because I had already banged the magic stick, so I thought of the awful parties you used to run here, and poof. Here we are."

Lucien sighs, heavy, and rolls his eyes, and then grabs my hand and drags me down the street. "I cannot believe the future of my species is in your hands."

"Hey!" I yank my hand out of his and walk in step beside him. "I will have you know I have come a long way."

His fangs drop when he lowers a salacious grin at me and winks. "You think so, little Horseman? Keep up then." He sprints at full Vampire speed down the street.

And I follow, keeping up with ease while using air magic to boost my already faster-than-most-people-can-see speed. Until I'm overtaking him and seconds from the Vampire Royal Council building and laughing at his out-of-breath wheezing.

"Keep up then."

We screech to a halt in front of the building I now remember as being as big a disappointment as when I found out the moon isn't made of cheese. Corporate building with plasmascreen ads on the windows.

"Beat you."

"You cheated." He catches his breath for a quick second, then places a hand on my shoulder. "Don't think I didn't miss the air magic."

"Pfft. Don't know what you're talking about."

Lucien laughs as we walk through the front door and head on up to the same floor as before, where large meetings are held. But unlike last time, I have full control of my Vampire senses and know that human blood is meh.

I have much tastier morsels at home.

"Ready?" he asks.

Fluffing out my skirt, ensuring my boobs are placed to effect, and dragging my hair back in front of my shoulders, I look to him with confidence. "Yes."

The door swings open on silent hinges and we're greeted by the full weight of the council watching us as we make our way past the couches and seats and human blood volunteers and settle up on the stage.

Now I just need to make one hell of a speech.

Lucien looks my way, but I gesture for him to start. It'll be best that way. Lure them in with someone they know and trust, then hit them with the cold hard truth.

He steps just in front of me and looks his father dead in the eyes, not afraid, not backing down, and for the first time I've seen, really taking his place amongst his people. "You are not going to like the conversation at hand today, but I implore you"—he gestures to the room, meeting a few eyes—"all of you to simply listen."

His father places the human woman on his lap aside and leans in, listening. "Continue."

"We have three enemies collaborating—the Fae Queen and her army, Prince Phillipe and his delusions, and the SC causing mayhem with every decision made—and we need to start eliminating the threats one by one, weakening the opposition. We don't know where the Fae Queen's armies are, and we suspect that Phillipe has joined her, which leaves the Supernatural Council."

He looks to me, wide eyes subtly asking me to join in.

I step forward, wondering what the fuck I'm supposed to say to these people. "I know you're scared, and I know that playing politics is the job of the council, but if we don't loosen the hold the SC has on our magical communities, we won't win this war. They're too strong with their alliance."

Grabbing the plasmascreen rod out of my bag, I place it into the air and turn it on, watching as the screen rises in front of us, showing the plan from earlier. "We are dealing with the human and Fae council members as we speak, undoing the damage done to them. But this still leaves two species, splitting the council in half. I don't know about you, but that's not good enough for me. I don't want to leave the fate of the world up to a 50/50 chance. Either you command a revote of the Vampire councilmen, or we leave the fate of the Vampire community up to the Shifters."

A deep breath leaves my lungs.

They don't like it. I can see it in their eyes. The king is shaking his head, as though the very thought repulses him. "You ask too much this time, Magic." He looks around the room and asks, "Anyone who opposes this plan, raise your hand."

Every hand in the room goes up collectively.

"You see," he starts, "if we have another vote, we cannot have another for a decade. And this council does not think the

SC are as big a threat as you make them out to be."

"Not as big a threat?" Lucien asks, rage slowly rising in his voice. "They have the biggest collection of armies in the world. If they choose to back the Fae Queen, or let themselves be manipulated and controlled by her, we will have a world war on our hands." His hair falls out of their perfect braids, falling around his face. "And you're just going to sit by and risk not only our people, but the people of every other species in existence? And why? Because you're a coward!"

"Watch your tongue!" the king booms. "Do not forget who you speak to."

"I speak to my future council. I look to the faces of those who will lead my people under my reign, in my stead when I am ill, who will be by my side when I make decisions for the benefit of Vampires as a whole, and not just for the ease and comfort of myself."

It's definitely going to be him, then? Lucien will be the next king?

The current king looks to me with a simple smile, answering my question. Then he turns back to his son with pondering eyes and a small smile hidden beneath contemplating lips. "We will discuss this further and reconvene tomorrow."

The breath Lucien releases is full of seething rage and frustration, but the voice in which he speaks is null, empty of emotion. "Thank you for your time and consideration, Father, council." He nods to the room and turns to me, gesturing me down the center aisle ahead of himself.

Chapter Forty-Three

Horseman of Magic Arrives at Vampire Royal Council with Prince Lucien

"He's so . . . Argh!" Lucien stomps back to his house, where he slams the door behind him. "I mean, does he not understand how important this is?" The fridge door slams shut him, and he carries various ingredients to the chopping board. "Is he that dense?"

"I don't think——"

"What does he think's going to happen? The Horsemen will ride to the rescue so he doesn't have to do anything?" Lots of chopped fruit later, and he's blending it all and adding it to a large glass jug. "You're not all powerful. You can't just snap your fingers and make shit happen."

"Maybe he just——"

Then he screws the cap off the vodka and triple sec and pours copious amounts in, before topping it all off with cranberry juice and ice. "It's like he doesn't want this shit to end." Grabbing two cocktail glasses, he pours us one each and hands me mine. "Like he's content to just sit there and do nothing."

The first sip is fruity, but with a sharp twist of alcohol that rolls around my taste buds. "This is really good."

Lucien stops ranting for a second to smile at me. "Might not be as good a cook as your brick wall of a boyfriend, but I can make a damn good summer cocktail."

"That you can." I raise my glass at him and wander out to the garden, where the large pools bring back memories of a previous life, of hate and violence. "They're all gonna find out one day, and it's like I'm sitting on edge, waiting for it to happen."

Lucien stands next to me, both of us basking in the heat. "Your past is yours and yours alone to bear. You don't need to tell anyone." He shrugs as he knocks back the rest of the glass. "You're still a person entitled to privacy, you know."

A small chuckle escapes my lips at the absurdity. "Have you seen the news headlines? The chatter online? The smear campaigns?" Taking another sip and a deep breath, I say, "Privacy is the very reason the Horsemen were in hiding for as long as they were."

"Really?"

"Uh-huh. They wanted their own lives, to be able to walk down the street without being hounded, to not be judged on every action." I take my boots and tights off, rolling them into a pile beside me, and dangle my feet in the pool. "I kinda ruined their lives."

Joining me, he ruffles my hair. "Yeah, but I bet you make up for it in orgasms." He turns to me, fangs descended, a glint in his eyes. "Seriously, how do you keep up with all four of them?"

I shrug. "Connie's the only demanding one. Nine and Dea are together, and Arrie and I are a new thing. Besides, it's not like they're not friends. They get it." The cool water and the iced cocktail are heaven in the beating sun, and I'm going to have to remember what Lucien did to make this drink. "And, you know, group sex."

Lucien splutters on nothing. "Group sex? You?"

"What?"

"Just never thought I'd see the day when a prude like you would be chatting about group sex with me."

My eyebrows raise in question. "What, Red not satisfying you enough?"

An actual blush creeps across his face. A blush! The satisfaction that gives me races through me.

"We haven't . . . We're not really . . . together."

"Why not?"

"Sometimes," he says with a laugh, "I forget that you weren't always as up-to-date with supernatural politics. Vampires and Witches. A Vampire prince and a Coven Witch, no less?" He grabs the rest of my drink and downs it in one.

"Never gonna happen."

"You're my choice, Lucien." When he looks at me in question. "When the king inevitably asks for my opinion on how to replace him, I choose you. Not because you're the next oldest or the prettiest—"

"You think I'm pretty?" he preens, running a hand through his hair.

"You know you're pretty, stop fishing." We both laugh, knowing I'm right. "But I choose you because you're the most capable of running a species, of inciting change, of standing strong. And I think that if Red is really someone you want, you'd chase her until the sun burned down the world, consequences be damned." I get up to grab another drink from in the kitchen, but I turn back around. "And who knows? Maybe a Vampire prince and a Coven Witch is just what you all need."

Just as I enter the kitchen and grab the jug to pour myself another glass, a small pop sounds, and Nine and Arrie stumble into the kitchen. "You were quick."

"I told you," Nine says. "Easy peasy. Did all three in less than two hours and even had time to explain what's going on."

"Briefly," Arrie mutters. The scowl on his face is my first clue, but the frustration lacing those eyes is the second.

Rather than boil in his mood, I push him up against the counter and lean into his neck, where I pepper kisses and tease sharp teeth along his most sensitive spots.

After a few seconds, he nestles his nose into my neck and wraps a large hand around my waist. "Magic . . ."

"Hey," I hear Lucien call as he walks into the kitchen, "no threesomes in my house unless I'm invited."

I snicker, but apparently Arrie doesn't find it as funny, because he snarls. "I'm not sharing with you."

"Stop being snarly. Lucien's just angry that I'm getting more than him."

"I can get whatever I want whenever I want."

"Yeah, but none of that is Red, so you don't want to."

"Red?" Nine asks, hovering near. "Really?"

Lucien shrugs, wanting the argument to end if his scrunched up porcelain face is anything to go by. "Probably not."

"Why not?" Nine asks, ever the gossip. "I mean, I know why." He taps his head. "But I wanna chat about it, anyway."

"Stupid Vampire Witch thing," I say, waving my hand through the air.

"Vampires live an awfully long time, Lucien. For a mortal, anyway. And let me tell you, in a hundred years, you're going to regret letting society tell you who to love."

"I am not letting soc—"

"Yeah you are, but it's okay." I pat him on the back, smiling. "I get it. You're scared. So you're choosing the easy road."

Arrie smirks at me, Nine smiles, and I just internally preen.

"I am not!" He slams a glass on the counter and it shatters into pieces, so he forces a breath out through his nose. "God, you're annoying."

"Yup."

"Fine!" He looks into the mirror in the corner of the room and sighs, then re-braids his hair. "I'll back by morning." Grabbing a teleporting crystal out of his pocket, he vanishes as quickly as it breaks on the floor.

"Guess I'll clean up, then." I use some air woo-woo to shove the glass pieces into the bin and brush my hands off. "So, what now?"

"Well, Dea and Connie are busy," Nine says, "so it's just us three for a while. Where are you with the Vampire king?"

"He's thinking about it. Thanks to Lucien." I walk back out into the sunshine and breathe in the warm air. "He'll make a great king one day."

"That he will, Killer." Arrie rests his hands on my shoulders, standing behind me, while Nine flies around the garden for a bit.

"You know," he shouts, "I will miss being able to fly."

"I'll make you a flying charm or something one day."

Yay!

Arrie chuckles under his breath, a smile peeking through— it's becoming more common hearing his laugh and smile.

"How are you doing?" I ask, looking up at him with my head tilted back. "I know how much you're struggling with moving on."

He shrugs, wordless. "I . . ." Then he sighs, running a hand down his face. "I am managing."

Nine stands next to us, floating down to the ground. "He is focusing on how happy you make him and enjoying your new relationship, but when things are quiet and everyone is busy, he can't stop feeling guilty."

"What he said," Arrie mumbles.

I wrap my hands over his on my waist and take a deep breath, organizing my thoughts. "When you're feeling that way, you should seek one of us out. It doesn't have to be me—I get why I might not be the best person to lean on—but it should be someone. You've been suffering alone for a really long time, so I think it's time to start trying something else."

"Ve's right, dude. You can't just suffer for another thousand years, and burying it all so you can be happy with Magic also isn't the answer."

"Then what is?" His hands clench into fists as his body goes rigid. "What else am I supposed to do? Our relationship is both the best and worst thing in the world for me. And I don't know what to do with that."

I turn in his arms and grab his face, yanking it to me. "You just have to feel. There is nothing wrong with love, hate, guilt, happiness, or anything else. All you have to do is feel." My nose meets his as our foreheads touch. "That is the healthy choice. To express emotion and let it flow through you. Doing anything else is immature and unhealthy."

Nine smiles at us in the corner of my eye. "Just don't aim your emotions at people."

"Okay." I pull away, thinking about the best use of our

time, then look to Nine, who's a ghost. Riiiight, so we can't really go too far afield. "Want to order in? Think of all the tasty takeouts they'll do here in New Orleans."

Takeout consisted of sugar—beignets, pastries, a whole nine-inch cake, and a sample of every ice cream flavor on the menu—and we popped the excess on the kitchen counter at home for Connie. With all the politics and organizing she's doing, she could sure use the sugar rush.

We're watching some lame horror movies on the screen when Arrie's hand lands on my thigh, brushing under the hem of my skirt and dangerously close to the "touch me and fuck me" zone.

"Arrie, wait, I—"

"Can I watch?" Nine asks, a wicked glint in his eye. "Pleeeease?"

"I was just about to say no to Arrie."

"Why?" Arrie asks. "Did I do something wrong? Is this about earlier?"

"Shhh." I put a finger to his lips, silencing him. "It's not you. I don't want Nine to feel left out considering neither of us can touch him."

"Oh." Something tells me he didn't think of that. But that's okay. It's my job to think of my boyfriends, not his. "Okay."

"No, wait," Nine says. "I maaaay have peaked on your first time a little." My raised eyebrows and Arrie's scowl make Nine sigh. "Heaven does have *some* perks, you know. But I missed loads cos it's hard to focus on Earth up there, and I really wanted to see." He pouts, lip sticking out and everything, like a child.

Arrie doesn't seem to mind, as he smiles and leans in to me, his kiss suddenly plundering my lips, his tongue suddenly slipping past my teeth, and his desire for me suddenly pressing into my stomach as he climbs on top and pins my wrists to the couch. He turns to face Nine with a smirk. "Any requests?"

"What am I, a porn star on demand, taking requests like a damn DJ?"

Yes, Nine says at the same time as Arrie says, "Tonight you are, yeah."

Fucking typical men.

Chapter Forty-Four

Top Secret Vampire Meeting: Are They Preparing for War against Humans?

"Hmmmm," Nine ponders. "What to ask for . . ." After a few more moments—a few moments of Arrie kissing down my neck and brushing lips against my cleavage—Nine says, *I wanna see ve on their knees, sucking dick like a pro.*

If he thinks I'm taking Arrie's dick like a pro, he's gonna be disappointed.

He trails kisses up the side of my neck and whispers into my ear, "Just do your best."

Apparently Nine is translating thoughts like he does when he's with Dea.

I want to say I'm not into this, that I don't have any bodily response to Nine watching us like we're starring in a porno, but I am into this. My body is responding. And if my boy-friend wants a show after being dead, then a show it is.

Arrie straddles my lap, leaning over me as he kisses me everywhere he can reach, my hands still unable to move from where they're pinned. His foresty scent washes over me, his neck exposed as his teeth rake over my shoulder, pain and pleasure shooting through me.

My fangs slide free, and they're sinking into Arrie's artery before I even think to ask. But it's Arrie. He likes it. And pre-dictably, the moment I drink, he groans and grinds into my stomach, seeking friction.

Everything lights up when he kisses my neck again, and now it's not just him seeking friction, moaning.

I want more. Need more. But I let him go, slipping free, and shifting us so he's the one pinned beneath me. Weaker than me. And now his rock-hard dick is mine for the taking.

Take his pants off.

Following orders, I sink onto the floor on my knees and undo his belt, whipping it off, then I unbutton his jeans and slide them off, leaving him on Lucien's couch in nothing but his underwear and a t-shirt.

The imprint his dick leaves in his underwear has my mouth watering and my body pulsing. My hand reaches out to run a finger from bottom to top, then dipping into the waistband.

His breath hitches.

Nine watches with rapt attention, eyes pinning my hand under his glare.

330

"Nine?" I whisper. "Are you able to take your clothes off?"

His nods. "Yeah, they're just ghost clothes."

"Good." My fingers wrap around Arrie through the fabric, his length hot in my hand as a groan slips free from his lips uncontrolled. "I want a show too."

Arrie scowls, impatient. "Just suck my dick, Magic." When I don't move my hand or go to undress him, he grabs a fistful of my hair and yanks his underwear off, then smirks. "Open up."

The sting of the pull on my hair zaps through me, lighting me on fire. And I can't help it, my mouth opens on a gasp.

Arrie takes advantage of the reaction and shoves the head of his dick in my mouth. "Yeah, like that."

My pants are flooded, and fuck I wish Nine weren't a ghost, because being filled from both ends sounds like a great way to defile Lucien's house.

I wish I could fuck you too. He settles beside Arrie, totally naked, dick in hand. *I really do.*

"Watching me fuck her will have to do," Arrie says between clenched teeth just as I slide my lips further down his length. "Fffuuck." His hand on my hair fists tighter, and he pushes me down further.

So far that I'm not sure I can take much more without gagging.

"Breathe in," Nine says. "And swallow the moment it hits your gag reflex."

Okaaaay.

(Cue doubt.)

I take a deep breath in through my nose, and Arrie slowly pushes my head further down toward his pelvis. He's trying to go slow, I can feel it, but he's pushing up against the back of my throat and I'm panicking. I know I did this with Dea, but it's different. So different.

Following Nine's instructions, I swallow, and Arrie sinks his length down my throat with a moan so wild I can't help but flit my gaze up his torso and watch his eyes roll back and his head hit the back of the couch.

Nine's watching too, his hand slowly moving up and down his cock—too slowly if you ask me, but hey, it's his orgasm.

Experimentally slowly I raise my head back up, Arrie's grip loosening, and swallow him back down. Again. Again. And again. Until I find a rhythm that's comfortable and has pre-cum leaking down my throat and Arrie's moans gradually getting louder.

Shit, dude, you look good. I want my dick sucked like that.

I'll give you all the dick sucking you want when I can. Promise.

For now, I do my best to suck and swallow at an even pace that increases incrementally. But when Arrie growls and tightens his hand, his hips rising up to meet my mouth, I don't focus on what I'm doing anymore and instead bounce my head in rhythm to his hips, letting him use me.

Letting him light a fire inside me so hot, I'd need all four of my partners to extinguish it properly. Or Connie and a bathtub, it would seem.

Shit, Nine groans. *When was that?*

Arrie moans louder, his eyes widening as they meet mine. "Fuck, one day I'll . . . I'll be there to watch that."

On our last date. Came so hard and so many times I passed out and woke up the next morning forgetting time had even passed.

I send Nine images of the various things I've done since he's not been with us, and by the sounds Arrie's making, he's sharing them.

Both of their heads roll back as they rock their hips at the same pace, Nine mimicking Arrie's, I assume.

I go to speed up, but Arrie pulls out of me and grabs me by the shoulders and shoves my skirt off, rips the tights and panties off, and shoves me on the couch, ass up.

He has enough sanity to slam two fingers inside me first, furiously ramming me apart, preparing me as best he can in whatever state his mind's in.

Not wanting that state of mind to end, I send more images—things we've done, things I want to do, and things I've read about—and Arrie's eyes glaze over as Nine chuckles at us both, his dick leaking.

There's preamble here, and I realize that he went easy on me before, afraid I'd break or some shit. But he knows better now. So he lines up and buries himself in me in one motion, not caring if I'm ready for him. He wants me.

"Something tells me he's getting you."

Arrie moans as he moves back out and slams back in. "So fucking wet." Then he says something in Norse, but I don't catch it.

He said you're tight and wanted something to shove into your ass.

Caught between heat and horror that anything more will fit, Arrie grabs my throat and squeezes so my head rushes. But I can still breathe.

I send more snippets Nine's way, and he shares them one at a time, slowly working Arrie into a frenzy I'm not sure my vagina will survive.

"Ffuuck," he groans. His fingers reach to my clit and pinch hard enough to hurt, rubbing between his thumb and forefinger. A growl whispers against my ear, "Come. Fucking come now."

And goddess damn it, my body explodes, fire spreading, moans leaking from my lips on the end of curses.

"Shit," Nine swears. "That's fucking hot."

"Ffuuck, yes. That." Arrie slams into me, his skin slapping against my ass, leaving bright red marks, no doubt. "Arrghh!" His fingers close around my throat so tight it hurts and I can't breathe as he comes, pounding me harder than anything I've felt before.

"Shit, shit shit." I watch as cum spills across Nine's stomach, his hips riding his hand in rapid movements until he's stopped leaking.

Arrie comes to a stop, his hand loosening around my neck, and he grabs my waist and pulls me back against him.

"I'm not done with you." He pulls out and slides his fingers in place instead, his thumb softly circling my clit.

It's in such contrast to the rough pounding he just gave me, I don't know what to do with it. But it's nice, like a massage and a thank you.

And I know in this moment that I'd marry this man if he asked. I'll never let him pull away again. He can have his space and be with me at the same time.

He shoves his knee between my legs, separating them, and the cum he filled me with leaks down his fingers and onto the couch. "Anything you want?" he asks.

"Ummm . . ." Aside from Nine inside me now? "I'm not sure."

He keeps up his movements, but he settles me in his lap and drapes my legs over the sides of his, pinning me apart. "Anything you wanna see, dude?"

I look back over to Nine, who's working his still-hard dick, but slower than before. His eyes are watching us, tracing Arrie's fingers and watching my pussy like someone who'd give anything to have their face down there.

Nine groans inside my head. *I'd give every tomorrow for a taste of you. Just a drop.*

"I want you. So much." A sob leaves me, and Arrie stops and pulls out, but I shove his fingers back inside me. "Don't stop."

"You don't have to," he says in my ear.

"But I want to. I want to have you fuck me and be as close

335

to Nine as possible." Tears leak down my face. "Please."

He kisses my cheek. "Anything for you, Killer." He looks to Nine, their gazes meeting. "Anything."

Nine moves to the front of me, watching Arrie's every movement.

Arrie tweaks my nipple with his other hand, and I arch into him, moans slipping freely, legs tense but like jelly at the same time.

"Curl your fingers and use the heel of your palm on her clit," Nine orders.

Arrie follows his instructions, placing a kiss on my neck at the same time.

And after a few seconds, the heat inside me rachets up, soaring through me like fireworks. "Nine . . ."

"I'm right here." He holds up his spare hand, a tear rolling down his cheek, as his hand speeds up. "I'm right here enjoying the show."

I can feel myself leaking all over Arrie's hand, a mixture of himself and me, but he doesn't seem to mind. He speeds up ever so slightly, increasing the pressure, and my body screams.

I'm so close.

"Don't stop."

"I won't," Arrie whispers, then peppers kisses up my neck and along my cheek bone.

My legs shake as my knees clench against Arrie's, and the moans slipping from my mouth border on screams as I clench around his fingers. Tighter than ever. "Ah! Yes, yes, yes." My

336

hands grip Arrie's elbows, nails digging in. "Niiine!"

"Oh god," Nine curses. "Yeah, Sweetie. You look so fucking good." He's staring directly at me, watching me orgasm on Arrie's fingers and drip onto the carpet, listening to me scream his name.

"Want you . . . inside me," I manage just as the orgasm peaks, lasting longer than usual.

Nine's knees buckle, hitting the floor, as more cum shoots from his dick. *Want to fuck you till you pass out,* he says as he screams my name.

We all just stay where we are, motionless. Nine hovers while Arrie holds me, and I'm still crying. I just want my boyfriend to hold me. I want them both.

I know, Sweetie. I'm so sorry.

"Not your fault."

Arrie sniffs behind me, and it's then I realize that he cried watching us. "I know this isn't the right time, but dude, even your cum is ghostly."

"Shut the fuck up," Nine groans.

Chapter Forty-Five

Lucien knows. I can tell by the stink eye he's sending us. We're walking to the Vampire Royal Council building early in the morning, getting some fresh air.

I look at him—really look at him—and realize that maybe it isn't me he's annoyed at. His hands haven't unclenched all morning, and I didn't hear him come home last night. He's also still wearing the same clothes.

"Sooo," I ask, "how did things go with Red?" Terrified of the answer.

He stops. He sighs. And for a moment, he looks like a man with a broken heart. "She said no."

We all stop, looking at him with sadness.

"Don't do that!" He waves his hands at our faces. "Don't look at me like I'm some kicked puppy. I'm not. I'm a Vampire prince." He straightens his shirt and replaces his braids. "It's time I fixed this stupidity."

With Lucien marching the way, the Vampire Council building soon looms, but today there are no ads or announcements on the plasmascreen windows; instead, there's a regal-looking picture of the king with the caption CHANGE IS COMING. We all look at each other with raised eyebrows, and Lucien brings up the interface to his datachip, scrolling through emails, messages, and other communications, looking for any inkling of an answer.

By the look on his face, he finds nothing.

Great.

We're going in blind. As usual.

Here's to hoping the king still likes me enough to keep me in the loop.

The council chamber is tense, with hushed whispers bouncing across the room like a playground fair, but we take our seats near the front and wait for the king to arrive. We're thirty minutes early for a change, so no dramatic entrances for me.

Lucien looks me up and down with a small smile. "You know, you're kinda hotter as a guy." He gestures to my jeans, shirt and waistcoat look I'm sporting today, stolen from his own wardrobe. "Especially when I get to dress you."

Should take Dea and go shopping together. Probably make a great pair.

Lucien's eyes light up for a second, but then he steals himself and takes a small inhale. "I would be honored." Which is Lucien code for he'd shit himself for the opportunity.

Shopping it is. Besides, I could use a better guy wardrobe. All I have are jeans and t-shirts.

Thirty minutes later on the dot, the doors swing open and the king storms in, followed by an entourage of guards and other personnel. His crown sits atop his head, and he's wearing what looks to be a very official robe.

I look to Lucien, who's sitting there with nervous hands clasped in his lap. Nine and Arrie smirk between them, clearly knowing something I don't.

Guess I'll just have to pay attention and find out.

"Good morning, everyone," he starts, sounding louder than I've ever heard him sound. "Yesterday we were asked a very important question, a request from the Horsemen and the embassy that has taken our council a great deal of time to discuss." He looks around the room, his gaze softening. "Many of us have not had the chance to go home yet, and for that I am grateful."

They haven't gone home? I look around the room, and sure enough, lots are looking tired and ragged, paler than usual.

"We came to a decision last night that we feel will have great effects for the community at large, as well as the world." He looks to me with a knowing look and smiles. "We have agreed to allow a revote for the Vampire Supernatural Council representative seats. We have already informed the SC, and the announcement is due to go public in a matter of hours. This is a lengthy process that will take time to organize, time I am sure the Horsemen do not have. It is therefore our choice to suspend our seats on the SC in the meantime. This will remove us from any position of international power."

He looks to me as he says those words, his meaning clear. He's putting himself and his people at risk for me. This could end badly for them if I don't protect the king's choice. If I don't help protect his people.

Clearly I've gained prominent clout with the Vampires.

Yay.

Lucien rises and joins his father on the small stage, a smile on his face. "We will bounce back from this stronger than ever, and no one will be left behind once we've dealt with this problem." He looks to me, trying to ask something, but I trust him. He can say whatever he wants. "The embassy already has pixie and Demon representatives in our efforts to share our position and world with supernaturals in politically lower stations. Hopefully, we can create a world where all species are equal and everyone's lives and cultures are protected."

A few clap, a few scowl, and a few don't seem to know what to think.

So I step up and join them both on stage. "I know this is scary. I do. And I know a change of this magnitude is a challenging path to walk as a community. But I promise to stand for you. For all of you. Once the threat has been removed, we will work to improve the Supernatural Council and rebuild it to what its original purpose was aiming for: peace between the magical and non-magical communities."

I think generally settled but uneasy is the best I'm going to get today. At least Nine will know how they're thinking and feeling. I hope.

Something tells me that helping to see the vote through will be the biggest pain in the ass ever, but I have to do it. It's my job. And you don't always get the luxury of loving your job.

We're sat in a café not far from the council building, when Lucien turns to Nine and asks, "How are the council feeling?"

"Everyone is stunned," he says from his floating seat next to me. "They haven't processed how insane it is to leave the SC. But there are quite a few councilmen who are happy to finally be challenging their rule."

Arrie sips his coffee in silence, happy to simply absorb the conversation, but his hand is on my knee, a comforting weight.

"Well, they have caused havoc for Vampires everywhere, and if not for Nine's blood supplement, they'd all be starving right now. It makes sense some of them are angry and seeking to fix things."

"Hopefully that anger helps us maintain control." Lucien stresses a hand over his wrinkled forehead. "I hope Father is up to taking control of this. He's not as . . . mentally there as he used to be."

"You're next in line, right?" I ask.

Lucien nods. "But I can't step up until he steps down or passes on."

"Could you not stand beside him, helping where he needs it? Like a united front?"

Nine smiles at me, then turns to Lucien. "I think he'd like that."

He looks at us with a gracious yet thoughtful look on his face. "I'll suggest it to him."

"Sooooo," I ask, getting to the good stuff, "what happened with Red?"

A huff of frustration leaves his down-turned lips. "Exactly what you're imagining. A humiliated Vampire prince on his knees begging a stubborn future Coven Witch to admit her feelings and work together to create a world where we can be happy."

"And she didn't go for that?" That sounds unlikely. Red might be stubborn, but she's an idealist, always thinking for herself and not just for her people. "That doesn't sound like Red."

"Well, then you go talk to her." He throws his hands up in the air in defeat. "Because I am done trying to persuade her to give us a chance. If she wants this, she can come and get it herself."

Ohhh, grumpy Vampire prince. Was this what I was like with Arrie? Ugh. No wonder no one wanted to hang out with me.

A little taste of your own medicine never hurt anyone.

Shut up.

I go to smack him in the arm, but lower my hand at the last minute when I remember that it'll go right through him. For fuck's sake. I need to sort him out a body.

You will.

I'd certainly rather be figuring that out than dealing with all this political bullshit. It's exhausting.

Yes. Yes, it is.

"I wonder how Dea and the ambassadors are doing with the Fae councilmen?" I ask, wanting to change the subject. "Maybe they could use our help in the meantime?"

Lucien looks up, a little surprised.

"All we can do right now is wait. Besides, I can teleport us back in no time."

Lucien waves a hand at me. "Go. Be free." His hand sinks into his other hand. "Come back for the announcement of the councilmen electives tomorrow. Father wants to do this as quickly as possible."

I wrap a single arm around Lucien's shoulder and change my charm bracelet into its staff form and leave, letting Arrie and Nine follow behind me. Once clear of other people, I teleport us to Rue de Rivoli, Paris.

Chapter Forty-Six

HORSEMAN OF DEATH SPOTTED IN PARIS WITH EMBASSY MEM-
BERS

Our scenery changes, and I'm suddenly standing on a street lined with old yellowish-brick buildings bustled together in a neat row, a wide road wedged between them.

"Does anyone know where Dea and the ambassadors are?"

Arrie says, "The two Fae councilmen are staying not far from the Fae palace."

"We've been there before," Nine says, floating away. "Follow me."

Here's to hoping it's not too far. Walking was not on my agenda today when I selected this outfit. Nor was Paris, which is a little colder than New Orleans. But oh well, live and learn.

Dress for all the places you're going in a day.

After twenty minutes of fast-paced walking (more like light-paced jogging), we round a familiar corner near the Fae palace, which is just a few left turns away.

"We don't actually have to go to the Fae Court, do we?"

"No," Nine says while laughing. "We wouldn't have sent most of our ambassadors into the Fae Court, Sweetie."

"Right." Of course. That would have been silly. "It's, what, six pm here?"

Arrie nods, checking his fancy time zone watch.

"Then they're probably at dinner somewhere."

Arrie pulls out his mobile phone—which, yes, we still use from time to time, and yes, I'll be grabbing us datachips the first moment I can—and phones who I assume is Dea, because after a few moments, we're changing direction and heading toward a nearby street with restaurants and plasmascreens lining the buildings with ads, and old-fashioned streetlights that curve at the top. Good old Paris' old and new mishmash never fails to make me gape in awe.

"They're in here." Arrie opens the door and speaks to the greeter, who guides us past tables seating couples, families, get-togethers, and business meetings, until we pass a curtain at the back, which leads to an exclusive area cut off from the main restaurant. And there, sat with six ambassadors, is my Angel of Death in a suit I've not yet seen with a placating smile on his gorgeous face.

He looks up when the curtain falls back into place and lifts a genuine smile the moment he sees us. He makes his excuses to the table and gets up to greet us. "I was not expecting you, Angel." He wraps an arm around my waist and tucks a thumb into my belt loop. "You look amazing."

"Thanks." A small blush creeps over my face. "Lucien dressed me."

Nine floats through us, making us shiver, and shoves his face into Dea's. "I'm here too."

Dea shifts into his Angel form and chuckles. "I know, Famine. You are impossible not to notice." He runs a hand down Nine's cheek, and I get to watch his shiver as his eyes close and his head falls ever so slightly back. "I could never forget you."

"Well," Arrie says, breaking the moment, "we've come to be help, if you need it."

"I will always take my team's help."

Nine grabs one hand while I grab his other, and Arrie rests a hand on my shoulder, as we make our way over to the table where servers are setting us seats and moving things around to accommodate our sudden arrival.

Red sits on the other side of Arrie, with two of our Shifter ambassadors on her right. And on the other side of Nine, who kindly hovers above his seat, sit our two Vampire ambassadors and our single Fae ambassador.

We have the full entourage today, it seems. A round house.

The two Fae sitting in front of us look stressed, if their sweating foreheads are anything to go by. But they pour over the paperwork and the videos and the rest of the evidence presented to them with fervor nonetheless. Enraptured by our experiences.

"This is all real?" one asks, his blue skin mildly white in the low twinkling lights of the green-and-brown-colored restaurant. "How do we know it's not all fabricated?"

"Oui," the other says. "Why should we believe you over our beloved queen?"

Red stifles a frustrated groan as the table goes rigid on our side.

"Because," Dea says, "we have no reason to lie. We are going to war with the Fae with or without you. All we are trying to achieve here is to the neutralize the threat the Supernatural Council produce."

"We are not asking for the SC's help," Red reaffirms. "We are asking that they stand neutral."

"I just . . .." The blue-skinned Fae frowns at the paper in his hand, his fingers shaking. "This is . . . unbelievable."

"One of our own got kidnapped under the Fae Queen's orders simply because she doesn't like us." I shrug. "I'm sorry, but she's not who she says she is."

"Magic is right," Nine agrees. "She's manipulative. She's purposefully blocking information to you and your people, even through your datachips, to make you see the world in the way she wants you to see it."

Maybe we could undo that for the Fae datachips, and then they'll see for themselves.

Not a bad idea, but a risky one. We won't know the outcome of that.

We cannot control what the Fae would do with such information, Dea echoes inside my head.

Don't they deserve informational freedom? Don't they deserve to make a decision for themselves, rather than have everything decided for them by a tyrannical ruler who wants to be placed above every other species?

No one says anything, and everything around us is clearly waiting for one of us to say something. Anything.

"Then undo it," the Fae with the blue skin says. "If you're so certain she's doing all of"—he gestures to the piles of papers—"this, then undo the block on our datachips."

Dea turns to Nine, who sighs. "I'd need access to the network to do that. Every species runs their own, as a way to segment people's information and control what gets shared, so she'll have that stored somewhere safe. Probably in the castle itself."

The two Fae look to each other, then nod. Serious expressions on their faces. "We are willing to let you into our datachip networks, so long as we can come with you and see everything you're doing."

Dea looks to everyone, who nod in turn. Then he turns back to the two Fae and agrees to their terms. "I wish to leave as soon as possible. As you can imagine, time is of the essence."

"It is not far from here, but getting you in might be a problem. It is heavily secured, and no unauthorized personnel are permitted past the doors."

Dea smirks, then takes his charm bracelet off, removing the permanent visibility spell. "That will not be a problem." He puts it back on in time to see the two Fae reattach their jaws to their faces. Dea turns to me and Arrie, then to Nine, and tells us, "Stay here."

"May I come with?" our Fae ambassador asks. "I've always wanted to see Earth's Fae Court."

"Of course." Dea whisks all four of them away, and we're left to eat dinner.

Well, Nine won't be eating, but the rest of us are.

"At least the food's nice," Arrie grumbles.

"Not as nice as yours." I turn to look at Red, who meets my eyes and then quickly darts them away again.

But I keep staring, and it must annoy her, because she turns to me and asks, "Do you have something you need to say?"

"Yes, actually."

"Magic," Arrie warns. "You shouldn't get involved in other people's affairs."

He's right. For once.

"Oh, pfft. Shut up the pair of you. Lucien is my friend." I give them both a withering stare, and they leave me alone. "You really hurt his feelings."

"He's a Vampire prince, I'm sure he'll be fine," Red scoffs, shoving a piece of her roasted duck in her mouth.

"He's still a person, Red. Being someone important

doesn't mean you don't deserve happiness."

"Maybe if you're a Horseman," she snarls. "The rest of us aren't so lucky."

I get the feeling she's not talking about Lucien anymore. She's talking about herself.

"I can't officially date a Vampire, okay. It's against Coven law."

"It's . . . what?"

"I'll be kicked out, disowned. I won't have a home anymore. Or a people. He knows this. But he's asking it of me, anyway." I can hear the sob in her words, the emotion that maybe I shouldn't have started out in the open.

I reach over and lay my hand on hers. "No matter what you decide, you'll always have a home in *Sheruta* and friends in us. And you'll keep your ambassador position on our side."

She looks to me with a thoughtful smile, a single tear running down her face. "Thank you."

"How long do you think they'll be?" Felicity asks, her gentle voice gracing my ears. "It's just . . ." She looks around, fidgeting. "I haven't been to Earth since . . . you know."

Oh, goddess. How stupid of me. "I can send you home if you like?"

She looks to the table and nods, a small gesture. "Yes, please."

"Here." Arrie hands her a teleporting crystal from his pocket. "Take this."

One day, I need to set up a production warehouse in

Sheruta for those damn crystals. Witches and Fae can make them together. Easy peasy.

Not a bad plan. Should get Connie to help. You know, afterwards.

Guess it's one more thing for the list, I think to myself as Felicity heads home.

Nine's hand goes to rest on my knee, but it hovers just above as he realizes he can't actually touch me.

"Okay people, if anyone has any ideas on how to make a corporeal form for my boyfriend, I am all ears," I address the room. "I am sick of not being able to hold his hand."

Everyone remains silent as not a single person offers a suggestion. Well, it was worth a try.

"Have you considered looking into death magic?" one of the Vampires asks.

And I have to hold in my audible groan.

How the fuck am I supposed to use that to create life?

"It's just that when I was Thailand, there was a Witch who claimed it could bring and take life at will."

I snap my head to him, eyes boring holes. "Bring *and* take life?"

He nods.

"Thank you. That's actually helpful."

He bows his head and returns to the conversation he was having with the Vampires next to him.

Death magic can give life, too? But how? It's called death magic, for fuck's sake. How can it give life? Aki never mentioned anything about it giving life. So maybe he doesn't know? Or maybe he knows and didn't want to tell me because he's a manipulative little shit with a god complex.

I'm so gonna kill him.

I'm gonna drive a dagger through his black heart, carve it out of his chest, and make him eat it. And then I'm going to ask Dea to find the gates to hell and make him drag him there.

Nine looks mildly horrified, but I wave off his concern.

Arrie's phone rings, and he answers, listens, and his eyes go wide for a moment before he schools his features and says, "We'll be right there." He looks to me, Red, and the others. "We have to go. They've run into some trouble."

Everyone runs from their seat, Red swiping her datachip on the way out to pay for everything, and come to a halt outside the doors.

"Does anyone know where they are?"

No one says anything.

"Sweetie," Nine says, "you can probably track Dea if you focus hard enough."

Track him?

Angel mated, Sweetie.

Oh, right.

I shift into my female form and focus on Dea, allowing the memory of him to fill me, the scent of smoky lavender and the feel of his Angel feathers running over my bare skin. And something in me sets alight and joins him to me. He's scared, alone, and panicking, and I need to get to him.

"Follow!"

I sprint toward him, but I slow down when I realize that not everyone can keep up with my Vampire speed.

Please be okay. Please be okay. Please be okay.

We jog down alleyways and speed across roads we should probably be more careful crossing, but it doesn't matter. Dea's scared. He's panicking, and I don't know why. And I'm not there.

Briefly I can hear Nine telling Arrie to just leave me be and let me do my thing, and I appreciate that. I don't want to hurt one boyfriend while trying to save another.

"We're close." A couple of more turns, and we're here. Somewhere. But it's just an empty plaza. Where are they? "Why aren't they here?"

One of the Vampires squints and gasps. "We're on top of them."

I look to the floor and roll my sleeve back. "Get out of the way." Air magic soars me high into the sky and hovers me a hundred feet above the plaza, and then I'm shooting down to the ground with my fist out in front of me.

The earth shatters beneath me as stone cracks and the plaza caves in, opening whatever is beneath us.

The others rush forward, craning around the dust to see the damage, and when it finally settles, a large hole has opened up beneath us. And in the hole is a shaking Angel on his knees surrounded by rows upon rows of computers glowing bright blue.

354

"Dea!" Nine is the first down, flying through the pieces of rubble without issue. "Dea?"

"Nine?" Dea doesn't look at him, but looks at the something in the distance that's not there. "Nine? Where are you?" Tears track down his face as his puffy eyes weep. "Why can I not see you?"

"I don't know."

I soon join them, but I can't touch him. He's surrounded by an impenetrable shield made of some kind of glowing green plasma. A Fae spell. "Just hold on, Dea."

"Magic?"

"I'm right here."

"Why can I not touch you?" He's reaching his hands out, but they're coming to a stop at the barrier. "What is that? I cannot see beyond the nightmare behind my eyelids."

"Nightmare?" I ask, shifting forms. I run my hands through the spell, feel for the key points and how they interlink and weave together. "What nightmare?"

"That day in the bedroom, when I could not feel anything, not even you."

"After Nine died?" I ask, still analyzing the spell. It seems to be some kind of mental illusion spell. Luckily, they're easily broken with a counterspell.

He sobs, his body shaking.

"Okay, just hold on a second. I'm going to break the spell." I raise my hands and trace several runes, joining them together in bundles that act at central nodes, and then slipping in an incantation. "That should just about do it."

The green glow blows away on the breeze, and Dea releases a heaving breath, hands slamming onto the concrete beneath us. Upon opening his eyes, he runs into us and slams both Nine and I against his body. "Do not get caught in one of those spells."

Everyone around us laughs a little, letting us have our moment. Even Arrie. Who is standing vigil in front of us, blocking us from everyone else, including the three Fae who accompanied Dea.

The one from our embassy is shaking like a leaf, his eyes shocked and the hair on his head singed off, leaving him bald.

"You okay?" I ask, not stepping out of Dea's hold.

"I've just . . . never seen a Horsemen fall before."

Dea stands up straight. "It was more of a trip." He shakes his shoulders out and looks to the other two Fae, who so far have done and said nothing. "Tell me where the damn thing is."

Everyone scrambles out of his way as he waves his wings, flapping the dust off them, and standing tall. My Angel of Death.

They rush to the other side of the room and point to a plasmascreen, where they scan their chips and enter their identities into the computer.

Nine hovers over them and orders, "Click on the button on the bottom right."

Dea follows his instructions, since Nine can't touch anything—he just goes straight through it—and after twenty minutes of trying to figure it out, they finally have the block removed from their datachips.

Seriously, I kind of daze out through most of it, since it's like they're speaking another language, but I trust they can do it. Especially Nine, he's a genius.

I try.

The ambassadors stand around, not quite sure what to do, but they at least have the sense to set up a perimeter so the general public leave us alone.

Red is coordinating with the local police officers who have arrived on the scene. And if I'm not careful, by the heat of their tones, I'm going to have to get us all out of here before we're arrested.

I shift forms so I can listen to their conversation better, but it's over by the time I manage to blink, let alone shift.

"Racaille," the officer mutters under his breath, his hand resting on his magigun at his hip.

We need to leave.

I Vampire speed toward everyone, carrying them into the center of the room, where Nine, Dea, Arrie, and the Fae are, and my staff pops into existence and soon we're hurtling through the aether toward *Sheruta*.

I didn't really think about it when I made the decision, but I may have brought the Fae councilmen with us. Oops.

I turn to them and apologize. "Sorry, fellas. But they were going to open fire in a few moments." I gesture to the ambassadors. "I might be immortal, but they're not."

Neither of them knows what to say, but our Fae ambassador says, "Maybe you should stay in *Sheruta* for a few days. See how we do things here."

"That's a good idea," I agree. "We can set you up in a hotel, and you're free to work, chat to other people, etc. You're not a hostage."

"Also," Dea adds, "it might be a good idea to go back after everything has died down."

They look to each other, frustration and unease on their faces, but they turn back to us and nod. Remaining silent.

We're in the main meeting room, and Connie and Felicity rush in, looking at us all with a mild amount of surprise on her face, probably wondering what we're all doing together. But she doesn't have time. "We have a problem."

Chapter Forty-Seven

Vampire King Announces Re-Vote of Supernatural
Council Members Amid Historic Political Move

"She's here," Connie says. "All three of them are here."

"Connie," Nine starts, "you're going to have be more specific."

"Aki, the Fae Queen, and Prince Phillipe are here."

Oh, for fuck's sake. I don't have time for this. I need to get back to Lucien.

Everyone looks to me expectantly, looking for guidance. Instructions. Something.

"Okay." I turn to the Fae ambassador. "Take these two to the hotel around the corner and put it on the embassy's tab. Then come back." Felicity is leaning against the wall with a worried look on her face. "Could you please contact Lucien and give him an update?" Then, without missing a beat, I ask Connie, "Where are they now?"

"Being held at the portal in the guildhall, but I don't think they'll stay there for long."

I turn to Rufus and the other *Sheruta* ambassadors. "Evacuate the center."

They look shocked, but I'm not taking any chances. Connie didn't mention an army, but even alone, those three are pieces of work. Not a single *Sherutan* is dying because my twin brother is a psycho.

"Nine, could you please fly high over the guildhall and see what they're thinking. Do not get caught. They still don't know you're alive."

He floats through the wall, gone, while everyone else gets to it.

"Red, Arrie, have our army on standby."

They march out the room, a feral pair if I ever saw one. Remind me not to mess with the two of them together.

"Dea, Connie, and I will go meet them," I say to the one Witch and two Shifters left in the room. "You alert the various councils and stay here, ready to step in if necessary."

Outside is chaos, people leaving their houses and business-es, and the guildhall is even worse. Employees are panicking, not knowing what to do. Everyone running around as though they have no heads.

"Everyone," I shout, "please leave and follow the evacuation procedure."

Everyone starts leaving, and soon I've found the fire alarm setting and pull it. The ringing echoes through my head like a siren, but I ignore it. Instead, I march to the portal room, where the doors are closed and six security guards stand watch, fear and determination on their faces. But relief floats through them when they see us.

"You're relieved." I wave my arm, dismissing them. "Leave with the rest of the evacuees."

"We've shut the portal down," one of them says on his way out. "No one can get in or out of *Sheruta* without a teleporting crystal."

I sprawl my senses out, drowning out the fire alarm, and check to make sure no one else is in the building. "Building's clear."

"Ready?" Connie asks.

Dea and I both look at her and smile. "Ready."

The doors swing open with a gust of wind, and we march forward. My staff is still out, gripped tightly in my hand, ready for use.

Stood in the middle of the portal building are three of my least favorite people, being led by Aki. And I'm about ready to roll heads when Nine says, *The Fae Queen and Prince Phillipe are here for peace. I still can't get inside Aki's head.*

Connie and Dea probably heard that, too.

Dea is the first one to say something. "Leave. You are not welcome in our home."

The Fae Queen smiles gently, her beauty gracing my senses. "Now, now. You own an entire realm. There must be space for us to chat somewhere."

"If you think we're listening to a thing you've got to say—"

"You will," Phillipe says, "when you learn what we have to say."

"You are a Horseman of peace, aren't you?" Aki says. Even his words sound false, dripping in poison. How did I ever believe a word that came out of his mouth? "I know you don't want war, sister."

The hiss that leaves my lips sounds feral, even to my ears. "You're no brother of mine. Leave!" I slam my staff into the ground and light my other hand on fire. "Or suffer."

Aki smirks, confident, annoying as hell. "So hostile."

"You tried to wipe out the main Vampire cities, created hostility between the magical and human communities, lied to and manipulated me, and killed my boyfriend among thousands of others." One of the charms in my staff spreads around the room, creating a smoke screen that covers everyone else, so thick you couldn't possibly see through it. "If you think you're anything but a villain, then you're as psychotic as I thought you were."

His smirk vanishes as rage contorts his mouth into a snarl, and his eyes flash daggers. "I am not psychotic! It's this world that's insane. Everyone just acting as though the Fae couldn't wipe them out whenever they chose or as though Vampires aren't draining everyone dry. Disgusting!"

"What are you talking about?"

"You're that cut off from society, you don't even see it, do you? How much everyone is struggling? Well, I can change that. I can put a real power in charge. Real control. Real safety."

His hands move into position, and I'm ready for him. His fingers twist and contort into waves of different stances, and a black sandy mist fills the room, sweeping beneath my fog like a disease.

"Aki, stop. You could hurt everyone using that."

"Don't worry, it won't kill your precious Horsemen. I already tried that."

"Then why?"

He doesn't answer; instead, he gathers the mist into a ball in front of him, sucking up every last drop, and he hurls it at me.

Like a boulder, I go flying, hitting the wall, and the spell creating the fog dissipates, leaving the room. Vanishing.

"Magic!" Connie yells, running at me.

"No. Stay where you are!" I hold out a hand and use air magic to push her back into place. "I can't fight more than one."

She reluctantly turns back around and comes face to face with a smiling Fae Queen.

"I thought you liked me," she coos. "I thought we were friends."

"We were, but my job is more important than any single

friendship." She sighs, taking a deep breath. "And Magic is right. What you're doing is wrong. Misguided."

"Is that your official opinion or just the one that's mirroring your girlfriend?"

Connie laughs a little, a small chuckle that snaps everyone's attention her way. "Sorry, it's just I'm not known for letting Magic think whatever they want. I'm always the one to put them in their place when they're being dramatic or just wrong." She places a strong hand on the Fae Queen's shoulder and looks her dead in the eye. "So yeah, it's my official opinion, Your Majesty."

Before I can even blink, she rams one of her daggers into her side, and blood spatters.

Aki cringes, a flicker of fear crossing his face. But he turns back to me, concentrating on his own fight. "You really have got them wrapped around your pathetic little finger, haven't you?"

"That's kinda how love works, Aki." I teleport myself to right in front of him, and blast fire at his face.

He skids backward, pain leeching from his screams.

But he steadies himself and forms a small dragon with his death magic, copying what I did in the cave where we found Lo. "Neat little trick, huh? Thank you for that."

I grab a ball of water and encompass his dragon, drowning it in salty water. "If all you're gonna do is copy me, then I guess this'll be easier than I thought."

Aki grabs a fistful of my hair and yanks, catching me off

guard, making me scream. He brings my face inches from his and breathes, "You're nothing but a rat. It should never have been you."

"I know." Tears leak down my face as my hands shake. "But it was."

"You're not strong enough." He yanks my hair again, pulling my body flat against his. Threatening.

"I know."

"You can't possibly hope to rule the world."

"I don't."

He throws me to the floor, a heaping pile of tears and shaking limbs. But I stand back up nonetheless. And I face him. I put my staff back on my wrist and produce fire in one hand and water in the other, dropping my fangs.

My hair sprawls out behind me as magical pressure surges.

Connie is kneeling on the Fae Queen's shoulder, keeping her down, and Dea has somehow pinned Phillipe to the wall, immobile and eyes closed.

"I am neither strong enough nor good enough for the position bestowed upon me, but I will stand up and fight, anyway. Because that is my job. My duty. And you are threatening the lives of an entire species. Threatening the way of life for millions, billions of people."

All at once, I hurl a fiery waterspout, sweeping him up and spinning him around the room. Aki's hair flails as he screams, tears leaking down his face when I zoom my vision in.

Nine, tell someone to turn the portal back on.

Already on it.

Thirty seconds later, the portal starts to whirl, and I drop the magic, dumping Aki's unconscious body on one of the chairs. Connie and Dea doing the same thing. And we turn around and leave.

"That went . . . unexpected," Dea says.

"What were they trying to do?" Connie asks.

"Aki had a camera on his coat. I couldn't break it. Some kind of spell has protected it. I couldn't break it without giving away that I knew what he was trying to do."

"Which was?" Connie asks.

"He's trying to frame us."

Chapter Forty-Eight

Could New Vampire Councilmen Really Change Any-thing?

"It's been a long ass day, I'm going for a nap." I look to the clock on the kitchen wall and frown. "I have to be back in New Orleans in a few hours."

"I've got a list of shit to get through," Connie groans. "Then I might go shopping." She turns to me and leaves a lingering kiss on my lips that tastes like peppermint tea. "Anything you'd like?"

"Cake."

She looks to everyone else. "Yeah, I guess if there's anything you guys need, I can pick it up."

Everyone lists off one or two items, and then we all head to bed, exhausted. And since I still haven't fixed Nine's body issue, he sleeps on Dea's other side, who stays in his Angel form, which is actually quite nice, because Angel mated cuddles are legit the best. Arrie is on my other side, asleep in seconds.

The poor thing. I think I socialized him too much today.

It's soooo weird that Nine needs to sleep. He's a soul. Why in the world does he need to sleep?

That's a great question, he says sleepily. *Maybe when we say we're bone-tired, what we mean is soul-deep tired. Maybe our souls can get burned out and need resting, too.*

Kind of like when we're more than exhausted. When it's not sleep we need, it's rest and recuperation and special interests and things that make us happy and comfortable.

Yeah, like that.

Sleep comes easily, and soon I'm drifting away into whatever recess of my brain controls my dumb dreams. Well, they've been alright recently, but it still puts me on edge.

Just as I'm dreaming about whose dick I get to suck next, the scene changes, and it's not a gorgeously naked Nine lying on my bed anymore, it's a blank space. Completely white. Kind of like what the Otherworld looks like. But also not.

There's something in the air in the Otherworld. Like it's nothing but not nothing. Nothing in the physical form. It's still something. But this feels like genuine nothing. Bone-deep emptiness. There's not even air around me.

And I realize I can't breathe.

Wait a minute, I'm dead. I don't need to breathe.

A figure shimmers in the distance, and I walk toward it, casually, confident that I can't actually be hurt here.

Where am I?

Who is that?

As I get closer, the answer to the second question becomes obvious. It's Aki. Only, he can't see me. Which is a good thing because Aki is crying on his knees in front of a tamaya *with our parents' pictures on and a charm bead I've not seen in a while—one of Dea's invisibility charms.*

"Aki . . ." I whisper.

He turns his head from side to side and frowns. "No, no, no . . ." His hands clasp at his head. "Go away, go away. Leave us alone!"

I back off, giving him some space.

He bows low to the floor and says a prayer, his tears staining the carpet below his knees.

That's when the rest of the room fills in, and I find myself in a rural home with sliding doors and chabudai *tables, with bamboo mats set to four place settings.*

This must be Aki's home.

But why am I here?

Aki gets up and stretches, then wipes the tears from his eyes, before he grabs a plate of sashimi from the fridge and sits to the table. "Itada-kimasu," he whispers.

He's really traditional in his ethnicity. Then again, I guess you would be if you grew up here. But I was moved to the US as a young child, so I'm less Japanese and more American. Maybe I should consider spending some time in Japan, getting to know my roots better?

Focus, Magic. Focus. You're here now for a reason. What is that reason?

Well, color me stupid, 'cos I don't fucking know. This seer shit is hard work. I don't know how the Coven seer does this all the fucking time.

This is the present, I think. Since Aki's got a bruise on his temple that I put there earlier. That also means he is indeed creating his own teleporting crystals. We need to find out which Witch is helping them.

But it's not until Aki has finished his meal and washed up, taken a shower, and then gone into his bedroom that I see it.

He's wearing something. Something that's glowing a faint blue. Something I didn't give him. It's hanging around his neck on a piece of rope. It looks like a piece of stone? As my hand hovers near, it glows brighter.

Aki gasps, then looks around the room. "You're here, aren't you?"

"Yup." Not that he can hear me.

He grabs the necklace and unties it, then dangles it in front of the mirror he's standing in front of. "It's nothing special, really."

There's a symbol on it. A symbol I've seen before. Of a horse holding a scroll in its mouth while standing on its hind legs.

That's the Horsemen symbol.

I wake up gasping, sweating, drinking in lungfuls of fresh air.

And the guys are around me in an instant, touching me, soothing me. Dea wraps his wings around us all as he places a hand on my stomach, all the while Arrie is running a hand up and down my back.

I replay the vision/dream/seer thing in my head, rolling that necklace around my mind like a puzzle piece. I look to

Nine, who's floating next to Dea with a shocked look on his face. "What is that?"

"It's part of the original Horseman seal he broke."

Chapter Forty-Nine

Future New Vampire Councilmen Threat to Human—
Vampire Alliance

Connie's not in the house right now—probably still running errands—but Arrie, Dea, Nine, and I go check out the vault with our seals in.

"See," Nine says, "these appear after a seal is broken, but the actual seals that get broken are stone tablets." He picks up one of the scroll seals and unravels it. "These are hidden inside the stone tablets."

"So he kept a piece of the stone seal?" Dea asks. "Why?"

"It explains why I couldn't read his mind. And why our powers are weaker against him."

"I don't think that's why he's wearing it, though." I grab the seal from Nine and roll it back up, placing it back onto the magically protected pedestal. "I think he just kept it because he didn't know what else to do."

Arrie scoffed. "He's an egotistical asshole." At my questioning eyebrows, he explains, "He assumed he was the strongest being on the planet when he broke the fifth seal. He's arrogant. There are all kinds of powerful Fae, Vampire abilities, and not to mention a fucking dragon."

"Lo wouldn't have counted," Nine says. "He's not magical in the same way we are. He uses a power older than Angels and Demons, and therefore older than our magical system." Nine leads us out, floating through the closed door. "I mean, he was around with the dinosaurs."

"Still, Aki's an asshole." He wraps an arm around my shoulder and squeezes. "He made Magic cry."

"That makes someone an asshole?" I ask, trying to hide my smile but failing.

"Yes."

"Dea's made me cry. Is he an asshole?"

Arrie shrugs. "He gets a free pass because he's your mate. He can soothe whatever part of you he breaks."

"Including the parts you break," Dea comments.

Arrie's hand balls into a fist, but I grab it, stretch it out, and thread my fingers through his. "It's okay. I forgive him."

Arrie stands stock still, like a statue, and turns to me. "Really?"

I wrap my tiny arms around his huge waist. "Of course." And I place a soft kiss on his chest, where my head rests. "I don't condone what you did, nor am I going to say it was the right thing, but I get it. You're struggling. I still see it in the way you mistake me for her first thing in the morning or when you notice me from a distance or when your kiss changes to something more hesitant." My hands rest on his shoulders. "But partners struggle together. And it's okay to be grieving, even after two thousand years." I gesture to Dea. "Do you see me hating Dea's gorgeous tattoo? No. Because Haji was important to him. Why would I take that away or fight it? I'm okay with you loving us both. But since I'm the one alive, we come first. Our feelings matter more than you pushing me away. They matter more than your guilt. You hear me?"

I point a demanding finger into his chest, but he grabs it and twirls me around, then lifts me up and wraps my legs around his waist. "We come first."

Dea coughs to get our attention. "If you two do not mind, we have a world falling apart. And Magic needs to get back to Lucien."

"Lucien! Shit." I climb down from Arrie, kiss him and Dea goodbye, wave to Nine, and then teleport to the reception of the council building, where Lucien stands waiting for me. "Lucien, hi."

"You're late."

"Sorry. Had to break into the Fae datachip center, fight Aki, eat, nap, then work out a seer dream. Been a busy twenty-four hours."

"You and me both." Lucien, I notice, is wearing a suit. A

business suit made to tailor with diamonds in the pick stitching and a shirt that's as white as his hair with a black tie and a pocket cloth. "Cannot tell you how much had to be done to get ready for the presentation of the candidates." He pulls a watch out of his suit pocket and mutters "shit" under his breath.

"Is that a pocket watch?"

"No time for fashion tips, we're late." He grabs me by the hand and drags me to a room somewhere on the first floor. He turns to look at me as we stand outside. "Tell me you have something better than that to wear?"

I shift back into my male form, who is still wearing the awesome clothes I borrowed from Lucien, if a bit dustier. I dust myself off, straighten things out, and then smile at him, smug.

"Looking good. Now, are you ready?"

"Thank you. And yes, I think so." I have no idea what a candidate presentation entails, but I can handle anything these Vampires throw at me.

We enter the room, and I'm met with dozens of cameras, the king, a backdrop that looks like a window over NYC, and three Vampires I don't know sat in seats beside him.

Okay, I'm so not ready.

"Stand over there, behind the cameras, and just watch," Lucien says. "The king wanted you here in support, so do as he says."

I shuffle into place as Lucien straightens his suit jacket

for the hundredth time and settles into the spare chair on the other side of the king. Who also looks handsome in a suit with diamonds in the pick stitching.

The director films, and we're off. Starting with the king himself.

"Hello, communities. Today we're going to introduce our candidates for the first round of the Vampire Supernatural Council seats. Each round will have three candidates, and one will be chosen each time by public polls. There are three seats available, so there will be three rounds."

Lucien chimes in with a smile and a dashing charm. "Remember, if you want to see change or you care about how your communities are governed, then you need vote. Without doing so, you might not see who you want in power."

"Let's have a look at our first candidate, Mr. Victor Hesham," the king says, gesturing to the man on his right. "He's been active in the political community right here in New Orleans for the past twenty-three years after being a turned Vampire abandoned by his sire."

Victor Hesham smiles gently at the king and nods. "That's right. I didn't know what to do, so I got a night flight from North Carolina to New Orleans and walked up to the council building and said 'hey, I'm a new Vampire, please help me.'" Everyone laughs, finding the idea hilarious, but I just find it sad. "But everyone here has been so generous, including the king himself, who took his time to walk me to the nearby turning clinic, who set me up with a job, a stand-in sire, and even an apartment."

Wow. What a clinic. They must really help their communities. I wonder who runs them or who created them.

"What kind of changes would you like to see?" Lucien asks.

"I'd like to see more laws protecting Vampires. I'd like to push for a law that makes it illegal to abandon a Vampire you turned. It was unfair what happened to me, but it happens to lots of people, even children." He smiles gently at the camera, then turns to the king. "I want to protect consensual Vampire feeding spots, make them legal, and I want to create more Vampire-friendly housing in non-Vampire cities, so those of us who don't have lots of money can choose to live wherever we like, just like everyone else."

Him. I'd vote for him.

The other two also get a chance to speak, but neither hold people's attention like Victor or feel as passionately or as strongly about Vampire freedoms. He'll get the seat.

Just when I think things are about to end, the king stands from his seat and gestures me forward. "Here today, in support of this part of our journey as a community, Magic, the Fifth Horseman."

Lucien and the candidates clap, straighten themselves in their seats, and smile as I sit down, taking the king's seat. Now the king stands behind the camera, watching me. And I have to say something.

I have no idea what to say.

I swear, I'll kill Lucien when this is over. He could have fucking warned me, the piece of shit.

"We, the five Horsemen, are happy to support the Vampire community during this time. And we wish the candidates the best of luck in their ventures—I'm sure you will serve your communities with strong yet kind leaderships."

Victor turns to me and shakes my hand, asking, "Tell me, how is the war going?"

Connie is usually in charge of this stuff. I never do it without a script or Nine's help. Shit. I don't know what to say.

"It's . . . umm . . ." Deep breaths, Magic. In, out. "We are doing our best to restore order, to spread truth to the world, and to bring peace between non-magical and magical communities."

It's a political answer, but it's the best I've got. I can't just go around telling them details and potentially ruining plans.

I shake the others' hands, and each ask me questions, and I do my best to answer, but it's the last question that catches me off guard.

The third candidate with the dusty blonde hair and the expensive suit looks at me with interest. "Is it true you can switch between a male and a female form? And that you identify as genderfluid?"

"I'm not sure what label would best fit someone like me. And I don't want to intrude on a community. But yes, I have a female and a male form." I switch and then switch back, demonstrating. "And I like the pronouns ve and they."

"How intriguing." He looks genuinely impressed for a minute before he schools his face and sits back down. "It seems like you're an interesting person, Magic."

"Well, I try."

Everyone laughs, and we get to work wrapping things up, where I hand things back over to the king, who I am also going to fucking murder later. But it's good to feel wanted. For a community to want me to be a part of it. I hope I eventually feel this way with the other pillar communities.

Chapter Fifty

Horsemen Cause Chaos in Paris: Vandalism, Injury, and Public Spending

"I'm going to murder you both," I groan as we walk back to a different room. "I swear, a little heads up next time. I would have prepared something." Well, I would have gotten Connie to do it.

The king laughs, his booming voice bouncing off the walls. "If I told you, you would not have been yourself."

Sighing, I shift into my female form, who's wearing a cute little black dress for the day. "Then one of you fuckers best buy me a donut, 'cos I'm starving."

Lucien, the darling that he is, buys me a dozen. Delivered. Ohhhh, how I love Vampires. They actually love me. Lucien tries to steal a donut, but I slap his hand. "Mine."

The king, however, I allow to take one.

Lucien whines. "But . . . but . . ."

"He's the king, little prince. He gets a donut."

"So when I'm king, will you share your donuts then?"

I just laugh. As if. "Nope. You'll always be a little prince to me, even with a dumb crown on your head."

The king laughs again—more times in one day than I've ever heard—before coughing to clear his throat. He looks tired. Less pristine. Old, almost. For a Vampire. They don't really do the whole "old and gray" thing. "Speaking of crowning princes, Lucien." He turns to his son. "I want to name you crowned prince. Officially."

Lucien looks to his father with stunned silence. "I wasn't expecting it so quickly. Is everything okay?"

The king laughs and shakes his head. "Such a pessimist. Everything is fine, but we don't know what will happen during this war. I want to secure our people's future."

Lucien doesn't look happy—in fact, he looks about ready to have his final emotion snap—so I grab his hand and say, "It's the right thing to do. It's always good to have a backup plan. Even if the first failing is unthinkable." I smile at his scowling face. "Trust me, you don't want to be in a position where there is no backup plan."

"Fair point, I guess," he says on a sigh. "We have to win this war, don't we?"

"If we don't, Aki and the Fae Queen will take over the Supernatural Council and govern the entire supernatural world. Humans will be their next target." The pressure on my shoulders is starting to wear me down. I'm ready to say fuck it and go on a month-long cruise somewhere. The world can save itself.

The king settles a hand on mine and smiles gently. "I know you're scared, but so were they when they fought in the first war. You're so much like them, and you don't even see it. You are doing well by the magical communities and the humans."

"Lucien? Do you mind giving me a moment alone with your father?"

He scowls but obliges, heading out of the room. "I'll be at home if you need me. I need a damn nap."

With him gone, I turn back to the king and ask the question that's been burning on my mind for the last few hours. "If a Vampire marries a Witch, what happens?"

He looks surprised. "That is not the question I was expecting from you." He thinks for a moment, lips down-turned. "While there are no legal ramifications, nor would we kick anyone out of the community, I'm afraid it would be difficult for the communities at large. And god only knows what kind of weird rules the Witches have." His eyes search mine. "Why do you ask?"

"I'm not going to tell you someone else's secret. Not even if you're royal." The smirk behind my smile makes him laugh again, and I realize that I just enjoy making people laugh. "Besides, I'm not sure he's ready for people to know yet."

The king's eyes go wide, a smile behind them, but caution

lies there too. "A Witch, huh? How . . . of the times."

I can see the wheels in his head turning, connecting the dots. Here's hoping he doesn't bring it up with Lucien, because he might try to murder me, and I really don't have the time to grow back limbs right now.

"When is the next thing you need me for?"

"The community has two days to vote, then the announcement is made and the second round starts."

"Then I will be back in two days."

"I'll have lunch ready. Brownies, I hear?"

"Always."

Back home, I'm ready to sleep. For, like, a decade. Maybe I could create some kind of Sleeping Beauty spell that would actually allow me enough time to recharge for a change. A hundred years sounds like enough time.

But just as my eyes start to drift close, Arrie walks into my room and asks, "You're back?"

"That's it! I'm done." I get up, throw on my lounge pants, and shove my hand to the wall. If you wouldn't mind creating a couple of doors for me, that would be great? One into and out of my study that isn't through my bedroom.

A smaller than usual rumble vibrates the house, and I go to inspect the house's handiwork. Perfect. A door leading into my study that's a few feet from my bedroom door and a door that leads to the garden on the other side. Complete with a path that leads to the outside of the property and joins up with the main path to town.

"There." I turn to Arrie. "I am dead tired. I'm sorry I yelled at you." I throw a quick kiss to his lips so he knows that it genuinely wasn't anything personal. "Is this an emergency?"

He shakes his head.

"Then if you're not joining me for a nap, please, respectfully, fuck off."

He chuckles as I remove my lounge pants once more and climb back into bed. He closes the door to my study that everyone usually uses and locks my bedroom door so I can't be disturbed, then climbs in behind me.

"Mmmmm, much better."

He wraps his strong arms around my waist and nestles his nose into my neck. "Sleep tight, Killer."

Chapter Fifty-One

Horseman of Famine Spotted as Ghost: Is He Alive?

"I did it!" my Fae trainer shouts. "I found a way to combine your death magic with Fae magic and Witch earth magic to give Nine a body." She heaves large gulpfuls of air into her lungs, catching her breath. "I swear, when I die, they best make a fucking statue out of me."

"I promise I'll build a giant statue in your honor." I roll my eyes at my grumpy trainer, her green skin looking more sallow than usual. "Now, are you going to share, or did you have some plan to use all of those pieces of magic on your own?"

She hands over the piece of paper she was waving in the air just a minute ago with a frown. On it, crudely drawn, is a diagram like the ones I often see in magical theory books. Not unlike the one in The Origin of Witch Magic.

In the center is a dark circle penciled in—and I'm assuming that's my death magic—but cutting through it are wavy lines in black pen that form a cross. What are those? But looking to the top right, I notice she's made a key. Wavy lines are Fae spells. Okay, so a Fae spell intersects the death magic. Got it. Then surrounding the edges of those spell lines is a circle in red pen which means . . . Quickly looking to the key. Aha! Earth magic. "So it's encased in earth magic?"

"No, it's laid on top of earth magic. You'll need to do that first."

"You want me to lay some earth magic down (which I can't yet do, by the way), then manage death magic while keeping multiple Fae spells alive, which are probably complex nonsense?"

"That summarizes it, yes."

I turn to her and politely, in my best customer service voice, say, "Your order has been processed and will arrive to you in three to four business days." She rolls her eyes at my sass. But I just flop into the chair beneath me. "Seriously, I have no idea how to do this. I love that you worked so hard on something that has no bearing on you, but this feels years away in skill."

"Maybe we can do it together instead?" she offers. "I can do the Fae spells, you can do the death magic, and then we just need to find an earth Witch."

"Collaborate?"

"Yes, then you can practise doing it together over the next few years until you master it. You'll have time to practise in a way that doesn't keep your boyfriend a ghost."

But that would mean exposing people—mortal people—to my death magic. Wouldn't that be dangerous? A stupid idea?

Nine floats over, having been browsing my book collection all morning, discovering new titles, and asks, "Can you grab a book for me and turn the pages?" He goes beet red, ashamed for having to ask.

"Sure." I go over to the shelf he directs me to and drag PORTAL MAGIC off the shelf with raised eyebrows.

He waves a hand through air as he floats over to the table and hovers in the chair next to mine. "Nothing important. Just curiosity."

I open the book's content page and watch him browse through. "Page 348, please."

I flick to the page, and turn when he asks, go back to the content page when he asks, and realize that I can't let him live like this. He'll need help with absolutely everything. So I turn back to my Fae trainer, who's watching us with sad eyes, and whisper, "Alright, let's do it."

Two hours later, we're outside in a random field no one uses, just the Fae, a friend of Red's, Nine and I hanging in a field, doing complicated, "should totally be forbidden" magic. And I would be lying if I said I wasn't scared.

Scared of hurting my friends. Scared of not being good enough. But mostly, I'm scared of failing.

The hope and anticipation on Nine's face is impossible not to see. But it might not work. It might be something that takes years to figure out. We might not even manage it in their lifetime. Which . . . fuck. We need to figure it out before the smart Fae lady dies. I don't know if I can do it without her.

"You were an interesting conundrum, Famine," she praises, happy as a cow, apparently. "Giving someone a physical body shouldn't be possible, but you're immortal already, which gave me an edge." She looks to us both with a wince, lowering her voice. "And I might have taken a sneaky peak at your scrolls, sorry."

I frown, scowl, and blister at her.

"Don't be too mad. I needed to see what made you immortal to begin with."

"And you just, what, analyzed an ancient spell, read ancient script, and figured that out?" Nine asks, clearly as annoyed as me.

"Yes," she says with a shrug.

Well, damn. Alright then.

Nine huffs but sighs. "Let's get this over with."

I think he's just annoyed that someone is better at magic than him. Which is adorable to see.

"If you're all done being hush-hush, I'd like to get this over with. I have a family dinner to return to." The earth Witch in question is stood a little ways over from us, her small stature almost comical if she wasn't slated to be a part of the next Coven. "Mom said I had to be back by six."

Oh, she's twelve. Did I forget to mention that?

Yeah, I'm putting a child at risk. Yeah, I know that's evil. No, I don't regret it. Well, I hope I won't, anyway.

We get into position, Nine and I at one end of the field, the others at the other end.

I can see them chatting for a minute, then the earth Witch, Zara, waves circles through the air, determination flowing through her. She stomps a single foot forward, and the grass uproots itself and floats into the air, forming a circle. Some dirt floats with it, gravel and bits of worms and beetles.

The Fae gives a lovely smile she never gives to me and then proceeds to encapsulate an energizing spell that pulls the earth's energy out of the floating earth pieces and forms a green bubble in the middle of the field.

Zara is straining, shaking, struggling to hold the ball of energy in its raw state. Something Witches have no experience with since they never work with Fae.

You can do it, Zara. You were made for this.

You'll be a great Mom one day.

He breaks my concentration with that sentence, and I flick my gaze to him and scowl. Now is not the time to be dropping the conversation of children, Nine. I snap my attention back to Zara, who seems to be doing better, the ball steadier.

She nods to us, and Nine floats as I walk into the energy. And it hits me like a truck. This energy is like coming home.

Like a steady rhythm beating my heart like a drum, keeping me grounded. This is why I can't do this yet, because I'm not steady or at peace. I'm as uncertain as the wind.

Maybe once the war is over, I can work on unlocking this power, but I don't think I'll be able to achieve it before then.

My green-skinned friend nods to me, letting me know it's ready for the next stage.

I face Nine, terrified and on edge. "I'm sorry if I kill you."

"Sweetie, I'm already dead."

Right. Of course.

I can do this.

I hope.

My hands rise into the air as I dig deep, into anger and uncertainty, into the stress of the role that's been thrust at me without a single care for whether it's what I fucking want. To the terror at losing Nine, the grief, the heartbreak of watching Dea fall apart.

C'mon, c'mon, c'mon . . .

Black sand seeps from my feet, filling the floor around us in like a black hole to hell. I gather it up and swirl it around us, mimicking the ball of energy. It flows through Nine, leaving him unharmed, thank the goddess, and I release my held breath.

Now it's time for the mystery step.

I can do this.

I swirl the black sand mist through the earth energy, pushing it through the aether molecules, splitting them up, then I grab their pieces and sew them back together, knitting them into something else. Something more.

Sweat drips down my brow, my nose, and off my chin. My clothes are soaked through. I've never held death magic for this long before. My limbs shake like leaves on a tree in a storm, only this time, I'm the storm.

Okay, Nine echoes the Fae's voice in my head. *You're doing well. Keep that in position. I'm going to thread the spells through one at a time. Don't worry about what they are, just trust me. I'll teach it to you another day.*

Okay. Go.

Nine is a mixture of black sand mist, green earth energy, and the weird reconnected energy that's dark swirly green. He reaches out a hand, and rather than pushing the magic through him, it bounces off him. And the smile he radiates fills me with so much joy, I nearly lose the death magic.

Steady.

I refill the magic, steadying it. And then breathe again.

Somewhere in the distance, I can just about hear Connie, Arrie, and Dea breathing, shaking. And I wrap their scents around me, allow them to fill me up, to fuel my senses with calmness.

The aether particles in the ball of magic stop moving. Frozen. And I can suddenly see outside. Everyone's face is frozen in shock, not understanding what's going on. But Zara is still struggling. So we have to continue.

Okay, I'm threading the first spell through. Magic, stand out of

Nine's way.

I move to the side of the magic, out of Nine's way, while holding the magic in place, still shaking, still struggling. It's like all the energy in me is being zapped out. Sucking me dry.

I could never have done all three of these things together. (Heck, I'm not even sure I can keep Witch magic alive while in my male form, or vice versa.)

Straining my hearing, I can just pick up on Arrie whispering, "You've got this, Killer."

Dea is silent, shaking, his hand laced in Connie's, who's also muttering under her breath. "I love you. You can do this."

The first spell breaks through the magic, passing straight through Nine, who's now tethered to the magical ball and spinning on the floor. She weaves the second one through the magic and then through Nine. But this time it ties itself to the new sewn-together aether particles, linking them all together, weaving the ball into a mesh.

The spell pops. Like a bubble. And my connection to the magic is lost. I look to Zara, and she's as confused as me, having lost the connection. Did something go wrong?

Nine gasps. *Magic!*

I snap my gaze back to him and gasp. The magic is flowing into him, lighting him up like a human Christmas tree, but it's clearly painful because he's wincing. "Nine?"

It's fine. I'm fine.

But he's gasping in pain, panting, and finally, when the last of the magic snaps into his form, he screams, flying high into the sky.

Not wanting him to be alone, I follow, lifting myself into the air with sheer momentum and using what little magical resource I have left. He leads me to the upper atmosphere, where we're still as statues, not breathing, not moving.

His eyes lock onto mine and hold on to them, scared. *I don't want to die again. I don't want to leave you and Dea alone again.*

Shhhh, it's going to be okay. I'm not going to let that happen.

His body is glowing, pain racing through him, and the screams he shouts leave my body pierced, scared. Guilty.

He's in pain, and it's all my fault. Because I was in too much pain to let him go. Because I wanted him back.

No. That's not true. He waited for me. He knew I'd come for him. He trusted me so much, he waited in the Otherworld for me to come get him, and I'm not letting him down now.

I throw myself at him, grabbing onto his shoulders and wrapping myself around him, giving him something real to hold on to.

His tears run back down my neck and back as his hands clench my t-shirt. "Magic . . . It's . . . working."

What? I pull my head back and gasp. I can touch him. He's . . . real. My hands land on his cheeks and force his eyes to meet mine. "You're real?"

"Real enough to do this." He throws his lips against mine, devouring them. One of those kisses that reminds you why you're alive, that fuels your heart and sets your soul alight.

"And this." He smacks my ass and laughs. "I'm alive."

We fly down, the magic still glowing lightly under Nine's skin, but it's slowly dying out, and we land on the grass, hand-in-hand, smiling.

The team rush over, but it's Dea who reaches us first, having fazed over. And he collides into Nine headfirst, pinning him to the ground with an oof. Arrie and Connie kneel beside them, both eager to touch Nine, to cement his skin to memory and reunite with a two-thousand-year-old friend.

But I turn to someone else standing just beside me. Someone I run to and wrap my arms around, squeezing the life out of. "Thank you." Tears stream down my face. "Thank you."

"Okay, that is quite enough." She untangles me from her and stands in front of me, pride shining in her eyes. "You are welcome, Magic."

Zara is standing just behind her, mouth agape, not having believed what she just helped do.

"And thank you," I say as I wrap her in a hug. "You did something amazing today. If there's anything you need or want, just let me know. We are forever in your debt."

She thinks for a moment, then asks, "Do you have an earth teacher yet?"

I shake my head, no.

"Then I'd like to train you." She looks to herself with doubt for a moment, then shakes herself out of it. "I know I'm only twelve, but I'm bright for my age, and I can do lots of things, and I—"

"I'd love that."

"Day after tomorrow at the Coven. Eleven am sharp."

I salute her as she grabs her teleporting crystal and smashes it to the ground. "Yes, ma'am."

Chapter Fifty-Two

Can We Really Bring Back the Dead? Experts Warn of
Side Effects to New Scientific-Magical Revelations

He smells like paper and ink and bonfires. Like reading a book on Halloween curled up next to the fireplace drinking hot cocoa and eating brownies.

"I'm grateful for my body and all, but you could not have brought my muscles back with me?" he complains when he's looking in the mirror. "Two thousand years' worth of work."

"I'm sorry the impossible spell didn't work quite as you'd hoped while I gave you a body."

Everyone laughs, the smiles never leaving their faces.

I wrap my arms around Nine's waist and rest my thumbs in his waistband. "I missed you." And then breathe him in like he's my addiction and I can't quite get down off the high.

Dea wraps his longer arm around us both, and we stare at ourselves in the mirror. Pride shoots through me and fills me up, leaving me happier than I ever remember feeling. Mortal or otherwise.

"So, Nine," Connie asks as he snuggles into the cuddle beside me, "what do you want to do first?"

"Anything you want?" Arrie asks.

Nine wiggles his eyebrows at us in the mirror. *A blowjob, please.*

He's just joking, but I'm dying to finally have Dea and Nine together. It's been empty without them both.

"So, umm . . . how does this work now?"

Nine chuckles, but the rest of them look at me like I'm a headless chicken. *Ve's trying to ask for group sex but doesn't want to upset anyone.*

I turn to Arrie. "I know we haven't talked about it, and we're still finding our feet, but—"

He silences me by throwing me onto the bed and asking, "Female or male?"

I'm not sure. "Both?"

Connie lies next to me, scraping my hair behind my ear. "Yes, please." She peppers kisses down my neck as Arrie grabs my hands and pins them above me.

Dea and Nine are making out by the mirror, their tongues sliding together as belts snap out of belt loops and t-shirts come off of heads.

Connie watches too, her eager hands sliding up my sweat-soaked vest top alongside Arrie's, who is pressing strong hands to my hips while he undoes my shorts.

Dea and Nine are in their underwear when Dea spins Nine in front of him and bends him over so his hands are flat on the bed by our feet. "Dea," he moans as Dea sits on his knees while yanking Nine's underwear down and palming his ass.

As Connie finds her way underneath my sports bra, she tweaks my nipple and nips my bottom lip. "I love your little gasps and moans," she says.

"I liked it when you screamed my name," Arrie croons in my ear.

But Connie hears, because super hearing, and she groans. "I want a movie of that night."

I play it in my head, starting from the beginning. "Care to help out, Nine?"

He tries to say yes, but Dea circles his hole with his tongue, so it comes out as a gasp instead. But he sends the memory to everyone. Which I only know because Connie's hips grind into my thigh as she says, "That's so hot."

I keep the memory playing, remembering how he pinned me to the wall and licked me like an ice cream in a world devoid of sugar.

Arrie's breathing heavy in my ear, gasping at the memory, his body shaking slightly. "Is that really how you remember that?"

"It was one of the best moments of my life." I unbuckle

his belt and shove his jeans down his hips, freeing his cock. "And I want more."

He throws the rest of his clothes off, then proceeds to get rid of mine with the help of Connie, and their rushed hands and lips and teeth seem to want nothing more than to get at me. To touch me. To smother me with pleasure.

On my knees, Connie bends down onto her elbows and kisses my hips, thighs, and doesn't let up, rushing to me with a stiff tongue that licks a stripe from bottom to top and sends my head back onto Arrie's chest.

Nine is still bent over, his fingers fisting the sheets as he muffles his cries into the duvet. Whatever Dea is doing to him is pulling him apart as he leaks pre-cum onto the floor as it drips from his dick. "Dea," he cries, "just . . . please."

"Shhh," he whispers. "Just lift your head and enjoy the show."

He does as he's told and looks up at me, orange-brown eyes on fire as they bore holes into mine. *You look like a goddess.*

Connie raises my leg and rests it on her shoulder to get better access as Arrie pinches harsh fingers on my nipples and twists and pulls. Connie puts her lips around my clit and sucks, sending my hips barreling into her face as I grind, seeking movement, friction, and she doesn't let up.

"Shit . . ."

Arrie growls above me, and I can feel the tension in his rigid body, waiting. Like a lion allowing his lionesses to get their fill first. But his patience will snap sooner or later. He does not seem like the sharing type.

Dea shoves two fingers into Nine's ass, stretching him, pumping him full, and Nine cries out. Connie's teeth graze my clit, and I'm moaning with him, struggling to compose myself.

Arrie's fingers seek me, stroking my wet lips as I try my best to spear them into me, but he has me pinned against him. Unable to move. Fangs out, eyes burning red, I hiss as he shoves a one inside roughly.

Connie's tongue works overtime as she flicks pleasure and licks circles around me, playing my body like a personal violin. And Arrie adds another finger, stretching me, and I can feel my body cresting over the hill, just needing one final push.

Dea sinks his rock-hard dick into Nine's ass, moving him up the bed slightly, closer to Connie, and he screams his name. "Dea!"

His body takes the pounding Dea gives, relentless. His wings pop into existence, his golden body lighting me up. "You left me," he growls. "You left me, and I couldn't do anything about it." His eyes are in pain, but his body is in heaven, and the mixture plays out across his face, twisted into some pain-filled pleasure that he takes out on Nine. "You're mine."

"Yours," Nine sobs. He keeps his head up, watching me ride Arrie's fingers and Connie's mouth as my hips piston between them. "Yours," he whispers.

Dea smacks his ass, the sound ringing out.

And I'm shooting over the edge, screaming Arrie's name

as he lifts me off the bed with his fingers, Connie fighting to stay with me by gripping onto my hips and sealing her lips around my clit.

"Oh god," Nine moans. "Fffuck."

Dea watches me, taking a minute to stop owning Nine and watch his mate, his eyes blasting golden light around the room.

As Arrie sets me down on the bed, he rips Connie's head by the hair off of me and bends me over, shoving my face into Nine's dick. "He wanted a blowjob." Arrie lines his dick up with my hole and thrusts in, groaning in relief. "Fuck, yes."

I suck Nine's dick as Arrie throws me up and down it with rough hands on my hips.

Nine's cries reach a fever pitch, but he takes the double pounding, as I hear Dea's skin slapping against Nine's.

"Fuck, just look at you, Magic," Connie whispers from beside me, her fingers deep inside herself. "Taking two dicks at once."

I don't like that she's left out, and it puts me off for a second until I get an idea. I throw the image Nine's way, hoping he's lucid enough to send it to everyone else.

"Are you . . . sure?" she asks. "I don't want to overstep anyone's boundary."

"Sharing within the group is fine, Con," Dea says. "Especially when we are all together. It does not mean you want a relationship with everyone."

With that, she climbs onto my back, rests her head on

Nine's shoulders as she plants her feet either side of me, spreading herself wide for Arrie.

"Get us both off," I say, holding Nine's dick in my hand. None of us are moving at this point, waiting to make sure everyone is okay. "I don't want my girlfriend left out while you're busy. So keep her busy for me."

Arrie doesn't hesitate (thank goddesses for his directness), and I feel him dive for her as she leaks all over my back while her fingers are still fucking herself with rough, harsh movements. He moves inside me again, picking up the pace slowly this time, tentatively finding the right rhythm for us all.

And I move the angle of my hips, allowing him to hit the back of me, slipping moans from my lips like curses on a sailor's ship. And I swallow Nine's dick back down my throat, swallowing when he reaches my gag reflex.

Fuuuck, Sweetie.

Connie moans as she moves her fingers faster, her knuckles grazing my back as I hold her up with ease. "Shiiit."

Nine turns his head and shuts her up, swallowing her next moan with his lips. "Shhh, I'm trying to listen to Magic's screams."

Just as he says that, both Arrie and Dea speed up, grabbing our hips and pounding, shutting us both up for a blinding second as pleasure shoots up my body, making it shake and somehow swallow Nine deeper so my nose meets his skin.

I'm gagging on Nine's dick, no one caring that I can't breathe, my moans sounding more like choked wet gasps as I

402

gurgle, drool dripping down my chin.

Arrie's fingernails dig into my hip as Connie's legs shake beside me, her moans delving into screams as Arrie brings her to release, gushing onto my back.

He races, thrusting harder, smacking my ass as he tries his best to break me. His hand once again finds its way to my neck, yanking me back onto his dick, but this time Nine's cock is in there, so when he screams louder and Dea swears, Arrie chuckles.

"Fuuuck, yeah," Nine groans. "Don't stop."

Arrie grips harder as I swallow faster while holding my breath, and from the sounds of things Dea rams into him harder than ever, flapping his wings to give himself more momentum.

I can hear Connie fucking herself beside me again, enjoying the show, getting what she's always wanted: to watch us. And I can hear Dea whispering into Nine's ear, "You are mine. And my mate and I will continue to own your body until you're begging us to stop. Never. Leave. Me. Again." He punches each word with a thrust of his hips. "Mine!" he shouts, punishing him.

Nine's sobbing, moaning, crying, and screaming all at once, and I have no idea if he's okay or if he needs to stop.

Don't fucking stop.

"Shit," Arrie swears. "Not gonna last." He grips my hip and throat tighter, bruising me, as he moans quietly in my ear, whispering my name. "Magic, fuck." His thrusts become erratic, and he's coming, filling me, releasing himself.

Nine swells in my mouth, slumped on top of my back, just taking it. Not being able to do anything else. But he swells, shaking, his knees buckling. Dea grabs him, continues fucking him but holds him up. "Dea . . . fuck. I need to come," he whines. "Please."

"Shit," Connie swears from beside me. "Nine, are you okay?"

I look up, and tears are streaming down his face as his eyes squint shut.

"Not stopping," Dea grinds out from behind clenched teeth, "unless he safe words out."

I hollow out my cheeks, sucking harder, doing my best to work his body, give him what he needs. But my own is singing, pulsating between my thighs in a needy ache that's starting to hurt. So I delve down, using my own fingers.

But Arrie bats them away, shoves three fingers inside me. "I'll do it." He shoves me onto Nine's dick. "I know you like my roughness."

I really fucking do.

Dea smacks Nine's ass loud enough I wince, and he screams out as Dea grabs his balls and squeezes lightly, his fingers grazing my chin. "Come for me." He's pounding him faster this time, a familiar pace I've seen before. Hard and fast. Just how Nine likes it.

"Yes, yes, yes," Nine cries. "Don't stop. Fuuck." He thrusts down my throat as Arrie thrusts fingers into me, slamming into the back of me. And then Nine's coming, screaming into the air and into our minds, coming down my throat that I have no choice but to swallow.

He falls fully onto my back, giving up hope of keeping himself upright, as Dea wraps his arms around his waist and pulls himself out and Nine out of me, then lies him down on the bed.

Arrie stops and goes to lie next to him, wrapping his arms around Nine's shoulders, comforting him. "I got it."

Connie is looking at Dea and I, eagerness in her eyes. But fuck, I just want to get some of her.

"Go," Dea says. "Go have your dessert."

So, being the good partner I am, I do as I'm told and bury myself between Connie's thighs. "Sorry, I didn't mean to leave you out or anything."

"You didn't. But I'll pretend you did if it makes you get up here."

I don't need to be told twice. I climb up her body and kiss her, but she shoves her tongue into my mouth without hesitation, groaning at the taste of Nine on my tongue.

Yanking her legs up, I bend them and pin her knees to the bed, opening her up for all to see.

"What do you have in mind?" she asks suspiciously, her eyes gleaming with mischief.

I shift into my male form and grin. "But with Dea in me, of course."

"Oh." She blushes.

"This okay?"

She nods. "I've never done it before, though."

I silence her concerns with a gentle kiss. "Me either, don't worry." I look behind me at Dea, who has his cock in his hand, watching us with rapt attention.

"Do not let me stop you, Angel. I am happy to enjoy the show."

"Or you could get in one of us and be a part of the show."

Connie grabs my breasts, tweaking my nipples and making me gasp. "Ve's done so much for everyone else today. Get in Magic, and we'll work them together."

Dea doesn't hesitate—doesn't even respond. My mate settles in behind me and lines himself up, ready to do what he loves. Take control.

"Now he gets to make us both scream." I giggle.

"Bet he'll be thinking about this for a few days."

Instead of responding, he smacks my ass, then Connie's, and we gasp. Laughing.

"Fucking you is always something I think about, Angel." And he slides in, filling me up. "But hearing you scream with your girlfriend will be a hot memory in the making, for sure."

We struggle to find the right rhythm for a while, something that pleases all three of us, but we figure it out, and soon we're all panting while Arrie watches and Nine sleeps.

Dea smirks over at Arrie. "Wishing you had not tapped out so soon, huh?"

"Shut up and get them off."

Connie's sliding against me, setting me alight, and Dea's pounding into me, stretching me. And I'm pretty sure this is going to be the quickest orgasm in the world on my behalf. But I want to last. I want to come with them.

"Come on," Dea groans. "You have no idea how hard it was holding back with Nine." He grabs a fistful of my hair and uses it to shove my lips against Connie's. "Kiss and come."

He speeds up, grinding us faster, and I angle my hips further, increasing the pressure.

"Shit," Connie curses. "Can't last."

"Fuck yeah." I pin her hands to the bed and let Dea work us both. "Come on. I saw how many orgasms you gave yourself earlier. You can manage one more for us, right?"

She nods and whimpers, bucking her hips into me. "Oooh, yeah." Connie grinds and moves her hips faster as Dea fucks me through it, his wings brushing all of us with delicate feathers. "Gonna . . . come." She moans into the air, her head tilted back on the pillow as she clenches around me.

And Dea's hips stutter as he's finally nearly there, but I think it's more intense than he thought it would be, because he drags me off of Connie and shoves my face into the mattress as he uses me. Pounding into me from behind as he bends over my hunched form. "Come for me again, Angel. For me. Please."

And fuck, I didn't know you could come from words alone. But this man is a work of art. I pulsate around him as he slams into me, and I sob into the mattress because it's too much too soon. Overstimulated. Overwhelmed.

But Dea's coming in me, leaking out, muffling his cries in my shoulder. And with one last slap on my ass he empties himself and flops on top of me. "Fuck, that was good."

"So good," Connie confirms.

I whimper, more than done. And rather sore from all the rough pounding from Arrie and Dea.

Arrie chuckles, still holding onto Nine.

"Is Nine okay?" I ask from beneath Dea. "He was full-on crying while you fucked the life out of him earlier."

Dea laughs and pulls out of me. "He is okay. He would have told me to stop if he wanted me to. I would not actually force myself on any of you."

He sounds kind of offended, and I realize that maybe I phrased that badly. "Sorry, I didn't mean it like that." I get us up and wrap my arms around him. "I know you wouldn't."

Dea rests his face in the crook of my neck, comforting himself, as he shifts forms, putting his wings and golden skin away. "He will be okay. Especially after cuddles." He turns to Arrie. "Thank you for the aftercare help."

"No problem. I missed him too." And looking at Arrie cuddling into Nine, holding him so gently, I remember that while it's not the same, they love each other too.

Chapter Fifty-Three

The Horseman of Magic: Their Pronouns, Magical Abilities, and Relationship Status

The next morning Arrie, being the early bird that he is, brings us waffles in bed. Yes, we were all served breakfast in bed by my boyfriend. How cool is that?

Living the dream.

"I don't really know what to do now. I mean, I'm on standby to help the Vampire king, but where is everything else?"

It's Connie's time to shine because she jumps in with, "Well, the community heads have been made aware of the situation with regular updates, the embassy are keeping their armies and the armies of those in support of us on their toes with regular training drills, and we're now fully equipped with magicomms for the entire army on a hierarchical network."

"So we either wait for them to come to us or look like the bad guys by going to them?"

"That is probably what they are waiting for, Angel."

"To make us look evil to get the support of the public at large?"

"It won't work," Connie says around a bite of her waffle. "We've done too much press. We've saved too many cities and people and changed too many lives—on camera."

"Then what else?" I ask, turning to Arrie. "If you were in their shoes, what would you do?"

"I'd remove public support. Isolate you. Force you to have fewer allies." He grabs a waffle, adds some strawberries, cream, and honey, and eats what looks like heaven on a lattice.

I want one of those. And so Nine proceeds to make me one.

"You don't have to—"

"You suck my dick, you get waffles." He hands me a heaping mountain version of what Arrie just made himself.

Connie gets a call on her holo, and she quickly shucks on some clothes and takes it in the study. But a few minutes later, she rushes back in with a frustrated frown on her face. "Aki released a really cut and edited video of the fight. It looks bad, Magic. Really bad."

I sigh. "I saw this coming." Turning to Nine, I ask, "Any chance the portal has CCTV?"

"Of course it does. We like to be able to keep track of who comes and goes." He also jumps out of bed and throws some clothes on. "I'll get right on that."

"I should probably call our **PR** manager and get things rolling," Connie says. She kisses me on the cheek on her way out.

"Just us three, then?"

Arrie corrects me. "Just the two of you. I have army stuff to deal with. Be back in time for dinner, though."

And he leaves.

"Are you busy today?" Dea asks me.

I shake my head, no. "Not until eleven, when I have an earth magic lesson with Zara at the Witch's Coven."

"So until then you are all mine, is what you are saying?" He drags me on top of him so I'm straddling his thighs. "We have hours before you need to be anywhere, and no one else in the house."

A few hours later, I'm dragging my butt to the Witch Coven in South Africa with only a few seconds to spare. I did not want to explain to my new teacher why I was late had I actually been late.

I teleport into the center of the Coven dead on eleven, and I'm met with a sassy yet happy twelve-year-old Witch. She might look small, but she's mighty. And the future of the Coven.

"You're right on time."

"I try." I look around in wonder, remembering how beautiful this place is. "Where are we training today?"

"In one of the caverns off the center. They have a few purposefully empty to allow for magical training. It's where I spend most of my time these days." She guides us that way, past houses made of earth and trees that have been coaxed from the ground by talented earth Witches.

"They're just trying to prepare you. The world is changing, and you'll help lead them during it."

"I know. It's just I don't have many friends." We climb up a rugged staircase that leads into an open hole in the wall next to some a sign that says TRAINING CAVERNS.

"Then I'm happy to be your friend and pupil, Zara."

"Let's just get training." She guides us down several winding paths until we reach a dead end, where we take a left into the biggest cave I've ever seen.

In fact, the only reason I can see the end is because I can zoom in with my Vampire vision.

"I've brought us to the cavern at the end because it's the farthest away so you can't hurt anyone if you do anything stupid. So don't hold back."

"Right. Good plan."

"Three rules: be as emotional as you can be; listen to every instruction, even if you don't understand them; and don't hit me with any death magic. I don't want to die."

I chuckle, finding her last rule hilarious. "Don't worry, it's hard to wield magic, so it won't just pop out by accident." Well, it's unlikely to.

She nods. "Then let's get started. First, tell me how connected to the earth you are. Remember rule number one."

Be emotional. So she wants the truth. Not just some wishy-washy answer. "I like the forest, and I love meditating and doing yoga outside. I even keep my curtains open because I like the moon shining on my face. It's peaceful, like I'm home and can never be alone because the earth is always there."

"Good news, you're definitely an earth Witch. But we already knew that. Accessing earth magic is harder than the other three. That's because it takes more energy and concentration. Some people theorize that it's because it's the most dangerous, so it's magic's natural barrier."

"More dangerous than fire?"

"Yes. You can bring down mountains if you so choose." My eyes widen, and she laughs. "With your level of power, you could reshape the Earth. Drown enter countries and raise land anew from the bottom of the ocean. You're mother nature reincarnate."

Is this really how some people view me?

"It doesn't feel that way. It just feels like I'm never enough for the challenges the world throws at me."

"That's because it's all boring politics. But when you have to use your magic, you'll be the answer everyone needs." She leans in closer to me. "Besides, you're pretty good at the politics stuff."

"You think so?"

"You've made such a difference around here. The energy is changing. More people want to come out, share our gifts with the world. It'll happen with the next council, we think."

"Not if the fire Witch has anything to say about it. She'll outlive me if she gets her way."

We both laugh. "Martha is such a hardass. Don't worry, you're not the first Witch to be caught by her hard views. And you won't be the last."

"That makes me feel better." I shake my limbs free from tension. "Right, so how do I access it?"

"You meditate until you get it right."

"Get what right?"

"The connection. It's different from other elements. You can really speak to the earth. It kind of vibrates back at you."

I gasp, looking at her with wide eyes. "What did you just say?"

"It communicates back at you. Like it's alive."

That's why the no one has seen anything like the Otherworld Gate! Because it's Witch and Fae magic together, and they haven't worked together since before the original Horsemen's time. It's earth magic I was feeling that day at the Black Gate.

"I think I've done that before, but it was a bit different then."

"Let's try repeating yourself, then. What were you doing back then?"

I'm not sure telling this child is a good idea. "I'm not sure I can say. I was dealing with a very old, very complex piece of magic, and as I was trying to figure it out, it vibrated back at me, guided me through the puzzle."

"Definitely earth magic of some type. Let's try to do that again." She sits on the earth cross-legged and closes her eyes, breathing in deeply. "Just try to feel your surroundings. Allow yourself to be open and let the magic come to you, rather than reaching out for it."

I follow her, also sitting cross-legged and closing my eyes. An open mind. "But my mind is always busy. How do I also keep it open?"

She laughs to herself. "Sorry, I just remember when I asked that question. My trainer told me to think through all my thoughts, all the possible combinations I can, and then live in the echoing emptiness that follows."

Think all my thoughts? "You're aware the entire world is on my shoulders and I'm a mess, right?"

"Yeah, I think this will take a while for you, but it's worth trying, anyway."

"Alright." Think all my thoughts. Well, there's the elections that are coming up for the Vampires, and I hope Victor wins. He's a decent Vampire with a great view of the world. And then there's Lucien and Red, who I really want to see happy but who are getting in their own way. Aki, the Fae Queen, Felicity, Arrie's insistence on working on our communication, Connie's hesitation last night with Arrie . . . And the list goes. But I allow every single one of them to pass through me. To think about them and move past them. Not let them hold sway over me. To not get stuck with them. I can always think about them tomorrow.

And when all the thoughts were done, when my brain had finally thought about everything on its to-think list, it was a little emptier. I'm not sure my worries will ever go, nor the pain and the bad memories. But it's roomier in here now. There's space to grow.

"Okay, I think it's emptier."

"Good. Now feel the surrounding earth. That feeling you get when you're walking through the forest or when you're breathing in the morning air . . . find that here's version of that."

It's just earth. There's nothing here.

But I reach my senses out, anyway. I heighten my hearing and my touch and my smell, and before I know it, my senses are filling with earth. The smell of the minerals, the organic matter, the worms tracing tunnels beneath me, the beetles scurrying across the ground, the spiders making homes in the crevices.

And something larger scurrying across the surface.

I hone in on it, traveling behind it, seeing where it goes, mapping the surface of the cavern out in my mind. It's like I can see, but I can't. My eyes are closed. But the entire cavern is before me in feelings, senses, and maps—all in my head. "This is amazing."

"Yeah, it is." She gasps, then instructs, "Open your eyes."

I snap my eyes open and see dirt and gravel floating all around us, frozen in place. "Are you doing that?"

"Nope."

"I'm doing that?" I ask tentatively as I stand and reach out for a small stone.

"Yup." She's smiling. "You're brilliant. It takes most Witches months to get this far. To connect. But it's like the connection is already there, ready for the taking."

"I can't believe I'm doing this." I jump a little, excited that I finally unlocked my earth powers. But the rocks around us fall, and I quickly zap up an air barrier above our heads, letting the stones roll off and onto the floor. "Sorry."

"And you can change between elements pretty quickly, too."

I grab a fireball in my left hand as I conjure a ball of water in my right, then send them zooming around the space.

"Both at the same time?"

"Uh-huh. I made a waterspout the other day by combining air and water. Famine reckons that the reason I was given so many individual powers is not simply so that I can fit in with multiple species but so that I can use them together and adapt to whatever situation I'm in."

"Flexibility," she confirms. "It's a power in itself. And this is just Witch abilities. You have Fae spells and Vampire strength and the ability to turn into any animal you wish."

"Don't forget the death magic." I laugh. "But seriously, maybe forget about it. I don't like people knowing that I have that ability. The world is already unsure of me."

"You're like marmite, Magic." She looks up at me with

reverence and fondness. "You divide people. But it's an honor to have such an important role in your growth."

"You are a very wise twelve-year-old, you know."

She shrugs. "People say I'm old for my age because I'm an orphan who has to look after her two younger siblings."

"Didn't you say Mom yesterday?"

"Grandma. She's Mom. But she's old. She can't really run around after Eli and Ferra."

"I understand your pain. I was an orphan, too. Though I only had myself to look out for, and I grew up with the Witches in the US."

"What happened to your parents?"

"Hunters. Angel-descended Witches are sought after and killed by the SC because of the power of their magic."

"Yeah, it sucks. They used to be the most powerful among us. Revered for their power. Well, that's what the ancient archives say."

"How far back do the archives go?"

She shrugs. "Not a clue, but at least a thousand years because I was reading about the Horsemen in the Middle Ages just yesterday."

"Hmmm, interesting. Thank you."

"If you want access to them, you'll have to petition the Coven Council."

A groan slips from my mouth before I can catch it, and we both laugh.

"If you were nicer to them originally, they wouldn't be so

hard on you."

"Hey! Some of them like me."

She holds up a single finger. "One. The seer likes you. For some reason." She gathers some dirt in her fingers and places it into the palm of my hand. "Let's try something else. Try the same thing you did earlier, but with this pile of earth specifically. Homing in the sensory connection is a skill. It might take time."

"Okay. Let's go." I had great success with the first task, I'm hoping that I'll be a natural with this.

Alas, I was wrong. I am shit at this.

Every time I try to hone in on the pile of stupid dirt, my focus snaps and I zoom out again. "It's like an elastic band."

"Right, but this elastic band can be trained to stretch further. Your homework for this lesson is to keep practising this. You can't really do much to topple the mountain without being able to ignore the earth around it first. Otherwise, pop goes the forest. The river. The land. The—"

"Yup. Get the picture. Pop goes Magic and their team, too."

"Speaking of team . . . Are you in a relationship with Famine?"

"Yes. And the rest of them too. We're a polycule."

"Like the seer and her two husbands?"

"Yeah, like that. But Death and Famine have a relationship together too."

"Oh, I see." She shoos me home, saying she has her own

training to get to.

Which makes sense, she's a child. She probably has some kind of formal education to get to.

But when I get home, it's darker than expected. "It's night?"

How the fuck does this time zone thing work across the realms?

Chapter Fifty-Four

Looking at the clock in the kitchen, I realize it's only seven pm, it's just getting dark a little early right now. Apparently. "I swear, this realm is as strange as me." Looking at the counter, there's a steaming pile of tacos and a note. Dinner can be reheated for five minutes in the microwave on full power. We're chilling in the theater — Arrie

Awww, he made me dinner.

I reheat the tacos, following the instructions to the T, and then find my way down the dark stairs and into the theater, where they're watching some cartoon about a talking dog.

Must have been Nine's turn to choose.

They're all lounging on the couch that's hovering in the

air, so I shoot myself and my tacos up there to join them, and settle on the other side of Arrie, who snakes an arm around my shoulders.

"Thanks for dinner."

He kisses my temple and says, "You're welcome."

"Shhh," Nine complains, "you'll miss the best joke!"

Yup. It's his pick.

Comfort films are allowed in this house.

No judgement here. Cartoons are fun.

Knew there was a reason I fell in love with you.

Do the others not like them very much?

Eh. I think they put up with them for me.

Well, no putting up here. I'll watch them with you whenever you like.

We watch another film after that one but on the bed, and somehow, we fall asleep there, in our clothes, all of us exhausted. And I notice that all of us are touching Nine somehow; whether it be a finger or a foot or an arm, none of us let him go.

Something tells me going to war again is going to be tough. He's getting the easiest jobs.

But in the morning, I'm the first one awake for a change. So I take advantage of the morning silence and go for a run through the forest, then start my regular yoga routine, where I attempt to do my homework, but I quickly get frustrated and have to do breathing exercises to calm down.

Eventually, I call it a day and head to the shower. The

nice, refreshing cool water dripping down my back and legs, cooling me off.

Maybe I could see Korby today and work on my bo stuff. I haven't seen her in ages. Or maybe just see her in general.

Breakfast is on the table by the time I reach the kitchen, and I gobble it up with vigor and then run off, kissing them all on the lips, lingering a little longer on Nine's. "Going to see Korby! Be back later." And I run out the door.

Korby is staying in an apartment above the pub, where she works most nights. I offered to buy her a place (or make her one), but she said she prefers living a modest life, where work keeps her busy and life keeps her entertained.

I knock on her door at nine-thirty, which I didn't think through, because she opens it with a scowl and growls, "What are you doing here at this stupid hour?"

"Oops. Thought I'd pop in to see how you're doing?"

"I've only been asleep for five hours, Magic!"

"I can come back later?" But I'm peering into her apartment, seeing what it looks like, being nosey, and she sighs.

"No, it's okay. But you're putting up with my bad mood until I'm fully awake."

"Deal. I'll even buy us breakfast."

"Done."

She lets me enter, and I'm seeing myself around, having a nosey, when someone steps out of the bedroom. Someone distinctly male. "Oh my goddess, I didn't know you had company. I'm sorry. I'll meet you in the café and—"

Korby laughs, flustering at my embarrassment. "That's what you get for coming knocking at such an ungodly hour."

She did this on purpose!

Korby and the guy have a quiet conversation that I don't listen to, at all, and then he leaves.

"He's just . . . a repetitive one-night stand. Nothing too big. Well . . ."

I snort over the glass of water I poured myself. "A repetitive one-night stand is a sort-of relationship, you know."

"Yeah, but he's a Fae. And I always wanted to settle down with another bunny. Create more bunnies."

I almost gag at the normalcy with which she says that.

"It's a Shifter thing. We do interbreed, but it's not common."

Curiosity peaked, I ask, "Why not?"

She shrugs. "We're just more attracted to our own breed, I guess. It's not a hate thing. Wolves especially stick to their own. In fact, most predators do."

"So being with a Fae is especially unusual."

"Precisely." She makes us coffee, and I just about go weak at the knees. "Want a cup?"

"Yes, please. And I'd marry you for some creamer. Seriously, they don't have that here, and I've been meaning to ask the house, but I keep forgetting."

Korby drags a carton out of the fridge and shakes it at me. "You Americans are good for two things: coffee and tacos."

"Just two?"

424

She shrugs. "Culinarily speaking, yes. But I'm Japanese. I don't put a lot of stock into non-fresh food." She holds up a finger. "Except tacos. You rule the taco world."

As we drink our cups of coffee, I once again apologize for waking her up and disturbing her morning after. "You know, you should consider keeping the Fae. They're super handy with spells and technology, and they dance great."

She frowns at her coffee mug.

"You're here, in *Sheruta*, and I don't think Shifters are so familiar here."

"No, they're not. I already asked. Nobody thinks me being with a Fae would be weird. In fact, there are other Shifter-Fae couples here in town."

"Then, what's the problem?"

"I like you. I do. But I didn't plan to stay here indefinitely, just as long as you need me."

I wrap her in my arms and breathe in her orangey scent. "You're my friend, I'll always need you. But you are just one teleport away. I'll be happy with wherever you're happy."

"And when I figure that out, you'll be the first to know."

"Come on, there's loads to *Sheruta* I haven't had the time to see, like the mall. Wanna go exploring?"

"Fuck yeah. But breakfast first, right?"

"Absolutely."

Shifters and their appetites always surprise me, but with constantly shifting back and forth, it's not a surprise. It takes serious energy. Maybe I should eat more and I'd be less tired.

Shopping with Korby is loads of fun—she has the enthusiasm and the stamina to keep up. We go into all sorts of shops on the way to the mall: tea, clothes, chocolate, various technology establishments, magical bits and pieces, including a hair dye and removal spell for Connie.

But when we get to the mall, my tiny little mind explodes into oohs and aahs as I look up at the ten floors you navigate by floating platforms that have plants spilling over the edges. Advertisement plasmascreens are everywhere, trying to sell you everything from certain Shifter scents to love potions.

"Love potions are bogus, by the way," I say to Korby. "Not possible."

"Yeah, most people assume as much. Wanna get lunch? I'm starving."

"We only just had breakfast . . ." I look to the clock on the tower in the center of the mall and gasp. "Four hours ago?"

"We've been shopping for a while," Korby says with a laugh. "Besides, don't you feed with your meals?"

Feed? "Oh, that. No, I typically just have some in the morning and then whenever I'm hungry."

"Well, we can order whatever we want from any of the restaurants from the food portals."

"Food portals?"

Korby points to the queues lining up in front of a row plasmascreens. "You order from any of the restaurants, and the food comes down the shoots." She points to the crowd of people awaiting their orders.

"That's clever." I assume it's not actual portal magic, but whatever, still cool. "Reckon they sell noodles here?"

"They have a pretty good ramen stall, actually. Not quite as good as home, but it still tastes great."

"Then let's go!" I grab her hand and yank her to the back of the line, which manages to go down pretty quickly despite its length. I shifted forms an hour ago when we bought me some more masculine clothes, trying out different styles until we found something that works. "Thanks for the help with the guy shopping. I hadn't been yet."

"Putting it off?"

"Yeah," I nod. "I'm more comfortable with who I am now, but it was shaky for a while there. And shopping for the part of yourself you're still scared of is kinda . . . unnerving."

"That reminds me of how some Shifters feel," Korby says as we reach the screen and she places her order. "Some Shifters have a hard time feeling comfortable with their shifted forms, like it's some kind of demon inside them." She shrugs. "It's more common with predatory species."

"I don't spend a lot of time in my Shifter forms either, to be honest." I place my own order. "I just spend so much time mastering my other forms. Their magic is harder, more complicated. My Shifter stuff gets left behind."

"The predators go for a run through the northern woods every morning, if you wanted to join them. Even Nigel goes."

"What about you?"

Korby smiles as she picks up our orders from the shoot.

"We prey species live together. The apartment I'm in above the pub is connected to the ones behind me. It allows us to feel safe and connected, and to have giant cuddle piles whenever we like."

After we sat and ate lunch, we started hitting some of the magic shops, because some of the best ones are here at the mall.

"Thinking of getting some of those air shoes that've just come out," Korby says. "Then I could hover around the bar and be quicker." So she picks up a pair and adds it to her basket. "It took me ages to get used to not being able to use my datachip here."

"Right. Everyone on Earth just scans the items and leaves. I forget about that." We don't have datachips, so we just take them up to the cashier. "One day, I'm getting a fucking chip. Fuck the others." I turn to the makeup behind me and oooh at a color-changing lipstick that I can't not pick up. You just squeeze your lips together and cycle through until you land on the right shade. Like a color wheel.

"I'm glad we went shopping today," Korby says as we head into a bakery on our way home. "You've been training too much."

"Agreed. But it's hard to take breaks knowing you could miss an important lesson that would save an entire species."

"Fair point." She takes a bite out of her pecan twist. "But counter point: you can't save the world unless you're the best you you can be, and you can't be that without taking breaks."

"So you're saying that shopping and pastries are me saving the world?" A laugh slips free as I also dig into my pecan twist. "I could get on board with that."

Magic? Emergency. Come home!

"Shit." I whip my staff out and teleport us to the kitchen, where Arrie is bleeding out on the tiles, looking like death. "Arrie!"

Chapter Fifty-Five

"Arrie!" I drop my shopping bags and rush to his side, where Dea's healing him. "What happened?"

Lo is circling above us, the size of my head. "We were attacked during training."

"So that's where you've been lately?"

"Been . . . training . . . in . . . Jura Mountains."

"Magic," Lo cautions, "they need help."

Okay. Okay, okay, okay. "First things first, Dea, stay here and help Arrie into bed and heal him." I look to Connie and Nine, both of whom have never been to the Jura Mountains and shake my head. Connie's the better fighter. "Connie, hand your plasmascreen to Nine and go grab your shit." I turn to Lo. "Go with Nine, help him update the embassy and grab the rest of our army, then teleport to me. I'll teleport back and take everyone to the Jura Mountains. Korby, you don't have to do anything—"

"I'm coming with you." She grabs our bags and places them on the dining room table. "But I need to get changed, so I'll be with Nine when you come and get us." She runs out of the house, faster than a regular human, but slow for a Shifter.

Everyone else disperses, Dea carrying Arrie up the stairs, Connie getting changed and grabbing her weapons, and Nine and Lo running out of the door.

After two dress changes—one in each form—and making sure I have my charms set to what I want on my staff, throwing knives strapped to my thighs and daggers to my hips, I'm ready to go.

Connie runs into me as I'm coming out of my room and grabs my arm before we teleport to the Jura Mountains.

The mountains loom in the distance, but I barely notice them behind the chaos exploding in front of me. Our army is spread thin, struggling to hold on, while the enemy decimate us blow after blow. Pushing us back.

We're losing.

And without Arrie, I don't know any of our defense strategies. Much less formations or attack combinations or anything like that. "I need the next in command."

Connie looks around and spots Red throwing fireballs, then drags my gaze that way. "There."

I fly us over and we land next to her. Three daggers fell the two soldiers at Red's back while a couple of arrows handle the two at her front.

"Red!"

"Yeah?" she shouts from a few feet away, out of breath.

"Arrie's down. We need you to take charge. Nine and the rest of our army are on their way, but it'll be a few minutes."

"I don't think we have a few minutes." She grunts as a knife scratches her arm and she flinches away. Then she spins and hurls a small fire tornado at the attacking group to her left. "We're outnumbered, and they took us by surprise."

"Shit." I look behind us and realize there are villages there. Innocent people. "We can't let them get through us. There are innocent civilians in those villages."

"I know that. I was hoping you'd swoop in and do your godly magic shit!"

"Err, right." I turn to Connie, use a spell to trip up the two soldiers trying their best to get anywhere near her, and watch as she takes them out with a single arrow to the head each. "Work with Red to retreat our soldiers to beyond the hill behind us. I'll cover us."

"Got it!"

I shift forms and fly into the sky, looking down from above, seeing if there's anything I missed. There are more of their soldiers coming through the mountains. Far more. We need to put a stop to that. Now.

Flying myself over there, I know what I need to do. Only,

I'm not sure I can do it. I settle on top of the rock on one side of the pass, kneeling on the rugged stone, taking ragged breaths of icy air.

My hands fall onto the stone, and I seek it out. The essence of the mountain. But I can't find it. Every time I go anywhere near it, it slips away like air in the desert. What did Zara say? To clear my mind and let it come to me.

Okay. Alright.

I block out the background thumping of the soldiers marching through the pass below me, the screams of the dying behind me, and the grunts and pants of our soldiers fighting for their lives. I simply focus on the surrounding earth. The rock beneath me, the little tufts of resistant grass poking through the cracks and the moss and lichen starting new life atop a mountain that clearly doesn't want it here. I reach out my magic and hold it out, inviting the earth in. And I wait patiently.

Okay, maybe not so patiently. But there is a war going on behind me.

Something lands on my shoulder, and the magical essence is familiar. "Lo. Hi."

"Hello, Magic. We are ready whenever you are."

"Be riiiight there." I breathe in through my mouth and out through my nostrils and wait in silence.

And I wait. And I wait.

Until eventually something touches the edges of my aether. Something strong and foreboding yet gentle and lenient in its giving. Hello mountain.

It vibrates under my hand, tickling my magic.

I need a favor from you. Would you mind breaking and blocking the path? If you would like me to fix you back up again later, I can, but for now, we need to block those footsteps from getting any closer to the valley.

And again I wait until it's ready to answer me.

Eventually, it links itself to me, and all of a sudden, I can push and pull, move the rock. Like it's joined forces with me. Wrapped its fingers through mine. I push on the edges of the mountain, and when it doesn't move, I push harder.

I push so hard that I can feel blood dripping from my nose and air huffing out of my mouth. But it crumples piece by piece, until it's falling down, the crash and echo of stone upon stone piercing the valley.

Thank you.

And I un-tether the connection, reminding myself to come back and fix it, if that's what it wants.

"Join the fight, Lo." I stamp my staff on the mountain top. "I'll be back with an army."

The army in question is in the field behind our house, I find out after flying over *Sheruta* to find it. Probably should have asked Lo where they were. Lesson learned.

Right now, I have to get them all to the Jura Mountains as quickly as possible. So I enlarge the spell's radius like I did in the tunnel in New Orleans and take a deep breath. Okay.

"Time to go," I make the wind carry to every soldier.

They take deep breaths and ready themselves, some holding knives and guns in their grips.

And I teleport four thousand soldiers into a battlefield in a single swoop.

Chapter Fifty-Six

Hikers Ordered to Return Home from Jura Mountains: War Ongoing

Chaos reigns. The sounds of gunfire, swords clashing, and fiery explosions ricochet off the mountainous rock around us, creating a valley of noise. The villages start a mile to the east, and we can't let them get that far.

But so far, our retreat hasn't helped.

A badass she may be, but Red is not a trained commander.

Nine?

Yeah? he asks, sounding out of breath.

We're splitting the battlefield into nine sections, I say as I fly high above, looking down on everything. Like a grid. And I'm going to maneuver you all around like chess pieces. I need you to relay messages to each section, so buckle up.

Buckle up? For whaaaaa?

I swoop down and grab him by the underarms, yanking him into the sky. "See this?" I think up a mental image of grid lines across the battlefield, dividing everyone up. "I want to use it."

Okay. What first?

See those two fire Witches in A2? Have them move to A1 and dispatch the Fae throwing water whips everywhere. Then move the bear Shifter in B3 over to B2. They're the biggest area with the most number of enemies, so they need heavier fighters.

Then let's move Cas and Dan from C2 up as well. They're the strongest Fae we have.

No, split them up. One to B2 and one to A2.

Done.

I watch the soldiers we picked move around the battlefield, barreling through enemies along the way, dodging others, until they're where they can do the most damage.

Once the fire Witches now in A1 have helped thin the water specializing Fae, I send them to B1 to help dispose of some highborn Vampires causing havoc with their stupidly good natural defense. Some unfriendly fire out to sort them out.

What next?

B2 are still struggling, but I don't see another move we can make.

Okay, send us to B2.

I fly us down there and drop us onto the field. It's more chaotic down here amidst the fighting, where I can't see the grid lines and I can't tell where section B2 ends and begins.

But there are three Vampires and a terrifying number of crows coming at me, so I can't afford to get confused.

I blow the crows into the nearest mountain rock with enough force to splatter blood over the surrounding tufts of grass.

The three Vampires charge at full speed and circle me before I have the time to react. Shit. I'm cornered.

Their menacing grins dagger at my insides as they hiss, hands in fists at their sides.

My best move right now is to counter.

The one on my left charges at me, fingernails the length of claws (and probably just as strong too), but it's the green liquid oozing off them that forces me to dodge him first swing. They're poison, I'll bet. He swings again, and I duck then roll out of the way. But when he swings again, I grab his arm and twist it behind him, then yank.

A sickening pop sounds. Followed by his screams.

The other two are in front of me now, but I have more room to maneuver, so I light them up, controlling the flames, not allowing them to travel farther than I say so. And upon my exhale, I extinguish them.

I'm starting to find all this fighting surprisingly calm.

I'm pretty sure that's not a good sign.

We can get you therapy later, Nine says as I turn around to find him straddling a Fae with an explosion rune in his palm.

"Nine, look out!"

Instinctually, I hurl a knife at the Fae's head and watch it sink to the floor with a thud.

Nine looks at me in surprise, his eyes wide and his mouth parted. *I knew that rune was there, Sweetie.*

Right. Of course he did. Telepathy, Magic.

But thank you for the assist.

One of Connie's arrows flies past my head, the fletching brushing my face. A shout behind me follows, then a curse. And I spin to find Phillipe crouching in the grass, his knee felled by an arrow.

She meant to hit him there.

Why?

Because the king requested him alive.

Oh, right.

I shift, and a binding spell slips from my fingertips like a breath of wind on a morning breeze. Easy. Effortless.

But Phillipe thuds to the ground, his limbs bound. "I'll gut you like the worm you are, Magic!"

"Yeah, yeah." I grab my staff and point the teleporting crystal at him, hoping my plan will work. "Get in line." And I send him to the embassy's holding cells I briefly remember from the tour everyone gave me upon opening. "I really hope he made it there."

Shrugging, I decide that I don't really care if he did or didn't. A happy accident in the making if there ever was one.

Nothing like an old Vampire prince to torture and maim. Well, alright, I'll probably not torture and maim him, but the idea still makes me smile. A person can dream.

Turning back to the battle, I blast air in several directions, hoping they'll smash against more rocks. But once I've cleared the surrounding area, I realize we're just getting rid of the last drudges.

"It's over."

"Yup," Connie says, putting an arm around me. "Wasn't that hard."

I eye her up and down—not a speck of a dirt on the woman—and laugh. "Only because I brought in reinforcements and sealed off the only path the enemy could use to get here."

"Oh, was that you?" she asks, sarcasm lacing her words. "Never would have guessed."

Red laughs besides her, then checks the wounded, including the enemies, and sets up a makeshift infirmary for us to use.

And I help. Because I injured a lot of these people. And guilt is gnawing its way into my heart.

Chapter Fifty-Seven

Man or Woman? What Does the Magic Horseman Mean for Non-Cis Gender Communities?

I send Nine home to check on Dea and Arrie, see how the embassy is doing. Many aren't fighters. And they need to be updated. Not to mention many of them relay information back to different species' councils and other bodies of important people.

In the meantime, Connie gets stuck in helping gently carry some of the wounded to the nearby village alongside some Vampire, Shifter, and air Witch helpers. All using their magic for good.

"Isn't it weird?" I ask Connie as she places another wounded down on the grass, this one missing a leg. "To be going from violent murder to gentle healer in the space of a few minutes?"

"This is what war is like, Magic. It's why we like to avoid it."

"She's right," a village healer called Kiara says. "You saved us today. And part of that meant defending against people who would do you harm if they could. But this"—she gestures to the rows upon rows of wounded soldiers, ours and theirs—"is a great mercy. It shows compassion."

Connie leaves, going back to continue carrying the wounded over.

The Witches and Fae have started helping us, creating fresh water, sterilizing needles and other equipment, getting a cooking fire going, cooling patients down with a cold wind, and creating comfier beds of grass and moss on slightly raised platforms.

I've been using my Vampire blood to save the most critical patients, and the few healers have been listing their injuries as I've gone. It's good system. But I need Dea. Only my blood can heal; I can't do anything for broken bones or non-critical things with the number of wounded in the thousands.

As if on cue, Nine teleports back in with a tired-looking Dea in tow. He fazes over and Nine teleports back. "What do you need?"

"Help. I'm helping the most critical patients, but some are in agony with broken bones and cracked skulls and missing limbs."

"I can heal the less major wounds, but I cannot do anything for missing limbs other than seal the wound and keep it clean."

Kiara steps in, putting her bowl of water down. "Then heal the broken bones so we can send those patients on their way. In the meantime, I will continue to help those missing limbs or organs."

"Use some of the fire Witches to help you cauterize the wounds in the field."

She nods once, the stern lady that she is, and rushes off. I have no idea what species she is, but she's a . . . to-the-point old woman.

Dea and I get to work, and by the time we've gotten through the soldiers already here, Connie and her small army of strong helpers bring in the next batch. So the moment there's a makeshift bed free for them or a new set made, they're laid down and we get to work.

This goes on for hours. And before we know it, darkness is setting in and the Witches are setting up witchlights along with Fae who are creating illuminating spell bead clusters that I desperately want the spell to. They're so pretty. (Or would be if, you know, they weren't illuminating the dying or critically wounded.)

Nothing, and I seriously mean nothing, feels better than the comfy patch of grass I find to sprawl out and nap in. The healers and makeshift nurses have been tagging in and out, using a nearby space they've fashioned into a sort of rest area.

I grab a large bowl of broth off the tray someone is handing out, and when he asks if I'd rather have something better from the nearby village kitchen, I decline and say this will be fine.

Then I tag back in and spread some more drops of blood around the most critically wounded and watch as their skin knits back together and their bones snap back into place. It looks painful, but they do nothing more than sigh a breath of relief. It might block their pain receptors at the same time as heal them. I don't know.

A familiar grumpy face storms over the hill carrying three bodies lain on top one another, his ragged hair in clumps over his shoulders. He places them gently into spare beds near me and forces me to spin around and look at him. "You're okay?" he asks, checking my head, shoulders, torso, then limbs. "Shift."

I shift into my male form so he can repeat the same process.

And I watch his face go from on edge to relaxed in a matter of seconds. "You're okay."

I nod, but I feel a little shaky, if I'm honest. "Just a little light-headed." I let another drop of blood fall in the Shifter lion's snout and watch its ribs crack back into place and its skin and muscle stitch back together. "There's many people to heal."

"How long have you been at this?"

"Well, it was light when I started. But I did nap and eat earlier."

444

Arrie growls low in his throat, clearly unhappy with my personal caretaking skills. He picks me up bridal style and carries me over to the edge of the makeshift hospital, then further to a rocky outcropping, where he places me on my butt. "Feed." He holds out his wrist. "Now."

"You've just recovered, Arrie. I don't want to—"

His snarl cuts me off. "Feed."

"Okay, okay." I snatch his wrist and sink my fangs in, letting his forest-tasting blood hit my tongue and trail a path of beauty down my throat.

The only sign this is having any effect on him is the slight heaviness to his breathing and the hand running through his hair and settling on his neck.

The moment I feel better, I stop. Pulling back.

"Better?"

I fold my arms over my chest and stand back up, heading back to work. "Yes."

Which makes Arrie laugh. "You are too stubborn for your own good."

I turn back around just before I hit the first line of beds. "Then it's a good job I have such a caring boyfriend."

Smugness radiates off him in waves, and I walk back to where I was with a pep in my step as I heal the next dying man, a Vampire I remember flying into a rock. He doesn't even notice it's me as I fix him up. But when he comes to, his leaking throat having stopped bleeding and sewn itself shut, he screams at the sight of me.

"Hey, hey, shhh . . ." I try to calm. "I'm not going to hurt you. I just healed you."

But there's no consoling him.

"Oi!" the wolf next to him whacks him on the shoulder. "Quit your hollerin'. She could have left you for dead out there, but she organized an army to help all wounded, regardless of side."

His eyes finally lay upon mine, widened shock in them. A short, gruff, "Thanks," rips from his lips. Then he turns over in his bed.

"You're welcome. Someone will be along with food in a moment. Blood pills are on hand, too." I move onto the next patient, trying to put his screams out of my mind.

This sucks.

And there's nothing I can do about it.

Aki is forcing my hand. I have to be the bad guy. But I so desperately wish I didn't have to be. Though, I guess I could have gone easier on the opposing soldiers—I even flew some of them into mush against the mountain—but I was so focused on the battle, on protecting our people, on keeping the villages safe, that I couldn't think of anything else.

Damn, this sucks.

I drop five drops of my blood into a wounded Witch's mouth and watch seven broken bones mend, a half fallen-off leg sew itself back together, and a sigh of relief leave his mouth.

"Thank you, Magic," he whispers before falling asleep.

"You're welcome."

Connie leads the charge once more, bringing more wounded through, but half of her soldiers come over the hill empty handed. Could it be?

"That's the last of them," she informs us. "The field is empty of survivors."

A sigh of relief escapes my mouth for the first time tonight. "Could you set something up for the dead? Organize them to be teleported back to their families in coffins?"

"Sure, but it'll take a while."

Brutus claps me on the back. "Some fighting there, Magic. Ma says we'll handle the teleporting and finding of the families if you supply the teleporting crystals and coffins."

"Done." Connie shakes his hand. "I'll have those to you in a few days."

"There's a batch of a hundred teleporting crystals in the baskets outside my room."

Connie nods that she's heard, but she's off, organizing food, supplies, and rejoining our army's hierarchy. Re-solidifying our defense. She was the best choice.

Yeah, she was. I spin on my heels to find Nine sat upon a rock at the edge of the last line of wounded soldiers. *C'mere.*

I seek him out and end up in his arms, breathing in his bonfire and ink and paper smell, letting it fill me up. "I missed you."

"I've not been gone long," he chuckles.

"I don't think I'll ever not miss you again."

"Dea says the same thing." We watch our Angel of Death make his way on unsteady feet through the final line of wounded, nearly collapsing. "We should probably . . ."

"Yup." We both get to our feet and walk his way, and just as his eyelids flutter and his knees give way, I catch him. "I'm going to take him home. I've done everything I can do here, anyway."

"Okay. Need anything from here?"

"Don't think so. Could you check in with Connie and ask when she's coming home? Sorry, don't mean to treat you like a relationship PA."

It's okay. I'll go check in with your girlfriend.

Thank you.

Arrie's standing behind me and grabs Dea for me, hauling his passed-out form over his shoulder. "Ready to go home?"

"Yeah, I've done everything I can do. And I need like three days' worth of sleep." We walk to an empty area, wait for Nine to return, and then I teleport us back to my bed.

"No sex. No food. No showering. Just sleep."

"Sleep," Arrie agrees. "We can shower and fuck in the morning." He lays Dea down on the edge of the bed and snuggles in on the other side, leaving the duvet open for us. "Ready?"

I yank all my clothes off and fall into bed beside Arrie, Nine joining me on the other side, snuggles between myself and Dea.

"What did Connie say?"

"That she wants to make sure everyone is well and the villages are okay before she leaves. And to remind you that she doesn't need as much sleep as us."

"Right. Never ending stamina. Forgot."

Chapter Fifty-Eight

Jura Mountains: Fae Queen Attacks Secret Base Orga-nization

I want to sleep in the next day, to join Arrie in my shower, to lie in bed with Dea and Nine, who are cuddled up under my duvet making out. But a little annoying prince is waiting for me in the kitchen. Like a dickhead.

"Best get going, Sweetie. You don't want to keep his high-ness waiting."

"Shut up." I squeeze my butt into the suit trousers, zipping up, and then I'm out the door without a second to spare. "Love you all!" I call behind me as I rush down the stairs.

Lucien does not look happy with how late I'm making us. His arms folded, a scowl on his face, his foot tapping away impatiently on the floor. "You're late."

"I don't know if you heard, but there was a fucking war at the Jura Mountains. I've only been back for, like, five hours. Back off."

He flinches. "Sorry. I'm still annoyed with Red."

"She fought well. And she's alive with nothing more than a few scratches."

You could practically see the panic and tension leech out of him. "That's . . . good. That's good."

"C'mon." I grab his arm and teleport to the Vampire Council building. "We're already late."

The king waits for us in the same room as earlier. And instead of the rude, impatient greeting I got from his son, he's standing there with nothing but a smile. "Magic, Lucien. You've managed to join us." He greets me with a kiss on the cheek (yes, even in male form, which is weird and endearing and wrong all mixed into one). "I was worried you wouldn't make it given recent developments."

"Everyone is doing okay, but we lost many."

"Magic is doing well on five hours of sleep," Prince Lucien comments.

"Only in this form," I joke. "My other form is still stuck in pajamas as I ran out of time to get both forms ready."

Everyone laughs, both of them finding my two form antics hilarious, apparently.

One of the Vampires running in the election chips in. "So, you can only switch into whatever clothes you were wearing in that form last?"

"Yeah. It's a bit of a pain really." I take a seat in the same place as before. "Thank goddess both forms share an energy source, or I'd have to eat twice, too."

"Wow. You're, like, one of the most interesting people I've ever met."

Interesting good? Or interesting bad? Eh. Never mind. Interesting good because I'm fantastic.

After five minutes of prep, the cameras roll, and the Vampire king announces to the world that the winner, by a landslide, is Victor Hesham. We all clap, even the losers, and everyone enjoys those fancy triangle sandwiches and blood that's been decanted into wine glasses. Which I pass on, naturally.

Once the cameras have stopped rolling, the other two candidates make their excuses and leave, but the four of us gather around and have a drink to Victor's success.

"Good luck, Victor. And I hope you make all the differences you dream of."

He shakes my hand with a warm smile. "I look forward to working with you."

A few minutes later, three new Vampires take their seats, all of whom I haven't met before, and we start the process all over again. I try to pay attention. I really do. But my mind is racing. And everything rushes around me like blurry cars on the highway.

When will the next attack be? Where will it be? How many people will die?

I know Aki's in Tokyo, so maybe I could find him and deal with him there, instead of waiting and always being on the defensive. But that would make me the bad guy, right? We're only supposed to help, to guide. Not to act out of our own opinions and biases. But he's my brother. He killed my boyfriend. How am I supposed to not hate him?

And what about the Fae Queen? What do I do with her? She's trying to take over the SC and put her species on top of the others, to rule with a Fae fist, as it were. But she can't. That defeats the point of the pillar communities and the Supernatural Council's very existence.

And Phillipe is in the embassy's cells awaiting whatever the hell I'm supposed to do with him. I've been meaning to tell Lucien and the king, but I haven't found the right time. I guess without all these ears around. Maybe after we're done.

Will taking Phillipe out of the fight even remove the Rogue Vampire Faction? Won't they just employ someone else? Or is he the only thing holding them together?

Pretty sure if we remove Aki and the Fae Queen, we can smooth things over and put someone else on the Fae throne. So that's something. At least.

Checking back in with my surroundings, the third Vampire is talking about creating a new blood supply to remove the need for the blood pills. And anger simmers beneath the surface. Nine worked himself stupid creating those. Stop being such an ungrateful ass.

Unbiased, Magic. Unbiased.

Goddess, I'm bad at this.

But it's over before I know it, and they're leaving to go back to whatever political candidates do in their spare time and I'm finally alone with Lucien and the king.

"We have Phillipe in a cell in the embassy," I say the moment the door closes. "What do you want me to do with him?"

The king gestures us to sit and releases a held breath. "It has been a long twenty-four hours. Let us have some more blood and food, and then we can update each other."

Nodding, we all agree.

"And, Magic, if you would like to switch forms, I care not for your pajama'd look."

Laughing, I politely decline. No need to tell him I'm naked and still aching from last night. I think I'll stick to this form.

A few moments later, a servant arrives with a trolley of more food and blood, which I obviously decline. But the muffins look good, so I help myself to yet more food.

"Stress eating, great. That's all I need," I mumble.

"If anyone has a good excuse for stress eating, little Horseman, it's you." Lucien smirks at me. "Do you have an update on how many we lost?"

I nod, not liking the figure Connie gave me. "Too many. 876, of which, 239 were Vampires."

Lucien and the king are both silent, their gazes to the floor. "I'm sorry."

"It is not your fault. We would have lost far more if you

454

were not there." He reframes his face and says, "The Supernatural Council messaged all the pillar communities this morning saying they're disbanding any military actions and removing themselves from the Fae Queen's side. They wish to remain impartial during this trying time."

I can't help it, I smile. "I'll take that. Impartial is good enough."

"And you caught Phillipe yesterday?" Prince Lucien asks. After I nod confirming, he continues. "So now it's just Aki and the Fae Queen."

"I know where Aki is, but I don't think a battle in the biggest city in the world between the two of us is a good idea. And if I lure him anywhere, he'll bring the entire army."

"You can't avoid the war that's coming," Lucien says, his wisdom voice turned all the way up. "Even if you manage to deal with your evil twin, we still have to deal with the Fae Queen and her army."

"Lucien is right," the king says. "We've had many battles over the past few months, but the one coming will be what we have been preparing for."

"I just wish I knew where it would be. That way we could plan accordingly."

The king smiles at me, a plan forming in his mind. "If you draw him out, and he brings an army, then you do not need to know. You picked the place."

"That is . . . right."

"I am not king for nothing, Magic." He laughs, lighthearted and amused. "There's juice in this old goat yet."

Which sounds ridiculous because he doesn't look a day over twenty-five. But he's really, really old. Like, close to nine hundred, I think.

I turn to Lucien, curious. "How old are you?"

Lucien chokes on his wine glass of blood and smirks. "Checking out a guy's age are we, Horseman?"

I shrug. "Yeah. Guess so."

"Well, I'm 251."

"Goddess, everyone I know is so old."

"You are literally fucking people two thousand years old," Lucien remarks.

"Yeah, but they're technically dead, so that doesn't count."

"That's worse."

"Says the Vampire."

"Okay, children," the king interrupts. "Enough bickering. I think Magic deserves to go home and finish getting rest."

"Right, yeah. I'm exhausted." I turn to Lucien. "Check back in with the embassy soon, because there will probably be a meeting for future plans."

"Will do." He mock salutes me before I stand back and teleport myself back to bed.

Chapter Fifty-Nine

As my eyes peel open from the perfect nap, I hear voices coming from across the room.

"A test?" Arrie asks.

"Yes. I think we should give their powers a final test." There's a smile to his voice, a hint of amusement.

Connie laughs, picking up on whatever Dea is hinting. But I don't hear Nine.

I'm lying on the other side of your bed, also tired.

Ah. What kind of test are they talking about?

He scoffs into my mind, clearly not on board with said plan, but answers anyway. *War games. We each get a flag and the first person to hold all five wins. We usually play around the house's grounds.*

Why do they want to test my powers in the first place?

Dea wants to push them. You don't find many opponents difficult because your magic is so adaptable, but fighting us might be harder.

Plus, seeing Arrie put me on my ass will make Dea and Connie laugh.

That too. Don't worry, Sweetie. I think you'll do better than they think.

"I'm up for war games," I say out loud. "But I think it would be more fun with teams from the embassy. Make it a real strategy test."

"Niiine," Connie moans. "I wanted to tell them."

"You are finally awake," Dea says with a beautiful smile. "You have been sleeping for ten hours."

I shoot up out of bed. "Ten hours? I don't have ten hours. Why didn't one of you wake me!" I try to hop into the jeans I left on the floor but stumble and shift into a crow, fly, and land on Dea's armrest instead. Then I shift back, groaning. "I don't have ten hours to waste on sleep."

Connie coughs to get my attention. "Remember when we talked about not running yourself into the ground?"

"I vaguely remember it . . ." I avoid her accusing eyes like they're darts on fire. "But war is coming soon. I don't have time."

"We are basically already in a war," Arrie grumbles. "This is what they look like. Many battles, much stress."

"They are not," Dea says, "like they are portrayed in the

movies, where it is all one big final, organized battle that determines the fate of the earth."

"Oh." I guess he's right. That is a little naïve to think. "Then . . . can I have brownies?" I look to Arrie before I go and sit on his lap, wiggling into place. "Pleeeeeease?"

He rolls his eyes, but the corners of his lips lift in amusement. "I'll go make another batch." He shoves me off him. "A large one, since you eat so many of them."

"They are like orgasms on a plate, Mr. Grumpy," I say as I head into the bathroom to shower. "Don't you dare take that away from me!"

After showering both forms and feeling cleaner than I've ever felt—more refreshed too—I follow my Vampire's nose into the kitchen, where I see a stack of the best thing known to mankind (or specieskind, I guess). Brownies.

"Yay!" But before I can snatch one from the stack cooling by the open window, Arrie hands me a plate with one on. "Okaaay, guess I'll eat this one." He also hands me a fork, but I'm not that posh. So I just shove half into my mouth.

And everything in me explodes. It sets my senses alight, draws my fangs forth, and has my eyes burning red before I can stop them. After I swallow, I turn to him and ask, "Is this the first prototype?"

"Uh-huh." He looks to the floor, almost nervous. And is that embarrassment?

"It's fantastic!"

He looks up and meets my eyes. "Really?"

I jump into his arms and wrap my legs around his torso, smiling down at him. "Best thing I've ever tasted."

A breath leaves him, and I realize he was worried. About my opinion and what I thought of something he loves. "That's good. I'm going to try a few other things, too."

"Ohhh, like muffins and lemon drizzle cake and those cute little apple pastries you sometimes make? What about—"

He shuts me up by kissing me. Lips press against mine in haste, but eventually the kiss slows down, deepens, and soon his tongue is dancing with mine and I'm remembering all the ways he's fucked me lately. All the eyes that watched us. All the amazing ways he sets my body aflame.

And if the small, under-his-breath groan is anything to go by, he's thinking the same thing. But he breaks for air instead, putting me back on my feet. "I have a few things to do today. Sorry."

He looks genuinely sorry. Like he doesn't know how to reject me. Or if he should. So I lean up to his face and pull him in for a kiss, a quick reminder that I still love him. "It's okay. I get it. You're allowed to say no." And then go for a stroll through the garden, managing to walk past the unicorns and a few fairy dens.

Everything is beautiful today. Even the sun shining is more beautiful than it usually is. It's amazing how much good sex, friends, and brownies can make you see the same world differently.

Remind me to fuck you with everyone else again in the future. You're basically glowing.

If a little tired still, but yeah. I feel great.

Nine laughs, but I don't know where he is in order to punch him in the arm.

If you really must, I'm with the horses.

Yes. I must. So I fly over to him, wanting to get to him quickly, and watch as he straddles a leg over his horse and grabs the reins. Then he flies across the field, jumping the fence, and gallops beyond.

His red hair flies in the wind as his legs hold on to the horse's sides (he's riding without a saddle, because of course he is).

You had to know how to do this in the Chinese army. They didn't like paying extra for saddles if they could avoid it.

So, not too dissimilar to most modern governments, then?

Not really, no.

I zoom down beside him and fly alongside the horse, keeping up with its speed easily. This is probably why I don't have a horse. That and I can just shift into one. Though, Dea could just faze or, so why does he get a horse?

His energy reserves aren't able to be topped up like yours, and he runs out quicker.

Well, at least he can control his visibility now.

Two thousand years of having to schedule everything around his visibility limit outside of the house. Just solved in one afternoon by our new partner.

I was thinking . . . When all of this is over, I'd love to

spend more time in Japan. There's so much to my culture I don't know because I was raised American, and I'd like to experience more of it. Could we do that? Just live in Tokyo or somewhere more rural for a few years?

We could. Nothing saying we can't.

Would be like an extended vacation.

Want me to buy you a house there? Then you can stay whenever you like for however long you like. In fact, we have a safe house there already. You can have that. Or I could buy you something better. Something that's totally yours, and—

Nine! I would love a house there. Thank you. But you don't have to do that. Houses are expensive.

You deserve everything you get from us. You were totally torn out of your world and shoved into an identity you had no idea how to navigate. And you still manage to focus on other people more than yourself.

And here I thought I was quite self-centered.

Everyone who goes through an identity crisis thinks about themselves a lot; it's part of the process. But that doesn't make you a bad person. It just makes you human.

I guess so. I would like to do more for all of you. Take you on dates, buy you gifts, shower you with love. You all need it. And I don't do it enough.

We haven't had the time, Sweetie. I promise that after this is all over, you can dote on our every whim.

I shift into my male form, then into a stallion, and I gallop alongside him, taking all the turns he does, jumping all the fences he does. Nine has to slow down a bit, since I'm not as

462

large as their horses, but we still have fun.

I'm so glad you're home.

Me too.

Later that day, we have a meeting at the embassy to discuss potential plans for drawing Aki and the Fae Queen out with their armies.

Rufus, our Shifter representative from here on *Sheruta* is sternly against the idea of us using *Sheruta* as a battlefield. "We would need to evacuate the entire town. Something that's never been done. We wouldn't have a home if things went wrong."

"But I can't evacuate other countries or cities, and I can this one. It's at least a possibility."

"One we cannot ignore," Dea says. "*Sheruta* was here when we were made. It is either as old as we are, or it predates us. It exists for a reason, just like we do."

I turn to him, surprised by his theory. "You think Fate created it for this purpose?" Then I turn to Nine and Connie, who usually have an opinion on such things.

"I always used to think that *Sheruta* was Fate's apology," Nine says. "That we might have gotten dealt a shitty hand, but here's an entire realm to yourself to do with as you please. But Fate is never that kind." He shrugs. "Maybe Dea's right."

Rufus scoffs. "You get to live forever. How is that a bad hand?"

Arrie scowls, meeting his gaze. "When you've watched every friend and family member and lover die for two thousand years, come back and tell me you'd still choose immortality. We will outlive everyone in this room. We will attend all eleven of your funerals."

At least Rufus has the dignity to look sheepishly to the floor.

Lucien's gaze softens as he takes us in, ending his pitying look at me. As though he's seeing us for the first time.

"We should lure the army to Margalla Hills National Park," Nine says after looking something up on the plasmascreen in his hand. "It's in Pakistan, and it's one of the largest open areas in the world. But it's not too near a city if we head to the north of the area."

No one seems to disagree, though they're still staring at us like we're dying puppies.

"Okay," I say, "enough. You can pity us later. We have a final battle to plan." At least I hope it'll be the final battle.

Lucien raises his gaze again, looking directly at me. "Father has made a choice about Phillipe." Well, that sounds dramatic. "Execute him."

The table gasps.

Red looks at him disapprovingly. "Execute him? You mean, his own father wants him dead?"

"Red, he killed hundreds of Vampires, wants to see the Fae Queen and himself sitting at the top of the world, and, might I remind you, he supports Aki and his ridiculous ideals."

"But he's your brother!" She seems genuinely horrified by the idea, but everyone doesn't seem that bothered.

Our single Fae seems on the fence, like he has something to say but doesn't feel like he can speak up.

I nod to him, encouraging him to speak. He's here for that reason, after all.

"While I don't wish to condone murder, it would send a message. Maybe the Rogue Vampire Faction will disband afterward."

"Or maybe they'll fight back harder," Red retaliates. "Maybe they might try to grow their ranks. Maybe it'll send discourse through the entire Vampire community and cause even more problems."

"We could just keep him locked up until everything has died down, then decide what to do with him," I suggest. Maybe everyone might be a little more inclined to show mercy when their people are no longer at risk.

Lucien is suspiciously quiet regarding his own feelings, which is unlike him, so I look to him. Really look at him. And it's clear as day on his face. He doesn't want his brother to die, but he has to respect his father's wishes. "I think we should interrogate him. See what he knows. Maybe he knows where the Fae Queen is."

Dea looks in agreement, along with everyone else.

"But who is going to interrogate him?" My hands wring in my lap, scared they'll ask me to do it. I don't ever want to do that again. Not after last time. Felicity meets my gaze and nods. She understands.

"That would be me," Nine says on a sigh. "I can extract information the easiest. And if I don't get what we need, and I can just force him to tell the truth."

I settle my hand on his leg and squeeze. "You don't have to do that. You never have to use your powers in a way that doesn't feel right for you."

"If you have fight and kill and do things you hate, then so do we. We can't just expect you to do all the hard stuff."

Connie agrees, nodding. "He's right. We have to step up and help you do the shit stuff. Or it's not a team effort."

Lucien pipes up, happy to help. "I'll help you, Nine. He might respond better if I'm there, or it might piss him off and make him slip up. Either way, it'll probably be of use."

"Thanks, dude."

"So," Arrie says, plasmascreen in hand, "the Margalla Hills National Park is owned by a council, controlled by the SC, so we should give them a head's up, try working with them better. It's also a completely open area with some buildings nearby, so perhaps evacuating those houses would be a good plan. But quietly, otherwise Aki and the Fae Queen will have time to plan ahead, and we want to draw them out suddenly, so they don't have time to strategize. That way we can capitalize on the time they have to spend communicating a defense. Just like they did with us at Jura Mountains."

Everyone nods, but I'm just proud. He's really come out of his shell these last few months, becoming more confident in his abilities and helping the team with them. He let us handle the decision around Phillipe, and while we were doing that, he spent time planning a strategy and the basic building blocks of a battle plan.

He's more intelligent than he looks.

Gah. I'm already disgusted by your newfound admiration for Arrie. It's gross.

Just because I'm not fawning over your brain this time. Jealous?

A little.

Oh, really? I'm sorry.

Don't be. Jealousy is normal.

Well, I'll make sure to tell you how smart you are and make you feel special this evening.

Thank you. I look forward to seeing this special interest. Will it involve your dick?

Maybe. If you ask nicely.

Please, may I have your dick? The snicker behind his mental voice is all too clear, and we both have to concentrate on not laughing while everyone discusses battle plans and numbers and defense systems with Arrie.

Yes, you may.

Maybe leave the domming to Dea, Sweetie.

Yeah, probably. Besides, he'd be furious if you subbed for anyone else. Trust me. He was so broken when he lost you. I show him the image of Dea crying on the floor, breaking apart.

But he goes silent, his face downcast, hands fiddling in his lap. *I hate that I caused so much pain.*

You didn't. Aki did. And I'll kill him for it.

Chapter Sixty

The cells in the basement are not what I expected. They're bright, with a small book collection, a TV every cell can see, and a menu ordering system (albeit limited and simple options) for the three meals a day.

At my surprised expression, Connie explains, "We're not running a prison. We just have this here in case we needed to hold anyone before we hand them over to whatever council they're represented by."

"*Sheruta* doesn't have a prison," Dea explains, waving a hand through the air.

Lucien, mildly shocked by this notion, looks at Dea quizzically. "Really?"

"We do not have a lot of crime here."

"Maybe the world can learn from *Sheruta*," he muses out loud, mostly to himself, with a small smile on his face.

I think he'll miss this place when he becomes king. He'll have to stay in New Orleans then. Maybe he'll turn the job down. He does have other siblings, I think. But he's the next strongest in the family line, and that's how succession works.

Phillipe is wearing the same dirty, blood-stained clothes I sent him here in—a black sleeveless tunic top with delicate embroidery and matching pants. His muscles flex in the natural lighting filtering in through the small window at the back of his cell. And he smirks from beneath heavy lids as we walk up to him.

"Ah, yes. I was wondering when you'd get around to interrogating me." His face is confident as he continues to lie on the bed, arms folded beneath his head, legs crossed. "Want to pilfer through my brain, Famine?"

"Yes." He's like stone, not a single emotion showing. "We need information to save the world from your friends."

"Pfft." He sits up, laughing. "Save the world? You act so justly, so righteous. It's just an opinion. And opinions can be wrong."

I wave his words away. "We're not here to chat. Sorry." Nine, don't let him get you talking. You don't want to accidentally send him information. If he escapes—"

I know.

Okay.

Lucien walks through the swinging doors, a mess of emotions on his face, lips downturned.

Phillipe changes, his posture going rigid. "Lucien." The words like poison spilling from his lips.

"Phillipe. You comfortable?"

"Sure. This is actually quite a nice mattress."

I bet Connie'll be happy to know her choices are liked, even by this asshole.

"So, how does this work?" Phillipe asks. "You enter my mind like Father does, then I spill the beans?"

Nine shrugs. "Something like that." He steps forward, hands on the bars and frowns. He concentrates, his brows furrowing, but nothing happens.

Everything okay?

I can't read his mind.

Lucien sighs. "For fuck's sake. What have you done now?" He stands just behind Nine, arms crossed, hair slightly out of place.

But Phillipe just shrugs. "I dunno, but it's probably nothing the great Horsemen can't fix."

Silver Leaf, maybe?

Perhaps. But this feels a little different. Like Aki and his mind barrier.

Of course he protected his allies. Why didn't I think of that sooner? I have no idea how he does that, though, so I can't undo it, even I wanted to. But it's safe to assume it's something like Silver Leaf; maybe even a spell that uses it.

But spells aren't a Witch thing.

So maybe it's not Aki's doing. Maybe the Fae Queen is behind this.

That is the most likely option, yes.

But wouldn't you have to continuously take Silver Leaf for the spell to remain active? So, logically, we just wait.

We don't have time to wait. Aki knows we have him, so he'll march before his time is up.

Lucien's voice echoes around us. "Really? You are the worst brother in existence." He storms to the cell's bars and stretches the metal, stepping through the hole he made. "Fucking stop being a dickhead."

"Lucien?" I warn.

"Relax, he cannot hurt me. Father used mind control on us siblings as children so we would stop hurting each other in fights and to better train us."

But doesn't that mean Lucien also can't hurt Phillipe?

As if to prove me wrong, he flings him across the room, and Phillipe flops to the ground, confused and in pain, bleeding from a bash to the head. "How . . . ?"

Lucien smirks. "Father removed the spell from me so I could help deal with you."

Phillipe snarls, anger flashing across his eyes. "That fucking ass."

Lucien slaps his brother across the face, forcing his head to snap back farther than it should logically go. Then he grabs him by the ankle and dangles him upside down. "Anyone got any spelled rope?"

"Sending for some," Nine says.

A few seconds later, a guard comes running in with some spelled rope in his hand.

Nine goes to take it, but I stop him and grab it instead. "Thank you. Please lock the door on your way out."

He nods and silently walks away, not even a flicker of emotion on his face.

I walk through the hole Lucien made in the cell's bars and grab Phillipe's ankles, fly myself into the air and tie his feet to the upper bars. "There."

"Good work. Makes him look lovely and pretty."

"Thanks." I have no idea what Lucien is going to do, but I know him. He won't kill his brother, not when we need him alive. And especially not like this. He'd leave it for his father to do. Which I don't blame him for. "I've been working on my villainy."

Then, in the speed in takes to blink, Lucien slashes his nails across Phillipe's neck, puncturing his artery. And blood spurts all over the cell walls and Lucien's white shirt.

Or maybe I was wrong.

Maybe he would kill him.

A highborn Vampire can't die this way. He's draining him dry.

Why? Ohhh, to get rid of any Silver Leaf Vain in his system.

And to weaken him. Vampires need circulating blood. It hurts being without.

Proving Nine's explanation correct, Phillipe tries to scream, but it just bleeds him dry quicker. A gargling sound escapes his throat, and I want to puke, but I hold it in. Lucien and Nine need me strong right now. They need pissed-off me. The me who doesn't care about flinging Vampires into mountains.

But apparently, I can't turn that on on cue, because I'm struggling with this.

Phillipe thrashes around, trying to escape the ropes binding his feet to the upper bars, but they dampen someone's strength, leaving them weak and without supernaturally powered muscles. So he gets nowhere. He just continues to struggle. Gurgling. Blood pouring everywhere, spattering the cell walls in dark red ichor that drips to the floor.

Lucien just stands there, immobile, watching his brother writhe in agony. Unable to even scream. "Anything yet?"

"Nearly." *I can read emotions, surface thoughts, but I can't dig deeper yet.*

"Then we'll keep going."

They're ruthless.

How are they . . .

Because we have to. You can leave. You don't need to be here for this.

If you have to do something you hate, then I'll stand by your side while you do it. This job can suck. But it's easier together.

A small smile creeps onto Nine's face, just a slight up tilt of the corner of his lips. A sliver of a smile. But it's all I need to know that he feels supported.

Phillipe continues to struggle, but to no avail, and eventually his movements weaken, his arms flop to the floor, and the blood slows to a trickle that rivers down his neck and off his chin.

"He's out cold," I say.

"Yup," Lucien confirms. "His mind should be free of influence now." He steps out of the cell and washes his hands in the sink of a different cell, patting a towel over his face. "You're welcome."

Nine's brow furrows, concentration lining his face, and he breathes out. "I'm in." *I can see everything.*

"Good. Can you—" Lucien begins to ask, but I shut him up.

"Don't distract him. Just let him do his thing."

"Right." He takes a seat on a cell's bed, head heavy in his hands. "God, this sucks."

Snickering, I sit beside him. "Still find Vampires saying things suck hilarious, sorry." A hand on his shoulder finds tense muscles and the weight of the world sat there. And I happen to know a thing or two about that. "The world will always be in danger, little prince. All we can do is help fix the pieces that fall our way. You're doing great."

"I just didn't expect to have to do that to my own brother. We used to spar as kids. Throwing each other around, not a scratch to be gained with the help of Father. He was always teaching me new things, sneaking me out to bars as we got older. But he changed once he married Felicity."

"Sometimes people do change. And there's nothing we can do but sit there and help them when they ask for it."

"He'll never ask for help. It's not his style. But he'll get it anyway, because I won't let Father execute him. I can't."

"You might not get a choice, but I'll stand by you either way." He looks to me, surprised. "Whatever you think is best, I'll support it."

"You trust me that much?"

"I trust that you want what is best for people. That you make choices to the benefit of you, your family, your friends, and your people. I can't ask more of someone than that."

Nine gasps as his eyes fly open, and he spins around to face us. "We need to stop the battle plan meeting. Now."

Chapter Sixty-One

JURA MOUNTAINS: FALLOUT IS WORSE THAN EXPECTED, RU-
MORS SAY, WITH LOSSES IN THE TENS OF THOUSANDS

"Wait, wait," I plead as we're running up the staircase. "Stop!"

They both stop and stare at me, frustration looming on their eyes.

"Nine, you need to explain. We need to think this through. Everything is delicate right now."

"But the longer we wait, the worse it gets."

"The worse what gets?"

"The Demons are working for Aki. They're going to betray us. And the one we put on the council is going to feed all of the information back to him."

"Okay." Shit. Fuck. "But if we rush in there, magic a-blazing, we out ourselves. They'll know we know."

"Yeeeah," Lucien says, clearly confused.

"But if we feed them false information, it can work to our advantage."

Nine looks stumped. "I can't believe I didn't think of that. Wow, I need a nap." He runs a frustrated, tired hand down his face, his eyes closed. "That is, of course, the plan."

"Okay, so what information do we feed him, because he knows what Phillipe knows?" Lucien asks, which is a valid question.

"We'll have to use real information," Nine says. "But give him false information about what we're going to do about it."

"Then reconvene with everyone else secretly and make a different plan."

Nine shakes his head. "That risks the Demons finding out. No, it'll be better if we Horsemen make the new plan and then send a secret message to the rest of the council. Messages are easier to keep secret than entire meetings."

"Right."

Everyone seemingly on board, we continue heading up the stairs, this time not in a rush. I think Nine needs time to think. He's the only one with all of their information and knowledge, so it'll be up to him to come up with the specifics.

The doors to the meeting room loom in front of us. Once light and welcoming, now they stand there all dark and foreboding, despite the white color and the plants and the plasmascreens that act as windows. But it doesn't matter, we have to go in anyway.

All Lucien and I have to do is act like we know nothing.

All I have to do is sell an entire set up.

Right.

I pat him on the back, sending him on his way.

You'll do great.

I sweep the doors open in a blast of air magic that makes us seem dramatic and in haste, and Nine rushes in, Lucien and I following at his heels.

"Wait!" He feigns being out of breath, holding up a hold while he leans on his knees. "Wait. We need to change . . . plan."

Arrie scowls, having already started to write the plan down, if the giant plasmascreen wall with diagrams and notes is anything to go by. "What's wrong?"

"The Fae Queen has more than one Witch. She has a small regiment of them from all over the world, promising them a home in her court where they can practise their magic openly away from the public's prying eyes."

"What kind of Witches?" Connie asks, worrying clouding her eyes.

"Fire and earth, as well as a few charm Witches. It's the charm ones I'm worried about. We have the upper hand by being able to mix Fae and Witch magic, but if they can do it too, Aki will use that to his advantage."

"Right," Arrie says, taking it all in stride. "We need to plan a defense strategy around the fact that different types of magic will be used, including teleporting crystals, charm spells, and mixed spells on the field."

Red looks worried. "Very few of us have faced that kind of magic before. Our armies aren't trained to handle that."

"Then we best get training them. Fast," Arrie says. "Take this strategy—I'll send a copy to you all—and Magic will work on best defenses for such attacks and hand you a dia-grammatic list." He looks pointedly my way, letting me know he expects that of me post-haste.

"On it."

"Anything else?" Dea asks, suspiciously looking at Nine.

"Nothing I think will be of use to us. But the Fae Queen and her army are hiding under the ocean, which is why we couldn't find them."

"Under the . . . ocean?" our resident Fae asks, surprise lacing his words. "I've heard of rumors of an old palace un-der the Atlantic Ocean, but I thought it was just a legend."

"Apparently not," Nine scorns. "They are there, but the defenses are many. It's built like a fortress. I think it's best we stick to the plan of drawing them out."

Arrie shakes his head. "They won't send the whole army. At least, I wouldn't. It'll be best if we have a small team infil-trate the ocean palace once half the army are gone. We have no way of knowing where the Fae Queen herself will be, but my bet is on the palace."

Everyone looks at him expectantly.

"I'll probably send a few Horsemen and elite soldiers, leaving our main armies in place for the actual battle. It'll be a stealth operation anyway, so splitting the army in half is just sure to make us lose the half we send to the palace."

His eyes come back into focus, and he looks at me with a smile. I wish I could tell you what that smile means, but it could be anything from 'I'm horny' to 'Look, I bought you a pet penguin'. Either way, I'm happy he's happy.

We end the meeting, and we Horsemen greet everyone as they leave, Lucien saying goodbye for a day as he helps deal with the election campaigns. Though he promises to come back for Phillipe in an hour or so. He's transferring him to their dungeons at the Vampire Royal Council building.

But the Fae hangs back, looking nervously at the five of us.

"Is there anything wrong?" Connie asks.

"Well, it's just . . . earlier, when you rushed in, I sensed something. Something magical happening in the room. But I couldn't tell from whom. So I thought I would ask if it were you?"

Connie looks to us with a question on her face.

"Not me."

Everyone else shakes their head.

"Shit," I curse. I quickly shift forms and scan the room, looking for Fae magic or tech that's out of place. And bingo, I found it. Hiding underneath the desk. I yank it out and throw it on the table, then set it on fire. "Listening device."

Everyone looks confused, but Nine and I just share a conspiratorial gaze.

"What's going on?" Connie asks.

"The Demon ambassador is working for Aki. All the Demons are, I say on a sigh. "It's why we forced Arrie to change his plans." Facing him, I add, "Do not actually change those plans."

"A false lead?" Dea asks. "Clever."

"Thank you." Pride rings through.

But the Fae looks at us concerned. "If the Demons are going to betray us, then that's . . . bad."

"Yes and no," Nine explains. "They don't know we know, so technically they've just handed us the advantage."

His eyes light up, understanding dawning. "I see. I will keep quiet, then."

"I will be personally informing everyone of the right plan the moment we have it finalized," Nine explains. "It's the only surefire way to keep it private."

"Then I best get practising some defense magic. I will see you all later." He leaves in haste, worry peppering his step.

"He's a little . . . odd," Arrie says.

"Jesus, Arrie," Connie scorns. "You can't just go around calling people odd."

"Why not? I waited until he was out of earshot." Frowning, he leads the way home, a little sour after being told off by Connie.

CHAPTER SIXTY-TWO

"ARE WE SAFE?" MEXICAN PRESIDENT ASKS

"Where's Arrie?" I ask Connie once I come in from my morning yoga session the next day. "He wasn't watching me like usual."

She shrugs.

But Nine looks up from the plasmascreen he's holding with a sad smile. *He's out by the fairy garden that leaves off the left of the house.* He sends me a mental image so I know how to get there. *Be gentle.* "I'm off to deliver the messages to the ambassadors." He turns to me. "Good luck."

Gentle? Good luck?

This part of the house is where the older rooms sit, and the gardens here have been left unattended, left to grow wild and free. But there's a small archway off what I think used to be a pathway, the stones since cracked and mostly sunken into the ground.

"Arrie?" I gently ask, hoping he's nearby.

But no one answers me. Shifting into my female form, I strain my hearing and try to find out where he is, and when I hear sobs coming from beyond the archway, I rush in, not expecting the image in front of me.

Arrie's kneeling at the back of the garden, his hands clenching the grass beneath them, straining for control. For something to hold on to. There's a gravestone in front of him, followed by smaller gravestones either side.

This is . . .

I don't say anything. All I do is kneel beside him, place a hand on his knee and the other on the ground. And a second later purple flowers shoot up around their graves, curling into the stone and around our feet.

Arrie looks to me with tears pooling down his cheeks, his chest heaving, struggling to take in breaths. It's like he's stuck in the past, still as raw as he was two thousand years ago. "Just feeling the emotions . . . sucks."

He did this for me?

I wrap tight arms around him, grounding him. "You don't have to push yourself. But it's lovely that you came to visit her. I'd be so mad if you didn't visit me."

He wipes his eyes as he pulls out of my hold, a gentle yet sad smile on his face. "Thank you for the flowers. She loved them so much, she would decorate the whole house with them. Used to drive me crazy."

"You do not strike me as the flower type."

He shakes his head with a laugh. "I didn't used to be. But I like my Zen garden bedroom the house provided. Always felt like a gift from her, telling me to let nature calm me."

"She sounds wise, like Dea."

"But strong. She'd wield a battle-axe like no other woman I've ever seen."

And that's how we sit for the rest of the morning, me listening to his memories as he shares them, talking about his wife, his children, and a whole life I wish I could have seen.

Chapter Sixty-Three

"So, the goal is to catch everyone's flag and not lose them. You have the entirety of the grounds, but not beyond. We don't want to be destroying buildings we don't own," Nine explains, excitement in his eyes instead of the unsteady somber from earlier. "As per Connie's request, there are plasmacams everywhere, so try not to destroy them."

Dea, Arrie, and Con are ready to go, geared up, and eager to get started.

"You have one hour before the horn will sound and you will have to start your strategy." He looks to me. "Understand, Sweetie?"

"Set up my strategy, and when the horn sounds, the game

starts. Whoever has all flags at the end wins. What happens if we're knocked out and no one has all the flags?"

"The winner will be whoever is holding the most," Dea answers.

"Everything clear?" Nine says, who is also dressed in strong cloth-like material acting as armor, but he also has a layer of carefully placed chain mail. "Just remember, try not to remove anyone's head. Take far too long to regrow."

"And it's horrifying," Arrie grumbles.

"Remember that time you got your head blown off by a rhino Shifter, Nine?" Connie laughs, unable to stop for a moment.

"Yes, yes. I'm sure it was hilarious." He does not look impressed. "Can we get started?" He looks to the time on the clock of the kitchen and smiles. "We have forty seconds before the cameras start rolling and we have to get going."

I'm a little nervous. This is like a final test of my abilities, but instead of facing regular opponents, I have to face them. Two-thousand-year-old beings with more practice in battle than I can ever hope to have. Also, the idea of facing Connie or Arrie in hand-to-hand combat leaves my knees knocking a little.

You know, just a tad.

And what about Nine?

He could make me do whatever he wanted. While he might not like to do so with other people, it would be okay with us. How do I combat that?

"Ten," Nine counts down, "nine, eight, seven . . ."

We step outside onto the porch and get ready to run. Well, they do, I just lift myself into the air and ready myself to fly.

"Five, four, three, two, one!"

Dea fazes instantly, blurring into the forest, whereas Arrie and Connie sprint at full speed into the distance, both heading north. But Nine and I stay still.

I have no idea what Nine is doing, but I'm flying.

We've had a whole twenty-four hours to prepare, and Connie prepared a live stream of the game so the public can be entertained and we can gain some more brownie press points. But it means I've had a full twenty-four hours to strategize and plan and prepare spells and charms that'll do some impact to my team.

None of us saw each other until dinner, where we sat in silence and stared each other down. But it was when Arrie strapped his dual battle-axes to his back that it started to feel real.

I have to actually fight them.

For real.

No holding back, which I'm pretty they've been doing with me until now.

I fly over the gardens, seeing if I can spot any of them, but the only person I know where they are is Dea, whom I can sense. He's somewhere near the forest. And while, yes, it seems like an advantage, I have to remember that if I can sense him, he can sense me, too.

Nine is still by the house, staring out into the garden, un-moving. But Connie and Arrie are nowhere to be found.

Hmmm . . .

Time to start laying my traps, then.

They're Fae spells I've rigged to alert me when tripped. Which will come in handy when trying to find everyone. Plus, they don't drain my magic here because we're on a leyline, so my biggest advantage over the others is that my Fae magic won't tire.

But I bet they've already thought of that.

Oh well, doesn't mean I can't use them.

I place three dozen traps all over the gardens, including in the forests, fields, fairy dens, and on the general pathways; though, I've avoided over-placing on the pathways because who will use those. Some are placed in trees, bushes, and un-der rocks, whereas others are placed just in the way but hid-den with an invisibility spell I may or may not have stolen from Dea while sucking his dick.

Hey, don't judge me. Use what you got.

And I've got dick-sucking skills I can use to distract.

We've spent twenty-three minutes of our prep time so far, so I have seven minutes to set my final trap. And this one is specific to Arrie. I'm hoping it won't catch anyone else, but I'm not sure if that aspect of the magic will work. I bury it in the ground near the house and use my newfound earth magic to make it look like nothing has been disturbed.

"That just about does it." Now I just have to prepare my

defenses.

I fly back into the air and head to the very back of the garden by the outer border fence, where there's nothing but a couple of fairy dens and fields. But behind the fence is the northern forest. And that's the point of being here.

There's magic in that forest. Magic I can tap into with enough concentration.

We are not, to my dismay, allowed to hide our flags. They have to be on show. And did I mention they glow, like dazzling pieces of shit giving away my location, even if I wanted to hide? So, instead of wrapping it around my bra strap (which was my original plan), I tie it to my belt loop just behind my dagger.

I'm armed to the teeth today: knives, daggers, my staff in charm bracelet form, and so many charms and spells in my bum bag that I'm genuinely worried they'll all spill out the moment I open it.

Fifteen minutes left.

Time to set up basic defenses.

I don't actually think anyone will struggle with these, but they'll stop them for a short pause, and that's long enough for me to see who I'm dealing with and choose my defense strategy.

I'm betting they'll be gunning for me.

And I don't have a clue what Nine is playing at, because as far as I can tell, he's still by the house.

Oh well, I don't have time to worry about him. I have to

lay some spells and traps down this end, and after doing that, I raise a wall of earth around me, then a ring of fire blowing high into the sky around that.

Without Nine playing yet, Connie and Dea are most likely to find me first. I'm hoping Dea will play fair and not tap into our mate connection, but I don't count on it, which would, hopefully, leave Connie as gunning for first place.

She's good, but she can't just walk through fire. Not to mention the wall.

But there's sound on the other side of the wall, and before I know it, blonde hair sails down from the sky in two plaits and a wicked smile. "Nice try."

Shit. She jumped the wall?

I push the wall outward, giving myself more room. But I don't take it down. The last thing I need is a two-on-one battle. She's enough on her own. Throwing all my strength against Connie might work, but I'll be too tired out to fight the others, so I have to find another way.

Luckily, I thought she might be first. Truthfully, I thought she would be second, but hey ho. Work with what you've got.

I throw a couple of testing knives her way and watch her dodge them with ease, as expected. But when I throw a torrent of fireballs her way, she whooshes toward me instead of dodging.

Slam.

I'm on the ground before I can even take a breath and prepare myself.

"Never gonna beat me with that weak defense, hon."

That's what she thinks.

I slam the flat of my foot on the ground and am rewarded with a rumble getting closer. Louder. Closer still. And soon a chunk of earth slices toward her, throwing her off me with a screech.

She jumps to her feet and smashes a charm bead quickly at her feet, floating her into the air. And she flies at me. Dagger in hand, she slices at my face.

But I fall to the ground, then shoot myself into the air as quickly as possible. Quicker than that spell allows her to follow. As soon as I'm above her, I zoom to the ground headfirst, gaining speed.

Her eyes flicker in fear for a quick second, but Connie stands her ground—steadfast, unmoving. She doesn't flinch. Until I'm literally three seconds from her face, when she rolls out of the way, and I smash my fist into the ground.

Pain lances through me, shooting up my arm. "Shit," I curse. My fingers break on impact and I can barely move them.

I switch forms and shift into a falcon, racing her around the sky, until she shoots an arrow at my wing. Piercing right through it. I fall to the ground. The pain is preventing me from shifting back to man, but I can shift into something else with a wingspan.

I try an eagle, and luck be with me, the injury doesn't transfer. That's some magical blessing right there. Fuck yeah.

"Well, that's just bullshit," Connie shouts.

I shift into a man and smile. "For you!" I grab my staff, flashing it into my hand. "For me it's perfect." Then I activate one of the crystals in the wood I'd spelled just for this occasion.

As I stamp the wood on the charred ground, Connie's legs sink into the dirt with a yelp. "What are you doing?"

One of her best assets is her stamina. I can't remove her perfect aim, but I can keep her in place while I knock her unconscious.

And so I shift back into my female form, fingers having healed—thank fuck for Vampire healing speeds—and I hurl a ball of water larger than her at her body.

She screams before I plunge her under. But the smile on her face as she's holding her breath tells me she's not really scared. She's just a drama queen.

I yank the water this way and that until I have a grasp on her bow, which I yank off her back.

Her eyes widen in surprise as she accidentally breathes in water.

Oops. I pull the water down to the ground, allowing it to rehydrate the burned areas. But I keep her pinned in place. "Don't panic, babe. I'll heal you later."

"Wha—?"

A bubble of air circles around her head, and then I pull the air out, leaving her without breath. And she quickly falls asleep, her oxygen limit reached.

I un-stick her from the ground and remove the air bubble, then lay her unconscious body on the floor, tucking a strand of hair behind her ear before grabbing her green flag and tying it to my purple one at my waist. "Sorry."

A loud crash in the distance has my head swiveling that way. Two of the guys are fighting. I resist the urge to check on Dea, and instead lower my defenses so I can see better. Once the walls of earth and fire are down, I zoom my vision east and see three trees being felled as Dea falls into them wings first.

That would be Arrie.

I leave them to it and sprint back to the house to find Nine, but he's not there. I can't see him.

But I know he knows where I am. So finding him is going to be a bitch. But maybe I can figure it out. I'm smart too. Okay, maybe not Nine smart, but smart enough.

Don't sell yourself short, Sweetie. You're very smart.

Don't patronize me.

He laughs in my head, echoing around my skull.

Instead, I push thoughts of his voice in my head aside and look at the surrounding ground. Maybe I can find tracks. It's not like he has any earth magic, so he can't just magically erase them (which is a very cool way I'm going to figure out how to use my powers later).

My mental list is getting out of hand.

Tracks, Magic. Tracks.

I scour the area, flying just above the ground so as not to

create footprints while looking. There! Just by the first fairy den is a lone set of footprints. Nothing leading up to them, nothing going ahead of them. They just stand there facing the fairy den like he vanished into it or something.

He wouldn't . . .

More trees crash behind me, echoing around the garden, so I know Dea is putting up a fight against Arrie. Unless Connie got free. That's a terrifying thought.

Crouching low to the ground, I hover in front of the fairy den, watching small, glowing little creatures whiz around the bush, traversing their home. "Hi there."

They all turn to face me, blank expressions. But one of them comes forward, standing in front of everyone else. "He said you would come looking for him here." Despite being so tiny, their voice is loud and clear.

"So he came through here?"

Their head bobs side to side, as if they don't know. "Not quite through here, no."

A grumbling groan escapes me. "If not here, then where?"

"I did not say not here, I said not through here."

What?

Not through here?

I look to the footprints below me once again and grin. "Not through here!" Not through, but under. I look to the fairy and smile. "Thank you. If there's anything you need or want, I'd be happy to help."

"More dens that lead to our sister dens farther south

would be nice."

"I'll get right on that when I have a free minute."

They bow, and the rest of the fairies behind them bow too. Then they fly away, leaving me alone.

Below me. Right, well. Time to dig.

My hand rests firmly on the ground. Earth isn't my strongest element right now, but I should be able to sense what's below me and maybe make an opening. I managed to move a fucking mountain earlier.

Hands run through grass as I cross my legs and settle on the ground, stretching my senses out. I block out the crashing from the others fighting and focus solely on the what's close to me. Like the fairies flitting across their bushes, flying around their home, the ants scurrying behind me and the beetle pushing dirt around his home. But below me, below the maze of the animals and the insects' networks, is an empty space followed by a series of tunnels.

He carved out the ground so he could travel anywhere in the garden.

The fucking asshole.

I think you misspoke genius.

Genius, asshole. I don't see the difference.

Taking a deep breath, I open a small entrance just large enough for me to fit through.

Either way, Nine. I'm coming for you.

Chapter Sixty-Four

Magic is Looking Strong, but can They Win Against the One-Man Army?

It's dark down here, surrounded by nothing but dirt. Even with a small fire in my hand, I can't see more than a few feet in front of me.

Where are you?

Somewhere around.

He's going to be an asshole to find. If only I knew how to turn on the block in my mind that blocks him out. I've done it a handful of times, and Aki has it perfected (because of course he does), but I don't know how to control it. I usually like Ninè in my head, but right now, I wished I had put more effort into learning how to keep him out.

But I have other senses he doesn't.

Yanking my boots off, I walk barefoot through the maze of tunnels, trying to sense the surrounding earth through my feet. I search for what must be around at least ten minutes. Maybe longer. But I can't feel anything other than insects.

Until for a split second, nothing longer than a blink, I feel a vibrating rustle coming from the tunnel to my left. The one on my right is empty, I think. But there's something down this one.

So I turn my fireballed hand left and follow it.

Well done.

I turn a corner, and there he is, feet on either side of the tunnel, split like a spider.

"Can't believe you found me so easily. Damn those new earth powers."

"Right? Aren't they amazing?"

"They are something." He hops to the floor, hand on his holster, eyes on me. "But then you are incredible."

"Thanks." Hands filling up with knives, I prepare myself to fight. He might not be as strong as Arrie or as perfect as Connie, but he's smart and can read my every move. Out fighting him is going to be hard. "Maybe I might be as great as you one day."

"Stick around long enough, and maybe the genius might rub off."

"Let's hope so." I grip the two knives in my hands and chuck them his way, testing the waters. "Or this whole immortality thing will get old fast."

He dodges them, ducking to the floor, but I bring them flying back, soaring through the air like bullets.

But this time, he turns and shoots them down, knocking them out of the air like leaves.

"Damn." I've never seen him shoot properly. Not really. "Didn't realize you were so handy with those."

He snuffs, seemingly offended.

"You'll have to give me a lesson one day."

"Stop distracting me." He shoots a couple of magibullets my way, but I block with a body-sized slab of earth.

A shield.

So he sprints at it, crashing through the earth like paper, and then shoots again.

But this time, I crash the earth on top of him, opening the tunnel up to the sunlight that pours in. I hop to the ground, waiting for him to join me.

He pops out of the rubble like a daisy, hopping to the grass as well. A wicked smile on his face.

Something tells me out in the open wasn't the right move. But why else would he have been down there?

So I could get to you without walking into Arrie or Connie.

Why is everyone gunning for me? That seems unfair.

Instead of answering, he grabs his second gun and shoots round after round of bullets at me.

I deflect them with whooshes of air, more earth shields, and more tornadoes of air, which seemed a bit overkill, even for me. But whatever.

He doesn't give up.

More bullets rain around me.

And I'm spinning in the air, dodging, deflecting, without time to even think.

So when an arrow lodges into my arm, I scream in pain and whiz around to see a furious Connie behind me.

Great. Two on one.

I yank the arrow out, then shift form. Shifting into a bear, I barrel toward her, swiping a sharp clawed paw at her face.

She jumps over me, landing gracefully on her feet behind me. Nine's now in front of me, having run around us. And now I'm caught between a bow and two magiguns pointed at me, not sure how to deflect them both at the same time.

Until something glints in the corner of my eye.

One of my traps.

If I can get one of them over there, I could take out one of them without having to deal with them both. But shit, now Nine knows the plan. Connie it is.

I kinda feel bad catching her in so many traps.

But it is the game.

Before he has time to communicate my plans with her and team up, I throw him into the field on our right, hoping to throw him out of the fight for a minute. "Sorry!" I scream behind his flying body and waving limbs.

Connie unhooks her fingers slowly, releasing another arrow, but I dodge at the last second, shift back into my female form, and use air to funnel it back to her.

She looks surprised, a wicked grin on her face. Pride floating through her eyes. "Nice."

I use that second to sprint to the other side of the trap, which should be invisible to her, encouraging her to chase me.

She barrels after me, not breaking a sweat.

My arm is healed, so I'm not in pain anymore, but I know she can outlast me in a fight. Never-ending stamina has its perks, but this is definitely one of the downsides.

Her feet plant into the ground as she pulls back the string, her gaze steady on me.

C'mon, just one foot. Just one foot forward.

I step back, edging away, hands up ready to blow the arrow out its trajectory.

And she steps into the trap and instantly screams—screams that pierce my ears and tear my eyes from her burning body.

Fire rages up in a storm around her, her hair burning to nothing instantly.

Shit, shit shit.

Too far.

Placing my hand to the ground, I disable the trap and watch her body collapse to the ground in horror. Her skin is pealing in places, charred in others.

"Connie?" I whisper. "Shit. I'm sorry."

Nine finally runs up beside me, having recovered from being thrown into a field. "Teleport her to the hospital." He looks for her flag but smiles at me when he notices it on my belt.

The makeshift hospital is just on the outside of the grounds, so I teleport her there, leaving just four of us left. I think. Then I spin to face Nine, who's out of breath and struggling to focus, his arm broken and shoulder ripped out of place.

He puts his hands up, admitting defeat. He hands me his orange flag with a smile. "I'm going to make sure she's okay."

He's letting me win.

I hate fighting.

I nod, turning to face Dea and Arrie, who are still going at it in the forest. I fly myself into the air, carrying myself on the wind with gentle caution, assessing the situation from afar. They're both skilled fighters, but one is my mate, and I'm not sure we can hurt each other in any real way. Not even for a game.

And then there's Arrie.

I find them in the forest. Dea's wings are broken, and he's on the ground, tears falling to his chin, as Arrie stands above him, both axes in hand. His eyes are burning, focusing on the battle.

"Dea!" I fly to his side, landing heavily on the floor. "Are you okay?"

"Fine, Angel. Just fighting Arrie." He looks to Arrie's burning eyes and watches him take a step back, focusing his attention on me. "Be careful."

Arrie has one blue and one black flag, having already taken Dea's flag.

I teleport him to the hospital with the others and face Arrie, gearing up for the real battle.

I don't have a plan for this. No matter what I thought of or came up with, it wasn't good enough. His battle strategy ability basically makes it impossible to plan because he'll outmaneuver me.

So instead I face him. Hands armed with throwing knives and fire magic, mind taking in my surroundings and minding his stance.

"Arrie."

"Magic." His voice is empty, devoid of emotion.

Chapter Sixty-Five

War VS Magic: Down to the Final Two

Nothing prepares me for the brute strength with which he punches me. The searing pain in the side of my head thrums as I'm thrown back into the tree, doing something awful to my spine. I can't move my legs. Can't wiggle my toes. I can't even breathe.

So I shift.

Using my male form to at least be able to run.

Using everything I have, I run. I use the wind rune in my staff to put some breeze behind me, giving me a small advantage. I'm faster than Arrie in both forms.

But he's thundering behind me. He might be big, but he's not slow. All that muscle is designed to carry him and his weapons, not falter and be slow.

There are cameras at all angles, flying above us, below us, and beside us, but we ignore them. The world wants to see us.

"Stop running, coward."

Coward? I grind to a halt, spinning to meet a face of thunder, battle-axes flying through the air. "Ah!" I shift into my eagle form, not trusting my falcon to be healed yet without speedy Vampire healing. I soar into the canopy, banking and spinning back around to face Arrie.

I can't believe he threw both battle-axes at me.

How fucking rude.

But rather than pick them up, he faces me with fists instead, punching my eagle in the face.

I sprawl behind, trying desperately to use my wings to bring me back to level. But I hit a tree trunk and slide to the ground, where roots cradle my cracked wing.

Shifting back into a man, I stand and grab my staff, ensuring I remember the words to the spell. When Arrie tumbles close, within range, I yell the spell.

And he grinds to a stop. Frowning. "What did you do?"

I'm not going to answer that. Arming him with more information to strategize with is not wise. I'm not the smartest, but I'm not dumb. Instead, I use a trapping spell to tangle his feet into the ground and watch his now-weak form try to get out.

"Why can't I . . . break free?"

Because you're weak, I want to say, but I refrain from doing so.

I edge closer, trying to be cautious yet fast. The trap spell won't hold him long, and I have no idea how long a weakening spell will last on Arrie. My hand is inches from the two flags at his waist. Nearly there—

Snap.

Arrie's arm grabs my throat and yanks me off the floor just as his feet are finally free. "I don't need super strength to beat you." He pins me to a nearby tree, where his hips pin mine to the bark as his hand closes around my throat. "You're mine."

Oh, I know.

I press my hips into his, showing him just how much his I am.

And his eyes focus out a bit, losing control over his battle focus mode, and I use it to my advantage to wrap legs around his waist and flip us onto the ground.

I shift to my female form, but the pain is still too great, so I shift back. For fuck's sake. I have no idea how to beat Arrie in my male form. I need my Vampire strength.

His fist meets my face in a riotous roar as my head pounds and my ears ring.

I don't know if I can do this. If I can beat him.

Not like this. Not without access to my Witch magic or my Vampire strength. Fae magic is all about strategy, but with his strategy ability, he'll just out maneuver me. The only skill that leaves me is my Shifter stuff.

But how do I beat the Horseman of War as a Shifter?

Wait a minute. I don't need to beat him. I just need the flags. Then it's game over.

I've got this.

I shift into a blue tit and fly high above his head until he's standing, then I shoot to the ground, shifting into a bear as I land heavily on the ground. Clawing at his face, I growl.

But he takes the swipe as he's pushed back a few paces, arms protecting his face.

So I shift into a panther and leap at him, knocking him to floor.

He lands with a whoosh, the breath knocked out of him. "Oof."

A chuff sounds from my throat as I claw at his arms, leaving gouges in his forearms the length of his radius.

The growl that sounds from him is half pain, half frustration, and eventually he throws me off, jumping to his feet. "Stop!"

Nope.

I shift into a rat next, so I can crawl up his pant leg and grab the flags, but he grabs me by the stomach, his hand engulfing my entire body, before I can make it above his knee.

So I shift into a beetle this time, something smaller and less easily thrown off. I scurry up his leg, underneath his pants, and make it out of his belt with ease. Now to grab the flags.

Keeping them tight between my mandibles and hoping for the best, I shift into a wolf. Please transfer the flags to my teeth. For the love of magic, please work in my favor.

Apparently karma is all out of favors, though, because I shift an inch from the flags, and Arrie digs a dagger into my shoulder the moment I appear.

I whelp and pounce backward.

Arrie looks at me, a snarl on his face, his eyes still glowing and his hair having long since fallen out of his braids. "Stop messing around."

I shift back into a blue tit and fly to his face.

Maybe if I blind him, I can just grab them sneakily.

(Don't judge me, I can just heal him later.)

I fly fast at his face, but he puts his arms up before I can get there. Taking advantage of the distraction, I change tactics and go for the flags. My talon snags one, and I chirp. Yes! I shift back into a man and yank, then look down at my hand. A black flag lies in my palm.

"Shit," Arrie growls. He tries to snatch it back, but I sprint as fast as I can away from him, using the air rune to give me a boost.

It gives me time to tie it to my belt.

One down, just Arrie's to go.

The light blue flag flows at his waist, and I eye it with greedy determination. I can do this.

I shift into my female form and sprint faster—faster than Arrie can possibly keep up with. And I laugh.

Turning, I stand with my feet firmly on the ground, ready to face him. Pain gone, I won't be caught off guard by him again.

Arrie nears, murder in his eyes and a smile on his face. He's going to beat me to a pulp, and he's going to enjoy it. The psycho. But I won't let him. He charges me, battle-axes somehow returned to his grip.

I dodge his charge, letting him tumble to the floor and roll back up to standing. Fireball in one hand and a boulder the size of my head in the other, I'm ready.

When he lifts his gaze to mine, I hurl both at him in succession. One. Two. Then hurl two more fireballs. And I keep going, hurling different elements at him, seeing how much he can handle.

He crushes the boulders with his axes, so I quit with those and instead focus on spinning him off step with various small tornadoes, his feet struggling to stay on the ground. Then I light him up.

Blazing him like the trap did to Connie.

But he races away, dodging in a zigzag, avoiding my aim like a pro.

So I stop that and instead chuck a tidal wave at him. But I'm out of breath, struggling to keep up the pace. And all of a sudden my heart is racing, sweat drips off my brow, and my breath comes out in pants as I'm forced to curl over, hands on knees. "Shit."

Arrie swings one of his axes at me, and I don't dodge in time.

I fly to the side, bracing myself for impact with the ground. I protect my face with my arms, and my legs come out fully intact, somehow, but my arms are crushed, bruised, and basically useless. So I can't cast or attack in this form for a few minutes.

Usually, that wouldn't be a problem, but a few minutes could cost me the game right now.

So I shift back to my male form and stand my ground, reminding myself that I have all kinda of spells, charms, and runes in my staff.

Time to use some.

"Come on, then!" I scream at him.

He smiles, his eyes still focusing, his breathing still even, but he's covered in scrapes, cuts, and bruises. And I'm pretty sure he's just ignoring the pain of a broken ankle.

The brightness of his eyes stuns me for a second, but it's the thud of his ax on the floor that widens my eyes in genuine surprise. He walks up to me slowly, arms out, feet in a fighting stance. And smiles.

I return the stance, ready for an even fight.

No magic.

Just a fist fight to the . . . incapacitated. Though I'm pretty sure Arrie could punch someone into the afterlife if he so desired, but maybe not someone who's also immortal.

He swings for me, but I duck and swing my leg out, catching his broken ankle and forcing him to the floor.

He grunts as his ass lands on the forest floor.

I swing my legs over him and pin him to the floor. I shift forms and use my Vampire strength to actually keep him down, my fangs dropping free and his arteries pulsing beneath me.

I can hear the rush of blood. I'm tired. Weak.

It's only Arrie.

So I go for it, refueling.

And when I feel his answering response, his hips rising into mine, I relax, my grip loosening. Blood floods my mouth, trickles down the back of my throat and heals my bruises, cuts, and broken bones. And I'm so grateful, because I'm going to—

Arrie throws me off him and shouts into the air, his fist pumping into the air carrying five flags. Including mine.

I lost.

Chapter Sixty-Six

Horseman of War Wings War Games in Show of Brutal

Strength

He's here.

I grab Arrie's hand and teleport us to the makeshift hospital, which is nothing more than a tent with a couple of beds in. Everyone's there, Dea and Connie in beds next to each other. Connie's skin has started growing back, but it's not quick enough.

"Angel?" Dea asks, gesturing to my lips. "You still have blood on your face."

Oh. I wipe my face clean and then sit next to Connie. "Sorry babe. I didn't think it would affect you that much. I promise not to burn you alive again." I take a fang to my index finger and make a small tear, then shove the finger in her mouth, which she opens diligently. "There you go."

I let her take as much as she likes, needing her to be on top of the world, before turning to Dea.

He takes a different bleeding finger, licking stripes across the pad and sending shivers down my spine.

"You won, bro!" Nine exclaims. "Well done!"

"Didn't think I was gonna for a minute there."

Nine turns to me with an amused smile on his face. "Better luck next time, Sweetie."

"I don't have time for that," I curse. "Where is he?"

"He's stood next to a Vampire I don't know by the embassy building. His army is coming through."

Connie shoots up out of bed, looking surprised and ready to go, her usual beauty back again with full force. "It worked?"

Arrie grumbles, "My plans always work."

"We drew him out," Dea confirmed. Then turns to Connie.

"Right. *We* have evacuated *Sheruta* to New Orleans, your traps are active and should funnel them away from the town, and our armies are in place."

Everyone nods, but I turn to Arrie. "You good? Not too exhausted?"

He shakes his head and grabs his battle-axes he somehow always manages to recover. "I'm good, Killer." He wraps an arm around my shoulder before handing me three vials of his blood I shove into the pouch hanging at my waist.

Dea and Nine do the same thing, arming me with special

go-go juice in case I need it, but when Connie hands me her three, I hesitate.

"Are you sure?" I don't want her to do something she'll regret or be uncomfortable with.

"It's the right thing to do." He green eyes land on me, shooting me with confidence in her decision. "You're going to need it fighting Aki."

"And remember," Nine says, "you need to remove that necklace if you can. He's more powerful with it." His eyes close for a moment as he concentrates. "He's looking for us. We need to move."

Everyone gets up, makes sure they have all their weaponry, and moves in separate directions to their designated positions.

We planned this. This is going to work.

Use the televised game to lure Aki in after evacuating *Sheruta*. Done. Prepare our armies and get into position. Done. Win the war. I guess we'll see.

I materialize in front of Lucien, Red, and the team of thirteen, preparing to traverse the town without being seen to lure Aki and the army away from the town and through our traps. And our secret weapon is currently curled up quietly in Lucien's pocket.

"You okay there, Lo?"

"I am well. Resting before the fight."

"Good."

Red smiles at me. "Saw you taking on Arrie on the plasmascreen. You were amazing!"

514

Lucien chuckles and then scolds, "Till you got distracted."

"Shut up."

The rest of the team are a mix of Shifters, Fae, Witches, Vampires, and a few pixies, just in case we need another method of communicating with the other teams. Every team has a few.

"Ready?" I ask.

Everyone stands and looks at me with determination on their faces.

"Good. C'mon." I lead them through the forest, down a few winding paths, and into the town center, where Aki is standing with a few Vampires, a smirk on his face. "Aki."

"Sister! Hello."

My illusion spell is working (well, it was a group effort), and not-really-people people are walking about, chatting, looking alive. But if you look closely, you'll notice they aren't interacting with anything but each other. Hopefully Aki hasn't noticed that.

"Leave. You are not welcome here."

"But I thought we were having a battle for strongest Horseman. Where was my invite? Surely I'm at least in the running."

I snarl, my fists curling. "You're not a Horseman."

His face changes from smirking to frowning in an instant, his eyes darkening. "More a Horseman than you." His team of Vampires are ready, preparing to charge, but he holds up a hand, stopping them.

"Leave, and you can just live your life. Free."

"Free? You think living as a mortal is freedom?" His voice breaks, and for a moment, I feel sorry for him. His mind is so warped with power, he can't see the real world anymore. "You think I can just leave the world in your stupid hands?"

I'm a few steps from him now, within grabbing distance; all I have to do is grab my staff and teleport us. But I don't want him stealing it from me—that would be devastating. And I don't trust him not to do exactly that. I throw it into my hand and quickly activate the sticking rune, then teleport us to the first stop.

Predictably, his hand wraps around the wood with a smile. "Dumb sister." But he can't grab it from me.

"Predictable brother." I yank it from his grip and walk back a few steps, putting some space between us.

We're on the beach, close to the water. There are a bunch of water Witches and Fae behind the cliff, ready to intervene if we need it. But the important thing is that there are no buildings here.

Our army isn't far from here, just over the other side of the hill, ready to charge on my command. Nine and Arrie are with them. Connie is elsewhere, taking care of the backup plans.

Dea, on the other hand, is getting the rest of the second squad ready. I'll join them when I can. For now, I need to help make a dent in this stupid war.

"Our army is on the way, Taylor," he snarls. "You won't

win. Not this time."

"Eh. I like our chances." I raise two fingers behind my back, and a few dozen Witches and Fae materialize behind us, a tidal wave in the making. I'm helping them slightly, giving it a little more stability and oomph. "We're not built on hate like you. We're unified."

"Unity?" Aki laughs. "Just a societal concept, nothing more."

Ugh. I can't with this asshole. I flick a third finger. "Now."

The tidal wave rushes over our heads and dives toward Aki and his team, throwing them over the hill. "Ahhh!" His screams are music to my ears.

Lucien gets Lo out of his pocket and chucks him into the air. "Go get 'em." He grows into his large form, circling the battlefield over the other side of the hill, waiting.

And there, in the distance, coming eastward, is the thundering sound of thousands of boots on the ground. An army. Made mostly of Vampires or Fae, but the Demons will join them, and then there are a few Witches they've collected too.

It'll be hell.

But I will win.

Chapter Sixty-Seven

We teleport to the cliff, looking on from a distance, out of reach of Aki and his impending army.

Swords clash, magic is thrown in every direction, and our friends are fighting for their lives, blood staining the sandy grass.

The Vampire king amongst them, he speeds around the battlefield removing heads like candy, and Lucien looks on with worry.

"He'll be fine," Red reassures, her hand on his arm.

"I just wish I could be there."

I look at Nine, my gut clenching. "Me too." But we have a more important job to do right now. "When they need it, they have the second half of our army waiting. Connie won't let them lose."

Everyone nods, solemn faces. Silent.

I have to trust that Arrie, Connie, and Nine can handle this without us. That Arrie can lead us to victory. We were always meant to work as a team, and part of that is trusting that they can do what they've been doing for two thousand years. In the meantime, I have a Fae Queen to deal with.

Dea teleports in with his team a moment later, bringing our team's total to twenty. It's not much, but then that's the point. "Ready?" he asks, his eyes on one figure in the distance.

"As I'll ever be."

I'll be fine. I promise. I love you both.

I love you too.

His eyes meet ours for a second, before some Vampire clambers onto his back, and he has to yank her off, sticking a knife in her heart, then cutting her head off.

I turn to face the team of twenty, Red, Lucien, Dea, my Fae trainer, our Fae ambassador, and I included. "Is everyone ready?"

They all nod.

"Then get ready, because this will be a little scary." I teleport us to the Atlantic Ocean, a memory I have of looking out a plane window, and many of them scream as we plummet to the ground, not really able to breathe.

Okay, air bubble. I gather the surrounding air, moving it into a bubble that will gradually lower us to the floor and give us oxygen.

"No one panic," Dea orders.

Lucien shakes his head, fear gripping him. "Your lives are fucking crazy."

"Yup."

But he's spinning in place, grasping for a surface that's not there. "Shit shit shit."

Red grabs his hands and spins him to face her. "Stop panicking. Just take deep breaths."

And Lucien isn't the only one listening to her, as I notice lots of people with their eyes closed following her instructions. Calmness slowly washes over everyone at her words.

I look to Dea, matching his gentle smile.

"Okay, we need to find the entrance."

The water Witches with us all turn and face the ocean, but one of them says, "We need to be a little closer. I can't get a read from this high up."

"Okay. Lowering us."

I can't read the water yet, my magical limits becoming more and more obvious the further complications I face. But I can glide us over it.

Nine's voice washes over me: there's nothing wrong with help. Working with the world was your idea after all.

He was right, of course. He's always fucking right. The genius asshole.

"There," the Witch from earlier says. "I can read from here."

And the other two agree, so I keep us at this height, trying to cover us with clouds and keep us out of sight, lest we do stumble onto some underwater Fae kingdom unexpectedly.

"Lots of fish, some sunken ships, but no underwater Fae kingdom. You sure it exists?"

"Yes," the only Fae with us says. "It's legendary among our people, even us on *Sheruta* have heard of it."

"We scoured old books and legends for days," I say, "it should be around this part of the ocean. I hope."

Red and Lucien remain patient, silently observing the work. Not really able to help.

A couple of hours later, and more frustration than I thought possible, and one of the Witches exclaims, "Wait! There!"

They all turn to where she's facing and analyze the water below. "That could be something. It's like an underground tunnel running beneath the ocean. But it's really deep."

"Nothing to worry about," I say with false confidence. I lower the bubble at speed so we're on top of the water, then I sink us.

The light quickly fades, and soon everyone who isn't a Vampire cannot see, but given the night vision thing, I'm good. "No one panic. I can still see."

"Me too," Lucien says.

A few of the other Vampires agree.

And everyone seems to take a collective breath, let it out, and then grab onto their own clothing, shivering.

"It is quite cold down here, Angel," Dea says.

"Oh, right. Huddle together for now. If I light a fire, we have nowhere for the smoke to go." I rush everyone into the center of the bubble, allowing them to share body warmth, and I do not miss how Lucien curls around the back of Red, keeping her closer to the others. "We're nearly to the floor, I think."

"Let's hope there's no anglerfish, like in Finding Nemo," Red says.

"Why?" I ask. "Why would you put that thought into my head?"

"Sorry," she winces. "Bad habit."

Lucien chuckles.

The other Vampires are also on the outside, along with Dea, who cannot die from hypothermia but who does have wings, allowing everyone else to have an extra layer of heat as he wraps them around the group.

Slowly, I rest our bubble on the bottom of the ocean floor, which is surprisingly empty. "Okay, we're here." I pop the bubble at the bottom, allowing my feet to find the floor and see what's down there. "It is a tunnel. No guarantee it's the one we're looking for."

An earth Witch nods and crouches low to the ground, helping us by creating a hole in the ocean floor. "Alright, I'm about to break through."

Two of the water Witches kneel beside her and curl their hands into tight fists. "We can't hold this for very long."

As the hole widens and light spills into the ocean, everyone rushes through, quickly and efficiently lowering themselves onto whatever lies beyond. My Fae trainer goes first, taking it upon herself to deal with whatever might be lurking in mysterious tunnel number one.

Once everyone is through, including Dea, who had to shift back in order to fit, I crouch near to the floor and grab the water they're holding back. "Go," I say through clenched teeth.

Shit. I have to make it through this hole, but I'm holding up the fucking ocean here. It's kinda hard work. Soon I'm panting, and eventually, I lower myself through the hole and look to the earth Witch with us. "Any time, babe."

"Right." She plugs the hole back up, and I release the water, hearing it roar overhead.

I release a panting breath, hands on knees. "Fuck, that was hard." But looking around me, I realize the hard part might be to come. "Where are we?"

Chapter Sixty-Eight

Big Players Nowhere to be Seen: Where are the Horsemen and Their Armies?

Hanging lanterns light the way at every few hundred meters, the metal gratings under our feet illuminating ominously in the partial dark.

"Sooo, left or right?" I ask the group while looking around, having raced both directions for a mile or two. "It's the same for a while in both directions, I'm afraid."

"Well," Lucien says, "that way is land, right?"

Dea nods, agreeing.

"So that way, farther out to sea." He does not look sure, but it's the best plan we have.

So left it is.

We head that way, various Vampires racing ahead every

mile or so, giving us instructions and choices as to what is coming up. But it's seemingly miles and miles of tunnels.

"How did the Fae Queen lead an entire army down here?" I mumble. "Seems inefficient."

"You'd be surprised what a community can do and how quickly when motivated," Red responds.

I hang back a bit, standing next to my Fae trainer, who has been remarkably quiet on this venture. "You okay?"

She looks to me with curious eyes. "Of course." But there's something there. Something strange I don't understand, and I get the feeling there's something she's not telling me.

But I trust her.

She'll tell me in her own time.

"Well, if you want to chat, I'm right here."

She looks at me fondly, if slightly irritated (which, on second thought, might just be her face), and smiles. "Thank you."

"We must be nearly there by now," one of the water Witches complains. "We've been walking for hours. And it was a few hours before that."

She's right. Connie, Nine, and Arrie are taking care of everything back on *Sheruta*, and they might not be okay. What if they're all dying and stuck at the bottom of the ocean?

"They are fine," Dea says. "I think we're nearly there. The lights are getting more frequent."

Lucien, who's up front, raises his fist, and we all stop. "I can hear voices," he whispers.

I walk up to him and strain my hearing, zooming in on the sounds coming from somewhere in front of us. "They're talking about dinner and their husbands."

"Guards," Dea says. "We should take them out and hide their corpses somewhere."

"I wasn't going to kill them," I scold. "Just throw them unconscious."

"It's too risky," Red says. "They could sound an alarm if they wake up, and we don't know how long this will take us to complete."

"I'll do it," Lucien says. He races forward before anyone can stop him, light footsteps making his almost as soundless as Dea, but if I strain, I can hear him. A small, almost unperceivable gasp echoes across the grates, and then Lucien races back. "Done. Just need to find somewhere to put their bodies."

We all move forward hesitantly, all of us on edge. But the corpses look merely asleep, no blood in sight. As I notice the small pinpricks in their necks, I realize he drained them dry.

A raised eyebrow is all I throw at him.

"Quickest and cleanest way to kill someone," he says with a shrug.

"See if this grating comes up," Red says. "Quickly."

Everyone manages to lift one of the panels that line up to form the walkway we're on, and we dump their bodies in the small space beneath, thankful for a Fae's lithe form.

"Okay. Moving on." I point forward. "Thank goddess we

picked the right direction."

"I'm not just a pretty face," Lucien jokes.

Everyone chuckles.

Another Vampire runs ahead, quiet and swift, and when he returns, he says, "Another hundred meters and there's a locked door."

"Locked how?" I ask.

"Digitally."

I crack my knuckles and smile. "Bring it on."

Everyone looks to me with surprise on their faces, but Lucien and Dea smirk, knowing my mortal past.

"I can have non-magical skills. Secret ones."

"If you say so," the earth Witch says.

We eventually get to the door, which is heavy, seemingly to keep out water if needed, and digitally locked with a pad on the left-hand side. I check it out, yanking off the cover, and nod.

I've done one of these before, when breaking into the Chinese SC HQ. Good job they used SC technology, or this might have been a bitch. Pushing all the right buttons and cutting all the right cables, and we're in.

"What were you, a burglar in a past life?" someone asks.

"Something like that," I mumble.

"Not to worry, little Horseman." Lucien pats me on the shoulder. "You'll always be the hero to me."

"Thanks." I remove his hand and open the doors. "Here goes nothing."

We don't know what's beyond this door. There could be an army waiting for us—or it could be empty. For all we know, the queen could be sitting on her throne right behind this door. Though I doubt it.

But when I swing it open, it's just an empty room with elevator doors on the other side. It's a squish to get us all in, but we manage.

"What button?" Red asks.

"What are the options?"

"One through five."

I think for a minute. "We're probably on one, so go to five. She'll most likely be there, at the top. Hardest to get to."

"Or she could on the bottom, which is hardest to reach to from the surface," Dea suggests.

"There's like a million tons of water above us, I doubt she's worried about that."

"I'm with Magic," Lucien says, and most people agree. "Level five it is."

Red presses the button and the doors close behind us, then we're sailing up, all facing the other entrance, ready for whatever it throws at us.

But it once again opens to emptiness.

"Where the fuck is everyone?" I whisper. "I'm starting to think we've been duped."

"Maybe they're hiding somewhere, knowing the other half of their army are fighting," Lucien suggests.

"They did not take their whole army, did they?" Dea asks.

"They wouldn't be so stupid," I respond. "He might be evil, my brother, but he's not an idiot." I take a deep breath, entering the atrium made of glass, the black, swirling ocean lying beyond the room like a terrifying ghost. "Onward, I guess."

There are a set of stairs to the left, another to the right, and a small door at the back. All of which might lead to her.

I check the door at the back quickly, but it's just storage, so that leaves the two small staircases. "Probably the spiraling one on the left, right?"

So Red goes right, checks what is that way, and comes back and nods. "Just empty bedrooms that way."

We all creep up the stairs, but something doesn't feel right. This has been too easy. Something is off. The air in here feels untouched, like it's been days, maybe weeks, since someone's been here.

"I don't think this is—"

"Shh," Lucien scolds.

"But something isn't—"

"Shut. Up." He strains forward at the top of the stairs and looks around, confused. "What is that sound?"

I can't hear anything, but then, his hearing is better than mine. Maybe he has supersonic senses, like Connie. Could that be his Vampire ability? I still have seen nothing in action from him.

The group dissipates, checking all the doors up on the stone platform quietly, quickly. And without stumbling. They were chosen for their stealth, this team, and Dea did not disappoint with that.

There is one door at the back, almost hidden, like it's tucked away, and we go for it, turning the doorknob against my better judgement, and are sucked in. Like it gobbled us whole.

Some of them scream, but some of us remain silent. But we're falling. Like, really, really, falling. Into pitch-dark blackness with zero windows or sources of light, and I don't know what to do.

Breathe, Magic. Breathe.

After a few ins and outs, I light a small ball of fire in my hand, keeping it close to me so as not to light the tunnel on fire; Red follows suit, keeping hers tight to herself too. And when it lights up, I realize we're falling beneath the ocean floor.

Dea shifts and gets his wings out, grabbing some of the others, while I get rid of the fireball and use air to bring us to a stop. "Where are we?" he asks.

"I have no idea, but we must be beneath the ocean floor? How much further until it's just magma or whatever is beneath the surface?"

No one answers—probably because no one knows—but I slowly rise us up to the top again, giving Dea's wings a rest.

"Thank heavens it's you," Red says. "Imagine if we did this without you?"

Once we're back on solid ground and we silently all agree

to stay the fuck away from that door, Lucien says, "Booby traps, then?"

"Would seem so." I stand in the center of the glass-domed room and raise my hands. "I need silence to concentrate," I tell everyone, lest they get the clever idea to talk. I shift to my male form and use my Fae magic to highlight any and all traps and magical circles, runes, and other spells in the room.

My Fae trainer looks around, taking it all in. "Seems this room is filled with traps, but there's a secret door over there." She points next to the door I went into earlier. "Might be something."

We all creep up to it, this time being a little more cautious. But I'm the one who opens the door and steps through. "I'll go first. Wait here."

Even Dea seems to think this is a good idea, as he says nothing, but he's feeling apprehensive. I look to him before stepping over the barrier with a smile. I'll be fine, I try to convey with my eyes.

He smiles back, nodding.

But before I can turn around, as I'm stepping over the edge, my surroundings change, and I can no longer see them behind me. In fact, there's not even a door behind me anymore.

It's an empty stone room with metal bars along one side and a small window on the other. "Fuck." That door teleported me to a prison.

Chapter Sixty-Nine

Where is the Fae Queen Hiding? Online Speculation is Growing Wild: Top 10 Ideas

As far as I can tell, there's nothing around me. The outside of the bars is black nothingness, the outside of the small window is pure white, and there are no stones, sticks, or anything pointy I can use to get out of here.

So that leaves me with what I brought with me myself.

But even if I manage to open the bars somehow or crawl through the window, I don't think it would help.

Pressing my face through the giant mental bars, I peer into the blackness. "Where am I?"

If I don't get out of here quickly, the others are going to come after me, and we're all going to be stuck here.

I grab my staff and try teleporting myself out—no use.

I analyze the surrounding spells, trying to see if I can de-puzzle them—they're too complicated.

I throw my female self against the bars, trying to break them—I'm apparently not strong enough. But that throws me for a second because I can probably lift a forest, and somehow I can't break through basic metal?

"What the fuck is going on here?"

I have my powers, but I can't seem to use them. Testing that theory, I try to shift into any kind of animal, but I can't. Something is stopping me.

Dick on a stick, I'm fucking stuck here.

Think, Magic, think. There must be a way out of here. I can't shift, so Shifter magic is out. I'm not strong enough to do any damage, so Vampire stuff is out. I could scan the Fae magic, so I seem to still have access, which makes sense, because otherwise how would they maintain the spells. What about Witch magic? I shift into my female form and try lighting up a fireball or conjuring water. I can't seem to shift any of the dirt on the floor, either. Dammit.

Okay, so just Fae magic.

I'm going to have to science my way out of here. Magic is just science with extra woo woo.

I sit cross-legged in the center of the small room, just a few feet either side of me where I can place my hands on the floor and feel the magic. It pulses through me. I can feel the intricate spellwork, the knots and tangles, where the runes affect the spell, where incantations have been replaced, and where certain ingredients have been combined into potions and used to impact the spell.

It's complicated.

Not quite as complicated as the Otherworld Gate, which I'll still be trying to decipher in two thousand years, but complicated enough that I'm worried about the time it will take. We've been here too long.

Connie, Arrie, and Nine have been fighting for hours, and we're no closer to the queen. Maybe we should have left earlier.

Putting those worries to the back of my mind for now, I focus on finding out what the spell does. It seems to mostly be a holding spell, but I can't really find out where I'm supposed to be being held. Or how to send me back.

I reach through the magic, following various rune circles and spell lines, until I reach a familiar presence. Someone whose spellwork I've felt before. She's there, searching for me.

So I grab on, tying my magic to hers, and then tying myself to my magic, and soon I'm dematerializing, vanishing from the weird room.

"Oh my God, Magic," Red says, exacerbated. "What the hell happened?"

"Do not go in there," I say, out of breath. "Teleports you to a room that blocks non-Fae magic."

My green-skinned Fae trainer helps me up, plopping me back onto my feet.

"Thank you."

"You're welcome."

I look around, not noticing anything else, and then look to Dea. "Maybe you were right. Maybe floor one is where she is."

"It is the next logical place to look." He wraps an arm around my shoulder. "Just try not to get caught in too many more traps, Angel."

"Better me than the rest of you." I shut the door before everyone turns around—because falling through that—and then something in the room clicks.

Barely audible, but it's there. A faint clicking.

Someone gasps. "What's that?"

I look toward where the earth Witch is looking and frown. There's a shimmer in the air. As though there's an invisible barrier surrounding us. Walking up to it, I reach my hand out. But I squeal when it zaps me. "Don't touch that."

The Fae trainer sighs and raises her hands, feeling out the room. And in a few seconds blue-glowing runes fill the air in a dome shape, interlinking in a complex weave that leaves my jaw dropping. "It's a trap," she says.

The elevator doors open, and the Fae Queen walks in with a few soldiers behind her, smiling. "That it is."

I slam my hands against the barrier, testing its strength, but it stays standing. Lucien swears, Red looks furious, and Dea's worried face makes my stomach roil. If I ever get stuck in a Fae spell again, it'll be an immortal lifetime too soon.

The Fae Queen looks us over, but her eyes widen in surprise as her mouth is rendered speechless when she lands upon a particular someone. "You." Her fists clench, her soldiers pull their weapons out, and the room's domed glass goes stormy, lightning striking and thunder sounding. "What are you doing with them?"

My Fae trainer, whose name I was never given, steps forward, solemn emptiness on her face. "Helping."

"Against your own people?"

"You have not been my people for a long time, assuming you ever were."

"Do you know how long I have been looking for you? Get over here. Now." Her tone brokers no argument, her eyes furious as her earlier smirk is now a thin grimace. "Ophelia."

Ophelia looks to me, sad eyes meeting mine, and says, "I'll take the spell down, but when I do, I need you to fulfill the rest of the plan no matter what."

I don't understand what she's talking about, but I nod anyway. Agreeing to anything my friend needs of me.

With a simple wave of her hand, she removes the complex spell and grimaces in pain.

"Ophelia," the Fae Queen whispers, an eerie, almost supernatural sound coming from her mouth, "come here."

Ophelia's feet take her to the Fae Queen, but her face tells me she doesn't want to go there. "Yes, Mother."

Chapter Seventy

BREAKING NEWS: ARMIES IN SHERUTA CLASH

Mother? Wait. She's the missing Fae princess the news has been on about for the last few years? That's why she wouldn't give me her name. Did she not trust me?

Fulfill the rest of the plan no matter what, she said. Even if it means hurting her to get to her mother.

Goddess, I don't like this.

Our eyes meet, and I can feel the sadness coming off of her in waves of grief. She really doesn't want to be over there. And I'm going to make sure she doesn't have to be for much longer.

I switch forms and brace myself, trusting that she'll take the spell down.

The Fae Queen smiles as she takes her daughter's hand

and goes to turn around, but Ophelia smirks at the last minute and jumps forward, slamming her hand against the barrier with a high-pitched scream that shoots through me.

But a second later, the barrier is down and we're free.

The Fae Queen drags Ophelia back, behind her contingent of soldiers, and sighs at her. "Really, Ophelia? When will you learn to behave?"

"When you stop being such a bitch."

"Stay there and don't move, Ophelia," she says in the same voice as before, that eerie, echoing magical voice I don't understand.

The Fae Queen stands in front of her daughter but behind her guards, like a coward.

Red and Lucien are upfront, ready to go, fire in hand, fangs lowered, and for a brief moment, I think to myself that yeah, they'd make a great future for our world. But my smile drops when one soldier charges Red and punches her in the face hard enough to swerve her head at a weird angle. And Lucien roars, fury consuming him.

His eyes burn a violent red as his fingernails grow into claws and his fangs descend further, his hair blowing back from the magical pressure in waves of white-hot anger. A single swipe of those claws is all it takes to have the soldier screaming in agony—drowning out every other sound in the room.

The soldier's face melts, burning and charring in places, as his eyeballs melt from his eyes. "Wha . . . What did you do to me?"

Lucien smirks at him. "Poisoned claws." He lifts his hand and stares at those very claws, admiration on his face. "Never really liked using them until now."

Red just looks at him with wonder and shock, matching my expression. But Dea doesn't look surprised at all. He just stands there in silence, a small smile on his face.

And then chaos breaks out as our team charges the other, not a one of them holding back. Itching for violence.

Dea flies overhead, picking off the soldiers one by one, then dropping them from the ceiling, sometimes charging them into the ground headfirst.

A Fae comes at me, a rune circle on his palm that I don't recognize, but I don't give him time to use it and find out its function. I grab him by the collar and throw him into the nearest wall. His head bashes inward, blood and brain matter spattering over the wall.

Then I rush the next attacker, a Vampire with muscles that might rival Arrie's. I duck under his first swing, then kick him in the balls before slamming his head to the tiled floor.

Thankfully, we don't have an entire army to deal with. But the smile on the Fae Queen's face tells me they're near. I need to get to her. To shove teleport her into one of our cells in the embassy. Then it'll break whatever hold she has on Ophelia.

I rush past one-on-one fights, two-on-one fights, and plain chaos as Red lights up the room. Until I'm face-to-face with Queen Bitch, who has a tight grip on Ophelia, a snarl on her face, and eyes the color of thunder.

I swear, she looks like an angry snake.

One I'm gonna poke with an angry stick and see if she's really poisonous.

"Magic."

"Hi, Your Majesty." I smile gently, sincerely, for just a moment. "Sorry, but I'm going to require my friend back. I've grown rather fond of her, you see, and she's an important part of my inner circle. Not to mention badass."

She scoffs. "The only reason she's as 'badass' as you say is because she received a royal education provided for her because she's my daughter."

I groan, a hand wiping down my face. "You're one of *those* parents. Spare me. You feel like because you spread your legs and ripped your pussy giving birth to her that you in some way own her. As though she owes you blind loyalty and love simply by existing." My hands crumble into fists. "Hate you break it to you, but love and loyalty are earned, even by those with whom we share blood." I clap my hands, congratulating her with as much sarcasm as I can muster. "Congrats, you provided the bare necessities to your child that qualify you to be a parent. You want a gold medal?"

Ophelia is holding back laughter, though not moving. Her eyes meet mine again, and I can see the thanks behind her irises.

But the Fae Queen is stewing in seething anger in front of me, clearly in disagreement with me. "See, the problem with you Americans is that you lack basic respect for other cultures. Here in the Fae Court we remain loyal to our parents no matter what."

"You have a culture of abuse? Seems like something, as a queen, you have the power to change."

No more words are exchanged as she steps forward and throws a rune at me, but I swipe it away, not even paying attention to what it was. And then I dodge her attempts to throw various spell beads from her necklace at me—again, not knowing what they are.

"Rusty?"

The shrill scream out of her mouth sends unpleasant shivers down my spine, but she manages to get a weak punch in before I'm grabbing her wrists and teleporting her to our prison.

But before I can do that, Ophelia yells, "Wait!" I stop and turn to her, but all she does is yank the crown off of her mother's head and smiles. "Okay, I'm good."

And I finally teleport her to the prison, where her magic should be fully dampened. "That was easier than expected."

Ophelia shrugs. "Queens aren't trained in combat."

I raise an eyebrow at her in question. Then why is she?

"Usually."

We turn to the last remnants of the fighting, just a few more pairs of magicuffs being placed onto wrists, and we're panting but free. "Move out of the way," I say to everyone, including myself. And I teleport them to the same prison.

I turn to Ophelia with a scowl. "So, what now, Your Majesty?"

The matching scowl she sends me withers me on the spot, and maybe I'm not ready to take her on scowl for scowl.

"There's something I need to do, but I'll meet you on the battlefield."

So I teleport everyone back to *Sheruta* as Ophelia goes somewhere else, probably to do some Fae royal nonsense, and the sight we're greeted with turns my blood to stone.

Chapter Seventy-One

Sheruta Barred to General Public as War Rages On

The battlefield is basically a graveyard. We're on top of the cliff, where we were before we left. And looking down on all our friends lying dead or injured has us all silenced in the space of a breath.

Dea flies off, probably in search of Nine, making sure he's okay.

I can't believe I abandoned them to this. I could have gotten anyone else to go—Nine would probably have managed that okay.

You didn't know what you'd face.

Nine?

Alive and well, Sweetie. But Arrie's pretty badly hurt. He's in the makeshift hospital with the other wounded that teleported out.

I turn to the team. "I'm going to heal the wounded, get them back out in the field. Nine and Connie are fighting at two separate locations: the north forest and the field in front of us. Divide yourselves between them."

Nobody asks questions. They just leave. And I teleport to the hospital, adrenaline and fear running hot through my veins. Arrie's easy to spot, groaning on a bed while trying to stand back on his feet.

Predictably.

"Arrie, if I see you get back up again," a nurse says, "I'll drop a building on your head."

I smile, standing at the edge of the bed. "Don't worry, I'll help."

Arrie's gaze snaps to me, and I swear I see a breath of relief flow through him. "You're okay?"

"Yup. Our operation was a success and easier than expected." I grab his chin in my grip and drip some blood from my finger into his mouth. "Now rest for a few minutes until that's done healing you, and you can go back out there."

Spinning, I turn to face everyone else and project my voice on the air. "You're not required to return to fighting, but I'm going to heal you all so you're free to do so. There are other jobs available, such as collecting the dead from the edges of the battlefields, helping the nurses here, and patrolling *Sheruta* to ensure they don't disturb the residences." Blood pours in a steady stream from my fingertips into everyone's mouths. "It takes a few minutes to fully work."

I turn to the nurse. "I'll come back as often as I can to help. In the meantime, keep up the great work." Then I teleport out of there to find Connie, who's in the forest somewhere, having engaged our backup plan a while ago, it seems.

More dead lie strewn across the forest floor, a mixture of ours and there's—the sight disgusts me. So many dead, and for what. So he can have more power. What a waste.

"Magic?" Connie screams from across the field before running through fights to get to me. "You're back? Did it work?"

"A raving success. What can I do?"

"You have to get to Lo. He's over there." She points westward. "Magic." She looks at me with serious eyes for a second before lowering her gaze. "I think he might be . . . dead."

Those words shock me to my core. And I'm teleporting farther down the forest in visual increments, trying not to teleport myself into a tree or a corpse, until I eventually find Lo's body on the forest floor, lying still. If you ignored the odd feeling in the air, you could almost pretend he was sleeping.

"Lo!"

I screech to a stop beside his body, anxiety and worry coursing through me.

"Maaagic . . . ." It's so faint, his voice, but it's there. "I'm . . . sorry."

I fly over to his face and watch giant tears fall into a small puddle on the strewn leaves. "Hey, hey. It's okay. You're going to be okay." I slice my wrist open, anticipating lots of blood being needed.

"No, Magic." His eyes meet mine. "It'll take far too much blood to cure a being like me, and then you'll be out of commission until you've slept it off. They need you." His eyelids droop. "The world needs you."

"I can't let the last dragon die, Lo. Even if it weren't you, I couldn't do it."

"Ah, there she is. My sister." His voice pierces through me.

This is all his voice. His plan. His violence. None of it had to happen. "How could you do all of this?"

"Me? This was your plan." Hand on heart, he smiles at me, blood covering his torso.

"Because we didn't have another choice. It was the only way to keep you from terrorizing the other species, and eventually the humans." Because let's not forget that he cares nothing about them and would have tried to mess with them, eventually. "You forced my hand."

Tears leak down my face as I gesture to Lo. "He's the last dragon in existence! What were you thinking?"

"Took a lot of magic, for sure. Nearly gutted me dead. But I managed it. Solo." He smirks. "Something you couldn't manage on Jura Mountains."

This is just a pissing contest to this asshole, isn't it? He just wants to be me. Though, why anyone would want my life is beyond me. All I want is a small apartment in Tokyo to live out a regular lifetime with those I love. But he wants the world at his feet.

I'm done with this.

I'm done holding back, letting him get away with shit just because I'm too afraid to hurt my own brother. He killed Nine. Lo is on his last legs—if he's not dead already. And he wants the world to serve him.

Shifting into my male form, I put my staff away and shift, moving my body into a new shape, forming something I've not shifted into before. And before I know it, I'm growing in size, growing wings large enough I have to be careful of the trees, and my feet with talons the size of people.

Aki's smirk wipes off his face as horror dawns.

And a dragon's roar rips from my snout as fire engulfs the air above the trees.

Chapter Seventy-Two

Fae Queen goes Head-to-Head Against Horsemen in Devastating War

I shrink my size to maneuver around the trees, mimicking the various sizes I've seen Lo in before, and I chase Aki, who's using teleporting crystals to jump a few hundred meters in front of him each time.

He won't be able to keep that up. He can't have that many teleporting crystals left. Eventually, he'll run out, and when he does, I'll pin him to the floor.

Arrows bounce off my wings and stick into my thick hide, fireballs the size of heads aim at my face, but I just open my mouth and swallow them.

If I weren't about to eat my brother (or maybe I'll torch him, I haven't decided yet), I'd totally be loving this moment, but the dead bodies beneath my wings and the smell of blood up my nostrils and the sound of Aki's breaths ragged and his whimpers, his sniveling grate my senses to shreds, and it's all I can focus on.

Aki.

Aki.

Aki.

I chant his name over and over again in my head, so afraid that if I stop, the rage will dissipate and I'll go easy on him. Right now, I need that anger to burn through me like a flame raging against the night. Right now, I can't be peaceful. Because if I am, the world loses.

So I'll sacrifice it all—my brother, my sanity, my innocence—so the world will forever beat on.

Aki's feet stumble as he pats at his empty pockets and scatters his limbs across the forest floor. "Wait, wait, wait. Please, don't—"

I grab him by the arm and toss him into the air, the open my mouth below him. Waiting.

He's inches from my teeth, seconds from being destroyed, and he's suddenly hit by a flying person sailing through the sky.

I spin around and roar, fire burning my throat, but I swallow it. I don't want to burn the forest down.

It's a stupid Demon that saves him. And not just any Demon, but Verity. I know he made the deal, but did he have to save his life? Couldn't he have just stayed by the sidelines and watched?

"What are you doing?" I roared.

"My job!" He shrugs. "Sorry." He plops Aki back onto his feet, and then races away, clashing with one of our Witches farther up field.

Aki uses those few seconds to adjust himself and raise his hands into the air. Black sand pours from them in streams until it floods the area around us and everyone, even his own people, die instantly.

"Wait, Aki, no—" He throws it at me, and I have to shift back to male, then to female, and catch it. "What are you doing? This is so dangerous!"

"Stop being so afraid and fight me already! The last one standing can be the Fifth Horseman."

Ugh. He doesn't get it, does he?

"It will always be me, Aki. Even if I die, it will have always been me. You can't change what Fate has decided." I hold the magic in my shaking hands, unsure what to do with it, but eventually I let it go, let it travel back to him at speed, like a death bullet.

He catches it, adds to it, and slowly seeps it toward me like a fog, and out of that fog sprouts a tiger made from the same stuff. It pounces at me, and I blow it away with air, making sure it doesn't seep beyond the boundary of bodies already dead.

"Stop this," I plead. "Please."

He gathers all the death magic into a ball and lets it fester, growing in size and power until it's so big, I do not know how I'll possibly be able to stop it. He says nothing. Just looks at me with salacious glee and dangerous intentions. Before lobbing it my way.

I scramble to catch it, widening my arms as far as possible, but it engulfs me. I can't breathe for a second, until I remember I don't need to in this form, and then I let out the oxygen in my lungs and relax.

Calm, Magic. Stay calm.

Black sand is in my eyes, up my nose, and in places it has no business being. But I have to stay calm. I can find a way to remove it all.

I light a fire in my palm, seeing if it will burn, but it's no use. It's not flammable. Then I try dousing it in water, shoving it away with earth, and blowing it away, but it comes back every time. So I grab my staff and activate the protection rune, drawing a shield around me. And like it was made for this circumstance, it removes all the sand from my body and keeps it out like I'm wrapped in plastic wrap. But it doesn't do anything else. The sand still surrounds my shielded body.

But now I can think.

I start siphoning it away, placing it behind me and storing it in a hill of black sand I'm keeping for later, until finally I can see my brother watching me. Assessing me.

He looks impressed, but I'm not.

I'm pissed. So I charge at him when he's not expecting it, and pin him up against the nearest tree. "This is ridiculous.

You're being a child." I yank a look down at his neck and see the rope. I just need to grab it. Then he'll be weaker, like the normal version of himself.

But if it doesn't work, then he'll know I know, and my only piece of information leverage will be gone.

He struggles in my grip, not strong enough to break it, but his kicking feet are annoying, so I use a foot to pin his ankle to the tree also, keeping him still.

"Going to kill me, sister?"

"Hush. I'm thinking. And it's sibling."

"Pfft, you're a woman who can grow a dick. Doesn't make you a man."

My eyes bleed red as my fangs descend, frustration ebbing at my self-control, and instead of overthinking it, I just use my free hand to rip the cord from around his neck with all my strength.

"Nooooo!"

And it comes free, dangling in my grip.

I don't know how to destroy it, but I let Aki go, jump back several hundred feet, and snap it in two. Stone crumbles in my fingers. It's just stone. "Huh." Thought it would be spelled or made of something stronger, but it's not. It's fragile. So I hold it in a small ball of water and wash it with small waves and twists and turns, essentially eroding it until it's nothing but crumbled wet dust in the palm of my hand.

"What have you done?" Aki screeches once he's finally caught up to me. "How did you? Why?"

I shrug, not really caring to tell him about my badly trained seer abilities. He's weaker now, and I should have no problems killing him.

So I grab the largest chunk of earth I can manage with my newly found earth magic and slam it against his body, sending him spiraling into the air. Where I grab him in a tornado that I do my best not to destroy trees and people with, and throw him into the sky. I meet him up there, not really understanding why he's screaming quite so pathetically.

"It's just air, Aki. Surely you can magic your way out?" I put a finger to my lips. "Oh, that's right, you're a useless mortal with regular magic now."

"Regular magic? Even as a mortal I'm stronger than you." His hands form a complex series of gestures, twists, and turns, and soon his death magic has taken on a life of its own as it swirls and twirls through the air.

Before I can predict what it's going to do, and as we're falling quickly to the ground, it strikes out like a snake, jabbing me in the side. Then again. And again. And again. Until I'm hurting all over and my skin is turning black as my skin rots.

"Shit." I lower myself to the ground, letting Aki simply fall. (Who cares?) "What is this?" I rip my t-shirt off and look at the damage, and it's like my skin is slowly blackening, charred like roast meat left in the oven too long. How do I fix it?

I don't know death magic enough to reverse the damage,

other than to try siphoning out of myself—but a quick try of that tells me it won't work.

I have daggers, knives, my staff, and my pouch with . . . I have Horsemen blood! But when I go into the pouch, there's nothing there but a pile of broken glass.

Aki lands on the floor on the back of a unicorn made of death magic.

"Shit!" I teleport back across the forest, away from Aki, who looked about ready to throw that unicorn at me.

"Magic," Connie says, almost sounding out of breath, "how's Lo?"

"I don't know—" A scream leaves my lips as the death magic spreads through me farther.

Connie notices me holding my side. "What's wrong?" She drags us away from three Vampires fighting and ducks behind a rock. "Let me look." I take my hand away, and she gasps. "What is that?"

"Death magic."

"He did this?"

"Yeah. Not sure it can kill me, but it fucking hurts, and I can feel my magic weakening."

She reaches into my pouch and sighs, coming to the same conclusion I did. "Fuck balls."

"Yup." Another scream rents the air, stealing my breath and forcing me to lie down. "Can't ask Nine, or it'll remove one of the guys from their position. The field already took too much damage while Arrie was down." Connie looks concerned for a minute, but I wipe it away with, "I healed him, don't worry."

Relief washes through her. But then she looks to me, brows furrowed, and a tear slips free. "Use me."

"No, Connie. I can't do that to you. Not after . . ."

"It's okay. I'm asking you to feed from me." She leans her head to one side, exposing her neck.

"But—"

"Magic. Enough. We need you. And right now, you're infected with something we have no cure for. No one in the world will have a cure to that. I don't have time to grab one of the guys and bring them here, and even if I did, doing so would kill too many people where they are. This is the best way."

Even so, her hands are shaking.

She's scared.

But she's right, I don't have a choice.

I'll never forgive myself for this, but I let my fangs slip and my eyes turn red. I push her head to the side so she can't see me feeding, and I sink in.

The rush of blood fills my senses, and her beautiful, powerful taste floods my tongue. It's like a summer's breeze, with exotic fruit and sunscreen and sand. Like a cocktail of sun.

The blood rushes over the death magic, allowing my body to have enough energy to fight it. It fizzles in my veins. Sending my torso white hot with pain until it fades. And then I don't feel anything. Not even the death magic.

Connie fists my hip, gripping tight, and I pull back a little, listening to her, but she groans. "No, don't stop."

So I take a little more and let her yank me on top of her. But we're in a battlefield and this isn't the time or place. So I pull back and quickly tuck away my fangs and calm down before I look at her. "If you ever want more, we can resume at a later date, but we do have a world to save right now."

"Right." She coughs, then touches the wound at her neck. But she shakes it off. "Go kill him. Then save our dragon."

She runs off before I can think to ask how she's doing, but I guess I can give her more time later. Afterward.

Right now, I have to fight to make sure we have an afterward.

Chapter Seventy-Three

World Awake Watching Horrifying War as Horsemen Defend their Home

Aki's doing something near Lo with a vial, so I smash more earth into his face, sending him flying, hopefully smashing the vial while I'm at it.

I'm done with this asshole.

I sprint at him, slamming him into the ground the second he gets up. But I don't let him move an inch, with several punches to his face that dent his cheek bone.

And when he finally stands after I let him, he stumbles back to the floor. "Magic . . . ."

"No!" I roar. "You killed him! One of few people I care about more than the world, and you murdered him trying to get to me." I throw him onto a lone sword sticking out from the ground, his shoulder pierced. "What did you think I would do after that? Let you walk around freely?"

I walk up to him, bend down to his dying body, and whisper, "I'll rip you apart piece by piece." I yank him off the sword and sink my fangs into his neck, drinking more deeply than I usually would. And when I rip myself from his neck, I rip an arm from his torso and throw it away.

Just as I'm about to take a deep breath, he grabs my sleeve with his only hand and tries to pull me toward him, so I lean over. "You'll never be good enough for this job."

"No, I won't. But perfection isn't the point. All I need to do is try." And I rip his head from his shoulders, then set the pieces alight. And I watch as he dies. Never having to deal with him again puts a smile on my face and sends peace rolling through me.

Nine, sends out the message that it's time for stage four.

Okay.

A second later, I get the mental message: *Stage three complete. All soldiers move to stage four.*

A cheer goes up from around us as everyone knows what that means. We have all three enemies dealt with, two in custody and one dead.

Phase four is tricky, but with Nine, it'll be easier. He gathers mental images from everyone he needs and sends them out to all soldiers, including the one of me ripping Aki's head from his body, which makes him wince. And then he announces, *You are free to leave with zero consequences. Go home to your people. Anyone still fighting will be eliminated.*

After that, I expected teleportation crystals smashing everywhere, but most remain, choosing their beliefs over their own life.

That still leaves half an army who are still fighting, swords and magics clashing around me.

Shit. Now what?

We keep going. We outnumber them.

I teleport over to the front field, spotting Arrie straight away. Nine's not far. And Dea's in the air, leading the part of the battle that's air born.

Just as I'm about to teleport Nine over to Connie, splitting us up a little more fairly, someone stands over the edge of the cliff we were on earlier. Someone whose figure I'd recognize anywhere.

"Ophelia?"

Zooming my vision in, I notice the crown on her head and a similar set of bracelets wrapping around her arms as her mother had. She looks . . .

She looks like a queen.

Her voice rings out loud and clear, "Fae, you are commanded to return home and wait until further instruction greets you."

As one, they drop their spells and weapons, and the ones air born fall to the floor. They do not look happy about it, but they retreat, poofing out of existence as they use their teleporting crystals.

She flies down to us, spotting me and standing beside me. "Sorry, I needed to do an important spell to gain the ability to do that."

Arrie smacks her on the back. "Well done, Your Majesty."

Dea also descends, standing with us.

No one moves. Not even the enemy. They're down to simply the Vampires and the few Witches that remain. Fae made up most of their army.

Nine, sends out the message again.

A second later, he repeats the same message, and most vanish this time, not wanting to lose, it seems. They're all smarter than I gave them credit for.

"And the rest?" Arrie asks, an evil glee in his eye.

I gesture my arm wide, letting him have at it. "Be my guest."

Chapter Seventy-Four

FAE QUEEN'S ARMY DEFEATED AS CROWNED PRINCESS OPH-
ELIA SENDS HER PEOPLE HOME

An hour later, I'm at the hospital, helping with the cleanup efforts and healing patients when the guys stumble over the ridge as the sun starts to set. Nine's hobbling on one leg, half propped up by Dea, Arrie's grinning, and Dea looks relieved to see me.

Grabbing Connie's hand, I speed us over there and hug everyone. "We did it!"

"You did it," Dea corrects.

"I nearly lost a leg out there," Nine complains, "we did it."

"If you wanted to keep your leg, you should not have walked into that Fae's trap."

"Well, I couldn't be bothered to keep fighting him," he explained with a wave of his hand.

As he does so, I drop a few drops of blood into his mouth. "Might take a couple of minutes. Seems to heal bones slower." I turn to everyone else. "Anyone else have cuts, scrapes, et cetera?"

Arrie holds out an arm as Dea lifts his wings with a wince.

Sighing, I heal them both before ordering them all to help with the effort. "How does the city look?" I ask Connie.

"Good. We managed to keep most of the fighting contained. Somehow."

"Good. Start allowing the residents to come back and send the ambassadors and their generals the signal to start sending people home."

She nods, going off, seemingly relieved to have something non-violent to do.

"Arrie, Dea, please help carry people to the hospital. We're starting them off here, then moving them to the regular hospital if they need to stay. Nine?" I turn to him, giving him an extra hug. "I'm so glad you're alive."

"Me too, Sweetie." *I love you.*

I love you too.

Breaking the moment, Lucien Vampire speeds over, concern flittering across his face. "Has anyone seen my father?"

No one says anything, but Arrie steps forward. "Lucien, I'm so sorry, but a lightning spell struck him a few hours ago. He's dead."

562

The look of horror on his face breaks my heart.

The Vampire king is dead.

I turn to him. "What about Red, Korby, and the others?"

Lucien looks to the ground, speechless. "I have not seen them." He looks up at us with sad eyes, tears staining his cheeks. "Excuse me, but I have to find his body."

Grabbing his hand, I squeeze. "I'll help. And we can look for Red and Korby while we're at it." I teleport us to the battlefield Arrie was commanding. "I'm so sorry, Lucien. He was a great man."

"And a great father."

We search the area, and eventually, after following the lightning patches that charred the ground, we find his crown lying next to his body. "Is it him?"

Lucien leans down and licks a little of his blood, then bursts into tears.

Not knowing what to do, I kneel next to him hand on his back, letting him say goodbye to his father.

An hour later, someone familiar runs over. "Lucien!"

He shoots his head up, looking at her with tears in his eyes and lets her come to him. "Red." He grabs her around the waist and hugs her tightly to him, not letting her go.

"Lucien . . ." Sobs rack her as relief courses through her. "I'm so sorry. Yes. Yes, I'll marry you."

Taken aback, I just sit there, not sure whether to congratulate or not, given the Vampire king's dead body lying next to me.

She looks to me, then to crown in my hands and the body beside me. "Wait, is that . . . ?"

I just nod, not having it in me to say the words yet. "I hate to ask, but have you seen Korby and Nigel?"

"Oh, yeah, they're helping with the cleanup effort, I think. Nigel's missing an arm though."

"What?" He's missing an arm?

"Go," Lucien says. "I'll be okay."

Red wraps her hand through his with a gentle smile as they both kneel at the king's side.

So I teleport back to the hospital, where I see Nigel helping to hand out supplies with his one remaining arm. "What are you doing up and about, old man?"

He looks to me and smiles. "Magic! I knew you were alright, but . . . you know, an old man's going to worry."

"Sit down right this instant." I point to a spare spot on the grassy floor. "I'll heal up the wound. If you had the arm, I could try to reattach?"

"Burned to a crisp, I'm afraid."

I unwrap his bloody stump, amazed at how quickly it's already healed, but with a drop of blood, it heals completely in no time. "There."

"I hate to ask, but is he . . . dead?"

I nod.

He looks sadly at the floor for a minute. "I knew it was needed, but he's still my godson."

"We can have a funeral, if you'd like?"

"I'd like that."

Before I can say anything else, someone rushes me from behind, and I'm so overwhelmed and tired that I genuinely don't hear or sense them coming. But Nigel smiles gently at me.

"You're okay," I hear Korby say in my ear. "I trained you well enough that you're okay." She spins me around to face her. "I was worried you'd be injured or something and it would be all my fault."

She's rambling, and I let her. It's so good to see Korby alive and well. And without a scratch on her, by the looks of things. She fought well.

"I can't believe it's over. I watched what happened to Aki. I'm sorry it had to be you."

I think there will always be a part of me that'll be haunted by the memory of me killing my own brother, but it was for the best. And I don't regret it. Not for a second.

"Well, I'm going to help cook food for the whole army. We'll catch up after, right?"

"I still have training to do, so of course. And shopping." And with that, I continue helping heal people, using my magic for good, like I'm cleansing my soul. Trying to outweigh all the murder with lifesaving Vampire blood. Other Vampires join in and help me. Their blood isn't as effective, but it does the trick.

As it gets dark, I sit on top of the hill where my *Shinto* shrine sits, still intact, and a few deep breaths has tears coming to my eyes. They're all dead. The king, Aki, and all of those people who have friends and family who love them.

If only I could have . . . found another way.

We tried. He gave us no choice. Their deaths are on him. Nine walks up to me, sits cross-legged beside me, and puts a hand on my knee.

"You never know what the future holds, so you cannot judge past actions with today's knowledge. It is not fair to yourself," Dea says, joining Nine's other side, his wing wrapping around us both.

"More words of wisdom?" Connie asks. "How predictable." She lays her head in my lap, looking up at me. "I'm okay."

The image of her scared face as I had to feed from her will forever haunt me. And that's one war wound I don't think I'll heal from.

Arrie sits on my other side, as silent as ever. But he tucks his arm under Dea's feathers and rests his hand on my shoulder. Then he breaks his silence to whisper three simple words that send my body flying high into the sky. "I love you."

"I love you all."

Author Ramblings

It's over. The story that kept me awake at night, that made me laugh, cry, and throw things has finally come to an end. And I think a part of me will always be here, with Magic and their team. Magic will always be a part of who I am.

This was such a tough ending to write. I've been so worried that whatever I write won't be enough, and I still think it's not good enough. But finally, FINALLY, I can talk about Nine. I have been sitting on that plot twist for a whole freaking year! With no one but my husband to talk to about it.

I hope you loved Magic and their story, but most of all, I hope you feel accepted by them. That you will always have a place to call home, regardless of everything else going on in your life. Thank you for sticking out Magic's journey and being part of their growth, for being my first ever group of fans (still doesn't feel real) and cheering me on from the sidelines. This book series exists because of you, so this ending was for you.

An extended epilogue will come in November with the epilogue, so stay tuned for that. And if you want to stay up-to-date on my work, you can find me on Instagram (@authorkilmari), Facebook (Kilmari's Keep), and TikTok (@freidakilmari).